NO LONGER PROPERTY OF
SEATTLE PUBLIC LIBRARY

FIRE & ICE

RACHEL SPANGLER

Ann Arbor
2019

Bywater Books

Copyright © 2019 Rachel Spangler

All rights reserved. No part of this book may be reproduced, stored in a retrieval system, or transmitted in any form or by any means, without prior permission in writing from the publisher.

Print ISBN: 978-1-61294-163-9

Bywater Books First Edition: October 2019

Printed in the United States of America on acid-free paper.

Cover designer: Ann McMan, TreeHouse Studio

Back cover photo credit: Will Banks

Bywater Books
PO Box 3671
Ann Arbor MI 48106-3671
www.bywaterbooks.com

This novel is a work of fiction. All characters and events described by the author are fictitious. No resemblance to real persons, dead or alive, is intended.

To Susie, who loves me even when I call the wrong shot.
This is all your fault.

Chapter One

"Curling?" Max Laurens self-consciously patted the dark hair that barely fell halfway down her forehead and was even shorter on the sides. The word didn't make any sense in this context of her job as a sports reporter. "Like hair curling?"

"Curling, the sport, with the rocks and the brooms on ice."

She shook her head slowly, trying to process those incongruous items together. "Wait, the one with the funny pants and all the yelling?"

"That's the one."

"No."

"Hear me out."

"No way." She planted her hands firmly on the arms of the conference room chair, ready to make a dramatic stand, but the man across the table only rolled his brown eyes.

"You can't just say no."

"I can."

There was no triumph in his voice as he said, "Not if you ever want to work here again."

"Look, Flip," she said in a grave tone, "I get that things have been a little crazy around here lately."

"Not around here, around you."

"Right, but I'm still one of this country's preeminent sports reporters."

He scrunched up his face from his tight lips to his receding hairline in a way that made him appear constipated. "Are you?"

"Yes!"

"You're still a great writer, you still have a great sports mind, and you're still good both in front of and behind the camera, but your credibility is shot."

"I can get that back."

"I believe you. I'm in the minority with that opinion, but I'm going to bat for you, which is why I'm offering you a chance to stay in the world of sports coverage."

"Sports? You said I'd be covering a curling team."

"Yeah, curling is the sport."

She shook her head vehemently again. "Curling is not a sport. It's competitive sweeping, for fuck's sake. That's not a sport!"

"It's in the Olympics."

"So is that thing where people dance around with ribbons."

He snorted, then regained his composure, feigning a seriousness she didn't totally believe. "Curling always sees a massive uptick in viewers during Olympic years."

"This isn't an Olympic year."

"Actually, it is."

"For the summer Olympics." She fought the urge to drop her head to the faux mahogany table. "Summer's the opposite of winter, which means these broom handlers won't get another shot at TV viewership for another two seasons."

"I can't do this anymore, Max." He sighed and stuffed a few sheets of paper into a manila envelope. "The network has the TV contract for Curling Night in America to kick off the season in October, the national championships in February, and the world championships in March. We're funding an embedded reporter for several months. Embedded, Max."

She grimaced. "Can we use a different word, maybe one that doesn't invoke the idea of 'in bed' and my stories?"

He made the constipated look again. "I only meant to highlight the fact that I'm offering you steady work for four months.

Whoever takes this job will be on-site doing personal interest stories during the early part of the season."

"Puff pieces."

"Once the competitive season gets rolling," he continued, without acknowledging her snark, "you'd get the TV coverage of the matches."

"Television? As in cable?"

"Well, probably mostly live streaming online and through our app for the small events."

"Internet coverage. Of course."

"The early rounds of the national championship will be televised on the cable channels, and the finals will air on network TV."

"Four months." She sat back in the chair. "Four months in a frozen penitentiary for failing to vet a single source."

"You know it was more than that."

She rolled her eyes to hide the sting of the truth. It *had* been more than that, for all the reasons he knew and a few he never would. "Four months in lockup."

"You never know. You might get time off for good behavior. Think about it more like probation."

She didn't want to think about it at all, or as anything more than a subpar offer she'd rejected outright. Sadly, the low growl in her stomach and the new constant dull throb at the base of her skull warned her not to be so rash. "Just for argument's sake, where would this possible good behavior take me exactly?"

Flip rolled his head, as if trying to crack some of the tension out of his neck, before forcing a tight smile. "Good news is you'd still be in New York State."

"And the bad news?"

"Buffalo."

A little whimper escaped her throat. She tried to cover it with a fake cough, but managed only to sound like an asthmatic puppy.

Sympathy flashed through Flip's eyes. She hated that.

"I'm fine." She coughed a little louder. "It's fine. I'll be fine."

"You will," he said seriously, then folded his hands on the table and leaned forward to adopt a less formal stance. "Take the job. Get out of the city. Get back to the basics. You'll find your feet again."

"Sounds like I'll have to find them on a sheet of ice."

He grinned. "You've been in slippery situations before. I'm sure a little bit of ice isn't going to break you."

She didn't know if the slipperiness he referred to was her career or her personal life, but she supposed it didn't matter if the end results were the same. Honestly, she hadn't been able to separate the two for a long time. Maybe he was right, and she needed some time to untangle herself. She had been through a lot. And she was still here. She had an offer for long-term work with a chance of advancement from puff pieces to network TV. At the very least, the job could keep her foot in the door with a major sports network. She'd been in worse situations, and she'd written her way out of them, or at least she'd worked her way up above them for a while. She had to fight down a wave of anger at the fact that she didn't think her crimes warranted such a drastic penance, but four months on ice in Buffalo wouldn't break her.

"Fine."

"Yeah?" He smiled his real smile, one of a little kid who's just been picked to be on his older brother's baseball team. "You'll take the assignment?"

She shrugged, more resignedly than hopefully. "If this is what it takes to move on, yeah. I can take it."

Callie Mulligan tilted the forty-pound curling stone onto its side and ran her gloved hand along the bottom to clear any possible dust or frost, then lowered it gently back to the ice. Bracing her right foot against the black block of the hack, she bent her knees and lowered herself into a crouch. With a slow, steady inhale, she tightened her fingers around the handle atop the stone.

Straightening her knees, she kept her chest low and her back level as instinct took hold. She could have finished the move in her sleep, but she willed herself to stay fully present in her body. Controlling for the angle of her hand, her line of sight, and the slip of her left foot against the ice, she exhaled and pushed off. She fully extended her right leg in a long, graceful line while keeping her left one bent severely toward her sternum.

For a second, she became pure kinetic mass and motion, an object at one with the laws of physics. She never felt more at home than she did in the slide, but as the blue line drew steadily nearer, other instincts overrode her sense of oneness, and internal equations began to solve themselves. The same way most people could drive and sing along to the radio at the same time, she calculated her speed, her grip, her trajectory, and her position only a fraction of an inch to the right of the thin black center line. Then, with a minuscule twist of her thumb and forefinger, she gently lifted her hand.

Easing her chest upright, she lowered her straightened leg, causing her own momentum to slow as the rock continued to spin forward.

"No," she called immediately. "Nope, no, never, never, never."

"We're not going to bleeping sweep it," Ella grumbled.

"Yeah." Layla yawned as she pushed herself down the ice, slider foot first, and her gripper shoe pumping along as if she were trying to kick some invisible skateboard into gear. "We haven't swept anything for twenty minutes."

"Twenty-five," Brooke called. "My feet have frozen in place."

Callie rolled her eyes at their exaggerations. If this stone landed where she wanted, she'd be ten for ten, which meant she couldn't have been throwing for much more than ten minutes, but she was still too focused on the rock to verbalize her argument.

Standing up fully, she followed the path her throw had taken. Striding more than slipping, she caught up with the rock just as it inched past the twelve-foot red circle painted at the other end. It had slowed dramatically, allowing it to spin more full counter-clockwise rotations in a shorter span of space. The increased spin gave the rock's arc the distinct curl that defined the sport. She'd seen it a million times, but the rhythm of her breathing still faltered slightly as the rock made another slow turn through an eight-foot-wide white ring.

"She's dying." Brooke held up a yellow stopwatch to prove her point.

"Nope," Callie said quickly, but with enough authority that neither sweeper lowered her broom.

"It's getting frosty here without all the old men blowing their hot air," Brooke said, her tone more teasing than warning.

"I accounted for that."

"But did you account for the fact that I'm now asleep standing up? And therefore not breathing as heavily, which means I'm not warming the ice as much around the stone?" Layla asked.

She heard the smile in her friend's sarcasm. "Yes."

"Of course, she did," Ella groused, sounding the least playful of them all, as the rock had now twirled through the blue three-foot circle of the bull's-eye-inspired target.

Callie's heart beat a little faster; she worried the stone might stop there, but as so often happened, the last spin held just enough torque for one half-swing around, which inched the entire stone just inside a white center circle barely big enough to hold it.

"Right. On. The. Button," Brooke declared unnecessarily, as they all stood directly over it, so close to one another the tops of their heads brushed together.

"Well, that's a perfect ten . . . again," Ella said, leaning back and flipping the padded end of her broom onto her shoulder. "Well done, team. Same time next week?"

"It's a date," Brooke agreed, hooking her own broom through the handle of the stone and pulling it toward her.

"Wait." Callie finally glanced up at them. "I wanted to work on—"

"No," they all said in unison.

"But it's—"

"Eleven o'clock at night?" Layla asked. "Yes. Yes, it is."

"On a school night," Ella added.

"Yes to that, too." Brooke turned and slid Callie's stone next to seven others with matching handles. "We're done."

"I thought we were going to try to go twenty-five for twenty-five sometime. Wouldn't that be fun?"

The "no" this time wasn't just unanimous, it was emphatic. She must have grimaced because Layla's dark eyes softened. "Look, it's for your own good. If we start enabling you with your twenty-five button shots in a row, next you'll want to shoot for one hundred."

She felt the thrill of a challenge tingle in her chest, but she knew better than to express her excitement. Still, she did want more. She always wanted more. Thankfully, she didn't have to inconvenience her team in the process. She had had plenty of practice pursuing perfectionism solo. "Okay, you're right. You all can call it a night. Good practice."

"'You all,' as in us, but not you?" Brooke asked, pulling off her stocking cap to reveal the havoc the dry static had wreaked on her shoulder-length copper hair.

"I won't be long. I just want to hang around another half hour or so, to see how the weight changes as the temperature drops a few degrees."

Her teammates shifted uneasily and glanced from one to the other. She could sense the guilt radiating off them. Their reaction would likely depend on what she said next. She was the skipper, the play caller, the leader. She could easily bend their emotions, their drive, their loyalty to her in order to make them stay, and part of her wanted to. Why should she let them off the hook when she still burned with a desire to push harder? But guilt was a poor substitute for passion, and loyalties too often tested bred resentment.

"Okay, okay. I get it," she said with a little laugh. "No need to stage an intervention. I'll call it a night, too."

The surrender sparked a series of relieved sighs, and she had to smile more genuinely. They cared about her, even if they didn't quite share her level of obsession. That had to count for something.

7

She exited the ice, and they all began to pack up their gear, shoving jackets and gloves into athletic bags. She went through the motions, going so far as to slip off her curling shoes and stash them away. When she did, her hand touched a slip of paper she'd tossed in there earlier. "Oh hey, I forgot to mention, there's a reporter coming to see us next week."

"From like *Buffalo Spree* or something?"

"No, like a big-time reporter. From TV or the internet. They were a little vague, but I got an official email from the USA Curling press secretary."

"Whoa." Layla sat up from tying her sneakers and flipped a few dark braids off her forehead. "Curling USA is sending someone *here* to talk to *us*?"

"The email said it was connected to the TV coverage of the season. I told you they're taking us seriously this year."

"Maybe I should make an appointment to get my hair done," Ella said, not exactly capturing "serious" with her tone. "I could use a little more on-screen work."

"Go ahead." Layla laughed. "I'll be right here waiting. No need to improve on perfection."

Callie shook her head. "All jokes aside, more exposure could be the first step in getting some endorsements, which would help fund travel to more tournaments. And the more we play, the better our chances of picking up additional funding. A couple more years of climbing steadily would put us in a great place as far as our Olympic chances go."

Her teammates' eyes glazed over as she talked. They'd all heard this before, but they smiled politely anyway, all except for Brooke, who nodded through a yawn.

"I mean, you never know, right?" she asked, reining in her enthusiasm.

"Anything is possible." Layla slapped her on the shoulder.

It wasn't quite the endorsement she'd hoped for, but even if her friends didn't share her vision for the next few years, she at least appreciated their willingness not to rain on her parade. Now it was her turn to do the same for them. "Anywho, it's a good step for the future of the team, but we won't have a team if we all drop dead from exhaustion tomorrow. Let's call it a night."

"Thank you," Brooke said, almost reverently. "We'll be back at it again tomorrow."

"I know." And she did. "You go ahead. I'll lock up and be right behind you."

Everyone slung their bags over their shoulders and headed for the lounge. Layla stopped to hold the door for her, eyebrows raised in both question and challenge.

Callie went so far as to pat her hoodie pocket and pull out a jangling key ring before turning out the lights over the ice. "See you tomorrow."

She walked them all the way to the door and made a big show of closing it behind her while everyone else crossed the parking lot. Pretending to lock the door, she waited until the sound of their tires rolled across the gravel lot. Turning under the amber glow of a streetlight, she waved as each one pulled onto the main road and headed off in different directions.

Then she turned and pushed the door she'd left open. She strode back past the lounge, switching on lights as she went. Tossing her bag on the floor, she pulled out her curling shoes and laced them up. She inhaled the sharp, clean scent of frost and stepped back onto the ice.

She always had work to do.

Chapter Two

Max's GPS remained adamant she was on the right road even as her own doubts grew. She seemed to have entered an industrial park of some sort. To her left, an interstate overpass hummed with the remains of rush-hour traffic, but to her right, empty loading docks gave an almost ghost-townish feel to the place. She'd always imagined Buffalo to be run-down and rusted out. While so far she'd only seen the airport and whatever this place was, she felt a little satisfaction to find she'd been right.

She came to a small asphalt cul-de-sac, and the woman on her GPS app announced she'd arrived. Slowing her rental car to a stop, she glanced around for a few seconds before noticing a small white sign with what she supposed was a curling symbol overlaid with a white buffalo. Below the sign, an arrow pointed to a gravel parking lot between two large buildings. She pulled all the way to the end without seeing any other signs.

"Now what?" She might have used the complete lack of signage as an excuse to go to her hotel and try again later if a green Prius hadn't arrived at the same time. A man and a woman hopped out, chatting animatedly, and bounded down a short set of metal stairs she hadn't even noticed.

"Okay," she muttered, as they disappeared down a low path that seemed part dirt road and part dirty alley. "I'm a New Yorker. I've been in worse places."

She followed along at a distance. In her experience, people who drove Priuses didn't usually lure tourists into alleys to mug them, but at the same time, nothing about her experience suggested that prospective Olympians trained in rusted-out warehouses down sketchy urban back roads, either.

Still, when she reached the set of glass doors the couple had used, she found them labeled in clean, white stencil: Buffalo Curling Club.

She went inside and let her eyes adjust to the fluorescent light as she quickly surveyed her surroundings. The entirety of the space consisted of one large rectangle, bisected by a wall of glass. On the side she currently occupied, a small, empty reception desk offered the only sense of order. Tables, mismatched chairs, and old couches dotted the concrete floor. Old lockers lined one wall, and a table overloaded with slow cookers took up another. Finally, two obviously newer drywalled boxes seemed to be bathrooms that had been slapped together as an afterthought.

She shook her head. *Where the hell am I?*

"Hey, newcomer," an old man in an oversized Buffalo Bills sweatshirt called. "You lost?"

"Maybe," she admitted. "I'm a reporter for The Sports Network."

He wheezed out a laugh. "Then you're definitely lost."

She didn't appreciate the vote of confidence, but she fished a piece of paper from her pocket and checked the name she hadn't bothered to memorize. "I'm looking for a Callie Mulligan."

Several more heads turned, and the din of conversation stopped. She shifted slightly under the collective gaze now pointed at her. Several people eyed her with interest, a few more with suspicion. Finally, the same man smiled. "Shoulda known she'd be the one who'd bring someone like you to Buffalo."

She raised her eyebrows.

"Surprised it didn't happen sooner," someone else added.

She didn't comment, generally preferring to reserve judgment until she had a good read on a room.

"Shoulda sent someone else." Another man grumbled from behind her.

She set her jaw but didn't turn. "If you could just tell me where I might find her or—"

"On the ice." The first old man cut her off. "She's always on the ice."

She glanced through the wall of windows to her right, and for the first time let herself take in the expanse of ice in the larger portion of the warehouse. Bright, white, and glistening, it was divided into six long, narrow lanes. And on every strip groups of people slid, swept, and called out a cacophony of instructions or encouragements she could barely make out through the glass. Men and women of all ages and sizes bustled about quickly, and round rocks dotted their paths. Nothing had made sense for a long time, and the scene before her only seemed to offer a visual representation of the randomness permeating every area of her life.

"Ah, come on." The man pushed up from his chair. "No need to go all deer-in-the-headlights. I'll show you."

She fought the urge to run and instead followed him through a door to one side of the glass.

"I'm Stan, by the way."

She nodded. "Max."

"Yeah, I know," he said. "I suppose a lot of people do these days."

She grimaced, wondering when this would get easier, or if it ever would. Maybe she'd been wrong to come here. Maybe she should've taken some time off or away. Not that it would be possible to get much farther from her own life than where she was right now. She stared up at the exposed metal rafters overhead and shivered as the ice made its way into her lungs. At least if she'd run away, she could've gone someplace warm.

"Actually," she started, just as Stan stuck out an index finger.

"There she is," he said. "First sheet, there at the near end. That's our Callie."

She needed no more description, and Max needed no more introduction. Callie Mulligan might as well have been the only woman on the ice, because the moment Max's eyes landed on her, everyone else blurred together. The woman was young and lean and totally unadorned with makeup or jewelry, but that did nothing to detract from her smooth complexion or her pink lips, or the way streaks of honey threaded through her loose, golden hair. Most captivating, though, were her hypnotic hazel eyes. A blend of gold and amber, they sparked with amusement as she called out to someone down the ice, and Max felt a pang of regret that she hadn't been the one to spark that emotion or the laughter that accompanied it.

The wistfulness of the thought hit her so hard, she lifted the heel of her palm to her chest as if she could somehow stanch the ache throbbing there. Everything about her tightened—her muscles, her jaw, her mind—as she slammed those doors and barricaded them with her most protective instincts. Business. She was here for business.

"Excuse me," she said weakly. No one so much as glanced her way. Striding closer across a raised platform framing the ice, she cleared her throat and tried again with more force. "Excuse me, Ms. Mulligan."

The woman turned her head and smiled. Max faltered again at the easy genuineness of the expression. Callie had a girl-next-door grin and an athlete's body. And again with the eyes. The combination threatened to melt her reserves like hot coal on ice, and she forced herself to look away.

Thankfully, her surroundings provided ample distractions. Everywhere, people slid along with brooms brushing vigorously. The absurdity of the sight helped Max regain some of her indignation. She shouldn't be here. She shouldn't be in Buffalo. She shouldn't be covering curling. And if anyone had taken the time to listen to her, she wouldn't have to stand here, sullen and cold, afraid to make eye contact with a woman beautiful enough to make her forget all that, even if just for a moment.

Her bitterness added a little bite to her voice. "I'm Max Laurens with TSN."

Callie's smile broadened. "How great to meet you."

"Likewise, I'm sure."

"I'm so glad you'll be joining us for part of this season."

Max couldn't even begin to formulate a polite response, so she kept her jaw tightly clenched.

"If there's anything I can do to help you get settled—"

"No." She cut her off. There was no way to help her settle, and even if there were, she wouldn't want to do so here.

"The only thing I need your help with is figuring out what this"—she gestured loosely toward the ice, then sighed—"is all about."

Callie tried not to bristle at Max's sharp tone or clipped words. She didn't even have a problem with the fact that Max didn't even know enough about curling to ask a real question. Most people didn't. However, she had to work a little harder not to be offended at the fact that this woman didn't even seem able to look her in the eye. Maybe if she had, Callie could have placed her. Her face was vaguely familiar in the way so many reporters' faces were. She had her coal-black hair cut short at the sides in a utilitarian way, but left longer and feathered flawlessly on top for a wisp of style. She had high cheekbones and a strong jaw, and though she stood a few inches shorter than Callie, her posture and presence seemed to command more space than her stature would indicate.

"What do you want to know?" Callie asked.

"All of it," Max answered drolly.

"Okay, well, walk this way." Callie strolled down the ice as Max followed beside her on the platform.

"If we need to start at the basics, those little round things with the handles on them are called rocks or stones. They're heavy."

Max snorted softly.

"The idea is to slide them to the other end of the curling sheet—that's the ice—and land them in the middle of those rings painted on the other end. Each team gets eight rocks per end."

"End?"

"Ends are like innings, or periods. In full-on Olympic-style curling, we play ten ends per game. Around clubs like this, you're more likely to play six, or maybe eight. But the main thing you have to know is that each player on a team throws two rocks per end in alternating fashion."

"And then other people sweep them," Max said flatly.

"Exactly."

"Who sweeps them?"

"Well, the second and vice sweep for the lead, the lead and vice sweep for the second, the lead and second sweep for the vice, and also the skip, because when the skip throws, the vice becomes the skip."

Max glanced up, and for a second Callie was struck by another jolt of recognition as she got a look at her blue eyes, so pale they were almost gray, or maybe that was the glaze of uninterest clouding them. Her happiness at the prospect of the network sending a serious reporter to cover their team was tempered by the realization that Max was already bored with her.

She kicked herself for going overboard right out of the gate. She always did that when someone asked her about curling and, more times than not, she got the same uninterested look Max had pointed at her.

Thankfully, they weren't at a party or, God forbid, on a date. In her experience, there was no salvaging this conversation in those situations, but today she was in the one place where she had home-ice advantage. "Actually, the rules and terms can get a little complicated. It's not a sport that's really meant to be talked about in the abstract."

"I've managed to understand slant routes and defensive formations in the abstract," Max snapped, then seemed to catch herself only enough to lower her voice without quite adjusting her tone. "I'm sure I'm cognitively capable of following curling."

Callie's face flushed hot. "I'm sorry. I didn't mean to offend you. I only wanted to suggest we might have more fun if I taught you how to play."

15

Max looked down her nose at the curling rocks between them. "Cute, but I'll pass. That doesn't strike me as my kind of fun."

Callie swallowed a sigh. This wasn't how she wanted this to go. Max was supposed to be different. She was supposed to take this seriously. She was supposed to help, not make snide remarks and pass judgments from the sidelines. It wasn't that Callie wasn't used to people like that. The opposite was true, and she didn't need one more person to scoff at her dreams. She had to bite her tongue to keep from saying so as the familiar tensions settled in her chest.

Thankfully, she didn't have to find a response, as they were interrupted by Layla hopping onto the platform beside Max.

"Hiya. You must be the reporter." She stuck out her hand so close to Max, she had no choice but to shake it.

"Max Laurens."

"Layla Abrams. I play lead."

Max shrugged.

"You have no idea what that means, do you?"

"I could hazard a guess," Max said.

Layla laughed. "Is that how you do all your reporting—lob a Hail Mary and hope you land near the truth?"

Max winced and took a step back before seeming to catch herself. She set her jaw and squared her shoulders. Everything about her posture flashed from bored to braced for a fight. "I may have gotten a few things wrong in the past, but trust me, this *sport* is well within my comprehension level."

"Comprehension level," Layla scoffed. "What are we in, fifth-grade English? Or are we going to curl?"

"Hey now," Callie tried to interject softly.

"Neither," Max shot back, ignoring her completely. "I'm here to report on your *sport*, that's all."

Layla stepped closer, and Callie shot out a hand to stop her. Sadly, there was no stopping Layla on the rare occasion she got revved up. "Go ahead and say 'sport' like that one more time, Pencil Pusher."

"Like what? Like it's beneath me?"

"Like you can't be bothered to get down off your high horse and earn the right to disdain what you can't even do."

Max rolled her eyes. "Is that some sort of schoolyard challenge?"

Layla shrugged. "Put up or shut up."

"All right," Callie said, more forcefully. "This is going so badly. Everyone needs to dial it back a notch."

Max and Layla both shook their heads.

"We'll keep it simple. Regular rules, two-on-two," Layla declared. "One end. You can have Callie. I'll take Stan."

"No." Callie put her foot down.

"Yes," Stan cheered from behind them, already shedding his Bills hoodie.

"I'm in," Max declared.

Stan handed Max a slider and said, "Put that on over your left shoe."

"Guys," Callie pleaded, her head starting to throb at what an awful idea this was. "Please stop."

"What's the matter?" Max asked, as she stepped into the slider and turned back to her. "You're the one who wanted me to learn on the ice."

"I wanted you to have fun."

Max grinned for the first time since they'd met. "Winning is fun."

She shook her head. Max wasn't going to win and, worse, she might get hurt, which, given her demeanor, would only hurt Callie's team's chances of getting the press they desperately needed.

"Come on," Layla called, already sliding herself toward the other end of the ice. "Are you going to do this thing or not?"

Callie stepped in front of Max. "Can we please slow down?"

Max didn't even meet her eyes as she sidestepped around her toward the curling sheet and called, "I'm in!"

Callie turned just in time to see her left foot hit the ice and go right out from under her.

Then Max went down hard and fast and loud.

⊙ ⊙ ⊙

"Oof." All the air left Max's lungs in a rush, but she stiffened against the reflex to curl into a ball. Gasping in the frigid air against the ice, she rolled onto her side and braced herself with a forearm.

"Are you okay?" Callie's voice asked from high above her.

"Fine." She gritted her teeth, then placed her palm flat against the ice, only to jerk it back again involuntarily when a searing shot of cold branded her bare skin.

"Here." Callie extended a gloved hand to help her up.

She shook her head, and this time steeled herself against the cold before pushing herself up. She wobbled slightly before jumping quickly back onto the carpeted platform.

"Are you hurt?"

"I said I'm fine." She glanced around to see that several other games had come to a stop as everyone stared at her. She squared her shoulders against their judgment.

"Want to call it?" Layla shouted down the ice, more amusement than concern in her voice.

"Not a chance," Max called back, then turned to Callie. "Just tell me what to do to get the game started."

Callie pressed her pink lips together tightly, but Stan stepped in, holding up a quarter. "Heads or tails."

"Heads."

He tossed the coin in the air, and it landed between them with the tail side up. Of course it did, because that was just the kind of year she was having.

Stan grinned. "That means we get the hammer, but don't worry. It won't matter anyway."

Callie opened her mouth, but Max held up her hand. "Just stop, okay? We're doing this. You can make it better or worse, but you're not getting me off this ice."

Callie closed her mouth, but her eyes still managed to convey her message of pity, frustration, and a flash of anger. She nodded a single time. "You're going to have to throw first."

"Why? The sweeping looks easier."

"It is," she agreed, picking up her broom, "but you're not going to land anything on the rings, so I'm our only chance to pick up a point. I need to go second."

Max bristled at the lack of confidence. She was new to this game, but she was smart and generally athletic, not that shot-putting a rock across ice took much in the way of athletics. Still, she'd been doubted enough to understand you didn't overcome disbelief with anything other than action. "Where's my rock?"

"You get to pick the color since you lost the toss," Stan explained.

She eyed the matching sets of stones. The only difference seemed to be the color of the handles on top, red or blue. "Blue."

The older man smiled. "It'll bring out your eyes."

She snorted at the absurdity of the comment and rolled her shoulders. "Okay, so I saw other people doing this. I put my right foot on that little black rubber thingy."

"The hack," Stan supplied. "If you're right-handed, you use the one on the left side, so the stone is in the middle."

She nodded. Seemed easy enough.

"You use the slider," he said, pointing to the flat-soled shoe cover he'd given her, "to slide."

She winced slightly at the thought of slipping any more than she had the first time she'd stepped onto the ice, but she wasn't about to back down now. She shifted some of her weight to press the white-bottomed slider flush against the ice. Then with a deep breath for resolve she stepped forward once more.

"No!" Stan and Callie shouted, and each caught one of her arms so she stood suspended with her left foot half an inch from the ice.

"Oh, you are a bright one." Stan chuckled.

"Don't lead with your slider foot," Callie said more kindly. "It has no traction. Step out with your more grippy shoe."

Well, that made a ton of sense, and her cheeks burned slightly with the embarrassment of not having thought of it herself. She switched feet and eased onto the ice.

This time she didn't fall, which felt like a sad sort of victory, but she didn't have time to reflect on the low bar she'd just set for herself. Stan used his broom to push a blue-handled rock her way.

"Now, the slide is going to be a little complicated." Callie started to explain.

"You lunge and push," Max said drolly, as she put her right foot against the rubber block Stan had called a hack. It wasn't unlike a starting block for a runner, and she felt infinitely more stable against it than she had on flat ice. "Gimme the rock."

"Max," Callie said in a warning tone.

"You're the sweeper, right? Go sweep."

Callie shook her head and bit the corner of her lip, but she did as instructed and walked a couple of yards ahead of her.

"She's supposed to call your shot." Stan sounded a little embarrassed.

"Doesn't matter," Callie grumbled.

"Yeah, I'll just put it on the middle." Max pulled the rock close to her, then gripping the handle, straightened her legs as much as the weight would allow. Then she bent her right knee and pushed off as hard as she could. Her whole body wobbled, then pitched forward, and the rock shot out from under her. She landed with a dull thud, right on her shoulder.

Layla's laugh reverberated all the way from the other end of the ice. "Sporty enough for you, Pencil Pusher?"

She righted herself on the ice and rubbed her cold hands on her jeans, then glancing around for the rock, noticed it only a couple feet away.

"That one's not in play anymore," Stan said, pulling off his gloves. "It had to get past the line all the way at the other end to even be a guard."

"So it's, like, out of bounds?"

"Basically. Means you lost your throw and it's my turn." He held out his gloves to her.

She rubbed her palm one more time and clenched her jaw.

"Don't be stubborn. You're going to need them more than I do. You still have three more to throw."

She accepted the offering and edged away as he got into position. For someone who looked to be pushing seventy on the generous side of her estimate, he had none of the trouble she'd experienced getting into position and pushing off into a fluid lunge.

As he released the rock, Layla walked calmly toward it and swept only a little bit before letting it stop a foot short of the big ring at the other end.

"Did you miss?" Max asked, scooting back into the hack.

"No, I threw a guard. You're not allowed to knock it out until the fifth rock. If you want to go into the house, you're going to have to go around it."

"Don't bog her down in details," Callie said from the other end. "She's got to get a rock in play before she can worry about guards."

Max stiffened at the challenge, and this time as she pushed off, she locked her elbow and kept her arm straight even as her slider betrayed her again. At least now she was ready to hit the ice, and she rolled to lessen the impact. Staying down, she watched her rock spin and veer down the ice like a drunken dreidel until it bounced off the side barrier.

"Let me guess," she grumbled, momentarily grateful for the glove between her and the ice this time. "Out of bounds?"

"Out of play," Callie called, sliding the rock back to Stan, who moved it behind her and the hack. Then he proceeded to throw a perfect arcing shot right around his first stone and onto the center of the rings.

She didn't have time to wonder about the angles or spin that produced such movement before she was slipping and falling again. This time she managed to get her rock about halfway down the ice before it spun to a stop, only to be told that area was also out of play.

The amusement in Stan's expression mingled with something approaching embarrassment as he curled around his guard in the other direction this time and pressed his third rock right against the second.

"Nice freeze," Callie complimented.

Or at least it sounded like a compliment to Max, who assumed that in a sport played on ice, a freeze was a good thing.

She gripped her fourth rock tightly. She didn't need anyone to tell her this was her last shot. She was proficient enough at math to know half of the eight rocks would mean four fell to her and four to Callie. She had to make this, even though she didn't quite know what making it would look like in this context.

By sheer force of will and in a superhuman feat of core strength, she managed to stay upright as she pushed off and slid down the ice. The rock stayed in front of her, and exhilaration mingled with panic as she realized she was actually sliding, but she had no idea what to do next. She didn't have much time to figure it out, either, as her momentum slowed much more quickly than it had for Stan. He had slid much farther, where she was grinding to a stop after only a few feet. As she quickly processed this development, she gave the rock what little extra shove she could muster, and sat back on her butt with a plop.

"Whoo-hoo," Stan called excitedly. "Sweep, Callie, sweep!"

The instruction was unwarranted as Callie took off, her long, lean body tilted forward as she worked her broom in short, rapid strokes just in front of the rock. She inched her way so fluidly down the ice she might have been on solid ground as she worked efficiently without so much as glancing up. The strokes of the broom were so fast they blurred in Max's vision, but Callie's body stayed fluid as she slid gracefully along. It was a study in con-trasts, and Max held her breath.

"Oh, it's going to be close," Stan mumbled behind her as she slowed to a crawl near the blue line. "Look at her go."

And go she did. Callie scrubbed the ice so hard, Max wasn't sure why she didn't see steam rising off from all the friction, but when Callie finally lifted her head, she flashed a half smile and a quick thumbs-up.

"I did it?" Max asked Stan, her chest already puffing up with pride.

"Well . . ." He shrugged.

"What?"

"I mean you did some of it."

"What's that supposed to mean?"

"She got it over the line for you."

She folded her arms across her chest. "But I threw it over the line, so that gets to stay and be a, what did you call it, a guard?"

"It does." He did a poor job of smothering a grin.

"Well, you got one over," Callie said, as she slid smoothly to a stop next to her once more.

"I threw a guard," Max said emphatically.

"You did," Callie agreed, before adding, "a nice big one . . . to guard *their* stones."

"What?"

Stan laughed as he got into the hack. "Thanks, Max. You made my job easier."

"What?" she asked again, turning to Callie for answers.

"You put your rock right in front of the rock I needed to hit if I wanted to knock theirs out."

"Why did you sweep it so hard then?" she asked incredulously.

Callie shrugged and smiled. "You just looked like it really mattered to you. I wanted to make you feel like you'd contributed."

She couldn't believe it. Her face flamed now, not only from embarrassment, but from anger at how condescending her own teammate had been. She'd made an epic save of a play, not because it was helpful, but to bolster Max's ego. Did she really come across as that pathetic?

"It's your turn to sweep." Callie extended a broom toward her. "You need to—"

Max snatched it from her hand with undue force and pushed off in a huff before she had a chance to finish. However, the moment she did so, her slider engaged and whipped out from under her, all the way up over her head. She had a split second to process her own helplessness, but not enough time to curl fully into a ball before she dropped like a sack of bricks. It almost felt like the ice rushed up to meet her as she landed flat on her back. She managed to tuck her chin enough that the back of her head didn't crack open, but every other joint in her body seemed to compress and pop. A shot of pain seared through her right wrist, and a rush of gasps whooshed around her, or maybe it had only whooshed out of her.

"Holy shit," someone mumbled.

"Don't move," Callie called.

Layla got to her first. Dark eyes, serious but not unkind, stared down at her. "You ready to call 'uncle'?"

She winced and used her abs to pull herself up to a seated position without putting pressure on her sore wrist. "Not a chance."

Turning her head, she felt her neck crackle in several different spots, but she held up a hand to Callie. "I'm fine. Go throw the damn rock."

Layla laughed. "You're a glutton for punishment."

Max hauled herself up off the ice.

"In curling, it's considered good form to concede when you don't have any legitimate path to win," Stan said, his voice undercutting the bite of the comment.

"That's a dumb rule," Max replied.

"Finally, something we agree on," Layla said, as she pushed off down toward Callie's end of the ice.

"You really need to—" Callie started, but Max cut her off.

"Less talk, more throwing."

Callie sighed exasperatedly before turning to get back into position.

Max rolled her head from side to side a few times, then readied her broom the same way Callie had. She didn't have to inventory her aching body parts. Everything hurt, but nothing was broken. She would not allow herself to be broken. She'd taken a beating in her love life, her professional life, her reputation, and her finances. There was no part of her that hadn't been kicked around over the last six months, but nothing had ever broken her. She'd be damned if she would let a game of Scandinavian Slip 'N Slide kill her.

Still, she had to wonder why none of these people were wearing helmets.

Callie released the rock, sliding so controlled and with the grace of a dancer. The tendons in Max's knee creaked as she braced herself, preparing to sweep, but as the rock approached and she tightened her grip on the broom, another sharp pain shot through her wrist and she yelped. The rock slid right past her, and she pushed off, trying to chase after it, once again managing only two steps before she sprawled, this time across her stomach, arms and leg splayed like Bambi on ice.

"Son of a bitch." She flipped over, yanked off the slider, and sent it hurling back down the ice toward Callie.

"You're only supposed to wear those when you throw," Layla said matter-of-factly.

Max turned to Callie as if she'd betrayed her. "Seriously, you couldn't have mentioned that?"

She shrugged. "I tried, twice."

She ground her teeth, not sure if she was angrier at Callie for not trying a little harder or at herself for not giving her the chance.

Layla's rock went by in a rush with Stan sweeping like some happy little house elf. And then Callie was back up. This time when her rock went by, Max managed to stay on her feet. With a better grip on her shoes, she even managed to take a few steps, sweeping in front of the rock that came up on her more quickly than expected. She had to move faster, a lot faster than it had looked when Stan or Callie had done the same. It took everything she had to stay upright and a half-step ahead of the rock. She didn't even try to sweep so much as just run her broom along in the path of the oncoming rock, only she didn't do it fast enough, and her broom clicked against it.

"Ticked it," Stan called, as the rock slid only a fraction of an inch off its previous course. "Out of play."

Max fought back a whimper at the realization that she'd just cost them yet another stone. She didn't care about this stupid game anymore. She'd never cared about curling. She had no desire to be good at something so absurd, but for the love of all things holy, she wanted to not feel like a total fuck-up for just, like, two minutes. Was that too much to ask?

Apparently so, because Layla flicked another rock right into the rings as Stan scooted by effortlessly. How could these people be so good at something that Max failed at so miserably? She hadn't expected to be amazing right out of the gate, but she couldn't even stay upright and sweep at the same time. And it wasn't like any of this took strength or speed. People of all ages and sizes and genders played alongside them on the other sheets. She'd yet to see a single one of them fall ass-over-teakettle. Really, "throw rock, sweep rock" were the only skills anyone appeared to need, and yet when Callie threw again, Max had to get a slip-sliding head start only to whiff, flail, and stumble again as the stone breezed by.

This time she scraped her chin across the ice and threw up her hand to cover herself as a loud, sharp crack reverberated down the ice followed by a loud grinding, growling noise she didn't recognize. She closed her eyes tightly and cowered, half expecting the whole rusted-out warehouse to come crashing down on top of her.

"Had enough, Pencil Pusher?" Layla's voice called.

"Stop it," Callie chided. "Cut her some slack."

"No," she croaked, and pushed herself onto all fours. "No slack."

She stood and brushed little bits of ice from her chest as she did a quick count. There were only three rocks left on the other end, and two of them belonged to the other team. She could do this. Or at least she could keep from dying while the others did the work.

"Great shot," Stan called, as Callie stood over the remaining rocks in the ring.

None of them were where Max had last seen them, and one of their blue ones sat almost exactly in the middle.

"What just happened?" she mumbled to no one in particular. There had been guards, there had been multiple red rocks in her way, and there had been Max's complete lack of sweeping. How had Callie overcome all of those things in the short time

Max had been cowering in the duck-and-cover position at mid-ice?

For the first time, genuine interest flared in her, but she didn't have time to reflect or process as Layla's next rock whizzed by and crushed Callie's out of the center.

"Damn," she muttered, less upset about the loss of position than the realization it was her turn to sweep again. Still she lifted her broom and shuffled back toward the center line.

"Don't!" Callie shouted.

She glanced up to meet the hypnotic hazel eyes and froze. There was a flash of something deep and damn near dangerous in them, but when Callie took a deep breath and blinked, it disappeared, and she continued in a calmer voice. "Please, just don't sweep this one."

"Not at all?" Max asked, unsure if she felt more relieved or offended.

"It's not you. It's me, okay?" Callie said, then flashed her a kind smile.

Her chest tightened, but she didn't have time to respond before Callie's entire demeanor changed. She fit herself into the hack with military precision and pointed, laser-focus straight ahead. Then she coiled like a spring, but instead of jumping forward, her pent-up energy melded into a strong, steady release. Easing her hand off the stone with a tiny flick of her fingers, she sent it spinning clockwise and with less speed than might be needed for a clock's second hand to make a full rotation.

"Nope, nope, nope," she said, though who she'd directed the comment to, Max couldn't tell, since her eyes never left the rock. She didn't even stand up, instead pulling both knees to her chest in a low squat. "Line's good. Weight's good."

Max would have to take her word for it. She couldn't tell good from bad on this sheet of ice. Well, maybe that wasn't completely true. Her whole body felt bad, but her presence didn't appear to have any bearing on the game as the rock slid right past her in a steady arc toward the rings. She watched, a complete spectator on her own team, while Callie's rock tapped Layla's clean out of the rings and took up the space it had only a second earlier occupied.

Callie grimaced, and pushed up off her own knees with a little grunt. "Didn't get the double."

Layla smiled, wide and unrestrained, as she sent a rock right down the exact same path Callie's had taken. Max watched what she could've convinced herself was an instant replay if the color of the handles hadn't been different. She didn't even try to make her brain process how the two women had managed to make the same minuscule movement while controlling for every possible variable that might have affected their shots. And neither needed anyone to sweep for them. Then again, maybe the sweeping didn't really matter within the context of a game that didn't matter, played by people whose opinions of her didn't even matter.

The thought did little to fortify Max's mood. She'd busted her ass, both literally and figuratively, all to not contribute in any meaningful way.

"Good curling," Stan said, slapping her on the shoulder.

"Really?" she asked.

He laughed and shook his head as he kept on walking. "No. It's just a thing we say."

She followed, more scooting than actually stepping across the ice until she met Callie at the other end. She didn't know what to say, so she repeated Stan's empty phrase in a more sullen tone. "Good curling, I guess."

Layla snorted. "Still think we're beneath you?"

Max shook her head. She did actually, but she understood the optics of saying so after the drubbing she'd taken. Instead, she tried to think of some way to deflect without actually giving them or their game of choice any undue credit. Shifting her weight from one foot to the other, she tried to lean on her broom for support, and in a turn of events that didn't appear to surprise anyone, it went out from under her. She slipped with about as much grace as a cartoon character who'd stepped on a banana peel.

She heard another series of "ooohs" and snickers as her tail-bone hit the ice first this time.

Several hands reached out to help her off, but she clenched her fists and pulled herself back up.

"Are you okay?" Callie sounded genuinely concerned, and for some reason that upset her more than Layla's smug smile.

"Are we done here?"

"I think you were done the moment you stepped onto the ice," Layla said, and Callie shot her a stern look.

"You're not wrong," Max admitted, her pride barely containing her urge to rub the spot on her backside where a bruise was no doubt spreading. "So, unless you have anything else you need me to endure today, I'd like to go check into my hotel."

"Of course," Callie said, before Layla had a chance to speak again. "We can talk again after you have a chance to settle in and rest up."

She shrugged, sure that would indeed have to happen, no matter how little she welcomed it.

"Let me walk you out," Callie offered.

"Please don't." She waved her off and stepped back onto the carpeted platform surrounding the ice. Her relief at being back on solid ground nearly buckled her knees, but before she had a chance to make a break for it as fast as her quickly seizing muscles would allow, Layla called, "Hey, Pencil Pusher!"

Steeling herself, she turned to see her tormentor's wide smile and extended hand.

She waited, unable to accept the gesture until her sluggish brain processed the hint of affection she'd heard in the nickname this time.

"Anyone who can take hits like that and keep going"—Layla nodded appreciatively—"can't be all bad."

Callie nodded, frustration radiating off her hard-set jaw and squared shoulders, but her eyes were kind. "She's not wrong. Most people would have quit."

The sentiment warmed her more than the icy room should have allowed, as she shook their hands. The touch was the most intimate human contact she'd had in ages, and she tried not to think about how long it had been since someone had said anything appreciative to her as she headed to the car. Still, she could accept a compliment, and even feel a grudging respect for Callie and Layla, while also standing firm in her now confirmed belief that she fucking hated curling.

Chapter Three

"Callie!" A cheer went up from the table as soon as she swung open the door to her parents' boxy ranch home. She smiled at the greeting. Her family always acted as if they hadn't seen her for years, when it was hardly ever more than a couple of weeks.

"Perfect timing," her mother called. "The pierogies are just about out of the skillet."

"I do have a knack for showing up just as dinner's ready." She shed her light jacket and stamped her boots to make sure she hadn't tracked in any wet leaves.

"It's a skill you've possessed since you were old enough to play outside by yourself." Her dad rose from his seat to hug her tightly. "How'd your week go?"

"Not too bad," she said, skirting around the table to drop a kiss atop her grandfather's bald head.

"But not too good?" he asked, honing in on the non-answer she'd tried to slip by him.

"It was fine." She tried to dodge again, this time sidestepping her mother so she could wrap one arm around her waist without disturbing the platter of pierogies and polish sausages she carried toward the table. "What's new here?"

"Nothing new here." Her mom slipped out of her grease-splattered apron and shook out her auburn hair before she took

31

the seat opposite her husband. "You're the one who's supposed to come entertain us on the weekends."

Callie sat at the only remaining chair. "That can't be true. I'm all work and no play."

"Not true," her grandpa said. He stabbed a sausage and dragged it onto his plate with a shaky hand. "Your work is part play."

"Or all play," her dad muttered.

Callie bristled at the comment, but her mom responded with a little cluck. "Now, she also works at work, too."

"Yeah, that's why I wasn't here last weekend. I picked up more hours at the store."

"We know you get here when you can."

"I do, but things are only going to get busier until Christmas. Thanksgiving is the only time I have off between tournaments and the store and dog sitting and—"

"Odd jobs and part-time hours." Her dad grumbled. "Where's the stability in that?"

"She's the most stable girl I've ever met," Grandpa shot back at him. "Have you seen her on ice—stable and steady and upright when most people would slip or cave under the pressure?"

The comment reminded her of Max. Every time she'd closed her eyes, for days, she'd had flashes of that poor woman hitting the ice. She'd crumpled into a heap so many times Callie couldn't count them all, but she'd always hopped back up, rigid, stubborn, defiant. Even with time and space between them, she couldn't decide whether she found the attitude admirable or foolish. Either way, things hadn't needed to end that way. Heat flushed in her cheeks. She shouldn't have let it end that way. She should have stayed in control of the situation. She usually did. Few people ever frustrated her on the ice the way Max had.

"Dad, I'm not talking about curling, and you know it," her father said to his father. "Curling's a fine hobby. I just want my daughter to have a career she can count on, a steady income, health insurance, a pension."

"You want her to take over the window business," Grandpa shot back.

"And what's wrong with that?" Her dad raised his voice, not quite to the level of yelling. "You started the business, and you got to hand it down to your kid; all I want to do is hand it to mine. I'm not going to live forever. I want to know my legacy and my only child are going to be cared for when I'm gone."

"Can we not have this conversation every season?" her mom asked, already sounding weary.

"It's fine." Callie cut back in to keep the peace. "I know he only wants what he thinks is best for me. He found those things selling windows, and maybe someday I'll get there, too. But, for now, I actually have a lead on some new curling opportunities that might bridge the stability gap."

Her dad started to grumble again, but her mom silenced him with a look and said, "Tell us, honey."

"Well, you know how we've been sponsored by the national team for the last couple of seasons?"

Grandpa Mulligan puffed out his chest. "The national team pays my granddaughter to curl."

She grinned at him. "They don't pay us enough, but this year they also sent a reporter to follow us. She's going to do some web stuff and some promo videos, and she'll cover us when our matches are on television later in the year, leading up to the Players' Championship."

"And you said you didn't have anything exciting to tell us." Her mom chided her playfully as she scooped a few more pierogies onto Callie's plate.

"Nothing's come of it yet, but there's some hope that more coverage translates into invites to bigger tournaments, and possibly more sponsorships. I mean, every curler I know still has a day job, but a few of them are pretty comfortable. Maybe this is a step toward that for me, too."

She glanced at her dad, who nodded slightly instead of arguing.

"I think it sounds wonderful," Grandpa said, forgoing his knife and picking up the whole sausage on his fork to bite off the end.

"And have you met the reporter?" her mom asked. "Do you know who he is?"

"Actually, it's a she." Callie said, remembering Max's blue eyes under dark lashes. She didn't know why she'd found the trait so feminine despite her other, more androgynous features, but she didn't want to ponder the question at her mother's table. "Her name is Max Laurens."

Her dad coughed and reached for his water.

"I've never heard of her. Does she usually cover curling?" her mom asked.

"No, I've heard of her, though. I think she does more general sports coverage for the network, but I'm not really sure since I only follow curling. I think she's got some catching up to do."

"Well, you can help her with that," Grandpa said. "No one better to bring someone new to the sport."

Her smile twisted into a grimace. "I'm not so sure. Things didn't exactly go well when she stopped by the club."

Her mom patted her hand. "I'm sure it was fine."

Callie suffered another flashbulb memory of the hardness in Max's expression as scabs had begun to form across her scraped chin. "I'm pretty sure she's not a fan of the game, or of me."

"Then you'll just have to work a little harder. You know what I always say, 'Kill 'em with kindness.'"

"Just maybe not too kind." Her dad cut back in, his brow furrowed once more. "Keep your guard up."

She raised her eyebrows at the comment that seemed a little more pointed than his usual grumbling, and yet still cryptic. "What do you mean?"

He shook his head. "Probably nothing. I don't mean to rain on any parades. I just think it wouldn't hurt to do a little opposition research on this woman before you put too much faith in her."

"I don't think Max is the opposition. I mean, she's clearly not a big curling fan, but she seemed serious and driven. I'm sure when push comes to shove, she's on our team."

"I'm not calling her friend or foe so much as saying that, with people like Max Laurens, it's probably best to keep them at arm's length."

"People like Max? I don't understand."

He shifted in his seat. "Good."

"Pshaw." Grandpa cut back in. "No need to frighten the girl. I'm with your mother. Even if this Max woman isn't a believer yet, you'll win her over. Everyone who meets you falls in love with you eventually."

She beamed at him, thankful for the confidence boost, even as her dad mumbled something that sounded like, "That's what I'm afraid of."

"Hey, aren't the Bills playing at one?" she asked, in a blatant redirect.

He glanced at his watch and pushed back from the table. "Five minutes to kickoff. You coming, Dad?"

Grandpa waved him on. "Yup, you go on. I'll catch up."

Callie rose when he did and began collecting empty plates. "You don't have to do that, dear," her mom said.

"I know, but I want to help."

"That's a good girl." Grandpa grabbed her hand and gave it a little shake as she came by. When he released her, she glanced down at the crisp new twenty-dollar bill in her palm.

"Paw Paw." She shook her head. "I don't need this."

He lifted a shaky index finger to her lips. "Neither do I."

"You can use it to buy some of that candy Mom won't let you keep in the house."

"No, she's right. My teeth can't handle the taffy anymore, but it's good for my heart to see my favorite granddaughter do what she loves. Besides, I always wanted to be able to sponsor my favorite sports team. Turns out, that's you."

"What about the Bills?"

"Blah." He made a sour face. "The Bills are terrible. If I had to pick them to go to the Super Bowl or you to get to the Olympics, I'd put on my money on you to do it first."

She laughed but didn't argue with him. If that were an actual betting line, she'd put her money on her team, too.

⊙ ⊙ ⊙

Max stared out her hotel room window at the expanse of Buffalo's downtown. She would've preferred a view of Lake Erie, but her budget didn't allow for the upgrade. Honestly, it wouldn't allow for *any* hotel room much longer if she didn't turn something in soon. She really needed to find an apartment, too, but both her mind and her body rebelled at the idea. Her brain told her that the moment she signed a three-month lease, she'd resigned herself to a stay in purgatory for at least that long. She didn't want to admit she still held out hope for a pardon of some sort, though, so she contented herself with the excuse that she was still too sore to go exploring. Blaming her bruised tailbone and scraped-up face felt much better than facing the facts of her current situation.

"Fucking curling," she muttered for the fifteenth time as she stared out the window. Outside, the city hummed by. Traffic weaved in and out of impressive art deco buildings. Much of it seemed headed for the minor-league baseball stadium down the road where some sort of festival seemed to be occurring. She'd seen the crowds and heard the music when she'd ventured out for an extra-large tube of Icy Hot last night. The hipster crowd in the streets and hanging from the wrought-iron balcony of a microbrewery had caught her off guard. She'd sort of expected this city to be either empty on the weekends or perhaps filled with old steel-plant workers trying to drown the misery they never stanched after the last recession took their jobs.

Wasn't that what Buffalo was known for? Not festivals and craft beers and trendy young revelers. Or beautiful, young, fit curlers.

The thought brought her up short, and she turned away from the window. She might be able to handle this city shattering the stereotypes, but she hadn't been wrong about curling.

She sighed in relief. When was the last time she'd had a judgment call affirmed? She didn't want to try to remember. She chose instead to cling to this one instance in which her gut instinct had been spot-on.

Curling sucked.

Taking her seat as gently as possible at the desk, she flipped open her MacBook and started a new document. She didn't even have a plan, but she had something to say, and when that happened, she wrote. She'd always been that way, ever since she was a kid, and Lord knows it wasn't a learned behavior. She'd never seen anyone in her family write or type a single thing longer than their own names, and none of them had ever encouraged her, so she always thought the habit must have somehow been inborn. Even after she'd gotten into broadcasting and found she had a passion for working in front of the camera, she still preferred to write first when she got emotional about something.

Curling is crazy, and not in the fun way. She didn't know if she had a working title or an opening line. She'd worry about the audience and forum later. Right now, she had more important things to get off her chest, and once she started, she wouldn't stop until she felt better.

She typed at blurring speed about how the game, and it was a game, not a sport, seemed most well-suited to sloths or tortoises, both slow and with low centers of gravity. She led with the story of busting her ass because she'd learned early that the best defense was conceding the points she couldn't win and saving energy to focus on the ones she could. She admitted that balance on ice wasn't a skill most people generally possessed, but then again, why would they? Humans had evolved because their opposable thumbs and large brains gave them the dexterity and the skills to develop and use tools, like skates that would make them faster, or shoes with traction to make them more stable. Curling, on the other hand, rejected both and tried to make its competitors both slower and more prone to falling.

The scoring, which she hadn't even begun to grasp, she labeled as obtuse, and the heavy stones that clacked and swerved without much reason, she suggested, harked back to a more Neanderthal pastime of smashing rocks into other rocks. Perhaps that's where curling had begun, and where it should have been left, in the caves of our Neolithic ancestors. Even in the off chance of a second ice age, she could've made much better arguments for the grace and acrobatic skills of figure skating, or the speed and strength of a bone-crushing hockey game.

She couched all of her snide asides in the form of jokes. Humor was another survival skill she'd learned early, finding she generally won more people to her side of an argument if her witticism made them smile, rather than if she launched a full-frontal diatribe. And as her current piece came together, she figured she had a solid market for a sports magazine if she kept her complaints veiled under the cover of sport humor. *Sports Illustrated* and *ESPN* magazine both ran these types of essays, though they might not want one from her at the moment. Still, it was harder for people to stay angry at you when you made them laugh or made them money. She hoped to do a little bit of both while exacting her verbal revenge.

She used the term "competitive sweeping" when laying doubts about whether the frantic approximation of housework actually did anything except legitimize cleaning skills your mother never quite managed to instill in you. Perhaps, she posited, that's where the game had originated, as a Tom Sawyeresque attempt to teach men the technique needed to clean up after themselves. If that was the case, she'd gladly tip her hat to the woman responsible for duping thousands of people, all the way up to and including the International Olympic Committee, and offer to fill out her paperwork for a MacArthur genius grant. In the meantime, she refused to elevate what she could only see as Canadian Ice Bocce Ball to the level of the other sports she covered.

Then, since she was stuck covering this piddly winter adaptation of a garden party game, she ended with a hook designed purely to make her sound more sporting than the "sport" she was trying to cover. She copped to this article being born out of a first impression and promised to watch closely for the rest of the season (without saying she didn't have much choice in the matter), but she defied anyone, at any point in that time, to actually change her mind.

Sitting back, she clapped her hands together, and immediately regretted the gesture, as it sent pain shooting up through her wrist, her elbow, and her shoulders. Groaning, she took some solace in the hope that her words would long outlive the pain.

Chapter Four

"What the fuck?" Brooke dropped the magazine onto the ice.

Callie sighed, but didn't look up from her lunge long enough to even read the headline. She didn't have to. She'd seen it at least forty times over the last twenty-four hours. Several copies had made their way around the club, but they'd also shown up at a couple of her other jobs, in her actual mailbox as well as her email in-box, and she'd been tagged in multiple social media posts.

"It's just satire." She reissued her now-standard response.

"Is this the reporter who's supposed to cover our team?"

She let her body weight, or perhaps the weight of her stress, press her deeper into the stretch despite the tightness in her back. "One and the same."

"Where is she now?"

"Nowhere near here if she knows what's good for her," Ella said, joining them from the other end of the ice.

"I'm sure she'll stop in eventually," Callie said calmly.

"Are you?" Layla asked with a little laugh. "Because I'd be surprised if she can even walk after the beating she took the last time she came in here. I wouldn't be at all surprised if that article is the last we hear from her."

Callie shook her head. Maybe that would be best for all of them, but she'd seen the fire in Max's eyes every time she picked herself up after a fall. Women like her didn't abandon ship just because the water got rough. Also, Max had issued a challenge in that hit piece of hers. She'd said the wide world of curling had four months to change her mind. Callie still didn't know what to make of that open ending, other than the fact that Max seemed to intend to stick around for a while.

"Guys, it's just a humor piece."

"She's a shitty reporter if she thought any of that would be funny to the people she has to work with for the rest of the season." Brooke kicked the magazine aside and settled into a lunge of her own.

Callie couldn't disagree, but she suspected curlers weren't the primary audience for Max's article, and from the comments she'd read online, a great number of people had found the potshots hilarious. Her stomach tightened again, but she didn't want to lose a whole practice to this topic, so she decided to move along. "We've got better things to focus on than the bad jokes of someone who can't even stay upright on the ice."

Several people around her chuckled.

"Yeah," Ella's fiancé, Finn, called from the next sheet over. "Who the hell is Max Laurens to be telling people what's legitimate and what's not, anyway?"

She frowned and straightened herself to her full height, intending to ask what he meant, but a hush fell over the room. She turned to see what could make a relatively full club fall unnaturally quiet, and locked eyes with the cold gaze of Max Laurens.

"She's got a lot of nerve." Finn started forward, but Callie shot out an arm and shook her head.

"Leave her be."

He scowled, but even though he wasn't on her team, he had sense enough to respect her position. Thankfully, the others in the club, either out of their own good nature or in a nod to her, followed along. One by one, each person turned their back on Max and returned to the games her mere presence had interrupted.

Max clenched her jaw against the chilly reception. She couldn't have honestly been surprised, but Callie still felt a little sorry for her. It didn't have to be this way. She blamed herself, at least partially, for letting things get so out of hand at their first meeting. She'd only meant to throw her a lifeline, something to hang onto in unfamiliar waters. Instead, she'd given Max enough rope to hang herself. Still, she couldn't be held totally responsible for what Max had done with it. Max was an adult, and Callie wasn't a babysitter.

She turned back to face her teammates, all of whom were now warming up with a diligence and focus she couldn't remember seeing during a regular, midweek practice. Gone were the jokes and the empty chatter as they each trained their gaze toward the same spot at the other end of the ice.

Max wandered closer and nodded an acknowledgment. Callie returned the gesture and picked up her broom. She had too much going on inside her head to decide how she wanted to play their next interaction, and like everything else in her life, Max would just have to take a backseat to curling practice.

They went through the motions. She called shots, and her teammates made them. She called a sweep, and her teammates bore down. She asked questions about prospective shots, and her teammates offered emphatic answers. No one complained. No one wandered off. Most importantly, no one missed.

The cloud surrounding Callie began to dissipate. Nothing had gone the way she'd wanted over the last week, and yet her team looked better than ever. She had hoped Max would help her cause by offering good press that would in turn lead to better funding. Max had gone in the opposite direction, but maybe that didn't mean all her hopes were dashed. What if Max's betrayal had actually helped more than it had hurt? What if she could use it as a rallying point to focus her team and give them something to push against? Nothing ever helped increase funding like winning, and if they played like they were practicing today, they had a good chance of winning.

She glanced down at the other end of the ice where Max extended her hand to Ella, who ignored her and picked up another stone. Something in Callie's stomach twisted into another new knot. Not long ago, Ella had seen Max as a thrilling new opportunity for camera time. Now she looked right past her toward the ice. Even Callie's most playful team member had her pride. Part of her was happy to see everyone taking themselves seriously, but part of her didn't want to burn other bridges completely.

As she traded places with Brooke to take her own turn in the hack, Callie made the mistake of meeting Max's eyes again. She saw nothing but steely resolve. Maybe the ice in Max's gaze should've fortified her, but she couldn't help wondering what had made such a beautiful face so stone cold. The expression predated her current chilly receptions. She'd seen it from the moment they'd first met. She probably should've taken the hint then. Still, her mother's reminder to kill with kindness floated back into her mind as she assumed her delivery position. She couldn't ignore Max and use her as a rallying point at the same time. She'd have to choose one or the other eventually.

"Callie," Max tried, after she'd released her first rock. "We need to—"

"Practice." Ella cut in. "*We* need to practice. *You* need to stay out of the way."

Max's jaw twitched.

Ella wasn't wrong. They had a limited amount of time together each week, and they rarely got practices this focused so far out from a major matchup. Callie's priorities would not waver in this area, no matter what she saw in Max's eyes.

Wordlessly she turned away from the woman who'd already captured too much of her emotional energy and set up to release another rock. She cued her process of clearing everything, first from her mind, and then from the periphery of her vision, until the only world that existed fit on a one-fifty-by-fifteen-foot sheet of ice. She focused on the sound of her own breathing as her fingers curled around a handle that had come to feel like an extension of her own body. Allowing her eyes to flutter briefly closed, she never lost sight of the spot she wanted, and then opening them once more, she pushed off fluidly. Weightless for those few seconds of suspended glide, she released the rock and the tension she'd felt only seconds earlier.

She didn't even have to wait to see the line before she called, "Never, never, nope."

"Draw weight," Brooke confirmed from the other end of the ice, and indicated the rock would draw right up next to the one she'd left sitting in the center of the rings.

"Perfect, Skip," Layla called back to her, "as usual."

She shook off the compliment attached to the end of the assessment. She was generally far from perfect, as a player, as a leader, as an emissary for the sport, but that wouldn't stop her from continuing to try.

With that heavy thought, she rose and turned to face Max. Only she wasn't there anymore. Sometime during the minute it had taken Callie to make the shot, Max had disappeared.

She noticed the door to the curling area closing and leaned to the side to look through the large plate-glass windows to the lounge. Sure enough, Max had her back to them all, moving swiftly away.

"Callie," Layla said, suddenly beside her, voice low, "do not run after that woman."

"Yeah." She nodded, her gut clenching again.

"Stay the course, Skip."

"Yeah," she repeated, her voice weaker.

Layla sighed. "You're going after her, aren't you?"

"Yeah." She kicked off her curling shoes as she sprang off the ice, and didn't even bother to slip into her street shoes as she watched Max use her stiff shoulder to push open the outer door to the club. Every head turned to watch Callie go, and she felt the early burn of shame, but it did little to slow her momentum as she weaved her way quickly toward the door. She caught it just before it slammed shut behind Max, and throwing it open shouted, "Hey!"

Max turned and raised an eyebrow.

"What the hell's the matter with you?"

"Excuse me?"

"Seriously." She stepped outside, the gravel of the alleyway pressing uncomfortably on her sock-covered feet. "What's your problem? Are you this petulant and pouty all the time, or is it a new thing you're trying on for shits and giggles?"

Max's mouth crooked up in a smile. "Wow."

"No, I want a serious answer, because you seem dead set on being as offensive as possible while still acting like the offended party. Did I do something to torque you off, or had you made up your mind to disdain me before we ever met?"

Max frowned, opened her mouth, and then closed it again. She turned her head to the side as if pondering the question for a moment.

"Are you kidding me?" Callie fired back. "You have to think about your answer that hard?"

Max shrugged.

"We're busting our asses in here because we have a job to do."

Max rolled her eyes. "That is not a job."

"You're a pretentious asshole, you know that?"

Max laughed. "I've been told a time or two."

Callie sighed. "Has anyone told you that you suck at your job?"

Max winced and offered no reply.

"Has anyone told you that you don't belong? That you don't deserve what little you have? That all the work you've done to get where you are doesn't mean a damn thing? Have you had people make jokes at your expense and publish them for the world to see, only to then turn around and treat you like you should be the one begging them for more attention?"

Something wounded flickered through Max's expression, but she still lifted her chin. "Actually, I have."

Callie stared at her, waiting, practically pleading with her to make the connection, but the mask of defiance fell back across her features as quickly as it had faded.

"Look, you may not like curling, and you may not like me, but this *is* my job, and even if that doesn't matter to you, writing about it's supposed to be your job, too. Don't you at least care about that?"

Max's shoulders slumped slightly, and she nodded. "I do."

"Then, maybe we could start from there. Your job matters to

you. My job matters to me, and for the time being those jobs intersect. So, I'm all in on your little challenge."

"What do you mean?"

"That temper tantrum you put into writing, you ended it with a challenge to change your mind about curling. I fully understand that you probably didn't mean it, or maybe you thought you'd made a safe bet, but I've been bet against before, and I don't like to lose any more than you like to surrender."

Max snorted softly.

"Go ahead and laugh." Callie gave her a dismissive wave. "But if you're half as good at your job as I am at mine, I'll see you tomorrow."

With that, she turned and left Max standing in the alley. She didn't even stop when she heard the door slam behind her, and she didn't mind that everyone inside was staring at her.

Swiping a copy of Max's magazine off a table as she strode through the lounge and through the door to the ice, she didn't stop until she reached the massive whiteboard where they posted announcements and planned strategy. A small crowd gathered as she neatly tore the article from the rest of the publication and used a magnet to fasten it to the metal frame of the board. Then, snatching up a black marker from the tray below, she scrawled two words, bold and big enough to be read from anywhere in the room: "Challenge Accepted."

The Buffalo Curling Club wasn't nearly as crowded as it had been the day before. Perhaps four o'clock on a Tuesday wasn't prime curling time. She had no idea when prime curling time might be. The last few times she'd stopped by after five, people had been here, so she hadn't had to stop and think that perhaps that wasn't always true. She glanced up at the rusted-out warehouse and wondered why she'd had to remind herself this wasn't like an Olympic training center.

Still, as she walked up to the glass and stared out across the ice, a handful of people were curling. On one sheet, there seemed to be a group of high schoolers playing around, and at the other side stood the solitary figure of Callie Mulligan.

She allowed herself the luxury of watching Callie unnoticed. Despite all of the things Max had said about curling not being a sport, Callie still managed to look very much the part of an athlete. Of course, her body type was lean, and her thigh and calf muscles were clearly toned and firm even under her long, yoga-style pants. But there was something else about her, too, some intangible quality that set her apart from the others, who bore the body language of hobby players. Callie moved with confidence, grace, and purpose all melded together. She wasted no energy and suffered no distraction as she arranged several stones a few feet apart on the ice, then crouched low as if visually measuring their exact distance from each other. She did that little foot-push slide down the ice that everyone in the place seemed to have mastered, and Max winced at the unbidden memory of her own feet going out from under her.

Thankfully, Callie's singular focus kept Max unnoticed, affording her a few more minutes to watch her settle into the hack, stone in hand. She straightened her legs, showing off impressive glutes that Max admired with a slightly less-than-professional appraisal. Callie pushed off, making the long, low lunge seem easy, and released the stone, then hopped up and trotted after her own throw.

Max knew enough now to marvel at the core strength and balance those moves required, but she barely had time to process how her understanding had evolved before the stone Callie had thrown connected with the first one she'd positioned at the other end, sending the stationary one out of play. The shot would have been pretty enough if it had stopped there, but it didn't. Callie's rock spun off in the opposite direction, sending it careening into the other stationary rock with considerably less force. The bump was enough to knock it back at least a foot, while Callie's stayed put this time, right in the middle of the rings.

Admiration got the better of Max, and before she could remember how much she resented having to be here she pushed through to the ice area.

Callie glanced up, her quick smile fading into a frown. Max wondered whether the opposite had become true for her, as she generally frowned first and made someone work for the smile.

"You're back," Callie said by way of greeting.

"It's my job."

"It was your job yesterday, too." Callie nudged her throwing rock with her foot until it slid away, its blue handle spinning merrily.

"And it will be my job tomorrow, and the next day, and the next week, so I suppose we should start getting ready for the first big match of the season."

"Season started last month. I think you mean the Masters tournament next weekend, which is our fourth event of the year."

Max ground her teeth. She didn't like not being in the know. Reporters dealt in information like currency. Having none was bad, but she'd just admitted to having worse than none. She had counterfeit information. Bile rose in her throat, but she forced it down. She hadn't made a real mistake. She hadn't done the research. That was her fault, but admitting blame did little to improve her mood. "I thought curling was a winter sport. It's only October."

Callie grinned and finished resetting her red rocks right back to the same spots she'd had them before her last throw. "The season starts when it starts. Sorry we didn't ask your permission."

She didn't respond as Callie slid back down the ice. What could she say? She couldn't change the curling schedule any more than she could change the fact that she had to cover it. Actually, she could probably change her current writing assignment much more easily than she could change the curling schedule. She could always quit. She'd never done so in the past, but other people did. They took time off. More than one of her colleagues and editors had suggested a leave of absence. She could call Flip right now and tell him she intended to walk off the job. She could go sulk or hide or spend a month drinking margaritas on a beach in Miami. She'd be warmer, and she'd probably have more fun, but she'd also have more downtime, and right now that prospect appealed to her even less than hours of watching curling.

Turning back to Callie as she played the exact same shot as she had moments earlier, Max wondered if this woman would haunt her daydreams the way others did. She shouldn't. She hadn't earned that spot in Max's psyche, but she'd taken up residence there nonetheless over the last twenty-four hours. Ever since Callie had blown up on her in the alleyway yesterday, Max had been able to think of little else.

She didn't feel guilty, not a bit, but intrigue certainly fell among her prevalent emotions, and unfortunately, so did interest. The woman was such a strange mix of fiery and mousy. Yesterday, as she'd shouted Max down, she'd seemed to war between sad and pissed off. Max knew that blend well. She also had an unfortunate familiarity with desperation, and she'd heard plenty of that lacing Callie's tirade, too.

Maybe that's why the hook had landed in her chest and stuck there. She saw so many of her own emotions warring in Callie that, for a moment, it really seemed like they were in the same boat. She looked away, unable to process the connection through the haze of confusion and resentment still pushing at her from the inside. She scanned her surroundings, trying to tether herself to the physical. The ice, the steel, the concrete—she took solace in their solidity, until her eyes fell on a dry-erase board against the wall. There, splayed out in full black and white, was her article with the words "Challenge Accepted" underneath.

She turned her head just as Callie's rock cracked against first one and then another with pinpoint precision, and she immediately started resetting them to go again.

Something inside her cracked. Callie felt the same way she did. She knew it. She saw all the swirling emotions, the anger, the sadness, the desperate pleading, the frantic clinging to any shred of hope, and yet she managed to display all of those things without an ounce of bitterness.

Callie had merely accepted the challenge before her and gone back to work. It was something Max hadn't quite been able to do in her life, no matter how much she'd tried. What sort of inner fortitude did this woman possess that she lacked?

Callie felt Max's gaze on her as surely as she felt the ice under her feet. She was used to throwing pressure shots with the game on the line. There was no reason for the indifferent inspection of a single bystander to throw her off, and yet the hair on the back of her neck stood on end when Max watched her. Finally, she couldn't take it anymore. Turning around, she asked, "Do you have any questions?"

Max stiffened as if the question had caught her by surprise, and Callie checked her tone.

"I mean, if you want to hover over there like a stalker while I work, that's fine, too, but I can talk and practice at the same time."

"With an offer like that, how could a girl refuse?"

Callie shook her head but fought a smile. Maybe Max just possessed a sardonic sense of humor.

"Where's the rest of your team?"

"Layla will be here later. Ella and Brooke are only here on Sundays and occasionally Wednesday if we have an event coming up."

"They only practice twice a week?"

"No." She shot back quickly, a natural defense against the scorn building in Max's voice again. "We only practice together twice a week."

"Why?"

"Brooke lives in Rochester. Ella's a little farther away, and honestly that's closer than most elite curling teams. Most of them only get to practice together around major tournaments."

Max's brow furrowed.

"We make do with what we have," Callie said, trying to cut off another insult before it could be delivered. "Curling's not like most team sports. We don't pass to each other like basketball or football. Our team works because everyone on it plays their own part to perfection, and we can each practice our parts at our own clubs."

"So, you just do this by yourself day in and day out?"

Callie nodded. "At least an hour every day, plus I generally work out with Layla off the ice every day, and on the ice three to four times a week. I also play in two different pickup leagues."

Max grinned. "I bet the poor local dudes love to show up to their beer league and see a professional across the ice from them."

Callie smiled at the second joke in that many minutes. "Yeah, they call me a ballbuster, but I suspect some of them secretly like having their asses handed to them by a girl they can't have."

"Wow." Max's eyes lit up a little. "That's some edgy psychology there, Doc."

She shrugged. "I call the shots. It's my job, and the title is 'Skip,' not 'Doc.'"

"Skip," Max repeated, as if committing that tidbit to memory so she could use it later.

The silence fell between them again as Callie reset her stones and launched another shot. She managed to take out both of the stationary stones again, but still finished about two inches from the center of the button. It wasn't off by much. Most people would have called it a perfect shot, but she thought she could probably do a smidge better, and in curling sometimes a smidge made all the difference.

"What about you?" she asked, as she moved her foot to put the red rocks she used as targets back into place. It actually would be nice if Max helped with this job. It didn't exactly take any great skill to slide stones into place, but she knew better than to ask her to step back onto the ice. "What's your title?"

"Right now? I guess I'm a sports reporter," Max said, as if she wasn't at all sure of that.

Callie straightened her shoulders, bracing for an argument about the legitimacy of curling as a sport, but when she met Max's eyes, she saw more doubt there than she'd expected.

"I used to call myself a journalist," Max continued slowly. "I could be an on-air personality or broadcaster at some points, too. Probably will hit that target on this assignment, along with some blogging, and multiple kinds of commentary."

51

"Which do you prefer?"

She shrugged and looked away as if she wouldn't answer, and Callie felt a prick of disappointment. She didn't know why she wanted to hear the answer, but she did. She'd almost given up hope, though, by the time Max finally spoke.

"I like big, comprehensive pieces," she said slowly. "I cut my teeth on reporting scores and doing play-by-play, but I prefer the intersection of human interest stories and epic battles in the physical arena."

"Like during the Olympics, when they run the five-minute features on who the athletes are and what they had to overcome to get to the podium?"

"Yes," Max said, more quickly this time. "I did a bunch of those in Rio, and I had a blast, but they're never long enough to really get under the skin. I'm talking about really studying athletes. What drives them? What pushes them to break their bodies in pursuit of near superhuman performance? I love the thrill of finding that fulcrum point in a life or a season or a game when a person has to either crumble or willingly bear the mantle of a near impossibility."

Callie nodded, spellbound, as Max came to life in front of her. Her eyes changed, her voice changed, her entire body language changed. It was almost as if she was pulling from the qualities she spoke of seeking. Callie didn't doubt she was an amazing storyteller.

"I mean, I'm sure you don't see much of it in curling, but I've watched the way sports teams or performances can lift an entire region."

Callie's mouth twitched a bit at the curling dig, but she didn't want Max to stop talking. She liked this side of her. She could identify with it.

"I did a cover story for *Rolling Stone* last year about Elise Brandeis and Corey LaCroix, who came out as both gay and a couple at the Olympics two years ago."

Callie nodded at the now household names of America's favorite skier and snowboarder. "That's a big story."

"It was, and everyone was telling it from the same cutesy angle, but there were all these different layers of grit and fear and physical pain and personality clashes that went deeper than hers-and-hers gold medals. I had almost a whole ten pages to dive in. Few places let you go that deep as a sportswriter."

"So, you like long articles better than the short video interludes?"

"I'd like not being forced to choose. I'd love to use every tool at my disposal to tell a truly multifaceted story, like a great sports documentary. That'd be the dream."

"You could do that here," Callie said, more out of a desire to see Max thrive than out of any self-interest.

Max snorted softly.

"What? You'll have the time. You've got months, and the better part of a season to construct a narrative."

"But I'm not sure curling can give me the gripping content I'm looking for. I need a sport with enough drama and heartbreak to inspire people from outside that circle to be better humans."

"I'd think that if you were a good enough reporter, you could find a way to convey the humanity of anyone who was actually human."

One corner of Max's mouth curled up, and she glanced over her shoulder to the dry-erase board. "That sounds like a challenge, Skip."

She hadn't meant it that way at all, but she didn't hate the hint of a thrill in Max's tone. Instead of transitioning back into her numbness, she seemed to be sparking her stubborn defiance into something close to a more engaged bravado. Callie couldn't help but get swept up in the undercurrent of excitement as Max met her eyes once more and said, "You make good on your challenge, and I promise I'll make good on mine."

Chapter Five

"So, how's the reception at the curling club since your last piece came out?" Flip asked, his voice pouring through the speakers of Max's rented Subaru as she merged onto the highway heading out of Buffalo.

"It's, pardon the pun, 'icy,'" she admitted, but didn't go into any details.

"You better find a way to heat it up, because it's been two weeks since I've seen anything new from you."

"I'm working on it. I've been to practice every day this week."

"How's the team?"

"They're . . . working hard." She made the vaguest statement possible because she didn't want to admit she hadn't actually seen the team function together. She'd watched Callie frequently and had observed a joint workout with her and Layla, but this afternoon would be her first session with the whole team. She felt a twinge of nerves when remembering how "well" it had gone the last time she'd tried to approach anyone else at the club.

When she didn't elaborate further, Flip tried a different angle. "And what about you? How hard are you working?"

"Did you call me to bust my ass?"

"Yeah," he said, without a hint of guilt in his tone. "I went out on a limb for you on this job, and so far all I've got is one humor piece mocking the people I sent you to work with, nearly two weeks ago."

"I didn't know we were running a paper mill here. I'm getting acclimated to a sport most Americans know nothing about and have no interest in watching. It's not exactly an easy sell. You need to give me a little time."

"You've *had* a little time, but it's running out, which is why I'm busting your ass right now. Our first TV coverage of the season is next Saturday. I have a cameraman arriving in Nova Scotia on Thursday to start shooting filler, and right now I have no advance press from you. None."

Panic rose in her chest, amplified by the doubt in his tone. She'd been aware she was pushing the deadline, but she hadn't let herself think about the full implications of not seeing something through. She'd already mucked up her career beyond recognition. If she got fired from covering curling, she'd be done. She would probably also take Flip down with her if what he'd said about going out on a limb for her was true.

"I'll get you a couple of blogs by Wednesday," she said resolutely. "You can have them online at the start of the tournament, and then we'll film a few short vignettes to have on air by the weekend when we go live with coverage. You can have your play-by-play man cut to me on the sidelines if you need to."

Flip groaned, and she heard a dull thud like his head might have hit the desk.

"What?"

"You are my play-by-play man . . . or woman, or reporter. I can't cut to you because you will be on the screen. Did you even read the damn contract?"

"I skimmed it."

"Did you make it to the part that says whenever the team you're covering is playing, you do the broadcast?"

"Yeah, but like color commentary."

"This isn't the big leagues anymore. We can't even guarantee a two-person broadcast. It'll just depend on who your team is playing."

Her stomach roiled now as she took the exit toward the curling club, her foot a little heavier on the gas pedal than it had been moments before.

"If you can't handle this, you need to tell me now so we can replace you."

All the air left her lungs in a silent sob at the words "replace you," and she bit back the emotion threatening to explode out of her again. She was not replaceable. She wouldn't let herself be, not now, not again. "I'll get the work done. Email me the specs on what you need and when. I will not miss the deadline."

"Yeah, but what about—"

"I'm at the club. Email or call later, but let me do my damn job right now."

"Fine—"

She'd heard enough and pressed the end-call button on her dash, then skidded to a stop in the gravel lot. Practically sprinting down the alley, she threw open the door and crossed the lounge in three strides, then pushed through into the ice area with so much force the door hit the wall with a clatter. People turned to stare at her, but she didn't have enough chill to act chagrined. She looked past all of them, searching for Callie, finally spotting her at the far end of the closest sheet of ice.

She stood stock still and straight in the middle of the rings with her broom out in front of her, hazel eyes wide in surprise.

Staying on the solid platform, Max skirted the ice until she stood only a few feet away from her. "Hey, what are you doing for practice today?"

"Well, hello to you, too, Max."

She rolled her eyes. She didn't have time for pleasantries. Her mind had already slipped into work mode, and she needed an angle. "This is a full team practice. You're the boss, right?"

"I'm the 'skip,'" Callie corrected. "I call the shots for the other three players on my team. That doesn't make me their boss, though—more like a leader."

"But you don't play lead."

Callie laughed lightly. "I'd never thought of that before. I'm the leader to my lead."

Max didn't find the wordplay nearly as clever as Callie seemed to.

"But Brooke calls the shots for me," Callie continued. "She's my vice."

"Vice," Max repeated. "Vice like sin? Vise like the grip? There's a play there."

"Vice as in vice-skipper, like vice president."

She frowned. Not nearly as interesting.

"But vise like the grip might be relevant today," Callie said jovially.

"Why?"

"Because here she comes, and she's not happy with either of us."

She turned just as Brooke slid to a stop less than a foot away, her long, stick-straight black hair still stirring on the breeze of her approach. "What's the problem, Skip?"

"I was just explaining our positions to Max. Have you two met?"

Brooke shook her head. "Nor do we need to do introductions in the middle of a simulation."

Callie shrugged and turned to Max. "She's not wrong. We'll talk later."

Then, before she could stop her, Callie scooted off down the ice.

Max made a move to follow, but Brooke shot out an arm to block her. She opened her mouth to argue, but when she met the dark, defiant eyes staring back at her, she closed it again, finally understanding Callie's comment about "vise grip." Stepping back, she decided that perhaps quiet observation might not be the worst tactic.

There were more rocks in the rings than she'd ever seen before, and a few out in front of them, too. Both red and blue handles were equally represented, and they were scattered more than clustered. All good observations, but what did it mean?

57

She heard a low rumble like a far-off jet engine, a sound she'd come to recognize as a rock sliding toward her. Callie had released a red one, arcing it around the ones out front of the rings, but it was losing speed.

"Yep, yep," Brooke called, and two women with brooms pounced in a scrubbing frenzy.

"Get it there, get it there," Brooke encouraged. "Hard."

The rock curved more and more as it entered the rings before finally spinning to a spot on the second biggest circle.

Brooke threw a big thumbs-up in Callie's direction, and the two sweepers headed back down the ice without so much as a glance toward Max.

"So, that was a good shot?" she asked to Brooke's back. She got about as much response as she expected, as in none. Instead, the vice plucked a blue stone and placed it right up next to Callie's and walked back to position.

"Simulation," she whispered, remembering what Callie had said. They were placing the other team's rocks in hard positions and trying to work around them. The thought piqued her interest. There weren't many sports where you could actually simulate a scenario better on your own than with an actual opponent. She gave Callie a nod of respect as she threw again.

This time the rock followed much the same line, but a tick faster.

"Gotta curl," Brooke called, then glanced down at a stopwatch in her hand. "It's hot."

The sweepers seemed to understand what those cues meant and stayed fully upright as they walked along beside it.

"Cleared the guard," Layla said, in another term Max didn't understand.

"Curl, baby, curl," Brooke urged, but the rock remained neutral to her pleas, only bending back toward the rings slightly.

Ella shook her head. "Not enough."

"It might get there," Layla said hopefully.

"Naw, let it go," Brooke instructed, as the rock slowed, then spun itself out a solid foot from where Callie's first rock sat.

"Sorry," Callie said, and Max startled to see her so close all of a sudden. She'd been so focused on the rock's trajectory she hadn't even noticed her approach. "Want to go again?"

"I just don't think a little tick is going to do it here," Brooke said, holding up her stopwatch as some sort of evidence. "You have to lose too much to get around the guard."

All four women stared down at the rocks for a few seconds.

"Push back?" Callie finally asked.

"Split the guards?"

"Or try to drive ours through."

Brooke frowned. "Tough angle."

"That's why we practice." Callie turned and glided away, while the others shook their heads.

"What's a guard?" Max asked.

No one answered.

"Seriously?" she asked a little louder. "Not even a vocab lesson?"

"We're a little busy here," Layla said without looking up.

"Can you at least tell me if a pushback means you're going to try to hit one of the rocks out of the middle?"

"No," Ella said and walked away.

"No as in you won't tell me, or no as in that's not the play?"

Again, no answer as everyone assumed their previous position.

Max's frustration rose. She was used to a general distrust in the press, and she understood all too well why someone might not want to bare their soul to her, but stonewalling a legitimate network contact in an official setting and capacity was unheard of. No one on the ice seemed to have the slightest clue how to be a professional athlete, and she thought about telling them that, but then she remembered the article stuck to the dry-erase board behind her. Maybe she needed a new tactic if this was the result her goading had yielded.

Callie launched a new stone, and this time, it didn't curve much at all. It didn't slow down as it barreled toward the rings either, striking one of the forward-most blue stones, sending it straight back into two others. The entirety of the rings and everything in them shuddered before settling.

Callie caught up to the sweepers, and they all converged over the remaining rocks.

"Not terrible," Callie said, inspecting the damage.

"If we assume the hammer, we sit at least one. Maybe two," Brooke said in a tone suggesting agreement.

"I wouldn't play it if they had the hammer," Callie said, looking back. "We stripped our own guard."

"So, the front one is the guard!" Max said, almost triumphantly.

Ella shook her head. "Are you special?"

"What?"

"Seriously, are you a little slow, like mentally? Or do you really not know anything about the sport you've been sent here to promote?"

"Cover," she corrected, "not promote."

"Yeah, so I'll take that as a no," Brooke said.

Max sighed. "I understand that you all have to land the spinning rock on the bull's-eye for points, like in darts. Also, you use the brooms to change the direction of the rock to make it get closer or hit another rock."

They all stared at her, a mix of disbelief on their faces, except for Callie, who seemed more amused.

"Wow." Ella finally laughed. "Everything you said there was completely wrong."

"No wonder you have to write assassination pieces instead of real reports," Brooke added. "Wouldn't want anyone to know how terrible you actually are at meaningful commentary."

With that, she turned and headed back down the ice, pushing two stones in front of her. Layla and Ella both followed in similar fashion, and Callie turned away, using her broom to send the last two blue rocks down the sheet.

Max's face burned. "So that's it? No explanation?"

"They don't like you," Callie said. "That's an explanation of sorts."

"Because I wrote a humor piece about curling?"

Callie leveled that hypnotic hazel gaze at her. "Don't add to the injury by trying to insult our intelligence."

Max stared at her feet, embarrassment washing over her. She'd never intended the piece to be good, harmless fun.

"You broke their trust before you even earned it," Callie said more softly. "It's going to take time."

The panic swelled in her again. "I don't have time. I'm working on a deadline, and I get that I'm partially responsible for cutting things close, but I'm trying to make up for my mistakes now, all of them."

Callie raised her eyebrows at the comment, but Max forged on.

"I get that no one here liked my first piece, but blackballing the only reporter here to cover you won't serve your interests either, and honestly, if you all want to prove to me that you're serious, professional athletes, you need to start acting like it off the ice, too. You want the bright lights of TV coverage, then you need to grow skin thick enough to withstand the scrutiny that comes with being professional athletes."

Callie pressed her lips into a thin, white line, but the little flecks of gold in her eyes made Max wonder if she might actually be trying to hold back a smile. "I don't actually disagree with your premise, but I'd like to turn it back around on you for a second, because for all your talk about us acting like professional athletes, you've yet to treat us that way."

"I already said I made some missteps with the article."

"I'm talking about right now. You've just interrupted our practice multiple times in the middle of a drill that requires both physical and mental focus. Would you do that with, say, a football team?"

Max clenched her teeth.

"Now who's refusing to talk?" Callie's tone was laced with both teasing and satisfaction. "Would you walk out onto the field unannounced in the middle of a Bills training camp to ask players how many points a kicker could get?"

"No," she admitted, "I probably would've gone through a press office, and then approached a coach or player rep."

"That's me. I'm the coach, I'm the rep, I'm the coordinator for my team. They call us Team Mulligan for a reason."

"I'm sorry," Max said, trying to hold the pouting in her voice to a minimum this time. "I don't know the curling hierarchy."

"Maybe you should learn," Callie said, "because the season has already started, and as far as I can tell, you haven't written or recorded a damn thing since you slung mud a few weeks ago. From where I stand, it looks like you need us a lot more than we'll need you next week."

Her stomach knotted at the truth of Callie's pronouncement. She didn't have the power here. She didn't have it anywhere right now. She'd resisted this moment as long as possible, but as much as it nauseated her to admit, her name and her reputation weren't going to open doors for her anymore. She had to revert to the skills she'd used to get her to the top in the first place. She cleared her throat. "You're absolutely right."

Another raised eyebrow managed to convey both surprise and suspicion.

"I haven't shown you the respect generally afforded to someone in your position. I haven't done my due diligence when it comes to researching curling. I'd like to remedy both of those things, and I'd greatly appreciate your professional insight."

"Thank you," Callie said. "I understand it probably hurt your pride to say those things."

"A little bit, but I do care about my job, which is why I'd like to learn the rules of curling. Can you please tell me if I'm correct in my understanding that a guard is one of those rocks out in front of the rings."

"You're correct."

"And can you explain to me the scoring system?"

"No," Callie said politely. "I'm still in the middle of a practice. I don't have the time or energy to give you lessons while skipping my team."

Max sighed and, lifting her arms slightly, allowed them to fall back to her sides with a flap.

"I will, however," Callie continued, "allow you to stay on the platform and observe. Afterward you can tell me what you've figured out, and I'll let you know if you're on the right track."

She started to shake her head and then caught herself. This wasn't a negotiation. It was an offering, the only one on the table. Lifting her hands in surrender, she said, "I'll take what I can get."

The next two hours were a blur of rocks and brooms. No one spoke to her. None of the players even looked at her, but as they moved through various scenarios, she did notice that after each of her final throws in a simulation, Callie would call out a score. She hadn't been doing that before, and Max leaned a little closer as if inspecting a puzzle.

Red had one in the middle. They got one point. Maybe the middle meant one point.

But then blue had one in the middle and got two points, even though their other one was in the bigger, white ring. She scowled. How many points were the other rings worth?

Then the red team had one in the middle of two blue ones, and Callie knocked it clean out.

Three points. That didn't make sense. Maybe the rings weren't point-based at all. Maybe it came down to the number of stones the throwing team got in the rings. One rock, one point? That seemed democratic enough.

And yet after a few more rounds, or what did she call them—ends?—she noticed Callie only called out the points for one team, even when both teams had rocks on the rings. Her frustration rose, and she began to pace around the back of the sheet looking at different angles.

Finally, after clearing another set of rocks, Callie smiled mischievously at her.

"Figure it out yet?"

"It's not a point system like darts," Max said, not quite answering the question. "The rings aren't like three points for center, two for red, one for white."

"Correct."

"It's not points per rock either, because only one team is scoring in each end."

Callie nodded her affirmation. "That's as far as you've gotten?"

"Maybe."

"And that annoys you, doesn't it?"

"Maybe."

Callie laughed.

The sound didn't grate on Max's nerves. If anything, it loosened some of the tension from her shoulders, but she didn't want Callie to know. "You enjoy tormenting people or something?"

"What you call torment, I call motivation. You like to know what's going on." Callie stepped a little closer. "You're not the only one figuring things out today, Max."

"Oh?"

"If I tell you, you'll lose interest. If I make you figure it out, you'll stay engaged, and I want you engaged."

Max swallowed the emotions that the comment and Callie's lower tone sparked in her as she fought to stay present in this moment. "Sounds manipulative to me."

Callie shrugged. "I'm the skip. It's my job to figure out what makes my people tick and use that to our mutual advantage."

Sirens went off in her brain, and the edges of her vision tinged red, but Callie didn't seem to notice. She just pushed off back down the ice once more, leaving Max to battle the demons crawling at her again. She had to hold them at bay. She had to anchor herself to this spot. Not to Callie, not to any person.

She forced her eyesight back into focus and onto the rocks. Two red stones right next to each other in the center. Two blue ones opposite them in different sides of the red ring, and Callie threw again to park a blue just inside the white.

"That's two for blue," she called.

Understanding sparked through Max as the final piece slid into place just like the last stone. She had it. Straightening up, she smiled broadly, all the panic that had nearly consumed her mere minutes ago fading as something finally made sense.

"You have it," Callie stated, as she came back to the other end.

She nodded. "Only one team can score per end. That's the team closest to the center of the rings."

"The 'button.' Yes, but how do we get more than one point?"

"You get a point for every additional rock that's closer than the other team's closest one."

Callie grinned.

"In this end, you had two blue ones closer to the button than the closest red stone."

"And what about all those other stones?" She indicated several farther away than the blue ones.

"No points for them, only the ones closer than any of the opponent's rocks. Only the winning team's closest rocks score points."

The grin grew, and it warmed Max so much, she briefly worried she might begin to melt the ice around her.

"All right," Callie called down to her teammates. "Good end. Let's call it a day."

They all sagged with apparent relief and pushed off the ice, collecting their gear as they went. Callie turned to join them, but Max reached out, catching her arm.

"Wait."

Callie glanced down at where Max's fingers curled around her firm biceps.

"Sorry," she mumbled, momentarily thrown off. She didn't usually touch the people she interviewed, and she certainly didn't touch women who hadn't indicated their interest. She didn't know what had come over her, nor what was stirring in her now that she'd felt those impressive muscles flex beneath her palm. "I just . . . well . . . did you keep practice going for everyone until I caught up?"

Callie laughed that same lilting ring that echoed off the ice. "You're a long way from caught up."

Then she slid away, leaving Max to stand there in the cold, trying to reconcile the fact that Callie totally had her pegged.

Chapter Six

"I'm at a tournament called the Canadian Beef Masters," Max said aloud, to no one in particular. No one else seemed to find it odd anyway. Maybe it wasn't odd in this strange world of curling, but for all the middle-of-nowhere, low-budget sporting events she'd covered on her way up the reporting ladder, she'd never been to one named for a generalized dead animal product. And she'd thought the Tostitos Bowl had been a silly name when she'd covered it last year. What she wouldn't give to be back in Phoenix instead of freezing her ass off in Nova Scotia. Seriously, she'd had to look at Nova Scotia on a map just to make sure she actually knew where it was, and the geography wasn't the only thing she'd been unsure of during this tournament. In fact, it had been the least of them.

"Whoa, Max Laurens," a man said in a thick Minnesota accent, or maybe the accent was Canadian. She didn't know the difference. "Didn't expect to see you all the way up here."

"Me either," Max said, stepping up onto a platform only about a foot higher than the ice.

"You're not covering Team Mulligan, are you?"

"I am." She searched the man's features, from his rosy cheeks to his full red beard. Nothing about him sparked recognition, and he must have seen it.

"I'm Tim Mathis. We both covered the World Junior Championship tournament in Reykjavik a few years back."

"Oh." She still didn't remember him, and if she'd been covering junior sports, it had to have been more than a few years ago.

"Yeah." He laughed easily. "You ran circles around all of us even back then. You could pronounce the names of even the third-string players on the Slavic teams. Shoulda known you'd climb the ladder."

"And yet, here we both are at the Canadian"—she cleared her throat—"Beef Masters."

"Oh yeah, well, Grand Slam curling isn't the NFL, but it's got its charms."

"If you say so." She took the seat next to him and slid her mic a little closer.

Tim shifted over a little bit, almost nervously. "I'm sure you've got lots of great stuff prepared. I could do play-by-play if you want to do commentary."

"You know," she said, "I'm still a bit new to the sport. Why don't I just follow your lead today?"

He puffed up his chest a bit. "Sure thing. It'd be an honor."

She should've been relieved. Most other reporters treated her like she had cooties these days. Still, she couldn't manage to summon any of her social charms as she watched Callie and her team take turns sliding out of the hack and down the ice.

"Your gals have had a stellar tournament," Tim cut back in.

"Have they?" She supposed it never hurt to be a semifinalist, but she didn't know enough yet to tell if they'd played well or if the competition had been subpar. Most of Callie's team still wasn't speaking to her, and even Callie had been distracted over the last forty-eight hours. Or maybe distracted wasn't the right word, as she'd been focused on the tournament, playing two matches a day since arriving, but all her focus on her job had meant she didn't have time to focus on answering questions. Max had been forced to watch from the stands, trying to make sense of a game that often seemed to defy logic. She'd even resorted to watching

YouTube videos to pick up some terms. She pulled out some papers on which she'd scribbled the terms and definitions.

"Yeah, when I heard they'd even made this event, I was a little surprised. Looks good for American curling, though, to have our second-place team eke their way into the top fifteen."

She stopped shuffling her papers. "Second place?"

"Yeah, they're team two of the American cohort," Tim said, then furrowed his brow. "But, you knew that, right?"

"Yeah," she said quickly. "I mean, they were seeded fifteen in this tournament."

"That'd be their world ranking then, wouldn't it?"

"Right," she said, even as she wondered why she hadn't thought of that. Fifteenth in the world wouldn't be the top American team. That's why they were playing another American team today. Why had she assumed her team was the only national team? Oh yeah, because that's how national teams generally worked. America didn't have three national hockey teams or three national soccer teams, and those were real sports. Why the hell would there be three national curling teams, and perhaps more embarrassing, why wasn't she covering the top one?

Closing her eyes, she inhaled deeply and slowly through her nose and blew it out her month.

"They really have overachieved so far," Tim said cheerily. "Who knows where they'll end up the season?"

"And your team? Team . . .?" She glanced at her notes. "Team Dawes?"

"First-place American team," he supplied.

"No, I knew that." She lied. "I meant, how are they playing this year?"

His smile widened. "Rocking the house."

"Of course they are." She'd tried to sound congenial, but it only came off as tired. Tired of being out of the loop, tired of not knowing, tired of getting scooped by two-bit local reporters like Tim Mathis. How had this guy been picked to cover the top team when she got relegated to the second tier of a cut-rate game?

Sadly, by the third end she thought she had her answer as he corrected her for the twelfth time. "Actually, that's not a takeout. That's called a tick shot."

"Right, right." She tried to cover, though anyone with half a brain and a working set of ears had clearly seen through that charade two ends ago. "And can you explain the difference between a tick and a takeout for the casual viewer at home?"

"Certainly," Tim obliged, ever the professional, and made to look even more so by her gross ineptitude, "since you can't move a guard."

"A guard being a stone in front of the rings." She cut in with the only part of this she understood.

"Yes, and you can't move them out of play until the fifth stone of any end," he continued, stating a rule she hadn't known. "Sometimes the lead player has to play what's called a tick, and Layla Abrams just did so beautifully there, because she managed to move her opponent's guard over enough that it's not in her way without taking it completely out of play, or leaving her own rock in its place."

"And now the other team can't knock Layla's guard out of play, either."

"No, but seeing as how her guard isn't really guarding anything, I think they are probably going to put another one right where they put their first one."

"Indeed," she said with more gusto than the comment warranted, and then quickly added, "let's watch and see."

She wanted to put her forehead down on the desk, but she didn't dare. Even assuming the whole two cameras on this match were both pointed at the ice most of the time, she didn't want to run the risk of appearing as though she'd actually fallen asleep on the job. She might sound like she was completely out of it, but she didn't have to look the part as well.

The player she'd come to think of as Tim's lead played exactly the shot he'd predicted.

"Well, she is consistent," Max said.

"That's a bread and butter shot for a lead," Tim said. "If your first player can't throw a center guard, you don't stand much chance of making the top fifteen in the world or staying there for long."

She quickly scribbled a note to that effect in the margins of the vocabulary notes she'd brought with her. "And what would you say are the bread and butter shots for the other players? You know, in case we have any aspiring curlers at home who want to know what to practice."

He raised an eyebrow as she kept her pencil at the ready, but his tone never wavered. "I'd say every curler worth his or her salt should be able to throw a rock that sits in any open spot in the house at any time. Also, a simple draw around a single guard right to the button."

She wrote even while asking, "And a draw means just a rock that sits in the house."

"Exactly."

She grinned. That was one of the terms on her list.

"And the last shot any good curler should be able to play is a clean takeout, where they hit any open stone in the house, and knock it out without hitting something else."

"And we have seen all of those shots today," she said almost excitedly.

"I think you'd expect to see most of those shots in most ends at the professional level."

"Indeed," she said again, and shook her head. Who the hell had she become? Reduced to asking apparently dumb questions and uttering inane asides or exclamations, she said nothing else until Callie delivered her last rock, but then the excitement of actually knowing how to keep score overtook her and she proudly declared, "That's one point to Team Mulligan."

"And I know she's disappointed with that," Tim said, with a shake of his head.

"Is she now?" Max's voice cracked a little higher. "I mean obviously she is, but in a game when only one team scores, I think many people would see it as a good thing to be the team doing the scoring, but not in curling."

Tim laughed, and she forced herself to laugh along, even though she wasn't sure if he was laughing with her or at her.

"You're not wrong," he finally said, "but Callie holds herself to higher standards. All the women out here today do, and when a team has the hammer, they're expected to take at least one."

"And remember," Max said in an almost Pavlovian response to hearing one of her vocab words, "the hammer is what we call the last stone of the end."

"Right, and when you get to throw a stone no one had a chance to take out, you expect to sit it pretty close to the button, but the goal is always to make a play where you score two or more points with the hammer. Otherwise, the other team considers it a sort of win, or a tie at least, because they get the hammer the next time. A lot of teams would rather take a zero for an end and hold onto the hammer for the next one in the hopes they can do better that time around."

"Well, Tim, that's not confusing at all."

He laughed again as the guy working the camera motioned that they were fading to commercial break.

Silence fell between them, and Max tried, as discreetly as possible, to check whether the sweat from her armpits had soaked through her shirt. Thankfully, she appeared to be faring better on the outside than the roiling mess of emotions inside her might suggest. Her stomach hurt, her head pounded, her heartbeat echoed through her own ears, and she was so hot. How was she so hot in a room filled with ice?

"You okay?" Tim finally asked.

No. I might be having a stroke. She held the words in and rubbed her clammy palms over her face. She couldn't remember the last time she'd felt this out of sorts during a broadcast, probably because she never had. Sports were her solid ground, the place where she had the answers, the topic she could always use to hold her own. And she'd covered plenty of sports, not just ones she herself had played. She'd always managed to come through, though. Grit, research, charisma, and an innate understanding of what drove people to strive for excellence always mattered more than an intimate knowledge of game plans, or at least it always had until now.

"We'll pick up this end in progress. We're running one of your personal interest pieces, Tim," the cameraman said.

"Do you know which one?" Tim asked.

"The one on your lead's ties to Scotland."

"Ah, yeah, the motherland of the game," Tim mused and shuffled some papers.

Max glanced down at her notes, which said nothing about curling being invented in Scotland. It hadn't even occurred to her to delve into the history of the game. She'd been content with understanding the scoring and a basic glossary of terms.

"Ready to dive back in?" Tim asked, concern evident in his voice as he added, "You look a little nauseated."

"Yeah, I might be coming down with something."

"I don't mind picking up the slack," he offered. "We all have tough days."

"Thanks," she mumbled. She might've found that thought more comforting if she hadn't brought this one on herself. Instead, she lifted her chin, and looked the camera dead on, bracing herself for another hour's worth of mental and emotional drubbing.

Callie dropped her curling bag next to a bench before flopping onto it with about the same form as the duffel. "Ugh."

"Yeah," Layla agreed.

"Fourth place," Callie said for about the seventieth time.

"Could've been worse."

"If you say, 'we could have been fifth place or sixth place,' I will choke you."

Layla's grin suggested that might've been exactly what she'd intended to say, but then, glancing around, changed course. "You could have been that dude."

Callie followed her gaze to see Max slouched against a wall in the other corner of the arena. She had her hands jammed in the pockets of her slacks, her shoulders slouched forward, and the set of her jaw sent a scowl radiating across the room. She looked so isolated and angry, Callie had to stifle the urge to go to her.

"I heard she shit the bed on TV."

"What?"

"Not literally, but everyone is joking about how terrible her coverage was. They had to bring in a different broadcaster to bail her out. The Canadian team started a drinking game for every time she asked a stupid question, and they all got hammered."

"No."

"Yeah. If you had a contest to see who had the shittiest weekend, I think she'd win. At least we managed to do our job, and then some."

Callie frowned at the reminder of their own failures. "Did we?"

"Come on, Cal, don't start that again," Layla said. "We finished fourth out of fifteen teams. We exceeded every expectation."

"Not mine."

Layla snorted. "Yours are a little crazy. You expect us to win every match."

"We're capable."

"Maybe in that anything's-possible-on-any-given-day sort of mentality."

"No," she snapped, then caught herself. "I'm sorry. It's just frustrating to see so much potential in us, and not be able to put it all together at the right time."

"Yeah, but we did actually put it together most of the time." Layla picked up her pep talk. "We ran through the first half of the tournament. We played out of our minds. Literally every team we beat was ranked higher than us, and we only lost to two teams in the top five of the world."

"But if we keep losing to teams in the top five in the world, we're never going to break into that group, and if we keep losing to other Americans, we'll never make it—"

"Don't say it."

"To the Olympics," she finished.

Layla hung her head so a few small braids that had come

untucked from her stocking cap fell down over her eyebrows. "It's two years away. Can we not do that to ourselves this season?"

"I've been doing this to myself every season since I was ten."

Layla sighed. "I know. I've been there through every one of them, but can we try something different now? Can we just practice hard and play our best in the moment and let the results be what they'll be?"

Callie shook her head. It wasn't that the idea didn't appeal to her. She'd love to be the kind of person who didn't always push for more, the kind of person who could rest on her laurels, or even the kind of person who could rest, period, but she wasn't. "I wouldn't be me without the weight of this goal on my back. I'm not sure I'd want to be me without it."

Layla kicked her foot lightly. "Then don't change, because I wouldn't want you to be anyone else, but come get a beer at the Patch, at least."

Callie rolled her eyes. "That's the last thing I need, and the last place I want to be."

"Too damn bad." Layla picked up her own bag and slung it over her shoulder. "If you're going to be morose and obsessive, the least you can do is buy me a drink. That's friend code 101, also basic curling etiquette."

"Actually, it's curling etiquette for the winning team to buy us beers."

"Yeah, Team Dawes totally owes us the first round, but the second one's on you, or I'm going to crank our hotel room heater up to ninety-seven degrees tonight."

Callie laughed lightly. "Okay, okay. You drive a hard bargain, but if I get to keep my Olympic dreams and the thermostat at sixty-two, I'll meet you at the Patch and buy a round for the whole team."

"Sixty-nine," Layla said with a snicker, "for the thermostat, not the beer . . . or anything else."

"Deal."

Layla pumped a fist triumphantly. "See you in there."

Callie rolled her head from side to side as her lead went to join their teammates and competitors at the area tournament organizers set aside at every stop on the tour for players, officials, and their more hard-core fans to hang out after matches. There'd be live music, drinks, probably some dancing, and tons of people eager to catch up or rehash the event. In other words, it'd be everything she didn't want right now. Still, she felt a little better after talking to Layla. Maybe she needed to be pulled out against her will every now and then. It wasn't like she could do anything about their results right now. If she went back to the hotel room, she'd only spend her evening staring at the ceiling and trying to do the math on what it would take for them to improve their world ranking next time out. Those equations rarely gave her anything more than a headache.

Placing her hands on her knees, she pushed herself up, ignoring the way her thigh muscles had stiffened even in the few minutes she'd been sitting. Maybe moving around a bit would help that, too. Grabbing her bag, she headed out of the arena and down a long, low hallway.

"Please, please don't cut me loose," came a voice from an off-shoot hallway. The voice was familiar, but the pleading tone was what really drew her up short.

"I know. I understand I was already on probation, but I need one more shot."

Callie peeked around the corner, and there behind the stack of brooms and refrigeration equipment huddled the shrinking form of Max Laurens. She seemed smaller than ever, and not just because she'd crouched down with her back against the wall and her knees to her chest. She pressed a phone to one ear and her finger to the other.

"Can't you put me on, like, double probation?" she asked. "Can't you make it a thing?"

Callie couldn't hear the answer, but she suspected it wasn't good, because Max only continued to fold in on herself. "Please don't fire me over this. I'm a good reporter."

The rawness of that statement made Callie suspect Max had said it as much for herself as for the person on the other end of the conversation.

"Okay, fine, I *used* to be a good reporter, and I can be again. I have to be. I've lost everything. This job is all I have left. Please don't take it away. I know I can do better. I can be better."

Callie's heart twisted in her chest. She knew that desperation and that desire. She also knew how it felt to watch something you love slipping away. She held her breath, waiting for some cue that Max's pleas hadn't fallen on a heart of stone.

"Okay," she finally said, her voice raspy. "No. I promise. I'll have everything to you far in advance of the next tournament. I'll prove it, Flip. I'm all in now. You can run the job advertisement, but don't replace me until I have a chance to file a couple more pieces."

That didn't sound promising, but at least it didn't sound like she'd quite gotten fired, either. Callie started breathing again and rested her shoulder against the wall just around the corner. Max would at least have the chance to keep her job, or maybe reapply for it; she wasn't sure. She also wasn't sure why she cared enough to lose a single breath over Max's problems. If she'd been as bad as Layla'd said, Max probably deserved to be fired. She certainly hadn't applied herself, not the way Callie and her teammates had. They'd killed themselves to get the little bit of progress they'd achieved while Max had wasted weeks sulking and making snide remarks, and then had spent the past few days trying to make them all do the work of bringing her up to speed.

Callie pushed off the wall and walked quickly away before the desire to go to Max could overtake her. She had nothing to feel guilty about, but she knew the haunting echo of Max's pleading would likely mingle with her own grasping and bargaining as she lay awake in bed tonight.

Chapter Seven

When Max arrived at the Buffalo Curling Club five days after the tournament, she found Callie curling alone again. She didn't know if that was better or worse than having the whole team there. Certainly, Callie was nicer and more prone to speak to her than any of the others, but she'd hoped to start working on that today.

She'd spent the better part of a week studying the sport of curling. She didn't have any other choice. Flip had already started shopping for her replacement, and she could only pray he didn't find someone before she had a chance to redeem herself. After the embarrassment she'd suffered at the stupid Beef Masters, her first task centered on self-education. Thankfully, most of her sports knowledge had been self-taught. She'd only had to go back as far as her own roots to dredge up the skills necessary. She'd read books and watched YouTube videos, some of which were admittedly more confusing than helpful, but she now had a solid grasp on at least the basics.

She had also watched enough full-length games to understand how much she still needed to learn about strategy. There was so much blocking, and building, and anticipating future shots, she'd come to recognize an almost chess-like quality to the mental aspect of the game. She might be able to work that angle going forward, but she also knew from her hours holed up watching replays that the charm of this game, if it existed at all, couldn't be shared with the casual viewer on X's and O's alone. She had to have a personal interest angle, or no one would follow her long enough to reach the appreciation level necessary to delve into strategy. And for the moment, she had only one person to choose from.

She sighed, then straightened her shoulders. She'd learned long ago she couldn't play the hand she wanted. She could only play the one she got dealt, and honestly, as she watched Callie's long. graceful form in a fully extended lunge, she had to admit she'd been dealt a lot worse in the past.

The woman had a body the cameras would love, paired with the face of a girl next door, set off by the most intensely focused hazel eyes. It wouldn't be a hardship for people to watch her, even on mute. Maybe if she'd seen that sooner, she could've run with it, but she'd passed the point where she could phone in some pretty pictures and inane prose. She had to find a way to truly engage readers, and she suspected that meant she had to find a way to engage Callie herself.

As Callie finished her slide, she stood up, but instead of following her rock down the ice, she turned and glanced over her shoulder. As her eyes met Max's, a corner of her mouth curled up slightly, and with a little tilt of her head, she motioned her forward. Then she went back to work. The invitation had been subtle, but it was enough to spark something that felt suspiciously like hope in Max's chest, and she followed willingly.

"Where's your team today?" she asked, pulling up next to Callie as she rearranged a few rocks at the far end of the ice.

"Life."

"I thought they'd be all amped up after the tournament last weekend."

"You'd think," Callie said drolly, then seemed to catch herself. "I mean, I'm sure they are, but life gets in the way."

"Life?" Max asked at the second use of that vague term.

Callie shrugged. "It's nearing the end of the heart of the semester for Brooke, who's in the last year of grad school. Ella's soon-to-be stepdaughter has strep throat, and Layla is working extra shifts at Dick's Sporting Goods to make up for the shifts she missed last weekend."

"Layla has a job?"

Callie snorted and kicked her rock back down the ice. "We all have jobs."

She followed her rock, and Max walked along beside her, pulling a small, compact video camera from her jacket pocket and flipping it on. "Even you?"

Callie nodded. "I have several part-time jobs. I tend bar on an as-needed basis. I work for a lawn care company all summer. In the winter, I do snow removal for the same company. I walk dogs and house-sit when I can. Mostly, though, I pick up shifts at a local, used sporting goods store."

"Why?"

"They're flexible, and they let me come in after hours to sharpen skates, resize golf clubs, or take inventory of new trade-ins."

"No, I mean why work so many jobs?"

Callie got back into the hack, spinning the rock until the handle came to a stop in the position she wanted. "Mostly for giggles."

"Really?"

Callie rolled her eyes. "Of course not. We're all broke. You may not have noticed, but there's not exactly a line of sponsors and advertisers beating down my door."

"But you get funding from the national team," Max said matter-of-factly.

"We do," Callie admitted, pushing off again and going into her slide with her usual grace and focus. She released the rock before popping up and strolling down the ice, broom in hand. She picked up the conversation right where she'd left off. "Our entire team got about $25,000 last year."

Max did the math in her head. "That's only, like, six grand per person. You can't live on that."

"Live?" Callie laughed and crouched down to inspect which rock was closer to the button. "It's not enough to even travel on. We have to pay for our flights, our hotels, and our meals at every tournament all season. Think about the last bonspiel—that's what we call the big tournaments—flights from Buffalo to Nova Scotia, five nights in a hotel, five days of eating on the road. It all adds up."

No, it didn't add up, not for professional athletes. Not for Team USA. Who would ever sign up for hemorrhaging funds while the national Olympics body raked in all the dough for merchandise and TV ratings? There had to be a missing piece in the equation. "What about winnings?"

Callie stood and frowned, her usually youthful features creasing with worry lines. "Sometimes we win individual tournaments, which adds a bit of extra money to our pockets. We have a better shot of winning smaller bonspiels, but the smaller the competition, the smaller the payout. Bigger events pay more, but the likelihood of doing well enough to make prize money shrinks."

"Who makes the call on which ones to play?"

Callie's shoulders dipped, only a little, but enough for the camera to catch the weight pressing down on her. "We get some guidance, some encouragement, but we also have a lot of freedom to make those decisions as a team."

"But you're the skipper," Max pressed.

"Yeah. I am. A lot of things fall to me."

"So, what do you choose? The bigger money, or the better shot to win?"

"Neither." Callie started sliding back toward the other end of the ice.

Max scurried behind her, briefly wondering why they hadn't begun to wear matching troughs down the middle of the ice and carpeted platform. "Uh, sorry, would you mind elaborating?"

"I choose our tournaments based on the ones I think will make us better. To be the best, you have to compete with the best. That's all I look for. The pool size, the location, the prize purse, they're all secondary to the quality of the curling. I want to improve our ranking, I want to improve our game, I want to improve, period."

The steel in Callie's voice left little doubt to her seriousness, and Max didn't question any further along those lines, but the issue of full dedication did loop them back around to the original issue. "But when you're working so many jobs, how do you find time to focus on curling?"

"I don't ever *find* time to curl. Curling is the focus, always. I have to find time to work around the travel and tournaments and practice sessions. That's why I have so many sporadic jobs. Paying the bills comes second to my passion."

"Does that make paying the bills hard?"

Callie's smile turned wry. "Hard is relative. Do I have to do without some things other people take for granted? Sure. Is it worth it to be able to spend my physical prime doing something I love? I think so, usually."

Max probably should've jumped on that 'usually,' but she was too hung up on the phrase "physical prime." Stealing another glance at Callie's long legs in those tight pants, she could only appreciate the term's aptness.

"So I spend as much time here as I can. I spend at least one hour a day working out, alternating strength and conditioning, and I spend one to two hours a day on the ice."

Callie quieted as she surveyed the damage at the other end of the ice, frowning slightly as those hazel eyes swept over the rocks before she quickly rearranged them and headed back to the hack again.

Max smiled at the understatement. "How many hours do you think you spend on curling-related activity in a regular week?"

Callie didn't even hesitate. "I shoot for thirty, but weeks when we have bonspiels I probably get closer to forty or fifty."

"Plus several part-time jobs."

Callie shrugged.

"How can you manage that pace over the course of months? Something has to give. There are only so many hours to go around."

"I guess I don't need as much sleep as other people." She wedged her right foot back against the hack and coiled her body once more, but Max didn't want her to push off again, not when she felt so close to something that the hair on the back of her

81

neck stood on end. Still, as those hazel eyes locked in on her target, flecks of brown and gold shifting like an amber kaleidoscope, she felt the woman before her shifting into another dimension. She wanted to grab for her, to anchor them both together or, better yet, be transported with her. Almost subconsciously, she zoomed the camera in her hand as if trying to get closer. But as Callie began to rock back, all her energy building to propel her forward, Max called out the only thing she could manage to blurt.

"Why?"

Callie froze, then slowly turned her head, until the focused gaze she'd leveled at the other end of the ice suddenly encompassed Max, in all its intensity and intimacy.

"Why choose to put in those kinds of hours and make those kinds of sacrifices for something that doesn't even pay the bills, much less offer fame and glory?"

"I didn't *choose* any of it," Callie said, her voice as cold and flat as the ice between them. "Not any more than my eye color or my sexual orientation. This is who I *am*."

With that emphasis, she surged forward—controlled kinetic energy, mass, velocity, and honey-colored hair blowing in the breeze of her own momentum.

Callie crouched and spun the rock in front of her until the yellow handle stopped, and she wrapped her fingers around it loosely. Clutching her broom in her other hand, she glanced up. She didn't see the scoreboard. She didn't have to. They were tied with the number-one team in the world, and the final stone sat in front of her. This was their last shot, and everyone in the packed arena knew it. She didn't look at Brooke's face, either. Her vice didn't want to play the shot she'd called, but she held her broom between two red rocks anyway. Callie would have to hit them both, simultaneously, with equally distributed force and enough oomph that her rock would continue to move forward rather than transfer its energy to one of the guards.

The shot wasn't a physical impossibility so much as a feat of physics. The thought comforted her more than it seemed to her teammates, whose nervous energy wafted down the ice to her. They wanted her to play a safe shot or burn the rock by throwing it short. They were all happy to tie the top team rather than risk bumping one of the red guards into a winning position for Sweden.

She wanted the win.

The choice really was that simple. The physics, the score, the tension, the overall rankings all fell in line behind a singular desire and her faith in her own ability.

The world around her fell silent. All of her periphery blurred. She saw only her line. With steely certainty, she pushed back, swinging the rock with her, before reaching her pendulum peak and reversing course. All her momentum swung forward, and with an extra shot of strength through her leg, she added her own thrust to the gravity of the movement. Arm extended to the front, leg extended to the back as though it were the most natural position in the world in which to fly down the ice, her hair fluttered back away from her face as the worry slipped from her shoulders. And then she let go.

She slowed to a stop but stayed low to the ice, trying to gauge the line of the shot between the bodies of both sweepers hustling down the ice. All the fear and uncertainty that had fled during her slide slammed back into her. She'd chosen a shot dependent on millimeters. Slivers of millimeters. The width of dental floss could make a difference here. She held her breath even when Brooke shouted, "Stay with it."

Then came impact, a flash and crack that reverberated through the cavernous space. Both Layla and Ella pounced, jumping over the spinning guards and sweeping furiously to eke every remainder of forward propulsion out of the rock, until finally, in the same instant, they stilled.

Six people stepped forward, trying to position themselves directly over the rock, but when the crowd cleared, Brooke shot one hand in the air, index finger raised.

Callie wobbled as every joint in her body threatened to give way. They'd won.

Pushing herself slowly up until she could trust her balance again, she let the applause of the crowd wash over her.

"We won."

"Be cool."

"We're in the finals."

"Act like you've been here before."

"We're the top Americans left in the draw."

The seesawing comments of her teammates floated all around her, but she could barely hear them over the sound of her own heartbeat throbbing through her ears as she shook the hand of the Swedish skip and managed to say, "Good curling."

She accepted compliments with nods and mumbled thanks, but their joy still eluded her.

They'd done it. They'd beaten the top-ranked team in the world in a stunning upset, and Callie was, well, stunned. It wasn't that she hadn't thought they could win going in. She always believed they could beat any given team on any given day, but being able to do something and actually doing it were two very different things.

A hand clasped her shoulder, and she turned to see Layla smiling broadly at her. "You okay, Skip?"

She nodded. "Yeah. I'm great."

Ella reached up and mussed up her hair. "Holy spit, that shot was flipping wicked."

"You're going to kill me," Brooke added, grabbing her by the scruff of her jacket and giving her a little shake. "Do you know the probability of making that shot evenly?"

She shook her head. "Please don't tell me the odds."

Brooke laughed. "Okay. You earned one night off from sciencing, but please, at some point watch the TV footage because I could hear the announcers behind me, and I think they geeked out so hard they might've blown a gasket."

Callie glanced over her shoulder, searching the riser where the commentators would've sat. She hadn't paid any attention to the press area during the match, but if Max had been so excited to call her hammer shot, maybe she should go congratulate her, too. It would also offer a chance to help pump up the press coverage. She internally justified her need to seek out someone only tangentially related to her in the immediate aftermath of a huge win.

"She's not there," Layla said, as if reading her mind.

"Who?" Ella asked.

Layla turned back to the general stands and nodded up to a lone figure still sitting in the front corner of the raised bleachers.

Max wore a baby blue dress shirt under a gray wool coat, and her dark hair was impeccably coiffed. Her professional attire made her stand out against the rest of the spectators, in brightly colored sweaters and stocking caps, but not as much as her slumped shoulders and downtrodden expression did.

"She's been there the whole match," Layla said, "not a camera on her."

"So?" Ella asked. "Did she get fired . . . again?"

"No," Callie said quickly, her chest tightening at the realization she didn't know that for sure, not any more than she knew what the "again" part of the question alluded to.

"More importantly, why would we care?" Brooke asked.

Layla shrugged. "Maybe she's not totally terrible."

"A ringing endorsement if I've ever heard one," Brooke said.

"She's been better lately," Callie defended weakly. "Besides, she's the one covering us. If she's not happy, we're less likely to get the press we want from a win like this."

"Not if she got replaced," Ella mused. "Then maybe they'll send someone serious to work with us."

The thought rubbed Callie the wrong way, but she didn't quite know why. Ella wasn't totally off-base. And yet, faulting Max for lack of seriousness didn't feel right, either. Max had always been serious, maybe even to all of their detriment, but more than that, she seriously seemed to be trying to save herself lately. The echo of her pleas on the phone two weeks ago still rang through Callie's ears every time Max entered the club. She'd seen the fear lacing the focus in her eyes as she attempted, time and time again, to interview people who didn't want to talk to her, which had been often, over the last week.

"Yeah, but I just think maybe—"

"But nothing." Brooke cut back in, giving her a little shove. "You just made the best shot of the entire bonspiel in an epically clutch moment. The only thing you should be thinking about is the finals tomorrow."

The last part of that statement stuck much more than the first. She'd made a great shot, she'd got a great win, yes, but no amount of celebration would've kept her from going to Max right now as much as the reminder that her own work was not done. She didn't have time to rest. She didn't have time to worry about anything but the work ahead. She was the skip of the hottest team in the tournament, and tomorrow they'd try to take it all. That meant tonight they needed to watch video of their match, study the tactics of their opponents, and talk strategy.

"You're right. Let's go get showered and changed, then takeout and review session in my room at six?"

Her teammates' smiles and nods of agreement all confirmed she'd made the right choice, but as they gathered their things and walked away, she couldn't resist glancing over at Max once more. She hadn't moved, and the forward set of her shoulders hadn't shifted, but she'd lifted her eyes, steely and gray. Callie froze. She couldn't say why, she couldn't even breathe, but something Max radiated surged through her, a sadness, a sense of betrayal, the determination of a drowning woman.

Then a group of people stepped between them, blocking her view and cutting off her connection as they shuffled past, totally oblivious to anything other than the air of celebration she no longer felt. By the time everyone moved out of the way, Max was gone.

Callie shivered. For a woman who'd spent all day on the ice, this was the first time she'd felt truly cold.

Chapter Eight

That's a perfect takeout for the Japanese skipper. Callie Mulligan will likely play the same shot with her stone, Max commentated internally. *It'll give her one point to close the gap a little, but not enough to take the lead, and she's running out of rocks to play.*

Her internal monologue wasn't exactly inspired, but she would've held her own. She didn't even have a cheat sheet of terms in front of her anymore. If she'd had Tim or some other commentator to bounce off of, she would've done even better. She'd already made up her mind to play the role of informed newcomer, a sort of eager emissary between the curling in-crowd and people new to the sport. If what Flip had said about slowly but steadily increasing viewership was true, there had to be hundreds, if not thousands, of people interested but not fully engaged in the game. She could serve as a sort of bridge for them. Or at least that's what she'd tried to argue when Flip had refused to let her back on the air.

Oh, he'd said "yet" and been adamant that they hadn't found a full-time replacement, but a whole hell of a lot that did for her now, watching the finals from the stands while someone else called the shots of *her* team.

The thought made her shake her head. When had she started to think of Team Mulligan as hers? Brooke and Ella still wouldn't even speak to her, and Layla had warmed but not fully thawed. Only Callie had really let her in, but damn, she couldn't help feeling like that meant something. Or maybe she'd just watched the footage she'd shot of her so many times over the last week that she'd internalized it. How could she not? That moment when Callie'd leveled those cat eyes of hers right at the camera and said, "This is who I am," still sent a shiver up her spine.

Who wouldn't want to be a part of that passion? And for the last week of shadowing her workouts and matches, Max had felt like part of it—maybe not the curling, but at least the sort of collective momentum Callie seemed to sweep people up in.

Even now, as her team trailed by two in the final end, she carried herself with an enthralling mix of command and affability. Max should've been the one to point out those details to the viewing audience. Instead she sat idly by while Callie made another perfect shot to curl around a guard, knock out the closest Japanese rock, and sit right on the button. Plus she made it look easy. Max had seen several others miss similar shots over the course of the bonspiel. It was textbook, it was beautiful, it was admirable even, but it wasn't enough. What a freaking metaphor for Max's life right now.

She didn't know how Callie kept from screaming at the frustration of doing everything right only to come up short. They'd both deserved a better outcome today, but as the match concluded and everyone shook hands, Max didn't find the loss nearly as disheartening as her distance from it.

"Hey, Pencil Pusher." Layla's voice cut through her pity party. She stood at the bottom of the metal bleachers, staring up between a few stray braids that had fallen over her eyebrows. "You look like you could use a beer."

She opened her mouth to say she didn't usually drink beer, then thought better of it. "Actually, I could."

"Me too," Layla called. "You buying?"

She snorted at the boldness of the question, but Layla's tone and implicit invitation amused her for the first time in days. "Where?"

Layla grinned. "The Patch, of course."

"Hey," Ella called, and gave Layla a "what the hell?" look.

Layla shrugged her off. "I'm gonna let it go, El. We got beat at our best, I'm broke, and the reporter looks a little broken, too. If she's buying, we're drinking."

Ella pursed her lips together, clearly not thrilled, but unable to argue with her lead's logic.

Layla turned back to Max. "So? The Patch, you coming?"

She sensed the invitation was tenuous at best and decided against asking questions. "Yes, please. I'll be right with you."

She collected her coat and the backpack with her camera, then clattered down the stairs to the arena floor. Thankfully, she still had a network press pass to flash to the pimply teenager working security, but she had to wade through a slew of random-looking fans all hoping to get an autograph from their favorite curler. The thought of curling groupies still sparked a little shot of snark, but she kept her mouth closed and wound her way to where Brooke and Callie had just joined Layla and Ella.

"What's she doing here?" Brooke asked. "I thought she got fired."

The droll blow made Max's chest tighten, but she'd had plenty of opportunity to practice not showing it. Forcing a smile, she said, "Sadly, not yet, so I guess I'm buying you all a drink in a patch."

"What?" Brooke asked.

Layla groaned.

Ella rolled her eyes. "What she means to say is that Layla invited her to come to the Patch with us."

"Right." Max nodded. "Not *a* patch, *the* Patch. A specific one."

Layla shook her head, but the corner of her mouth curled up. "Talk less, buy more."

With that she walked away, followed by Brooke and Ella. Max got the sense she should follow. Instead, she turned to Callie.

"You threw a good game today, or called one, or played one, whatever terminology I'm entirely too much of a noob to know."

"Thanks," Callie mumbled, seemingly uncharmed by Max's self-effacing humor.

"Congrats on making the finals."

Callie sighed. "It's a start. Congrats on not being fired."

Max nodded slowly, then shrugged. "It's a start."

Callie had to brace herself against the din of the rock band on the stage and the tinny vibrations of their chords against the arching metal roof, a venue that resembled a small airplane hangar.

"This is not really the image that comes to mind when someone says, 'the patch.' I was envisioning something with grass, perhaps a few cows," Max said loudly enough to be heard even in the crowd.

"It's November in Thunder Bay, Canada. No one is partying in pastures," Layla shouted back.

Max shrugged. "You people spend all day on sheets of ice. It's not unreasonable to think you might be acclimatized to the cold."

"Acclimatized. That's a good word. Can one become acclimatized to, say, the keg room?"

Max turned to Callie. "She's not really known for her subtlety, is she?"

"Not really," Callie admitted. She could see the humor in Max's droll attempts at conversation, and under normal circumstances she might've even enjoyed her wit, but tonight she couldn't help wondering why either of them was even here.

The Patch clearly wasn't either of their scenes, but at least Callie had the excuse of being a curler. These were her people. They'd expect her to make an appearance after what most of the field would consider a tremendous showing for Team Mulligan. Even though they'd lost today, they had, once again, far outplayed their official ranking. She didn't doubt that, come Monday, they'd see another bump in their world standing. Curlers were a genuinely friendly group, and they'd no doubt want to offer their congratulations. The only problem was, she didn't want to accept them.

They'd lost today in a game they might've won if only she'd made better calls or better shots, or been a better leader. They could've played better, and to her mind they should've played better. She couldn't quite settle into a celebration with that knowledge hanging over her head, so all she could do tonight was play the part everyone expected of a skipper. She'd be gracious and social. She'd buy a drink for her team and accept the drink curling victors owed the vanquished. And then she'd make an excuse to sneak out early. Or at least that's what she would've done if Max hadn't been watching.

"Earth to Callie."

She blinked away the haze of her own daydream and focused on Max and Layla, who were both staring at her. "What?"

"You okay?" Max asked.

"Yeah, I was just . . ."

"Planning her escape route," Layla said matter-of-factly.

Max raised her eyebrows.

"No," Callie said weakly.

"Yes," Layla cut back in. "She's silently seething about the loss, and she doesn't want to be here making nice, but she respects the game and the community enough to do her part even while counting down the minutes until she can leave."

Max looked from Callie to Layla and back again before asking, "So, you all have known each other awhile, huh?"

Layla laughed. "You could say that, but let's say it over drinks."

"Deal." And off they went, leaving Callie to follow along with a little smile.

Max hadn't argued. She hadn't asked any probing questions. She took the pressure off Callie and rolled with Layla. She'd actually been kind of perfect so far, and the next thing Callie knew Max was paying for drinks. Well, she tried to ask if they had a nice Malbec, but thankfully Layla stepped in and ordered five Labatts. It was a minor misstep, and to her credit Max didn't complain. She accepted her bottle and waved Layla off with three others for herself, Ella and Brooke. If Max noticed their disappearance, she didn't seem bothered by it. And yet, she didn't seem quite happy, either, as she slid the remaining beer over to Callie.

"You don't have to babysit me," Callie said, as she sipped her drink and surveyed the crowd.

The corner of Max's mouth curled up. "I was about to say the same thing to you."

"Why would I babysit you?"

"Because I don't belong here, and everyone knows it. Actually, maybe not everyone, because if most of these people knew who I was, they'd probably have jumped me by now."

"No," Callie said quickly, "curlers are a very easygoing crowd. Everyone knows everyone, and there's a gossip mill to be sure, but it's too small a circle for people to be jerks. Not to stereotype or anything, but most people would say curlers are friendly almost to a fault."

Max snorted and took a swig of beer. "Yeah, I've noticed that around the club in Buffalo. Everyone's so welcoming."

Callie shook her head at the sarcasm. "You didn't exactly get off on the right foot there."

"You're not wrong." Max shrugged. "What about you? Why would you think I'm babysitting you?"

"Because Layla wasn't wrong, either," Callie admitted. "I'm kind of a downer at these things when we lose. You notice she ran off as soon as she got her drink."

"Actually, I hadn't, but now that you mention it, seems like she found the only two sad sacks in the arena, paired us up, and bolted."

Callie hadn't quite connected those dots yet, but Max hadn't made a major leap in logic. Layla knew her well enough to recognize she wouldn't be great company tonight, but she was also a good enough friend not to want to abandon her completely, so she found her a sad buddy in Max. She didn't know whether to be appreciative or offended and didn't see why she had to choose one or the other.

"You really did play well today," Max finally said, her tone a little lower as the band took a break and some previously recorded music took over at a more reasonable decibel level.

"Like you'd know good curling if you saw it."

Max's jaw twitched, and she took another drink. She didn't defend herself, and somehow that gave Callie the space to feel a little guilty.

"I'm sorry. That was rude."

"And deserved," Max admitted. "I'm trying to get better, though. I've been studying. I've watched a lot of matches. I mean, I can't keep stats or anything else because I don't know the strategies well enough, but I've learned to recognize what shot is being called and whether or not you do what's asked of you. You executed all afternoon."

Callie nodded. "I made my shots."

"But you couldn't make everyone else's," Max finished for her.

"We all got into a hole early." Callie dodged the implication about her teammates' play. "And we couldn't scratch our way out, not fast enough, anyway."

Now it was Max's turn to nod pensively, her eyes distant, her jaw tight, and Callie felt a strange connection to her.

"You know how it feels, don't you?"

"Yeah," Max croaked, her voice strangled. "I've dug my own grave a time or two."

"Is that why you weren't working today?"

"I was working." A hint of the old defensiveness flared in Max's voice again, but before it had a chance to take hold, her shoulders fell. "But not on camera. Apparently, I haven't earned that right back yet."

"Because you shit the bed on the last webcast?"

Max grimaced, and her voice rose an octave. "Should we phrase it quite that way?"

Callie hid her grin. "Sorry, I didn't see the footage. I just heard from a few people."

"Great. So much better that tales of my bed-shitting are floating around the wide world of curling."

She laughed. "No, just our club. No one else watches us on TV."

"You're a real inspirational speaker, you know that?" Max asked, but with some dry humor back in her tone.

She shrugged. "I'm the skip. It's what I do."

"Well, I envy that about you, Skip. I have no idea what I need to do. I mean, I get that I didn't turn in my best work off the bench. I came into this sport cold, and I didn't warm up fast enough. I've turned in top-notch stuff to my boss these last few weeks, though. Well, I mean as top-notch as curling can get."

Callie rolled her eyes, but before she had a chance to let the comment sting, Max plowed on.

"I didn't mean what you think I meant. Curling is a hard subject to write about for a general audience. I can't assume much prior knowledge of the sport, and therefore I can't talk to them the way you all talk to each other. However, I turned in several solid pieces in both film and writing. I covered some basics like the history of the sport as well as an introduction to Team Mulligan, despite the fact that three-fourths of them won't consent to an interview. That's no easy journalistic feat."

Callie nodded thoughtfully. Max hadn't made things easy on herself, but then again, neither had anyone else.

"And my boss admitted I'd done a fine job walking an even finer line."

"But?"

Max shook her head, and the first strand of her heavily styled hair fell out of place. "I don't know any specifics. Maybe I missed a moving target, or maybe the hole was deeper than anyone could climb out of in two weeks, but my boss said, given how the team performed in the last tournament and my lackluster coverage of those events, he wanted a more seasoned reporter on this week's webcast."

"So, you played well enough to stay in the game, but not well enough to win," Callie summed up.

"Yet," Max said quickly. "Until the final whistle blows, there's always a 'yet.'"

"Or the final rock is thrown." Callie added her own metaphor because she needed it. She needed to believe Max was right, and neither of them had topped out their talent or potential yet.

"Hello, Callie." A hand fell on her shoulder, and she spun quickly, surprised to find someone else standing so close, even in the crowd. Somehow, she'd forgotten the crowd, which generally only happened on the ice.

"Good curling," the Japanese skipper said in clear, but heavily accented, English.

"Thanks, Pancakes. You played perfectly."

The woman gave a little bow of her head.

"Are you enjoying your Canadian tour?"

"Very much so. A very friendly country, always."

"Indeed," Callie said, and the conversation ground to a halt. She should say something else. God, why was she so bad at these things? She was a friendly person. She made small talk at work all the time, but these post-match conversations always felt so forced. Still, Pancakes was trying to keep up her end of the bargain, and she wasn't even a native English speaker. Callie glanced around for something to kickstart the conversation again, and her eyes fell on Max, who was slowly inching back toward the bar. Callie shot out a hand and caught her around the biceps, reeling her back in.

"Pancakes, have you met Max?"

Max gave a little shake of her head and extended her hand. "Pancakes? Really?"

"It is my English nickname," Pancakes explained, just as she likely had multiple times. "When I began to travel to the bonspiels, I wanted an easier name for the other players to say."

"So, you named yourself 'Pancakes'?"

"I enjoy breakfast."

Max grinned at her, then turned to Callie with a look on her face that seemed to ask, *is this for real?*

"Pancakes is one of the top skips in the world right now."

"Of course she is," Max said, amusement creeping into her voice. Turning back to Pancakes, she added, "Congratulations on your win today."

"Thank you, but also thanks to Callie, who beat the Swedish team yesterday."

Callie nodded. "You could do the same on any given day."

Pancakes nodded her appreciation at the compliment, but Max arched an eyebrow. "Do you beat the Swedish team often?"

"Not often at all," Pancakes said, and then her dark eyes went wide. "I will buy you a drink now as my way of thanks and good sportsmanship."

"I'd appreciate that," Callie said, eager to move this little tradition along. She held up her almost empty bottle for her to see. "Another Labatt would be great."

Pancakes stepped up to the bar and immediately had the full attention of the bartender.

"You know this whole thing is a little surreal, right?" Max asked, when she was out of earshot.

"Whatever do you mean?"

"I'm in a raucous Canadian curling party talking to someone named Pancakes, who just won a tournament, and who now has to pay for your drinks."

"Drink, singular," she corrected.

"That doesn't make it any less weird."

Callie shrugged. "It's just how curlers do things."

"You know that's not how any other sport works, right?"

"I'm sure they've all got their traditions that seem odd to outsiders. I mean, I have a cousin who's into NASCAR—"

"Don't." Max held up a hand. "Do not try to use NASCAR as a logical justification for anything."

Callie laughed, a real laugh that shook her core. "Fair enough, but I still maintain that being friendly with your opponents is a nice way to stay civilized in a competitive culture. But, I'll admit, some people are better at it than others."

"And where do you fall on that spectrum?"

"I have no animosity for anyone. Honestly, I genuinely like the vast majority of the people I curl against, but in the wake of a loss, the wound is usually a little too raw for me to want to party with anyone, much less the people I came up short against."

As if on cue, Pancakes returned with two beers in hand. Callie accepted the first but was surprised to see her hand the other one to Max.

"Are you not drinking tonight?"

"Please don't tell our hosts," Pancakes stage-whispered, "but I find the stuff terrible."

Max laughed. "Pancakes, you are really upping my estimation of curlers overall."

Callie stiffened. The comment shouldn't have bothered her, but it did. She'd thought she'd built a rapport with Max. She didn't know why. They hadn't spent any real quality time together, but lately it seemed as if they'd connected, as if they understood each other. And that connection seemed earned, even hard won, given how they'd started off. To think Max would so easily bond with someone else over a distaste for bottled beer made her remember how little Max wanted to be here.

"Is your team on the dance floor?" she asked abruptly. "We don't want to keep you from them."

Pancakes grinned. "Layla was teaching them a cha-cha slide when I left."

"Well, you won't want to miss too much of that," Callie said. "I'll see you next month?"

"Yes. Safe travels," Pancakes said amiably, then turned to Max. "Nice to meet you."

"Likewise." Max lifted her beer in salute as they both watched Pancakes recede into the crowd.

Callie sighed and took a long pull from her bottle, the new beer cold and crisp, but not enough to soothe the burn still heating her cheeks.

"So which one of us annoys you more?" Max asked. "Me or Pancakes?"

"I'm not annoyed," she snapped, then shook her head. "That didn't sound convincing."

"Not even a little bit."

"It's been a long couple of days."

Max snorted. "No kidding. Is it over now? Do you get to make your escape? Or are there more curling traditions to be observed?"

"Now our team buys their team a beer."

Max chuckled. "You know what, I'd like to take back my earlier assessment about the absurdity of these customs."

"Oh?"

"In my initial rush to judgment, I misread the whole let's-go-to-the-patch-and-buy-a-consolation-beer as a simplistic nod to some nice Canadian politeness, but after being in the crowd for a while—" she gestured to the throng of people dancing and shouting to be heard over the music—"I see you're all geniuses who've developed an elaborate decorum as a cover for getting a little tipsy."

Callie cracked a smile. "Well now, that's some top-notch investigative reporting."

"Hey, it might be an in. Beer is a common draw across a lot of sports."

"We drink whiskey, too, and rum," Callie said, "all under the guise of staying warm on the ice."

"Now you're talking. That's a selling point most of America can get behind. Get drunk, throw stones. Actually, that sounds a lot like our political climate."

Callie laughed again. "I think I should be offended by that summation, but honestly I'm just so tired."

"Physically or emotionally?"

"Why choose when I can have both? Add mentally to the pile as well."

"Ah, the trifecta. I know it well." Max held out her beer bottle. "To being too exhausted to take offense."

Callie clicked her own bottle against Max's.

Max grinned and took another swig of her beer, then swallowed with some force.

"You don't have to drink that."

Max took another big gulp, this time barely holding her grimace. "If we drink faster, we get to leave sooner."

Callie thought about saying they didn't have to drink it at all. They could just leave their bottles on the bar and walk away, but suddenly she didn't want to. Something about Max's gray eyes, or the mirth in her grin, or the flicker of challenge in the set of her shoulders as she lifted the beer to her lips once more made her want to stay.

Callie mirrored the movement and began to drink. She kept her eyes locked on Max as they both swallowed gulp after gulp, neither one stopping to breathe, much less take a break until they'd both drained their drinks completely.

Lightheaded and fighting back a laugh, Callie slapped her bottle onto the corner of the bar. "Done."

"So done." Max plunked her bottle down, too.

"Shall we?"

Max motioned for her to lead the way, and she did. She threaded her way back through the crowd, brushing off blurry well-wishers and muffled congratulations as she went. She didn't stop at the table where Brooke and Ella sat. She merely dropped a few bills on the table as she passed and called, "Next round's on me," and kept on walking, secure in the knowledge Max was right behind her.

Max didn't know what had come over Callie. Maybe she didn't chug beers very often, but neither did Max. And as she swerved a little bit off the snow-dusted sidewalk, it became apparent why. She didn't like feeling out of control. Not even a little bit. As Callie squinted at the dimly lit path before them, she sighed, and Max had to wonder if the skip had a few control issues of her own.

"I'm staying at the Best Western." Max pointed to a green, rambling, two-story building in the distance.

Callie slapped her on the back. "Me too."

"Aren't we living the swank life."

Callie laughed. "I'm rooming with Layla. How's that for splurging?"

"Wow, high roller. At least I got my own room, and it's on the second floor, so I have an expansive view of the parking lot and the back of the convention center."

"Me too. We've got this."

It hadn't occurred to Max that they might not have this until Callie felt the need to state it.

"No problem. Do you need me to help you carry your stuff?"

Callie lifted her empty hands and stared at them for a second. "I don't have my stuff."

"We can go back in there—"

"No!" Callie covered her mouth. "I mean, please don't make me go back to the table. Layla will make me stay and have another beer, and I usually only have two, and I nurse them all night, and shhh, don't tell, but I leave the second one by, like, the leg of the table instead of drinking it all."

Max eyed her more carefully. The buzz she felt humming about the edges of her own nerves seemed amplified in Callie's pink cheeks and the grip she still held on her shoulder. "Wait, you normally nurse basically one beer all night?"

"Only at bonspiels," Callie corrected.

"What about at other places?"

"I don't drink at other places."

"Okay, so you normally drink one beer every few weeks, and tonight you chugged two of them?"

"In"—Callie squinted at her Fitbit—"thirty minutes."

"Okay, Skip," Max said with a light laugh. "You're going to stay right here."

Callie looked back over her shoulder at the curling arena. "How about against that wall?"

"Okay, sure. You lean against the wall, and I'll be right back with your stuff."

Without waiting for a response, Max bolted around the main building and back into the Patch. The music and strobing lights assaulted her senses once more, but she pushed through the undulating masses on the dance floor to the table where she'd last seen Brooke and Ella. Thankfully they were no longer there, but a set of long black duffel bags were stashed under the seats.

Max crouched down, trying to figure out which one was Callie's.

If they all belonged to Team Mulligan, surely someone could bring Callie's along later, but as she thought of the skip, tipsy and propping up the wall outside, she didn't want to let her down.

The realization made her chest ache. She wanted to do something good. Something right. Something independent of what she'd been paid to do. And she wanted to for someone else.

Callie.

She wanted to make Callie smile.

She had such an amazing smile, sweet and broad, and when paired with those intense cat eyes of hers, the combination offered such—

A hand gripped the back collar of her coat and yanked her up.

"What the hell do you think you're doing?" Brooke snapped.

"Whoa."

"What, ripping on us in print wasn't enough?" Ella asked. "Now you have to rifle through our stuff?"

"No." Max shook her head, which only made her vision blur. "I wasn't—"

"You're under the table picking up our bags. Did you really think no one was going to notice?"

"No. I didn't think about other people, I—that sounds bad. I wasn't thinking about you at all."

Brooke snorted and gave her a shake. "Great excuse."

"No, I was thinking about Callie."

Their eyes narrowed, and she suspected her little bout of truthfulness hadn't helped her cause. She glanced around to see several groups had turned to stare. She forced herself to take a deep breath, which wasn't easy, as Brooke still had her practically dangling from her own peacoat. "Look, I'm sorry I made you think I had bad intentions."

"Which time?" Ella asked.

"Any time." Max sighed. "Callie's outside. She didn't want to come back in here to interrupt the festivities again, so she asked me to grab her bag."

Ella snorted. "Sure she did."

"She might have," another voice said behind them.

Max craned her neck as much as she could in her current position and caught sight of Layla.

"Layla, thank God. You left us together, remember?"

"Yeah, let her go," Layla said.

Brooke obliged grudgingly, and Max took a couple steps back until she bumped the table.

"I get that you all don't trust me."

Brooke snorted.

"Fair enough, okay, but you all saw me walk out with Callie, and I only came back in here at her request." Seeing only stone in Brooke and Ella's expressions, she turned to Layla for help. "You can go outside and check if you want."

"Yeah, I want," Ella said. "I'll take the bag."

"I'll do it," Layla said quickly. Pointing at Max, she said, "You come with me."

"We'll go, too," Brooke said. "Party's over."

"Nah," Layla shook her head. "Party's just getting started. Hold my beer."

Ella pursed her lips and folded her arms across her chest, but she didn't follow as Layla gave Max a little shove toward the door.

The cold air hit her with sobering crispness as she pushed back outside. They didn't say a word to each as they walked down the snowy path and rounded the corner. There, leaning against the metal wall in the glow of a floodlight, stood Callie Mulligan with her eyes closed and a dreamy little grin on her face.

"There she is," Max said. "Go ahead and ask her."

Layla shook her head slowly. "I'm good."

"What?"

"I said 'I'm good,' Pencil Pusher. You want me to rethink that assessment, or you want to walk her home?"

Max met her dark eyes, searching for some answer or explanation.

Instead, Layla just held out the bag. "Take it."

"Thanks," she mumbled, wrapping her fingers around the handle, but Layla didn't release it.

Looking up once more, she saw a warning where there hadn't been one a second earlier.

"Don't make me regret this," Layla said flatly.

"I promise I'm not going to go through the bag or write something . . ." Her voice trailed off as the dead focus in Layla's glare made it obvious that wasn't what she'd meant. Her chest tightened again, and she glanced back to Callie, so beautiful and relaxed in this unguarded moment with her long hair stirring on a soft breeze and her lips parted softly.

Turning back to Layla more slowly, she shook her head. "I won't, I mean I can't, because I'm not, we're not—"

"Good night, Max." Layla released the bag and it fell with a flop against Max's leg, the weight of it a tangible reminder of something she hadn't asked to be saddled with.

"Wait," she called, but Layla retreated around the corner.

"Wait what?" Callie asked, pushing off the wall. "Oh, you got my bag. That was really nice of you."

Max bit her lip and shook her head. "I'm not really a nice person."

"I have noticed that about you," Callie said with a little laugh.

"Really?"

"Yeah, but it's okay. I'm working through it."

"You're *working* through the fact that *I'm* not a nice person?"

Callie nodded and joined her. "Shall we walk and talk before you freeze?"

She hadn't really noticed the cold with all the heat coursing through her, but she did feel the need to move around as a sense of unease overtook her. "By all means, lead the way."

Unexpectedly, Callie looped her arm through Max's, and with a little tug off they went.

"So, where were we?" Callie asked.

"Me not being a nice person?"

"Right," Callie said. "Well, you haven't been, which we both agree on now, but I think I get it, because I think I'm starting to get you."

"How so?"

103

"I think you're really driven, and you like to be in control, or at least in command."

"You're not wrong."

"You see curling as beneath you, which kind of hurts my feelings, but it shouldn't, because you don't even really understand curling and you don't really know me, so it says a lot more about you to dislike something you don't even know about."

"Ouch," Max muttered, as the javelin landed in fair territory.

"Right?" Callie asked, sounding oblivious to the barb in her last comment. "No one likes to be judged, but I think maybe you did it because something happened that made you feel out of control, or maybe you actually are out of control, and you just wanted to get back in control as fast as possible."

"Did I now?"

"Yes, and so instead of taking the time to really get to know me and my team and curling as a sport, you freaked out and decided it would be easier to just put us down. That way you get to feel a sort of control without doing any long, hard work."

She frowned and let the words hang in the frozen air between them. Is that really what she'd done? Had she put someone else down to make herself feel better or stronger? She'd already realized her attitude hadn't been helpful, but until this moment she hadn't thought of herself as a bully. She didn't like doing so now.

They reached the hotel, and Callie started up the stairs to the balcony circling the second floor. Max was just lost enough to let herself be led without thinking about their direction. Maybe that should have bothered her. Maybe a lot of things should've bothered her before now.

"I didn't get into this business to tear people down," she finally said. "I was drawn to sports because I liked the way they would bring out the best in regular people. I liked stories of people rising above."

Callie smiled sweetly and slowed to a stop. "Me too. I like those beating-the-odds kind of sport stories. Rocky, or Rudy, or Callie."

Max grinned back, despite the aches still pulsing at her core. "Callie? I haven't seen that movie."

"Maybe you're watching it now. Maybe you could write it, or film it, or whatever you do. I really don't know yet, but you said yourself that sports can inspire us to be better, to push, to grow and to face challenges."

Max released Callie's arm and turned toward the icy darkness that had settled over a grassy field. "I think I forgot that lesson when I needed it most."

Callie propped her elbows on the wooden railing and rested her chin on her hands. Together they stared out at the starless emptiness. Everything felt so still and vast and cold, except for Callie huddled close beside her.

"I'm sorry," Max finally said.

"It's okay."

"It's not okay to put you down in order to lift myself up."

"No, but it's okay to feel scared," Callie whispered.

"I'm not scared," Max said reflexively.

Callie took all the zing out of her defense by simply saying, "I am. I'm scared all the time."

"Why are you scared?"

"Have you ever stood on the brink of everything you ever wanted, so close you can feel the breath of your dreams on the back of your neck?"

As if on cue, a soft breeze stirred her hair. All Max could say was, "Yes."

"I'm there, Max," Callie whispered. "A few more steps, a couple more stairs, and I can't seem to take them. What if I never can? What if I've maxed out right here, and I don't have what it takes to lead my team any further? What if I fall short mere meters from the finish line?"

Max fought the urge to offer simple assurances. They weren't hers to grant, and they were both too smart to believe them. Part of what made the sports stories they clung to so enthralling was the very real possibility of failure that hung around every encounter. Instead, she said, "I'm sorry I didn't see that until now, either."

Callie shrugged. "You didn't want to. I don't want to, either. Neither does my team, but we all live with it. I think you understand those fears. When I look into your eyes, sometimes it's like a mirror to all the things I don't want to see in myself."

The thought hurt. Max hurt. Everything had hurt for so long, and no matter how much she tried to pretend it didn't matter, she'd ended up hurting other people, too.

Then Callie said, "It makes me feel a little less lonely."

"What?"

"To see you fighting. To see you refusing to give up no matter how many times you fall on the ice, or how many times someone refuses to be interviewed, or how many times you get benched. You just keep going. I'm not always sure why you do, but I'm glad you do. It makes me feel better about refusing to let go of my own drive even when everyone else looks at me like I'm asking too much, or pushing too hard, or being too unreasonable in my expectations."

"What if they're right about both of us? What if you and I are the crazy ones?"

"Then maybe we'll just have to be crazy together." Callie rested her head on Max's shoulder. "Like just be obnoxiously driven to succeed at our own goals, but together."

"That sounds both really dysfunctional and kind of nice all at once."

"But I thought you weren't a nice person?"

"I haven't been." Max sighed. "But I am trying now."

Callie stepped away only far enough to look up at her. "I see that."

"Do you?"

She nodded and furrowed her brow. "Can you see the same thing in me?"

Max nodded. "I do."

"Good." She gave a little half smile. "I don't feel so tipsy anymore."

"No? Well that's good," Max said, amused by the non sequitur.

"Yeah, seemed important to mention before I did this." Then she leaned in, cupping Max's face in her hands, and kissed her gently on the lips.

The move was just another in a long string of surprises Max had experienced since meeting Callie Mulligan, but it was by far her favorite. She would have to analyze and possibly even freak out about that later, but right now, with Callie's soft lips against her own, she couldn't manage to think of a later. Or her job. Or her fears. There was only Callie, her cold fingers, her warm breath, the press of her mouth, sure and skilled and so very right.

Max leaned into that kiss, not pushing or even asking for more, but accepting, the same way she accepted everything else from this woman. Callie managed to be sweet and fierce, strong and vulnerable, serious and stunning, and now sexy beyond belief as she tenderly bit Max's bottom lip before pulling away and smiling.

"Good night, Max."

She couldn't even find the words to say good-bye. She stood there dumbly as Callie opened the door to her room and disappeared inside. She didn't know what she should've done or said differently, but as she finally found the coordination to shuffle off to her own room, she figured she'd probably have all night to lie awake pondering those questions and so many others.

Chapter Nine

"Yes, you're going to want those to come right up to that dimple in your chin, but not until you've got your boots on." Callie kneeled in front of a pigtailed little girl to help her push into the unforgiving ski boots.

"What about my helmet?"

"We don't need it to measure you, but you need it to protect your noggin anytime you step on the slopes or a rink. Promise me you'll wear it?"

"I love my helmet. I put Wonder Woman stickers on it," the little girl said gleefully. "I wear it when I ride my bike, and when I ski, and when I skate."

"And when you curl?"

The child's brows knit together. "I don't curl."

"Well, we can fix that!" Callie snapped the last of the buckles and stood. "Curling is super fun, plus if you're under sixteen, you have to wear your Wonder Woman helmet."

"Do you do it?"

"I do," Callie said, grabbing the skis and holding them up in front of her like a measuring stick. The curved tip rose right up to the level of the kid's lower lip. "Pretty close, with a little room to grow."

"I'm still growing," the girl said.

"Good." Callie handed her the skis. "Me, too. Just in different ways."

"So, we're all set to start shredding some snow?" the girl's young father asked, a hint of excitement in his voice.

"Almost. You'll want to take these up to the register, and my buddy Jason will get the bindings set for her boots." She turned back to the girl. "It'll only take about five minutes. Then you'll be ready to rock, and in the meantime you can go look at our curling brooms."

"Okay," the girl said. "Let's go, Dad."

He smiled back at Callie as his daughter clasped his hand and tugged. "Thank you for your help with the skis, and for being so encouraging with her."

Callie shrugged. "Encouraging the next generation of sportswomen is never a burden. Good luck on the slopes!"

She grinned as the girl pulled him away, her heavy boots tromping loudly down the central aisle of the small store.

"Another happy customer," a familiar voice said behind her.

She turned to her boss, Heath, standing in the doorway of the storeroom wearing a vintage Sabres jersey and worn-out blue jeans. His hair still hung down almost to his shoulders, even though the brown had begun fading to gray around his temples. His nose had a wide, raised bridge that often made her wonder if he'd had some Roman ancestor, or merely suffered a childhood collision with a hockey puck. She grinned, both at the thought and at her general affection for him. "Hey, what are you doing here?"

"Mitch called in sick . . . or more likely hungover."

She grimaced. "You know you're going to have to fire him eventually, right?"

"Not until I find a reliable replacement." He eyed her expectantly.

"No."

"You're the best employee I've ever had."

"Thanks, but I can't take on more hours."

"You say 'can't,' I hear 'won't.'"

"We've been through this." She sighed. "I like the job, but the thing I appreciate most about it is how you offer me the flexibility to set my own hours. If I take on the manager position, I'll have to accept a more set schedule. Plus, I'll have to fill in every time someone else flakes out. Those responsibilities don't dovetail with my curling career."

"Career? Come on, what'll it take for you to put this job above curling, Callie?" His voice took on a new level of seriousness. "I've got money to pay what you're worth. I've got a good insurance policy for a small business and two weeks of paid vacation. Can curling give you any of those things?"

She shook her head as her stomach clenched. Even at the highest level of the sport, she would never have the kind of security he spoke of.

"Look, I'm not trying to break your spirit. I know your dad is on you about the family business, but I'm not talking about selling windows. You could still be connected to sports here. You can still spread the gospel of curling all around Buffalo. You'd still have plenty of free weekends and evenings to play, but you'd also have a real job that's worthy of you."

A muscle in her jaw twitched, and she had to breathe deeply through her nose to keep from snapping back at him. She had a real job. No one else in her life seemed to see curling that way, but she did. Not a hobby or a game or a dead end. A job. But, more than that, she also had a real passion, and while it didn't come with any of the perks he and everyone else around her seemed to value so highly, it had something more. Curling offered her a million intangible risks and rewards that came from the quest to be the best in the world, but she didn't know how to explain them or the sense of fulfillment she sought to someone who aspired only to steady income and dental insurance.

"I'm honored," she finally said. "Really. It means a lot to me that you'd consider putting me in charge of a business you worked so hard to build, but you deserve someone who can devote them-selves fully to the tasks, and right now my heart's not in it."

He smiled sadly. "I know. I don't want to bully you. I just don't understand."

"It's okay." She shrugged, some of his sadness seeping into her. "I've never met anyone else who really does."

● ● ●

"So, he said I could go ahead and attend the bonspiel next week in Minnesota, even though the network doesn't have any coverage rights to it, because no one else has TV rights to it, either," Max explained. "I won't get any formal credit, but I won't be stepping on any toes, either."

"But, if no one has broadcast rights, what are you going to do there?"

"I'm going to write, of course, but I'll also do some blogs and maybe even some live videos for our social media pages. There are limits to how much actual game footage we can share." Max felt herself getting more excited as she spoke. "If we break it up, I can probably get away with doing one or two ends a day, then pair those with some interviews or maybe even instructional videos if you and your team are willing to take part in those."

"I am, but—" Callie glanced over her shoulder at the others huddled near the far end of the ice.

"It's okay. You don't have to try to speak for them," Max said quickly, trying to stem the flashbacks to Brooke's fist on the collar of her coat, and the tone of Ella's voice as she all but called her a thief. "I'm well aware of how they feel about me."

Callie sighed. "I won't sugarcoat things and say any of them will be easy to bring around, but you're making an effort now, and we all need to do the same. They aren't going to like me pulling rank, but I'm the skip, and it's time for me to lead."

She turned resolutely, but Max caught her arm and pulled her back.

"Don't."

Callie stopped and glanced down at the point where Max's fingers curled around her biceps.

The muscle flexed under the thin long-sleeve shirt, and all coherent thought left Max's brain. In that moment all she wanted was to kiss her again. Her eyes flicked to Callie's lips, feeling their softness from memory.

"Don't what?"

111

The question didn't make sense to her. Very little made sense with Callie so close and her body so firm at the only place they connected. And yet she'd asked a question about something Max had said. Something about what she'd intended to do. She tried to mentally retrace their steps. Callie had been walking away from her toward her teammates. Max looked past her to see those teammates were all watching her now. She quickly dropped her hand back to her side as everything came back into focus. "Don't let me come between you and your crew."

"Sorry if I gave you the wrong idea. You don't have enough power to drive a wedge between me and this team."

"Um, good?"

Callie laughed. "I only meant we'll be fine, and I intend to lead by example. They'll fall in line. Come on."

With that, she headed off down the ice, and this time Max followed. She might not share Callie's optimism, but she did trust her assessment of people's willingness to go where she led.

"Hey all," Callie said, as she drew near the rest of them. "Max will be traveling to Minnesota with us next weekend to start work on some interviews and video footage. I'm going to give her some quick lessons on sweeping. Ella, I'll set up a draw for you. Play it clean to the button."

Ella steadfastly refused to acknowledge Max, but she nodded and said, "Sure thing, Skip."

They all took their places, and Callie motioned for Max to join her.

Without thinking, she started to step forward, but at the last second, she caught herself and drew back. "Um, actually, I think I better not."

"She can be taught." Callie grinned ruefully. "But seriously, if you weren't wearing loafers, you'd stand a better chance of staying upright."

"You want me to take them off, and what? Go barefoot on the ice?"

"Put on some grippers." She pointed to a bucket of black

pieces of rubber. "They fit snugly over the bottom of your shoes, like short booties, and provide a bit of extra traction."

Max obliged and tugged two of them over her slick soles, then tentatively put one foot onto the ice. To her great relief, it didn't immediately slide out from under her.

With an economic nod of satisfaction, Callie turned back to her team and made a few sweeping motions with her broom as if relaying signals, but before Max had the time to fully find her feet, much less ask questions, Ella reared back and sent a rock their way.

She shuffled right up behind Callie as it slid toward them in an arcing loop.

"Nope," Callie called. "Stay with it."

The sweepers walked along calmly beside the stone as it skirted around a guard.

"Gotta curl," Callie said, and as if on command, the slowing rock began to spin its way back toward the center of the ice, its handle rotating counterclockwise, and it eased into the outer ring of the house.

"Now," Callie instructed.

Both sweepers pounced like cats who'd spotted a mouse.

"All the way."

They scrubbed the ice mere millimeters in front of the stone as it continued its inward trajectory with dying speed.

"There you go," Callie said, as it came to rest, then turned to Max. "What'd you see?"

"When the rock started to slow down, they swept it to make it go in the direction they wanted."

Brooke snorted, and Layla shook her head.

"Wrong answer?" Max asked, a wave of embarrassment threatening to rise in her again.

"It's a common misconception," Callie said kindly. "Sweeping cannot change the direction of the rock. We set the angle of the throw out of the hack, and the direction of the curl with that little twist of our fingers when we release. Nothing we do after the fact will change either of those things."

Max frowned. "So, if you can't change the way the stone is spinning, why sweep in front of it?"

"Look at the ice." Callie crouched down. "See these little bumps?"

Max carefully lowered herself until she could run her fingers over the slippery surface. Sure enough, it wasn't smooth. Tiny raised dots peppered the sheet of ice.

"We spray little drops of water over the ice to give it a texture. It's called pebbling, and it's too fine to see from a distance, but the rock can pick up every one of them as it skims along the top. We use the friction of brooms to heat up the surface enough to create a thin layer of water for just a split second."

"And the water changes the direction?" Max asked hopefully.

"Seriously?" Brooke asked. "She just told you, sweeping doesn't change the direction."

"But I saw it with my own eyes. A rock that was thrown to the right of that guard came back and ended to the left of it on the back side."

"Because of the rotation, the spin Ella put on it, and the faster it spins, the more it curls. Light spin makes for a straighter line, and heavy spin makes it curl more."

That made sense given everything Max knew about curveballs and dreidels or tennis serves. What it didn't explain was what the sweeping did.

Her confusion must've shown on her face, because Layla clasped a hand on her shoulder and grinned. "It all comes back to speed, though. Heating up the rocks with our broom makes them move faster, which means it makes fewer rotations around any given patch of ice."

"And remember, the ice is pebbled, so it's naturally working to slow the stone down," Brooke jumped back in. "So, a faster-moving stone gets fewer rotations, and a slower moving stone gets more rotations."

"And the number of rotations is what determines how much it curls!" Max practically shouted when it made sense.

"Physics," Brooke declared emphatically.

"Did I mention Brooke is getting a PhD in physics?" Callie asked, leaning casually against her broom.

"If you did, I wasn't paying proper attention," Max admitted, then extended her hand toward Brooke. "I'm sorry for that."

The woman stared at her hand for a long few seconds, and Max braced herself for another rejection, but just when she was about to retreat once more, Brooke clasped her hand.

"Apology accepted."

"Sometime, if you have time, I'd love to talk about the physics of curling," Max said. "There's a lot I don't know."

"There's a lot no one knows," Brooke said, her soft brown eyes lighting up behind the square lenses of her glasses. "There's actually a ton of controversy around why sweeping works at all and how much value it actually has—"

"And, we're going to lay that to rest right now," Callie cut back in. "Set 'em up again."

At the command, her team snapped back to attention, shuffling Ella's rock back down the ice. Callie moved another one even with the first guard, but a couple of feet farther to the right. "Last lesson for today. Sometimes we need the rock to go straight, sometimes we need it to curl, and sometimes we need it to do one, then the other."

"Makes sense."

"For the shot I'm calling now, I want it to shoot the gap between these two guards."

"And, for that, you need it to go straight out wide," Max supplied.

"Yes, but then once I'm sure it will clear them both, I want it to curl in behind the first guard and sit there."

"Which will leave it protected from a clean takeout shot."

"Exactly."

As Callie called the shot, Max envisioned the play, for the first time seeing clearly the path a rock would have to take to accomplish the goal. If not for the lesson on sweeping, she would've thought that type of turnaround defied the laws of physics. Now she understood they were actually using those laws to their advantage.

Sure enough, as Ella's rock shot straight toward the outside guard, it barely veered from its path, but as it began to slow, the rotation became more pronounced.

"Gotta curl," Callie called, and Max finally understood the command to mean "let it slow down."

And it did. It slowed, and it spun, until the new trajectory sent it right between the guards like a perfect field goal, but as soon as it angled in, Callie shouted, "Yep, yep, yep. Hard!"

She, Layla, and Brooke all scrubbed the ice with everything in them. Max watched, transfixed, as Callie leaned in with her team, a fierce look of determination creasing her beautiful features, as the hard line of her body pressed into the broom. She flashed back to the strength of the flexing biceps she'd curled her fingers around, and a flash of heat spread through her. Strength, speed, ferocity, heat—none of those attributes meshed with the ideas she'd had about curling when she'd arrived in Buffalo, and maybe they still didn't apply to the sport as a whole. But there was no denying now that they absolutely fit Callie Mulligan.

"Happy Thanksgiving," Callie said, as she slid by on her way down the ice.

Max snorted. "What are you doing here?"

"Working off the tryptophan. What are *you* doing here?"

"I wanted to see if you'd be here on a national holiday."

"You mean a day when we celebrate what we're thankful for, and all my other jobs are closed?" Callie set herself back up in the hack. "Where else would I be?"

"Don't you have a family?" Max asked. "And I know you've got friends."

"Sure, and I saw them all afternoon." She pushed off and enjoyed the seconds of total immersion before she released the stone and rose to track its progress. "My mother pulled the turkey out of the oven at noon on the nose. Layla stopped by for the first helping, which we devoured with a multitude of side dishes before the football started at one. We all fell asleep in the living room by two and woke up feeling sluggish by three."

Max glanced at her watch. "Which put you at the club by four."

"Not a bad day, huh?"

Max shrugged, and Callie slowed her path back down the ice to take a better look at her. She wore charcoal slacks with a soft blue sweater and a dapper scarf, which hung along the lapels of her chic gray coat. She hadn't traded her loafers for tennis shoes yet, and as usual her short dark hair was perfectly feathered back at her temples so as not to obscure even an inch of her classically smooth face. She would've cut a strikingly handsome figure if not for the dark smudges under her icy eyes.

"What about you?" Callie asked, careful to keep her voice casual. "Didn't go home to see family?"

Max started to roll her eyes, then seemed to catch herself. "No, we're not big holiday people. Or family people, really."

"Wait, then what did you do for lunch today?"

"I had some leftover Chinese takeout that I heated up in my hotel room."

She'd made the statement evenly enough, but Callie's chest constricted at the image of Max all alone with a box of reheated lo mein for Thanksgiving.

"Anyway, what shot are you working on today?" Max asked, quickly changing the subject.

"Nothing fancy. Just a button shot. I play a fun little game where I try to shoot ten for ten, then twenty-five for twenty-five. Sometimes I just shoot the same stone from end to end over and over, but tonight I'm leaving the first stone on the button and trying to use my next one to knock it out of place and to sit exactly where it was."

"Boy, you sure know how to have a good time," Max said wryly, but her voice had lost all the bitterness it held early on.

"Yeah well, who's more pathetic, the woman who spends her holiday doing practice drills or the woman who spends the holiday watching her?"

"I think everyone would agree I am the more pathetic of us." Max pulled a folding chair right up next to the ice and made herself comfortable. "However, at least I get to kick up my feet and enjoy the view."

Callie's cheeks warmed a little at the comment. It was the first flirty thing Max had said since their kiss. She tried not to overthink it as she headed back to the hack. Mostly she'd been glad neither of them had made a big deal about the kiss, but part of her had begun to wonder if Max had even enjoyed the encounter. She'd seemed to at the time. She hadn't pulled away, and she'd had the most wonderfully dreamy look in her eyes when they'd parted.

But, ever since then, she'd been nothing but politely professional. Then again, so had Callie. Was Max waiting for her to make a move or set the tone? That was a good thing. She liked to be in control, and yet that wasn't completely how she felt around Max.

Her slide was as effortless as usual, but as soon as the stone left her hand, she could tell it was light. The line was perfect, but her heart began to hammer as she realized it didn't have the distance without sweeping.

"Sweep!" she called, moving toward the rock that was moving away from her. "Hard."

"Who?" Max asked.

"Me," Callie said, then laughed. "Or you. Earn your keep, Laurens."

"More like bust my ass," Max shot back. "I don't even have a broom."

The rock tapped the other one sitting on the button, but didn't have enough force left to move it, much less replace it.

Callie shook her head. "Streak broken."

"How many did you get?"

"Seventeen." Callie play-pouted. "Would've been more if you hadn't shown up."

"Wait a second, how do you figure? If I hadn't been here, you still wouldn't have had a sweeper."

"You distracted me."

"Me?" Max laughed. "You, of the infinite focus and fierce eyes, who can tune out entire arenas full of people? I don't buy it."

Callie opened her mouth, then closed it again. She had been distracted by Max, but she wasn't sure she wanted to admit that to herself, much less anyone else. She sighed. "Fine. I missed."

"What happens now?"

"Normally I'd reset and start again, but . . ."

"But?"

She shrugged, not trusting herself to get back into the hack yet. "It's Thanksgiving. I think I'm going to knock off and have some more turkey."

"Oh." Max frowned quickly, then forced her face back to neutral. "Right. Gotta get back to your family."

Callie shook her head, hearing the sadness behind Max's casual façade. "I meant I'd have some turkey here. My mother sent enough leftovers to feed an army, and I brought it all to the club in the hopes I could pawn some off on anyone else crazy enough to be here at dinnertime on a holiday."

Max's grin spread slowly, and she made a show of glancing over each shoulder before saying, "Does that mean I'm the winner of the crazy contest?"

"Clearly. Winner, winner, turkey dinner."

Within ten minutes, they sat at the low bar facing the plate glass windows to the empty ice, a plate full of leftovers in front of each of them.

Max groaned as she shoved a fork full of turkey and mashed potatoes into her mouth. "Your mom is my hero."

Callie would've laughed, but her mouth was also full.

"I can't remember the last time I had a home-cooked meal," Max continued, while reloading her fork for another bite.

"You don't cook?"

"I'm passable if I have a full kitchen, but I've been living in hotel rooms and efficiency apartments for so long I've almost forgotten what that's like."

"Did you give up your apartment in the city when you came out here?"

"I actually gave up my apartment months before that. I was never home enough to warrant the astronomical payment. I'd probably slept in my own bed less than fifteen times in the previous six months."

"Because of work?"

"Work and other stuff."

"Vague."

Max stiffened a little bit, and Callie worried she might have stumbled onto something inadvertently. Why would Max be sensitive about things that kept her out of her bed at night . . . ? Then pieces fell into place with a sickening twist. "Are you seeing someone?"

Max choked on her food and coughed several times before she recovered enough to croak out a few words. "What? No. Why?"

Callie shook her head. "Work and other stuff keep you from sleeping at your own place? Oh my God, did I kiss you when you have a girlfriend?"

"No, I don't have a girlfriend."

"Oh shit, a boyfriend?"

Max grimaced. "Double no!"

"Did you even welcome that kind of attention from me? Is that why we haven't talked about it? Because I thought we were just being professional and adults and busy, but what if I sexually harassed you?"

Max's eyes turned a stormier shade of gray. "No."

"Seriously?"

Max took her hand and intertwined their fingers, then looked her in the eye. "Callie, I promise. I was not offended by the kiss. It was not inappropriate. I welcomed the moment. Hell, I reveled in it, then and many times since then."

Callie sat back, some of the tension easing from her shoulders, but she didn't break the contact between their fingers. "I didn't mean to freak out. I just, I guess I'm sort of used to calling shots and relying on my gut, but you saw my last throw in there. Sometimes I come up short, or even miss completely."

"Can I just say how much I love the fact that you're dissecting a kiss with me in curling terms?"

Callie rolled her eyes. "I don't get out much, okay? I'm not good at the whole 'deep conversation' business. I just sort of assume everything is on the up and up unless I hear otherwise."

"And you didn't hear any such thing from me," Max concluded. "So, let's stick with that plan. We're both strong, competent, driven women who really get each other. I mean, isn't that what led to the kiss in the first place?"

"I think so." She smiled at the memory. "I was really worked up after the tournament. So much hope and adrenaline courses through me for those few hours, and when I win, it turns to euphoria, but when I lose, there's just no outlet. The stress stays bottled up, and sometimes I worry it breaks down my ability to reason logically."

Max's complexion paled and she pushed her plate away. She nodded. "I know what you mean. You want something so bad you visualize it into being, like a dream brought to life, and then when you wake up and have to face reality, it's disorienting. You want to cling to anything or anyone who ties you back to the last place you felt good."

The sadness of both the comment and Max's eyes caused an ache to build in Callie's chest. "That sounds kind of pathetic. Am I pathetic for getting my personal life all tangled up with my curling life?"

"Not at all. I think it's very common for elite athletes to find solace in other athletes, or at least people who feed that energy, who affirm the obsession that makes them successful. It's fundamentally human to want to be understood."

"You made me feel understood that night." Callie closed her eyes and pictured Max standing on that balcony, that single wisp of hair falling out of place, the sparks in her eyes, the warmth of her proximity. Fluttering open her lids again, she added, "And you're doing the same thing right now."

Max sighed. "Which is why, even though I don't think we did

anything wrong, I do still worry about how easily these things can spin out of control. The last thing I want to do is pull your mind off your most pressing task in the middle of a season."

"See." She gave Max's hand a little squeeze. "That's exactly what I'm talking about. You get it. You can acknowledge that we're attracted to each other."

"Considerably attracted."

"And that we're building a sort of unexpected connection."

"Pleasantly surprising, but true."

"And yet you're not pushing, or rushing, or asking for explanations or labels I can't offer."

"Because, once again, we're in the same boat," Max said. "I'm in no position to demand things of you that I can't offer in return. Even if I could, I wouldn't be inclined to tie anyone else, especially someone I respect, to my life right now."

"Again, we are on the same page," Callie said, feeling lighter and breathing easier. "We're both on the brink of big things. We each understand what the other is facing, and we wouldn't want to screw anything up for either of us."

"Which, to answer the original question, or at least I think it was one of the original questions, is one of two major reasons why I didn't freak out about the kiss. There's no need to discuss something we're already on the same page about."

"Good." Callie nodded. "But just out of curiosity, what's the other reason?"

Max got quiet, her lips pressed together in a thin line for only a second before she broke the contact between them to reach for her fork once more. Stabbing a piece of turkey and forcing a smile, she said, "Because, if I screw this up, I won't get any more of your mom's cooking, and that would be a travesty."

Chapter Ten

"Where the hell am I?" Max asked herself for about the hundredth time. She knew the technical answer was Eveleth, Minnesota, but in her head, she'd started referring to the tiny town as "Way The Fuck Up There, Minnesota."

She'd initially been pleased to see a tournament in the USA on the schedule, but honestly they were close enough to the Canadian border she might as well have crossed it. She'd had to fly into Duluth, rent a car, and drive an hour outside of a city that wasn't at all a city, but rather a town smaller than most subdivisions she'd visited around New York.

Even the Mesabi Curling Club was more of a modified civic venue that, in addition to the tournament, seemed to host weddings and holiday get-togethers in the all-purpose room overlooking the ice. That wasn't to say the place wasn't well kept. Every surface gleamed, but there were only four curling sheets with a single red carpet running between the middle two, leaving little space on the sides for spectators or commentators. There were two small sets of three-row bleachers stuck along one side, but they filled quickly with coaches and family members. She'd actually had to stand behind the glass wall separating the ice from the bar to watch Callie and her team play two games back to back and win them both easily.

Then they disappeared into a room off to the side, leaving Max sitting in the hallway while a toddler in a paper crown ran up and down, suggesting he might be celebrating a birthday. The whole thing felt like sort of a joke. She'd spent over a month with everyone trying to convince her, and had even started to believe, curling was a legitimate professional sport, only to find that an apparently important event took place in the middle of nowhere in a multiuse facility where fans weren't even allowed to watch from the same room.

She leaned her head back against the cold concrete as frustration built in her again, and she began to contemplate retiring to her hotel room, but why? Thanks to her distance from the players all morning, she had nothing new to write and no new footage to edit. Still, she was about to give up when the door to her side swung open, nearly colliding with the hyper toddler. Max grimaced and looked away, not wanting to see the moment of impact, but as the kid came careening around her, she assumed he must possess some mad running-back skills, and she breathed a sigh of relief.

"You okay, Pencil Pusher?" Layla's voice asked, with its usual mix of humor and sarcasm.

"Uh, yeah." She hopped out of her folding chair and ran her hands over her shirt as if she might have wrinkled it in her cowering. "Good games."

"Thanks." Layla grinned. "We've got a good draw."

"But we're not taking anything for granted," Callie called from behind her.

"Of course not, Skip," Layla said, "which is why we spent the last two hours dissecting video of a morning where we barely made a questionable call."

"You rewatched your entire matches already?" Max asked.

"Yes," Layla said, at the same time Callie said, "No."

"Not the whole games," Callie said, her voice tight.

"We fast-forwarded through some of the other team's throws," Layla explained.

"And the times when we were discussing strategy." Callie stepped forward around her lead to address Max directly. "But

124

yes, we played our eight o'clock match and immediately reviewed it so we could make adjustments for our 11 a.m. match, and then we reviewed that one so we can make adjustments for tomorrow. It's what we do. It's a vital part of our planning and strategy."

"Makes sense," Max said, a little impressed they had the focus and fortitude to not only play two matches in a single morning, but also dissect them both immediately. Lots of athletes used video in practice and preparation sessions, but few teams held them immediately before or after games.

"Makes me hungry," Layla said, then called back into the room. "Anyone want to go to that pizza place down the road?"

"Nope," Ella called. "I'm eating healthy. I've got a dress fitting this week."

"Can't," Brooke added. "Gotta study."

Layla rolled her eyes. "I'm about to starve to death."

Max's stomach gave a low rumble, and she looked up hopefully. "I'd be up for some pizza. I mean, if I'm invited."

Layla turned to Callie, her eyebrows raised, either in invitation or in a request for permission, or possibly both.

Callie glanced at Max, and the worry lines along her forehead smoothed slightly. "I guess since we're done playing and reviewing for the day, I could consider this my postgame interview with the press?"

Max grinned, recognizing that Callie probably didn't want to shirk her responsibilities, and gave her an easy excuse to consider the outing part of her duties rather than an escape from them. "Exactly. I'd love to ask you both some questions about this event. Totally a working dinner on my end."

"Whatever you two gotta tell yourselves, as long as I get fed," Layla said, then threw an arm around each of them and steered the conversation toward the door. "I'll answer whatever you want as soon as there's food."

And, true to her word, no sooner had the waitress taken their order for two wood-fired pizzas than Layla turned to Max and said, "What do you want to know? Ask me anything."

She blinked at the abruptness of the statement and the

complete reversal of course, for while Layla had been Callie's friendliest teammate as far as social graces went, she'd been no more forthcoming than the others until this very minute.

Max glanced at Callie as if silently asking whether this was some sort of a practical joke, but the skip just shrugged, a bit of humor sparking in her tired eyes. "Don't look at me. You're the reporter."

"Right." Max straightened her shoulders. "I sort of forgot that for a while, seeing as how we're in the middle of freaking nowhere for what seems like a bush league event compared to the others I've been to, and yet you all are as tense and focused as ever, if not more so."

"Totally more so," Layla agreed.

"But why?"

"Two words," Layla said. "Merit points."

"Could I have a few more words?"

Layla laughed, and even Callie's lips quirked up.

"This tournament may not look like much without the Japanese and the Swedes and all the others you see at the World Cup events. Fewer teams, smaller venue, a lot less fanfare, but don't be fooled about what's at stake."

"And what's that?"

"Our national ranking," Callie said flatly. "Those merit points she mentioned factor directly into our national ranking."

"I thought all the events had ranking points to them."

"They do," Layla said, "but there's a multiple ranking in curling. The World Cup has their own rankings, and only the top fifteen get to play top-tier events. The second fifteen play tier two, but those are out of the whole world. Our national rankings include only teams from the USA."

"Of which you're trying to become number one," Max concluded.

"Bingo," Layla said, "and without the rest of the world in this tournament, we also get to go head-to-head with our competition for that top spot. I mean, with the smaller field and so many teams here we already outrank, we also have a chance of scoring some coin to help with the cost of all the travel we're doing."

Max nodded, making mental notes.

"But it's more than just this paycheck. Our national funding and support are also very much in play depending on how we play."

"Plus, expectations are higher," Callie added, her voice still emotionless.

"National expectations, or your own?"

"Yes."

Max waited for her to elaborate, but when it didn't happen, she couldn't quite bring herself to push for more. She got the sense Callie was conserving her energy and her emotions, so she turned back to Layla.

"So, bottom line, you all have to perform well here if you want to move up in the rankings and have a real shot at the Olympics."

Layla sighed. "We are years from an Olympic bid. I just want to point that out because I don't think it's helpful, but you're not wrong. You don't get a chance to be the best in the world if you can't prove yourself to be the best team in America."

"And this event is your shot to start making your case for world domination," Max supplied. "Well, that explains some things."

"Like the giant crease between my skipper's eyebrows?" Layla asked, then gave Callie a little nudge with her elbow. "Come on, Callio, we played well today. We've already beaten half our pool. Even if we drop one tomorrow, we still make the championship bracket."

"I know." Callie nodded, but a little twitch in her jaw suggested that knowing something and liking it were two different things.

"We won't even face the other American team above us until the final round," Layla explained to Max. "We're in different pools because they want us to meet in the finals."

"Who's 'they'?"

"Everybody," Layla said, then nodded toward Callie. "Well, maybe everybody but her."

"No," Callie said quickly. "That's definitely the best-case scenario. I want to face them on the biggest stage possible. I also want to win. And I can, but only if I'm perfect."

The flint in her voice and the flicker of fire in her eyes reminded Max of the day she'd stared straight into the camera and said, "This is who I am."

Max had watched that video at least thirty times since then, but even the memory of it still gave her goosebumps. The sense of destiny seemed to circle invisibly around Callie, the weight of it pressing on her shoulders and crackling in the air. Either out of respect for that gravity or out of a desire to help her protect herself, Max decided again not to push in this moment.

Turning back to Layla, she asked, "What about you? Do you feel the push toward perfection?"

Layla laughed. "Sure, I feel pushed to perfection, but not from some internal or cosmic force. I feel it radiating off her."

Callie rolled her eyes, but Layla continued. "That shit's contagious, and I got infected from repeated exposure over the last twenty-five years."

"Twenty-five years?" Max pulled out her phone and started recording video.

"Callie and I met in preschool," Layla explained, unfazed by the camera. "She just decided I was her best friend and announced it to me. Whatcha gonna do at that point but go along? So, that's what I did. I went along with her all through elementary school, and then when she got the curling bug in middle school, I went along with that, too."

"So, you didn't come to the sport on your own, like through your own family or a community group?"

Layla snorted. "Seriously, how many other black curlers have you seen?"

Max didn't have to search her memory hard to find the answer. "Zero, but I haven't been around the sport very long."

"I have been, and let me tell you, it's just me here. I swear at the National Championships last year, I was waiting out front of the hotel, and people kept handing me their keys thinking I was there to park their cars."

Max glanced at Callie, who nodded. "Sadly true."

"Does that annoy you?"

"Depends on the day. Sometimes I want to scream. Some days I enjoy the look on their faces when they realize who I am. Once or twice I thought about just accepting the keys and driving off in their cute little cars."

Max didn't know whether she should laugh. Layla's tone was light, but the subject wasn't. Most other sports she'd covered had been extremely diverse. It was one of the things she loved about professional athletics. In those arenas, at least while the game lasted, barriers of race and class could be blurred by ability more frequently than in other areas of society. "Have you ever thought about walking away?"

"Sure," Layla said casually. "All the time, and not just because I'm black or gay. I still have these moments where I look around and wonder how this became my life. I mean, professional curling, how is that even a thing?"

Max laughed, inordinately relieved to have someone in Layla's position verbalize that. "So, what makes you stay?"

Layla grinned and glanced at Callie. "It never occurred to her that I didn't belong here. It never occurs to Callie that any of this is unreasonable. Like, she just takes it for granted that I can be a superstar in this sport. She's done it with all of us. She's willed this team into existence."

"Come on." Callie's face turned pink, and Max angled the camera to include her in the shot.

"It's true," Layla continued, "and it's powerful. When someone like her looks at you like you're special, like you're a winner, like you can do whatever it is she expects you to do, the funny thing is, you start to believe it. She's believed us right into the top tier."

Callie shook her head. "She's being funny now. She's one of the top leads in the league. In any league. She can throw a guard to any spot with her eyes closed."

"She's not lying," Layla agreed.

"See?" Callie looked down at her empty water glass. "Anyone else need a refill?"

They both shook their heads, and she pushed away from the table. "Be right back."

Max watched her walk to the bar before turning back to Layla. "You were saying?"

"I said what I said. She is this team. And it's true we can all make our shots, but she's a big part of the reason we do. We all want to be the people and the players she's never doubted we are." Layla sighed and sat back. "Brooke and Ella would tell you the same thing if push came to shove. We're all playing above our abilities, and we're doing it to keep up with her."

"Do you think you can be Olympians?"

"Me?" Layla shrugged. "It'd be a trip, but still feels a little far-fetched in my world. Callie, on the other hand, if she moved to Minnesota and asked the national team to assign her to a group from their high potential program, she'd be an Olympic shoo-in. Hell, she could probably have a spot on the number one team tomorrow if she asked for one."

The thought made Max's stomach clench. "Why doesn't she?"

Layla shrugged again. "You'd have to ask Callie."

She should. It was a perfect lead-in, and a question that deserved to be answered, yet when Callie returned to the table, her brow furrowed and her eyes seemingly focused on something no one else could see, Max couldn't bring herself to form the words. She didn't know exactly what had come over her, but as she flipped off her phone, she suspected she might not be any more immune to Callie's powers than anyone on her team seemed to be.

Seven games in three days. The pace had been intense even by bonspiel standards, and Callie could practically feel the muscles in her neck and shoulders beginning to fray from the strain. Her sides ached from the abuse she'd put her stabilizer muscles through as she slid up and down the ice for days on end. No amount of practice or planks could negate the toll of playing under pressure in this many back-to-back, high-stakes matches.

The physical fatigue had set in by the fifth match, but the emotional and mental exhaustion worried her more going into the final game. That's what had cost them their only loss in the last game of pool play. They'd dropped the final end to an inferior team, and it'd cost them a better slot going into the championship round. Her stone had been less than an inch farther out than her opponent's, and while that fact still burned, she chose to use the fire to keep her awake and vigilant against mental errors that could prove deadly in a game of millimeters. Still, knowing something could hurt you and preventing it from doing so were two very different things. For some reason, the thought reminded her of Max.

Glancing over her shoulder, she felt a little thrill to see her standing sentinel at the other end of the ice. She wore her long gray coat again today, this time over an emerald oxford shirt. Next to her stood some poor teenager Max had either paid or cajoled into serving as a cameraperson. The setup seemed to fit their surroundings. There were no flashy sponsor logos, no TV breaks, no high risers full of fans, but whatever the crowd lacked in number, they made up for in proximity. As Callie crouched down into the hack, she could practically feel the spectators breathing on the back of her neck.

Four ends in, the score was tied up at one, and something had to break soon. If she didn't crack a hole open in the game, she worried something might crack inside her. Again, her eyes flicked to Max. Callie could feel the steel of her gaze even from a distance. With a slow, deep breath, she let the emotions wash over her, then she pushed them away as she pushed off with her back foot. Everything faded as she slid, weightless, across the ice. The only thing she felt now was the breeze of her own momentum, and all she could see was Brooke's broom acting as target at the other end of the ice.

As she released the stone, she knew she'd hit her mark. No need to crouch, no need to hold her breath, no need to call commands to her team. She simply stood and strolled along behind her rock. By the time she reached the other end, there was nothing left to do but accept a few compliments and wait for her opponents to throw their last shot of the end.

"Team Mulligan is in a position to take the lead here, as they're currently closest rock to center," Max's voice said from somewhere close behind them. "Any point is, of course, a victory, but like most things in curling, this play isn't always as simple as it seems on the scoreboard. When a team has the hammer, they're expected to score at least one point. However, since the team who doesn't score in this end will get the hammer for the next end, it's easy to just trade one point for another and never pull ahead. To make a real impact, you want to score two or more when you have the final shot."

Max's point was spot-on and the reason Callie hadn't felt any great exuberance over her textbook throw. She had an important decision to make now. She did, however, feel a little shot of pleasure that Max understood her dilemma. Max seemed to understand more and more every day, and not only about the mechanics or strategy of curling.

As if to prove that point, she continued speaking to the camera. "In fact, sometimes a skipper will purposely burn the last rock, forcing the other team to take a point. It's a risky proposition, because you've, in effect, given the other team a lead, but with it, the hope of throwing up a bigger number on the scoreboard next end. I suspect that's what Mulligan will do here if the other Americans knock her out cleanly."

Callie smiled in spite of the decision quickly careening toward her. She enjoyed Max's confident commentary and, even more, she enjoyed the confidence Max had in her. Even admitting the risk, she expected Callie not only to accept it, but to make something of it. Somehow it was easier to believe those things about herself when Max stated them with such authority.

As expected, Danielle, the other skipper, used her last shot of the end to play a clean takeout. Callie's team huddled around her.

"They're sitting two." Brooke stated the obvious. "You want to play the same shot you nailed last time?"

"Nope," she said emphatically. "Let's force their hand."

"We've still got four ends left to play," Brooke said unnecessarily. "We might get a better shot later."

"We might." Callie agreed. Anything was possible, but she was tired of waiting and tired of playing safe. She didn't just believe she could create her own opportunity; she knew it. "Let's give them one here, and then take three in the next end."

Ella snorted. "Sure, yeah, three stones against the best team in the country. Seems reasonable."

"No," Callie said quickly, "not against the best team."

She glanced around at three sets of raised eyebrows. "*We* are the best American team, and I'm going to prove it, starting right now."

She didn't wait for any more argument or affirmation, but as she reached the other end of the ice, she did steal another quick peek at Max, and this time she didn't try to hide her smile.

"Callie Mulligan is having fun," Max said, part in statement of fact and part in amusement. For someone who'd had the weight of the world on her shoulders all week long, or maybe for years, she suddenly seemed not only cool and calm, but actually happy. Max didn't know why or how Callie was finding joy in this moment, but the twinkle in her eye and the slight curl of her lips made it clear she wasn't bothered by the group of rowdy teens who filled the low bleachers right in the periphery of her vision, or by the number one team in the country standing just off the other side ready to pounce on even the slightest mistake. She didn't seem concerned about the untold number of national team officials, scouts, and coaches watching from the glass-enclosed balcony above them. And yet the grin that had graced Callie's expression since she'd burned the shot in the fourth end never faltered.

Some athletes thrived on the pressure, but Max had watched Callie closely for nearly two months now, and she'd always gotten the sense that while she managed the tension like a pro, she didn't relish it. On the contrary, Callie seemed to be thriving not because of the pressure, but in spite of it, which made her apparent joy all the more impressive. Pleasure, pressure, pain, purpose—they weren't mutually exclusive, and she juggled them all with aplomb. For her reward, she'd come within a literal stone's throw of beating the only team standing between her and the number one spot in America.

Ever since she'd given up the point in the fourth end, she'd been fully committed to going for it, whatever "it" seemed to be in any given situation. From bone-crushing takeouts to tick shots where centimeters made all the difference, she'd called them all, and her team had made them all. Max felt proud of her, and also of herself for starting to see the finer points in the game. She could tell the difference between hitting a rock and freezing to one. She could anticipate the physics of a curl or the bounce a rock might take off another. And she could see the adjustments, literally hundreds of them, that Callie made throughout the course of a game.

Now she held her breath as Callie assumed the delivery position one last time. Her heartbeat accelerated as the tension amplified. Max shook her head. This was curling, for crying out loud. Competitive sweeping mixed with shuffleboard on ice. Nothing happened in any sort of grand athletic sense like shattering hits or powerful, arcing shots to deep left center, and nothing offered the explosive surprise of a goal being scored from midfield. And yet, when a stone slipped past, so close to another stone that you couldn't get a strand of floss between them, her whole body went slack in relief. There was a beauty and drama to it all that she still found unexpected.

And then there was Callie.

Max's racing heart kicked out of its rhythm as the woman pushed forward once more. How many times had she seen her do that over the last few weeks? Why hadn't she grown immune to her grace in motion or the fierce focus of those hypnotic eyes? Max had spent more than a decade of her life around impressive people with powerful personas and magnificent bodies. Why should this one call to her on any higher level? She was merely another subject to cover, to inspect, to break apart. Why was she here in the middle of nowhere

Minnesota holding her breath in the fervent hope that Callie would hold it all together?

She didn't have the answers. She didn't even have the will to search for them as Callie's stone ground around a close guard, tapped another out of the way, and stopped exactly in the middle of the house.

Max nearly collapsed and had to chastise herself as she turned to the kid holding her camera.

"There you have it, folks, a perfect shot to cap off a perfect run through the championship bracket."

"Easy peasy," Brooke said behind her, in a tone that made it clear the shot was anything but simple.

"Yeah," Callie said, a sigh in her voice. "Good curling."

"You getting this, Pencil Pusher?" Layla asked close behind her.

She turned to see her broad smile. Max nodded for the camera kid to adjust the shot. "I'm right here with Layla Abrams, lead curler on our championship team. How's it feel to finish number one?"

"Better than it would've felt to come in second."

Max grinned. "You were the underdogs coming into this match—"

"Nah." Layla waved her off. "No one's an underdog with Callie Mulligan at the helm. She never lets us feel second-best. She calls a game like she expects us to be champions."

"And now you are," Max concluded.

"And now we are, baby!" Layla jumped off the ground for emphasis, and Max fought the urge to do a little jig alongside her. In an attempt to hold onto her last shred of professional cool, she scanned the crowd of people streaming onto the ice. Then her eyes met Callie's. They were lighter than she'd ever seen them before and filled with so many emotions, Max couldn't begin to separate them. Instead, she let herself get swept away, the same way she'd let herself get swept up in the moment before.

She had no idea how long they stood there, staring at each other, or how many unspoken agreements passed between them, but

135

when their silent conversation was interrupted by a tournament official steering Callie in the direction of the winners' presentation, Max knew one thing for sure: Everything had changed.

The rest of the team must have felt it, too, or maybe they were all so high on the endorphins of their win that they simply didn't mind Max's presence as the celebration kicked into high gear. She hadn't meant to horn in on their party, but as Layla gave her a little shove toward the Patch, she had no inclination to refuse. Now, after two rounds of drinks and countless country rock covers from the band on stage, she hadn't moved from Team Mulligan's table.

"Good curling," another group of Canadians called as they danced their way over.

"Thank you," Callie shouted back.

"How's it feel to just accept a compliment?" Layla teased.

"Actually, pretty good." Callie tipped back another beer and turned to Max. "It's not a skill I get a lot of practice at."

"Accepting compliments?"

"Yeah. Apparently, the proper response to 'good curling' is 'thank you,' or maybe 'you, too.'"

"What do you usually say?"

"I usually tell them in great detail how I could've curled better."

Max laughed. "I understand the impulse. How are you holding it at bay tonight?"

Callie's smile widened. "I'm not. I couldn't have curled any better today if I'd been Wonder Woman."

"You were Wonder Woman," Ella said, genuine awe in her voice.

"Even your misses hit," Brooke added. "That one in the third end was off line from what you called, but you adjusted the sweepers before I even saw the problem."

Callie didn't brush off the praise this time. "I knew it was a possibility before I threw. All I had to do was switch to plan B."

"Do you always have a plan B?" Max asked, sitting forward and pulling out her phone.

Layla shot a hand across the table and covered the lens. "Yes, she does, and no, you don't get an interview tonight."

"Oh." Max withdrew the phone. "Sorry. I didn't mean to turn your celebration into a work function. It's a bad habit I have."

"Something else you two have in common." Layla motioned between her and Callie. "But, it's not just our celebration, Pencil Pusher. I heard you working on your little highlight videos during the game. You were legit calling the points back there."

"Yeah?"

"Yeah," Brooke said, in a tone that still held a little grudging. "You didn't suck today."

She tried to withhold her smile. The compliment wasn't exactly enthusiastic praise, but she appreciated it all the more. She hadn't sucked today. It was a huge step up, and one she was inordinately proud to take with these women. "Okay, so how does a non-curler celebrate a non-embarrassing performance around here?"

Layla, Brooke, and Ella all answered in unison. "Dance!"

"No," Callie and Max said in stereo.

Everyone laughed.

"Come on." Layla hopped up. "You win, you dance. Curling rule."

Max turned to Callie, eyebrows raised. "Is it really one of those unwritten curling rules?"

Callie's smile widened. "No, but she's not wrong. We're both winners again. Might be time to loosen up on the rules a bit."

Max returned Callie's smile. How could she not? Electric, magnetic, contagious—all the good and elemental forces passed between them. Callie thought she was a winner. She wasn't sure she believed it, but in this moment the fact that Callie did meant more.

"Okay." She pushed back from the table and rose slowly. Extending her hand, she said, "If winners dance, I guess we better boogie."

Callie accepted the pronouncement, and slid smooth fingers along the length of Max's palm and then tugged them both toward the dance floor.

Somewhere behind them, Ella blew out a low whistle. "I think those people in heck might be about to get some ice water."

⦿ ⦿ ⦿

Max moved much better than expected. Callie blushed at the thought. She hadn't realized she'd given any actual thought to how Max would move, much less held expectations on the subject. And yet she apparently had, because as Max twirled her playfully in a circle, she found herself pleasantly surprised.

"I can't remember the last time I danced like this," Max said, loud enough to be heard over the band currently butchering an Allman Brothers cover.

"I can't remember the last time I actually had fun while dancing," Callie admitted.

"Well, I suppose winning goes a long way toward lightening the mood."

Callie thought about that as she moved her feet to the beat, shifting a little farther away from Max to merge with the large crowd. The winning certainly didn't hurt her mood. A weight had been lifted off her shoulders halfway through their final match, and while she knew it would resettle on her eventually, it hadn't done so yet.

"You had fun out there today," Max said, as she danced closer once more.

"I did," she admitted, "from about the fourth end on, and I think I may actually have you to thank for that."

"Me?" Max raised her brows, and her gray eyes reflected the little flashes of light around them.

"I was on the fence about whether to take the safe shot or try to make my move when I heard you explaining the concept to your camera."

"Really? You could hear me?"

She nodded her head to the rhythm of the bass guitar. "I could, and that's unusual for me. Normally, I've got a complete cone of silence around me when I'm in the zone."

"You'd have to. The crowd was so close today, they were, like, literally breathing down your neck."

Callie grinned. "And yet, I didn't hear them. I heard you."

"Was I a distraction?" Max frowned.

"No," she said quickly, "or maybe you were in the strictest sense, but in a good way. You were so coolly competent. You stated my options in this really concise way, and you had this matter-of-fact kind of confidence that they were all valid."

"Weren't they?"

She laughed, a spark of joy in her chest. "They were! Like, both options had pros and cons, and both options could've been right or wrong depending on how we executed, but when you're out there in the heat of it all with so many people looking to you for some magic answer, it's easy to forget that."

Max nodded thoughtfully.

"Either way I was going to have to execute eventually, right? Either in the fourth or the fifth or the eighth end, I would need to steal an end, and when you just said so, like it was a foregone conclusion, I realized what I'd known all along and got the job done then. So, thank you."

"You do know I didn't actually do anything, right? I'm still no expert on curling. I didn't even manage any truly enlightened commentary. Everyone in that arena was thinking what I said."

"Yes. Myself included, but we were all caught up in the tension. You were stating facts."

The song ended and the strobe lights slowed as a female singer stepped close to the mic, and a fiddle vibrated out a long, low note. All around them, people made split decisions to either move closer or exit the floor. Max and Callie both froze, seemingly the only two left rooted in their indecision as a ballad took hold.

They stared at each other, eyes locked in question. Max had amazing eyes, unlike any Callie had ever seen before, almost the color of cloudy ice, but warmer, deeper, softer, like her perfectly smooth complexion. Everything about Max was smooth, her cheeks, her lips, the sheen and cut of her always unruffled hair. The symmetry was almost too much to bear, and for way too many beats, Callie got so lost in the sight of her, she forgot the unspoken question between them. Max finally broke the stalemate. "We've reached that awkward moment where the Patch turns into a middle-school dance."

Blinking, she turned to see everyone had either paired up or was looking on from the sidelines. "And all our friends are watching."

"All *your* friends," Max corrected. "Half the people here want me drawn and quartered."

Callie shook her head. "Way more than half the people here have no idea who you are."

"Ouch." Max flattened a hand across her chest. "It burns."

Callie stepped closer, placing one hand over Max's and the other on her hip. Together, they began to sway to the music.

"Thanks," Max whispered, "for saving my pride."

"Thanks for putting your pride aside enough to follow curling for a while. I'm glad you're still with us."

"Me too," Max admitted, "but in the name of journalistic integrity, I do have to fess up about something."

"What's that?"

"Earlier you said I stayed analytical while everyone else got swept up in the tension."

"Yeah."

"I have to admit, I got kind of swept up, too."

"What?" she asked, not fully processing.

"I did, and it still surprises me a little, but when you made your last shot, I held my breath the whole time."

A slow smile stretched Callie's cheeks, and something harder to define stretched in her chest. "You like curling!"

Max laughed, and the low, easy sound shook through the points where their bodies connected along their chests, stomachs, and thighs. "I don't know if I'd go quite so far."

"No, don't backtrack now. You were making real progress."

"Well, I wouldn't want to regress," Max said playfully.

"You like curling. You can tell me. You can tell the whole world," Callie teased. "Max Laurens, the curling convert. I can't wait to read that article and—"

"Hey now—"

"Go on, admit it."

"I'll admit I saw some of the appeal in today's match."

"Seriously? That's all I get? You can't say, 'Hi, my name is Max, and I like curling'?"

Max shook her head and pushed her lips tightly together.

Callie's shoulders sagged.

"I'm not ready to commit to the full shebang yet."

She sighed and looked down at Max's loafers, not sure why it mattered. She didn't need Max's unwavering approval or validation. She loved her job. She loved the sport. She loved knowing she'd played a damn-near flawless game. And still, as she took slow, steady breaths filled with the scent of Max's cologne, her body and her mind both seemed to be waiting for something more.

"Hey," Max whispered, wrapping her arm around her waist a little tighter until there was no more space between them.

Callie glanced up, her gaze connecting with those gray eyes once more, and her heart gave a little flutter.

"I might not be ready for the full-time commitment to the game of curling as a whole," Max said softly, her tone almost intimate even in the crowded room, "but I will gladly tell anyone who asks that I genuinely loved watching you curl today."

All the breath left Callie's lungs. She probably should've focused on the curling aspect of that statement. Max the sports reporter had enjoyed a single game of curling. It was a big step in the right direction, professionally speaking. And yet, there in Max's arms, their bodies warm and flush, Callie's reaction felt anything but professional, because all she'd heard was Max enjoyed watching *her*.

"Does that still count as good progress?" Max asked, close enough that her breath ran warm across Callie's neck.

She nodded, and rested her chin on Max's shoulder, not sure what they were progressing toward, but certain it did feel good. When was the last time she'd just let herself feel good? When was the last time she'd let go? When was the last time she'd let herself want something that didn't involve ice or a broom? She ran through years of memories but couldn't isolate a single one. She'd had so many accomplishments, so many experiences. Why hadn't any of them have made her feel as purely happy as she felt right now? She didn't have the answer, and she didn't even know what she should question more, the sum total of all those other moments or the magnitude of just this one.

The song faded to a stop, and Max slackened her hold but didn't break the contact between them. "Want another drink?"

"No." She closed her eyes, not wanting the moment to end, and yet knowing it had to. "I think I better call it a night. I'm feeling a little lightheaded."

"From the beer?" Max leaned back only enough to read her expression. "I have a car here. I could drive you back to the hotel."

"No, not from the beer, from, well . . ." Her cheeks flushed hot. "Maybe from you."

"Oh." Max's eyes went a little wide, the emotion in them shifting from concern to something that caused her pupils to expand. "In that case . . ."

"You have a car here and you could drive me back to the hotel?" Callie asked, unable to hide a small smile.

Max's mouth opened, but no words came out. Instead, she managed only a half shrug and then a nod. The move was endearing, and when paired with the heat radiating between them, Callie didn't know how she could resist the fire building within her. More importantly, she wasn't sure she wanted to.

Chapter Eleven

She'd played it cool while Callie had collected her things and assured her team they need not cut their celebration short on her account.

She'd played it cool on the five-minute drive back to the hotel.

She'd played it cool through the lobby, and on the elevator, and during the damn interminable walk down an absurdly long hallway.

At no point in that entire process had Max actually felt cool, though. Honestly, her cool had vanished the moment Callie touched her on the dance floor. She didn't know what had come over her. She's wasn't some teenager at prom. She'd been with plenty of women, and moved a lot faster with them, too, but much like the game Callie loved, she had an uncanny ability to stoke tension in some wonderfully unexpected ways that left Max off balance. When she'd placed her hand over Max's own and stepped so deliciously close, every thought blurred. Now it seemed like their boundaries were about to do the same.

"This is my room," Max managed as they reached the end of the hall. "I don't have anything to offer you for a nightcap. I didn't really expect to do any hosting while I was here."

Callie smiled with that wonderful mix of amusement and confidence she'd used on the ice earlier. Then she kissed her. If Max had had trouble thinking clearly before, she lost all ability to do so when Callie's lips touched hers. Thankfully, what her brain lost in the ability to think, her body made up for with the ability to feel. Every sense and nerve ending went into overdrive as the kiss escalated. Cold noses and hot breath, soft lips and skilled hands, she registered all of them at once. Callie's hands on her hips held them close, and Max appreciated the anchor as she began to melt into her.

Callie's tongue swept across her own in a brief, testing pass, and Max parted her lips more fully, welcoming the exploration. Maybe it was just that she hadn't been kissed in so long, but everything about this was better than she remembered. Callie's mouth moved with purpose from a full-frontal approach to feathery brushes at the corners, to a little nip with her teeth on Max's lower lip, then back again with a deep, soulful press that left her certain she couldn't remember being kissed like this because she never had been. How was this woman so good at everything?

She'd always heard people talk about not rushing the foreplay or spending hours making out without going any further, and she'd never understood those impulses until right now. She wondered briefly what else she'd never understood until Callie kissed her, but then their tongues tangled once more, and a soft moan replaced any remnants of conscious thought. She wanted to live in this kiss. She wanted to crawl deeper into it, deeper into Callie and all the feelings she inspired. She wanted, oh how she wanted. It surged up in her like a fire or a beast, or a fire-breathing beast.

She barely had time to even smile at the absurdity of that image, because before she fully processed it, it consumed her. Instinct, raw and hungry, took hold, and she cupped Callie's face in her hands. Callie had been kissing her, and Max had gleefully accepted the gift, but now she was engaged in returning it. Running her fingers along smooth cheeks and into soft tendrils of honeyed hair falling down around her temples, she pulled Callie even closer. They stole the same breath and echoed the same rapid heartbeat.

Fleetingly, she became aware they were doing all of this in the hallway of a Best Western, but as all her brain cells were occupied with processing more sensory information, she had little wherewithal to determine what to do about that until Callie's hands worked their way around her waist and into the back pockets of her slacks.

"Hmm." She hummed a little noise of encouragement, and Callie responded by pulling them so tightly together their hips gave a satisfactory little grind, seemingly of their own accord. That hadn't been what she'd intended, but she wasn't complaining. Still, if she wanted to get any closer, she would have to shift more than her hips.

"Key," she managed to mutter with her next quick intake of breath.

Callie slowed, as if trying to make sense of the word.

"Room key." She gasped again and then on her next pass added, "Back pocket."

Callie smiled against Max's mouth and clasped the wallet she'd already been so close to. Extracting it skillfully, she handed it to Max. Together they fumbled on the exchange, nearly spilling all the contents before Max found the strength to break the kiss and then, snagging the key card, jammed it in the lock.

She swung open the door, and with a nod to Callie managed to pant, "Inside."

Callie froze, her eyes sparkling and her cheeks flushed. "I didn't mean to give you the wrong idea."

"I got no ideas," Max said, her head spinning with the abrupt withdrawal. Had she gone too fast? Too far? Had she misread where they were headed? It wouldn't be the first time. Her stomach clenched at the thought, but her libido didn't fully release her either, causing a mental and physical tug-of-war inside her. "I honestly don't even have any coherent thoughts right now."

Callie laughed and stepped into the room, pulling the door shut behind her. "Good. For a moment there, I worried you thought you might be in control."

"I don't know what gave you that impression. I haven't felt

fully in control of anything since the day I met you and my feet went right out from under me."

She shook her head. "You know those two things weren't actually related."

"They totally were."

"Well, they didn't have to be. You could've done this the easy way if you'd made different choices."

"The story of my life." Max frowned as an old fear curled like smoke rising through her chest. "Actually, I've made a lot of poor choices in my life, Callie. Maybe you should—"

Callie kissed her again, silencing the unspoken. They made out across the room, until with a little shove Callie broke the kiss and sent Max onto her back across the king-size bed.

"Maybe you should stop overthinking," Callie suggested, as she shed her winter coat and kicked off her shoes.

Max nodded.

"I feel good." Callie pulled down the zipper of her warmup jacket. "Better than I have in ages. I want to revel in that for a while, if it's okay with you."

"Very okay."

Crossing her arms at her waist and clutching the hem of her tight, long-sleeve athletic shirt, Callie did a sexy little shimmy to work it up over her head.

Max started to sit up, but with a little shake of her head, Callie stopped her, still supine and propped on her elbows. She stared up in awe as Callie stripped out of her sport bra.

"You're not used to lying back and letting things happen, are you?"

"Nope."

Callie slowly peeled back the waistband of her yoga-style curling pants. "How are you doing so far?"

"Surprisingly okay with my new role here," Max managed, through the mix of awe and lust overwhelming her.

"You're a quick learner," Callie said, with a grin that raised the temperature in the room several more degrees. Then, pulling the pants away, she straightened up in nothing but some navy blue Team USA briefs with a red and white waistband.

Max had never been so conflicted about flag-themed apparel in her life. She didn't know if she should try to lower the banner or stand and salute the perfection it encased. Either way, she felt certain no one in the long, proud history of American sports had done the red-white-and-blue prouder than Callie Mulligan. She was a work of athletic art, a study in contrast between hard planes and soft curves. As she bent forward and crawled onto the bed, her body extended over Max in all its elongated and flexed glory, the only thing she could think was, "God bless the USA."

And then they were off again, a blur of bodies and blankets, as Callie had apparently done enough slow stripping for both of them and set about removing Max's clothes in more rapid fashion. Her skilled hands made short work of buttons and belts alike, while Max busied herself with the business of kissing the newly exposed skin along Callie's collarbone.

She did have to stop long enough to kick off her shoes and help push her own slacks toward the floor in a move that wasn't nearly as graceful as Callie's had been, but she knew better than to start comparing their levels of grace. Callie had her outmatched in every area. Still, Max hoped that what she lacked there, she made up for with gusto as she kissed and bit along Callie's neck and shoulder. Of all the body parts she'd ever found sexy, somehow she'd missed shoulders until this moment, or maybe she'd simply never had the pleasure of knowing shoulders like Callie's existed, so strong and muscular. She ran her tongue along the ridges and grooves that shifted and flexed as Callie held her own body weight suspended above her.

"You're incredible," Max whispered against taut skin.

"Not bad yourself."

She started to scoff, but Callie captured one of her nipples between her teeth, causing a strangled breath to be pushed out and sucked right back in. She arched her back up off the bed, pushing her chest forward for more of the attention Callie was currently providing. She wasn't surprised Callie paid attention to detail or had an above-average capacity for precision, but she was impressed at what having those abilities applied to her own body could do to her. She sank back into the bed, only to arch up again with each pass of Callie's skilled tongue, and then, without breaking her concentration, Callie began to work her hands lower.

Somehow able to focus on so many things at once, Callie demanded the same of Max as she stroked her way across stomach and sides and then, with a maddeningly quick pass, moved down to her thighs. She needed precious little pressure to ease them apart, but even with the task accomplished took her sweet time working back up to their apex. Max couldn't figure out what she found more enticing, the light scrape of fingernails along the inside of her legs or the graze of teeth along her breast. Thankfully she didn't have to choose, as Callie seemed fully capable not only of maintaining both, but also of escalating them simultaneously.

She whimpered and threaded her fingers through Callie's long, amber hair and reveled in the contrast between its softness and the hard body pressing against her. Everything about this woman felt like raw power laced with luxury. She could get lost in that delicious mix and never want to return, but Callie wouldn't let her slip away in any sense. Insistent and accomplished in everything she did, she kept drawing Max's focus back, this time with a teasing run along the center of Max's need.

The fleeting contact sent a jolt of electricity through Max, causing her hips to buck completely off the bed. Callie smiled against her chest, a sure sign she both understood and enjoyed her power in this situation. Still, now that they'd gotten to this moment, she didn't appear much fonder of waiting than Max, and instead of pulling back, she continued to steadily tighten her circles, homing in on the place they both wanted to be.

"Yes," Max whispered, then said more hoarsely, "please."

She didn't have to beg. Callie obliged, circling and increasing her pressure at the same time. Max's vision swam, and she shut her eyes against the onslaught of nerve endings in overdrive, immediately regretting the move. She wanted to see Callie, wanted to look into those hypnotic eyes that had held her spellbound more times than she would admit anywhere but here and now. Forcing lust-laden lids open, she used a majority of her remaining fortitude and, tugging lightly on Callie's hair, urged her up until their eyes were level once more.

Callie seemed to get the message and held Max's gaze, continuing the rhythm they'd established. She was so freaking beautiful, so strong, so skilled, so intensely focused Max couldn't withstand the combination for long. She managed to maintain contact with those hazel eyes as the first wave of orgasm shook through her, but then crumpled in on herself as every muscle in her body contracted. Eyes shut tight, and her mind blinding white, she surrendered completely to Callie's stable presence as she shook. Callie pressed their foreheads together and used the weight of her body to hold them both tightly, to one another and the bed, her strength absorbing the impact of Max's shaking form. Her persistence never wavered as she continued to stroke and coax every bit of energy she had to give. Then, continuing to hold fast, they relaxed into each other.

"I am mush," Max finally mumbled.

Callie's lips curled up.

"You reduced me to a puddle of flab and contentment."

Callie opened her eyes and allowed them to flick a quick course across Max's supine form. "I'm glad about the contentment part, but I beg to differ about the flab."

"Says the woman with biceps that could strangle a python."

Laughter bubbled up inside her. "You're such a writer. My biceps are totally average in my line of work."

"That's like saying Batman is totally average for the Justice League."

Callie shook her head. "You're so quick with those comebacks. Does it get tiring always having something witty to say?"

"Positively exhausting." Max's grin took on more of a Cheshire cat quality. "But speaking of quick comebacks, how can I repay the favor?"

"You don't have to." Callie noted that despite Max's bravado, she had yet to so much as lift her head off the pillow. "You can take a little time from being mushified."

"Don't have to? Good Lord, woman, I may not be a professional athlete, but I have my pride."

"Wait a second." Callie leaned back far enough to look into eyes that seemed more light blue now than gray. "Did you just call me a professional athlete? Like, not a curler, or a sweeper, but an athlete?"

Max groaned, but couldn't manage a scowl. "Fine. I'll admit it. Your body is every bit as athletic as any I have ever seen."

"I won't stop to think about how many bodies you can include in your sample size. I'm going to focus on the fact that I just got the great Max Laurens, queen of the curling contrarians, to admit she was wrong."

"When I'm proven wrong, I always admit it," Max said. Then with a full smile she added, "I've just never enjoyed being proven wrong quite this much."

"Because you like my athlete's body?"

Max gave a low growl and sprang up off the pillow, surprising Callie enough to send her flat onto her back. Not that she would've resisted even if she'd seen the move coming. The mix of mischief and raw attraction in Max's eyes was enough to make her forget she'd made the offer of a longer rest time.

Max kissed her on the mouth, deep but not slow, as she ground her hips down until they fit fully between her legs. Callie groaned as even the little bit of pressure made several very sensitive nerve endings buzz.

She was so close already. Something about Max made her want to go faster, to take chances she wouldn't normally take. She had a fleeting realization that being in bed with her now was a perfect example of that trend escalating, but then Max's hips bucked forward a little harder, and all trains of thought went right off the rails. She gasped and threw back her head at the jolt

150

of electricity surging through her, and Max took the opportunity to kiss along her exposed neck. Of course, this woman would go for the jugular. Callie had known it from the moment they'd met. What she hadn't expected was how much she would enjoy it.

Max's body felt like heaven and her lips like sin, as she pinned Callie to the bed and sucked a path down along her shoulders. The muscles didn't seem to know if they should contract or just melt under her mouth, and thankfully she didn't have to live in limbo long, as Max kept right on moving.

"You're delicious," Max mumbled as she ran her tongue around one taut nipple, before pulling it between her lips.

Callie was about to say something in response, but she forgot what as Max rolled her hips forward again. There were no words. That move, the perfect, rollicking circle that managed to undulate on exactly the right spot for just long enough to ratchet up her heart and breath—she felt certain it might be the end of her. She didn't care.

Max played her way across Callie's chest the same way she played at anything, full tilt and fully focused, her tongue drawing out sweet, hot, teasing patterns that might have been light or loopy if not for the fire they left in their wake. Thorough without lingering too long in any one spot, the only constant in Max's trajectory was south.

Then her hips were gone, leaving a cool void for a few endless seconds before being replaced with the heat of her mouth. Callie almost levitated off the bed when Max's lips closed around her. She pushed her fingers through Max's dark hair, rumpling the perfection before locking onto the short strands and holding her closer. She was excruciatingly close, but the conflicting desires to hold on and let go nearly tore her in two. She'd never been one to lose control, not quickly, not completely, and yet as Max began to work her tongue in circles that threatened to turn Callie's body into a puddle, she realized oblivion was more than an option. It was a real possibility. And then, suddenly, it became reality.

Light flashed red, then white, as the force of her orgasm rocked through her. Her fingers clenched in Max's hair, and her toes curled while everything in between contracted, then released only to convulse again as wave after wave shook her. Max remained relentless in her dedication to riding them to completion, then relaxed, allowing Callie's body to sink into the bed.

Then she started again.

Momentarily confused, her nerve endings buzzed as if someone had turned a dimmer switch low, only to spin it back up again.

Callie groaned. "I can't."

Her body disagreed, and so did Max as they worked in tandem to bring glowing embers roaring back to life. Callie couldn't think, couldn't process. She could barely move, but that didn't keep her breath from growing shallow once more. Everything was a blur this time, everything but Max and her mouth. Callie didn't know how either of them had the energy to keep going, and yet they did. Max sent her careening off the cliff once more, and Callie soared gleefully for several more seconds before crashing back to earth.

"Holy shit," she finally managed, between gasps for air. "You're going to kill me."

Max sat up, wearing the satisfied grin of the self-assured. "But what a way to go."

Calle laughed weakly and felt the muscles in her sides ache. "I think you wrecked me more than I did you. So much for me having the more athletic body."

Max shook her head and lay down beside her. "No, you definitely do. You have all the impressive muscles. I just have the one."

"Oh, but you use it so very well." Callie sighed dreamily. "I've never done that before."

"What? Fallen into bed with a suave sportswriter?"

"No. Well, actually, I've never done that, either. I've never fallen into bed with anyone so easily in my life. Oh geez, I didn't really think this through, did I?"

"No need to start now," Max mumbled, as she placed a kiss on Callie's shoulder.

"Okay, right." She blew out a deep breath and forced the rising panic back down into some darker recess. "I only meant I'd never had two orgasms in one pass."

"Oh, that's a shame," Max said in a playful tone. "Your body's like a Porsche of bodies. Who would be content with only one lap around the track?"

"Um, did you just compare me to a hunk of metal and motor oil?"

"Yes, but a very nice one."

Callie laughed. "Again, with the comebacks."

"You didn't seem to mind the first time . . . or the second."

Callie rolled onto her side, noticing the single tuft of dark hair falling across Max's smooth forehead. For some reason it revved her engine to know she'd been the one to shake it out of place, and her blood began to pump a little faster again. "Well, then, in that case, why not push our luck?"

"Are you calling for another lap around the track, Skip?"

She grinned. "Did you just mix your sports metaphors?"

"NASCAR and curling are not—"

Callie cut her off with another searing kiss. She didn't need to hear the end of the sentence to know she'd have to add it to the growing pile of things to deal with later. For now, she had the more pressing issue of Max's body against hers.

Chapter Twelve

"Shit-shit-shit," someone's voice muttered through the haze. Max reached for the pillow, intending to pull it over her head. She'd been having such a good dream. And warm, she felt so warm, then suddenly not warm as a shaft of cold air rushed against her naked skin. She abandoned her blind hunt for the pillow and grasped fruitlessly for the comforter.

"Max," someone whispered.

"No," she grumbled.

"Yes. We overslept."

"No."

"Okay, maybe you didn't, but I did."

The words grew louder and more rushed. Still, they didn't make sense, or at the very least they didn't sound like her problem.

"It's seven o'clock." The voice punctuated the point by yanking open the curtains, and Max recoiled from the onslaught of light like a vampire who'd been pushed out into the midday sun.

She flopped onto her stomach and threw her arms around her face, trying to bury herself in a mattress that smelled like Callie.

The thought made every one of her aching muscles relax. Callie. "Callie."

"Yes, so lovely of you to remember," Callie said, her voice softening only slightly.

Max forced herself to ignore the stiffness in her muscles as she pushed up to sitting and squinted against the light. It hurt her brain to focus, but slowly the white spots in her vision gave way to shadows, then a blurry image of Callie zipping up her tracksuit-style jacket. She suffered a momentary pang of regret that she hadn't gotten to see her all golden and sleepy in the early morning light.

She shook her head, trying to wipe away the thought and the haze surrounding it. "What's wrong?"

"I overslept. I have to go."

"Stay. Catch a later flight."

She shook her head. "I can't just leave the team wondering where I am. Layla will . . . oh Lord, Layla. It's a miracle she hasn't already sent out a search party."

"She knows we left together."

Callie sighed. "As does half of the curling world, no doubt, but Layla's the only one who knows I didn't go back to our room."

Max hadn't stopped to think about that last night. She hadn't stopped to think about anything, and from the ashen shade of Callie's complexion, neither had she.

"I'm sorry," Callie finally whispered.

She shook her head. She didn't want to go there. She didn't want to even peek behind that door to who knew how many regrets. "Don't apologize."

"My team." Callie offered the sum total of her explanation.

"Yeah." Max gripped the sheet and pulled it to her chest. "I get it."

Callie's shoulders slumped.

"It's okay." Max tried to sound more convincing.

"It's so much more than okay." Callie closed the distance between them, kissing her with all the passion of the night before, but when she pulled away the sense of endless possibility fled with the contact.

"Go," Max said firmly.

Callie opened her mouth as if she wanted to say something, but whatever it was would have to wait. The clock had struck

155

midnight hours ago. Callie grabbed her heavy coat off the floor and bolted out the door.

Max sighed but refused to let herself fall back onto the bed. She'd been here before, or at least someplace similar, and she refused to linger in the void of silence surrounding her. She threw off the covers and turned on the TV, then flipped through the channels until she found SportsCenter. She turned up the volume as high as could be considered socially acceptable in a hotel, and padded to the bathroom. She avoided the mirror and turned on the shower hot enough to see steam before ducking under the spray.

Warm needles pricked at her back, and she relished the feel of something other than Callie against her skin. She was fine. Or she would be. She wouldn't panic. She wouldn't let her mind spin out of control, or make connections she didn't want to make. She would focus on the here, the now, the different. And, mother of all things holy, was Callie different.

She was powerful and passionate. She went after what she wanted without being pushy or manipulative. Everything had escalated so quickly last night that Max still wasn't sure how they'd gone from a reluctant slow dance to horizontal in no time flat, but she suspected the answer started with "Callie." She had been in control the whole time, and for the first time ever that didn't bother Max. Perhaps because Callie had been so good at everything she did.

It might be tempting to tell herself the sex had simply seemed stellar because it had been so long since she'd had sex, but Callie hadn't even left her that excuse. The sex had clearly been amazing because Callie was amazing. At everything. And, as she raised her hands to scrub her hair, the ache along her obliques drove home the point. She didn't know how many times she'd climaxed last night, but she did know it was all her poor contracting core could handle. And then she'd helped Callie do the same.

She smiled at the thought and rinsed the soap from her hair. Callie's body was so amazing, and the command she had over it even more impressive. The command she'd had over Max's body was pretty great, too, but she liked to think Callie might say the same for her. While she had no doubt that Callie was her better in many cases, last night they'd found something akin to equality, another rare occurrence in Max's life. Her last relationship had been a lot of things, but equal was never one of them.

The thought caused a little shot of pain in her chest. Why did she even let her mind go there? Or perhaps the better question was, why hadn't she gone there last night? Had she gotten too swept up in the moment, in Callie, to remember the lessons she swore she'd learned? Why had she waited until now to summon that terrifying realization?

She shut off the water and threw back the shower curtain. She couldn't believe she was doing this again. Of course, Callie wasn't Sylvia, but once again, she'd leaped without looking. And now what did she have to show for herself? Another woman who had to run out the door lest anyone know they'd been together.

Her stomach lurched, and she held onto the towel rack to steady herself as she dripped water onto the tile floor. She couldn't start another relationship like this. She didn't even want to. Maybe Callie didn't want to, either. She hadn't exactly left with a promise to get together anytime soon. She didn't know if that thought should make her feel better or worse. And yet, that kiss. If she'd followed it up by crawling into bed, Max would have yielded again and again. She had no ability to think clearly around her. She was weak and dumb and powerless, the same way she'd always been, no matter how well she had learned to hide.

"No," she said aloud, taking comfort in the way the tile amplified her voice. This wasn't the same thing. Callie wasn't that person. Max wasn't even that person anymore. She'd just been caught off guard last night, and she had to cut herself some slack on that front. Who wouldn't cave when a beautiful, passionate, sexy woman suddenly asked you to take her back to your hotel room for the night? Surely better humans than her had fallen in similar situations and lived to tell the tale. She could stay calm, gather her wits, and move forward with a clear head.

She didn't have to make the same mistakes twice. And Callie

wasn't the kind of person who would let her. Callie wasn't manipulative, helpless, or needy. The thought helped lighten her mood considerably. Callie had been the antithesis of needy last night, or this morning, or ever, really. She was a star on the ice and in the bedroom, and anyone who saw her in any area would know without a doubt that Max couldn't offer her anything she didn't already possess in spades. But then again, few people would ever get to know Callie unless she got some more press coverage.

Her stomach flip-flopped again. "No. No. No."

This wasn't that. It couldn't be that.

She wrapped a towel around her waist and padded out of the bathroom to begin collecting her clothes. ESPN moved to coverage of last night's hockey games. "In what's shaping up to be the feel-good story of the year, Victor Garrick scored a hat trick last night as the Rangers beat the Red Wings."

Her chest seized at the name, and she scanned the room for the remote, ready to make a dive for it, but before she got the chance, a familiar voice coming from the television froze her in place.

"I'm trying to move on. I'm trying not to let anything take away from my final season," Victor said to a room full of reporters. "I think my teammates deserve that. I think I deserve that, too."

"Hard to argue with that." The reporter cut back in. "You'd have to have a heart of stone not to root for this guy after everything he went through during the off-season, between the—"

Max abandoned the remote and slapped the off button on the television. She couldn't take this right now.

She couldn't take it ever again.

Callie's rock slid between the two stones she intended to bounce off of and kept right on sailing until it hit the backboard.

Layla threw her hands up in the air and said, "Field goal!"

She shook her head. "Not helpful."

"Maybe not, but you have to admit we just witnessed a rare feat, Skip. You managed to miss both rocks in one shot. When was the last time that happened?"

"About ten minutes ago."

"Oh yeah." Layla grinned. "I guess the event was only rare up until this week. You ready to talk about why that might be?"

"Lack of focus," Callie grumbled.

"Sure, we can accept the surface explanation, but wouldn't it be more fun to get to the bottom of why you're not focusing?"

"Fun for who?"

"Me, clearly." Layla laughed. "I suspect you already had your fun last weekend."

Callie's cheeks burned even in the cool of the curling club.

"Come on." Layla nudged. "Let's take a break."

She rolled her eyes. "There's no time for breaking when I'm playing so poorly."

"Look," Layla said, her tone carrying a new warning. "I get that you're not all into talking about your feelings, but I have waited the mandatory three days before I can lay down the best friend card, and I'm playing that ace right now. You know the rules of friendship. Sit down."

She complied, largely because she did know the rules. She and Layla had established them over more than a decade of friendship. Layla had given her ample time and space to process, but now she'd come to collect the goods.

"Time to play 'Yes or No.'"

Callie slouched in her chair and stared up at the exposed metal roof of the club. "Fire away."

"Did you leave the Patch with Max Laurens last Sunday?" Layla always started with the easy ones since she liked to build to a crescendo.

"Yes."

"Did you, at any point in the night, come back to our hotel room?"

"No."

"Were you with Max that whole time?"

"Yes."

"And what percentage of that time was spent having hot, freaky sex?"

"Foul," Callie called. "That's not a yes-or-no question."

159

"I'll rephrase," Layla conceded. "Was more than half of the night spent having hot sex?"

Callie sighed, but the sound ended up more dreamy than frustrated. "Yes."

Layla laughed. "Go girl, it's your birthday, your sexy sports reporter birthday."

She rolled her eyes.

"Okay, sorry. Yes or no, the sex was in the top ten percent of all the sex you've ever had?"

"Yes."

"Top one percent?"

She didn't hesitate. "Yes."

"Aha!" Layla said triumphantly. "I rest my case."

"What? That's not a case. There is no case. You would make a terrible lawyer."

"Right?" Layla flopped into the chair beside her. "Could you mention that to my mother next time she starts banging on about me needing to choose a real career?"

"Sure."

"For real though, Cal. What happened with Max?"

"I don't know." She hung her head. "I mean, I know how things ended up, but I'm still not sure how they got there so fast. I mean, it was kind of a big day for both of us. But I've won bonspiels in the past and never jumped into bed with anyone."

"And it's not like you haven't had that chance."

She snorted. "Maybe, but I've never had any urges to take it."

"So, maybe the more important question isn't how it happened, but why it happened with Max."

She blew out a slow, steady breath that fluttered a strand of hair away from her face. "It would be easy to say she just happened to be there, right place, right time, but there were hundreds of people there. I remember there being a crowd. Other curlers wanted to talk. The fans were on the dance floor, but I just didn't see any of them."

"You only saw Max and that square jaw and that hair that doesn't move."

160

"It moves," Callie said with a little grin.

"There you go. Give me the details. Did you ruffle her all up when you rocked her world?"

"Maybe." Her face flamed.

"Give me more."

She shook her head. "I can't."

"You could if you loosened up a little. At least tell me she's not so damn stoic in bed as she is at the events."

"She is not," Callie admitted, as a thousand memories flashed through her mind. "She's cocky, and she's got this, I don't know, swagger almost, but she backs it up with skill and a hint of playfulness."

"Playful doesn't strike me as her MO."

"I know, but it's there, underneath all the stubbornness. She's actually really witty and kind of funny when she's not grumpy. And she's passionate. It's so intense. That's what did me in."

"Is 'passion' a euphemism for 'good in bed'? Because if so, I feel you."

"No," Callie said quickly, then laughed. "I mean, the two may be related, but I got swept up in it before we got to bed, and I think that comes from seeing her struggle and fight and claw her way back into control."

"She had a long way to go on that front after her first day here."

"But she did it. Or at least she's working hard to do so. She knows what it's like to take hits and get back up."

"Indeed," Layla said with a shake of her head. "Pride is strong with that one."

"She gets what it's like to want something when no one else believes you deserve it. She knows what it's like to pour everything you have into something no one else thinks you can or even should do."

"Ah." Layla's smile turned a little sad. "So, this wasn't, like, a one-time wild night off? You two bonded?"

"No," Callie said quickly. "I mean, we hit it off, but it was totally a one-time thing. We are not—I mean, I cannot, because curling, and work, and focus."

"And Max knows this."

"Of course."

"Because you talked to her about it?"

Callie bit her lip.

"Oh, Cal. You've talked to her, right?"

"We overslept. You saw the shape I was in the next morning. I barely made it to the car before Ella and Brooke got there. I didn't have time to talk to her Monday morning."

"It's Friday," Layla deadpanned. "Tell me you called her."

Callie grimaced. "Am I supposed to call her? Why isn't she supposed to call me? I mean, we're lesbians. There's a fifty-fifty chance she's supposed to call me. Right?"

"Please don't tell me we're doing *that*."

"What? Am I wrong? She knows where I work. She works here, too, and she hasn't been in. What if she's avoiding me? What if she thinks we made a terrible mistake and she's right?" The words all came out in a rush that suggested they'd been pent up for a while. Maybe a lot of things had been pent up for a while, given her behavior lately. How long had it been since she'd lost herself in something other than curling? Doing so with Max had been a big deal for her, and while she hadn't expected it to go anywhere, it stung to think Max might be avoiding her now.

"Who jumped whose bones?" Layla asked, cutting to the heart of the matter.

"We both jumped. Again, lesbians."

"Who jumped first?"

"Um . . ."

"It was you, wasn't it?"

She nodded.

"First of all, high five!" Layla extended her hand above her head, and Callie slapped it halfheartedly. "Second of all, call her! She hasn't been to a practice in almost a week. That's not like her. You know who it's like?"

"Please don't tell me."

"I'll tell you. It's like someone who had great sex with a woman who ran out on her the next morning and hasn't called in a week, so now she's worried things are going to be awkward at work."

"No."

"Yes. And guess what is also awkward at work: you missing shots you can make in your sleep."

She slumped. "See, this is exactly why I shouldn't have slept with her. It was amazing—"

"How amazing?"

"Indescribably amazing, but now we're in a mess. Our reporter has disappeared, I'm distracted and missing shots, and you're sitting here talking about my sex life instead of practicing."

"Talking about your sex life is more fun."

"For you, but for me it's a reminder that I let my emotions and my libido get in the way of what really matters. It can't happen again."

"But—"

"I mean it. Please respect me here. I don't want it to become a thing. And I don't want Brooke and Ella to know. It's bad enough I pulled you off track. I couldn't take it if my lapse in judgment derailed our whole team."

"I think you should have a little more faith in them."

"It's not about them. It's about me."

"And Max."

"No," she said emphatically. "There's no 'me and Max.' It's just me. My life, my dreams, my career."

Layla held up her hands. "Okay."

"Okay, you won't tell them?"

"Yes."

"Okay, you'll let this go?"

"Okay, for now."

They stared at each other for several seconds before Callie realized that was probably the best she could get, given the magnitude of the conversation. "Okay, we can get back to work?"

"Yes."

She nodded resolutely. "Okay, then, let's do that."

Chapter Thirteen

Max sat in the car outside the curling club. She needed to go in. It was time for a full team practice, the first since their big win last weekend. She could easily wave off not stopping in all week as Callie practiced at random times, and none of the other players were guaranteed to even be in town. She had video to edit and articles to submit, plus she'd started working on a series of curling primer blogs for the run-up to the Players' Championship in a few months. She'd had plenty to keep her busy, working, without watching Callie trying to make the same shots over and over again in those tight pants with those amazing arms flexing and her hazel eyes so intense.

She shivered more than the dropping temperature warranted. Winter had arrived in Buffalo, with freezing air and an inch or two of snow, but neither of those things had helped cool the heat still burning inside her. Heat from lust, heat from embarrassment—they both boiled in the pit of her stomach. She didn't even know if she could separate the two in her mind anymore. How could she ever explain the mix to Callie?

At least with the whole team together for a full practice the two of them probably wouldn't have much chance to talk about anything other than work. The thought made her feel a little cowardly, but also helped her get out of the car.

Nothing had changed about the club. She didn't know why

she thought it might have. Because she'd changed? No, she hadn't really changed. Because Team Mulligan had won a big match? There was no more excitement or sense of greatness surrounding them now. It had been only one match out of hundreds. Everyone had simply gone on with their work, and she intended to follow their example.

She pushed through from the lounge to the ice and immediately saw her team huddled together around the white board where Callie drew up some sort of play. There, to her right, still magneted to the board, was Max's article under the bright, bold heading of "challenge accepted."

Oh, how she wished she'd known then what she knew now. She didn't know if her assessment of curling's qualifications as a top-tier sport had fully changed, but it had certainly become more complicated. Her assessment of Callie's athletic fitness had certainly evolved. And she would no longer question any of the curlers she'd met in their dedication or competitive spirit. More importantly, though, now that she knew how that challenge would draw them closer together, pinning their dreams and drives to each other's, would she have made the same choice? She feared she might've, which only made her feel worse.

"I got it," Ella said, breaking from the group. "Let's roll."

She nodded a brief acknowledgment in Max's direction, which was more than she'd freely given her in . . . maybe ever.

"Hey, Pencil Pusher's back," Layla called, as she slid by to take her position, broom in hand.

"Did you miss me?" Max asked, and then grimaced that her voice sounded more needy than sarcastic.

"Actually," Layla said, "I sort of did."

She grinned, bolstered, then turned toward Callie. She hadn't moved from her spot by the board, but her gaze landed on Max. Those hazel eyes held their usual intensity, but their familiar openness had been replaced by an almost catlike air of mystery. She didn't know how long they stood there, but long enough for the chill to creep through her clothes. Surely something had to give. No one could feel this many swirling emotions without something taking precedence or priority. Or then again, maybe she felt all the things, and Callie felt nothing. Would Max have to break first?

The thought was disconcerting, and Max failed to rise to the challenge, merely flashing a weak smile before looking away under the guise of finding a chair. She sat several feet back from the ice and watched practice without noticing much of anything, including what the team happened to be working on.

She was good at reading people—or at least she always had been, until Sylvia. Even after everything had calmed down and her initial heartache had been replaced by other emotions, the thing that hurt the most was how much her misjudgment had shaken her sense of self. What did it mean that someone who derived their living, and even their sense of self, from their ability to ask the right questions, to read between the lines, to see the truth through the layers, had gotten all of those things so horribly wrong?

And now, when she needed most to tell herself she wouldn't make the same mistakes again, she stared into Callie's generally expressive eyes and saw . . . nothing. Her palms started to sweat, and she rubbed them together. She didn't like feeling off balance or out of the loop, and she hadn't for several weeks. Her body rebelled at the thought of going back there, her shoulders tightening and her stomach beginning to churn.

The crack of two rocks colliding reverberated through the cavernous space, drawing her attention back to the ice. Or more accurately, to the players on it.

"Whew," Layla called. "What a shot, Ella."

"Hot darn," Ella said, with a huge smile on her face. "I'm going to come up with an I-nailed-it dance because this is becoming a thing for me."

Brooke laughed. "How about an Ella-nailed-it break, Skip?"

Callie nodded. "Sure. Take ten."

The team didn't need telling twice as they all made a break for the lounge, all except for Callie. She sighed heavily enough for Max to see the rise and fall of her shoulders even from a distance. She had a sudden memory of kissing along those tight muscles and had to tamp down the urge to do so again.

"Glad you're back," Callie said, as she used her foot to scoot a couple of rocks into different positions.

"Yeah?"

"I'd started to wonder."

"Me, too," Max admitted, "about a lot of things."

Callie nodded.

"And I had work to do."

"Work?" Callie finally glanced up. "That sounds . . . good?"

"Yeah," Max said more confidently. "Work's good. Work's important."

The corner of Callie's mouth curled up. "I'm glad to hear it."

"And you?"

"Work is getting better."

She raised an eyebrow.

"I was off for the first few days after we got back here. Distracted, I guess."

"Oh." She didn't know what else to say. "In a bad way?"

Callie's smile grew, and she stepped off the ice toward Max. "There's not really a good way to be distracted in curling."

"Right. Sorry."

"It's not your fault," Callie said, then added, "I mean, you certainly played a part in the distraction, but I don't blame you. And, I don't have any real regrets about the events that sparked the distraction."

"Events," Max repeated, a little more playfully. "More than one?"

"Several, if I remember correctly, but things got a little blurry, and that's risky in my line of work."

"Mine, too."

"Which is why you stayed away for a few days?"

"Partially."

"Then we're on the same page." Callie pulled a chair near enough for them to talk quietly, but not close enough to touch. "We both needed to refocus and get back to thinking about work."

Max nodded. She didn't disagree, and she even appreciated Callie's ability to recenter herself so quickly and completely, but those qualities also made her worry Callie had never fully stopped

167

thinking about work in the first place. The fear might not have been fair or rational, but fears rarely were.

"So then, tell me about your work," Callie prodded. "You were doing things related to the last tournament?"

"Yeah, some stuff along those lines."

"Some stuff?" Callie teased. "Vague."

Max's cheeks burned. "Sorry. I did a couple of write-ups for the new blog, and then I edited a few highlight videos to share on social media."

Some of the sparkle returned to Callie's eyes. "That sounds fun. I mean, I assume you included all my best shots and cut the ones I flubbed, right?"

Max felt her expression twitch. "Uh, probably."

Callie stared at her as if waiting for more.

"I don't remember exactly what shots went into which pieces, but you won, so it's got to be pretty flattering."

Callie frowned. "We don't have to talk about it if you don't want."

"No," she said quickly. "It's fine. I just wasn't prepared to defend my coverage of you right now."

"I didn't think I'd asked you to defend anything. I was trying to show interest in your job, because I know it's important to you. I wanted to be supportive."

She wanted to believe her, and she did, at least intellectually. Callie was kind and genuine, but Max was scared, and she hated that.

"It hadn't even occurred to me that you had anything to defend until right now." Callie glanced over her shoulder quickly at the white board. "Do you?"

"No. I mean, I don't think so."

The response did nothing to soothe the hurt swirling in those hazel eyes now. "Did you write another hit piece?"

"No!" This whole conversation was spinning out of control. She understood the need to focus on work, but now work felt so much more complicated than it had felt last week. Never again would anything she wrote about Callie be a neutral process. She couldn't just be a reporter giving unbiased press to a random curler. All those lines and their motivations were muddled. She would love to go back to talking about their jobs, but she didn't know if she'd ever be able to separate her coverage of Callie the curler from her feelings for Callie the woman, and that was the very crux of her job. And, so very dangerous, both personally and professionally.

She couldn't sit still as the panic rose in her once more, so she hopped up under the guise of stretching.

"Max," Callie said, her voice placating. "I'm sorry we didn't have a chance to talk on Monday morning."

"It's fine."

"I don't think it is." Callie rose so they were closer in height once more. Too close.

"Yeah, you have to do your thing. I have to do mine. I mean, we have to do things together, but work things, also separately." She was going off the rails now. She knew she sounded crazy. She couldn't seem to stop. But she had to stop. She had to pull herself back together. She couldn't have a panic attack. Not in front of Callie. She forced her lungs to take one deep, slow inhale, then pushed it out with more force than she intended.

Callie's brow furrowed, and worry filled her eyes.

"Hey, what's going on?" Ella called, striding up to her with the same expression she'd worn when she'd accused Max of stealing Callie's bag.

"Nothing," Callie said quickly. Then turning back to Max said, "I'm sorry."

She shook her head almost frantically. "No, it's my fault. I'm sorry."

"What did you do?" Ella snapped.

"Nothing," Callie said again.

"It doesn't look like nothing," Ella said, edging a shoulder between them. "What did you say to her?"

"This isn't really any of your business," Max said halfheartedly. "Can you please respect our privacy?"

"Oh, you're one to talk about respecting privacy," Ella practically

169

spat. "Care to call Victor Garrick and see how he feels about your right to privacy?"

All the air left Max's lungs.

"Did you really think we didn't know about that?" Ella pushed into Max's personal space. "Did you really think any of us trusted you?"

She shook her head, not in an answer to the question, so much as an attempt to stem the rising tide of bile in her throat.

"Ella," Callie said quickly, "stop."

"No, Callie. I don't care what kind of press coverage this woman comes with. She's not worth whatever's going on here. It's not worth selling your soul for a few extra matches on TV."

Max took another step back, reeling at the blunt impact of that statement. Is that really what Callie had done? Sold out for the TV viewership? She couldn't believe it, and yet that's likely all anyone else would believe if they ever found out.

Then Ella spun on her again. "How many more lives and careers and families are you going to destroy before you learn to leave people alone?"

Max winced, the pain of the comment causing her to take another step back, and then another.

"Okay, really," Layla said, looking from Max to Callie, her dark eyes pleading. "I think we all need to cool down here. Maybe talk some things out."

"No," Max croaked, "she's right."

"She's not," Callie said quickly.

"She is," she said more emphatically, but her conviction might have been undercut by the way she continued to back away from them. "Listen to her."

"Max." Callie reached for her, but she pulled farther way.

"I'm so sorry." It was all she could manage before she turned and fled.

Chapter Fourteen

Callie stared at the door Max had practically sprinted through, trying to process what had just happened. Things between them had been awkward from the moment they'd made eye contact, but to say they'd escalated quickly would've been a radical understatement, and she couldn't understand why. Certainly, Ella's arrival hadn't helped, but she seemed to have aggravated the situation rather than caused it. Thankfully, Callie wasn't the only person trying to put those pieces together.

"What the fuck," Layla said. "I left for, like, five minutes and come back to find everyone had a personality transplant."

"No," Ella said, a subtle seething in her voice. "That woman hasn't changed her personality at all. What did she do to you, Callie?"

She blinked a few times, trying to make sense of the question. Max had done several things to her, but none of them warranted the venom in her teammate's voice. "We were just talking. I think the bigger question is, what did she do to you?"

"Nothing," Ella said. "I'm not giving her the chance."

"The chance to what?"

"Seriously?" Ella stared at her, then turned to the others.

Layla shrugged, but Brooke nodded almost reluctantly. "I know you want to give everyone the benefit of the doubt, Callie, but with her past, and the way she looks at you, I mean, you can't blame us for worrying. We care about you."

"Looks at me how? Wait, worry about what?"

"She's got sort of a bad track record with women," Brooke said.

"Sort of?" Ella scoffed. "She broke up a marriage and tried to end a good man's career so she could steal his wife."

She heard all the words, and intellectually she understood them. But the sentence made no sense to her.

"It's true," Brooke said, again seeming to feel a little bad about it. "I mean, you never know for sure what's going on in someone's relationship, but I read some of the stories after Ella told me, and the facts are pretty hard to dispute."

"What story? What facts?"

"Yeah, I'm going to need to be filled in here, too," Layla cut back in.

"Don't you two ever follow hockey even a bit?"

"No," she and Layla said in unison.

"We live in Buffalo, for fudge's sake. Victor Garrick has been a star forward for the New York Rangers for, like, ever. And he's totally loved by everyone, but last year Max ran a story about how he was juiced up on steroids and violent to his wife."

"That's awful."

"Yeah, 'cause none of it was true. Max made it all up to make him look bad."

She shook her head. "Why would she do that?"

"Because she was banging the wife."

Her stomach lurched.

"It's true," Brooke said softly. "She's never really denied that part."

"What part did she deny?" Layla asked.

"She said she got bad information from the wife, but I mean, really, that was her only source, the woman who she was cheating on the guy with?"

"And he was humiliated. He had to hold a press conference and tell the whole world he was diabetic and this would be his last season playing hockey and how he wanted to go out on his own terms. Max took that way from him, along with his wife."

Callie eased back into the chair. So many things made sense now. Her dad's warnings, the reason Max was even covering curling in the first place, all her anger and resentment. She shook her head. Actually the last part didn't quite make sense. Why would she be mad at other people if she had been the one to dig her own grave? And where was this other woman now? Surely, if Max had gone through all that for her, she had to love her a lot. Or maybe she hadn't. Maybe Max slept with women like that all the time. Callie certainly wasn't in a position to argue otherwise.

"You okay?" Layla asked. "You've gone a little green."

"I don't know what to say."

"How about, 'thank you for getting rid of her'?" Ella asked. "Did you see the way she turned tail and ran when it became clear we knew her game?"

Callie flashed back to that moment. Max had run, but she hadn't looked like someone who'd been caught, so much as hurt. Her eyes had gone wide and wounded. And if she was someone who slept with sources on a regular basis, she certainly hadn't acted like it earlier. She hadn't been smooth or carefree today or ever before. She hadn't even chased after Callie or really pursued her in any way. Perhaps she should feel a little offended about that. If Max fell easily into bed with women she covered, or connived and cheated to get what she wanted, why had Callie been the one to kiss her first, to invite her back to the hotel and jump her as soon as they got there?

She couldn't make sense of Ella's story with everything she'd experienced herself, and yet if Max had never denied the allegations . . .

She shook her head again.

"Come on," Brooke said gently. "Let's get back to work."

Ella sighed. "Yeah, okay. Maybe we'll be able to focus better now."

"No," Callie said softly.

They all stared at her.

"I don't think I'll be able to focus."

Brooke laughed nervously. "You can always focus on curling."

She shook her head again, this time with more force. Something was off. Something in her, something in Max, and it was off even before Ella had burst in. Max had gone from twitchy to scared to hurt. That thought overrode all the others.

She kicked off her curling shoes and tossed her broom to Layla. "I gotta go."

She would owe them all an explanation eventually, but for right now she needed to get a few of them for herself.

Max's hand shook too badly for her to get her key in the ignition. She hadn't had a full-blown panic attack in months, and she had honestly thought she'd moved past them. Another thing she could add to her long list of stupid assumptions. At least she was still breathing, albeit rapidly and shallowly. Still, she didn't think she would pass out, and as soon as her arms stopped spasming, she could drive. She could leave the club, leave Buffalo, leave the country if she wanted to. She'd seen signs for Canada not far from her hotel. Maybe she could apply for asylum, not that they would give it to her since she was still clearly a social pariah. The thought made her chest tighten painfully. So much for breathing.

She pushed her seat back and tried to double over as best she could with the steering wheel in her way. She tried to think of something else, anything else, anything concrete, the shudder of a winter wind against her car, the squeak of the rubber floor mat against the trembling soles of her shoes, the sharp rap of knuckles against her passenger side window.

The last item on the list finally burned through the haze, and she glanced up to see a face pressed close to the glass.

She screamed and jumped so hard she smacked her knees on the steering column. One hand shot to her leg and the other to the center of her chest.

"Sorry!" Callie called. "Oh, I made it worse again."

She shook her head, but she couldn't draw a deep enough breath to offer any consolation.

"Can you come out here?" Callie asked. Eyeing Max more closely, she said, "Or do you mind if I open the door?"

Max shook her head again, finally sucking in a full gulp of air. Callie opened the door and leaned her head inside. "Hey."

"Hey," she managed to rasp.

"You okay?"

Max stared at her, still gasping but no longer fruitlessly as her lungs began to expand again.

"It's okay," Callie said, her voice calm and steady as she eased into the seat beside her. "I'm right here."

"Why?"

Callie's eyebrows shot up.

"Why are you here?" Maybe not the best first sentence to mutter on the comedown of a panic attack, but it was all she could think of.

"I don't know," Callie admitted, still staring at her with concern.

"What do you need?" Max asked, certain that no matter what the answer was, she couldn't provide it now, anyway.

Callie shrugged. "I'm not sure, but . . . I think, maybe, wings?"

Max blinked several times, wondering if she'd lost consciousness, and perhaps this whole encounter was actually a hallucination.

"Chicken wings, not like actual wings to fly with, though those would be good, too, I suppose, but I really meant the kind you eat."

"Buffalo wings?"

"Yeah, but"—she grinned sheepishly—"here we just call them 'wings.' You want to go get some with me?"

Max turned her head to one side and then the other as if she might rattle her brain back into place. When nothing shifted, she said, "That's not what I expected."

Callie grinned. "I get that, but I mean, you are in Buffalo, so wings should never exactly be *unexpected.*"

Max tried to consider that point. She supposed it was no weirder than anything else that had happened in the last ten minutes, and maybe it was exactly what she needed to jar herself out of her downward spiral because she did actually seem to be breathing better now. Callie had a habit of breaking off in wildly different directions, but none of them had actually led her too far astray . . . yet. "Okay."

"Okay? To wings?"

She nodded. "Okay to wings."

"Good." Her grin spread. "Want me to drive?"

"Yes, please."

And that was all she'd had to say. Suddenly, she went from lost and cold and scared to cruising along the highway in Callie's little Subaru hatchback with a tiny curling stone on top of the antennae and Team USA stickers in the back window, because, of course.

"So, you know about the whole wing controversy in Buffalo, right?" Callie asked with a casualness in her voice that didn't betray any of the freaked-outedness most people would've felt in a similar situation.

"I know Buffalo wings were invented here."

"Right, but where?"

Max shook her head. "No idea. Where?"

"That's the controversy. Two different restaurants claim to be the originator of the Buffalo wing. Both the Anchor Bar and Duff's have stories about inventing our city's signature dish, which incidentally makes Buffalo the only city that's also a flavor."

Max snorted. "That's quite a claim to fame."

"Right? I mean, you don't get Detroit-flavored chips, or Cleveland sauce."

"Nor am I sure I would want to."

Callie laughed. "But it's important to know where you come from, and Buffalo isn't quite sure where her signature taste began."

Max thought about that, grateful to have something else to fill her mind and push out the horrible questions that had crowded the space earlier. "Well, which place do you think is better?"

"There's great debate around that as well. It splits the city down the middle. Everyone here has a pretty set opinion on the subject, but I wouldn't want to taint your taste buds with my bias. I think you need to try both for yourself."

"Fair enough, but which one are we trying today?"

Callie clasped her hand on Max's shoulder and gave it a playful squeeze. "My friend, you have so much to learn."

"I don't doubt you," she said seriously, "but that still doesn't answer my question."

"Both," Callie said with a grin. "The only way to do a proper taste test is by limiting all the variables and trying one right after the other."

"We're going to two wing places in one day?"

"Of course we are."

Max laughed, but the sense of absurdity surrounding her now stemmed less from the overindulgent meal plan and more from the woman suggesting it. After everything that had happened between them, Callie should've taken her chance and run for the hills. Instead, she had run toward her.

Max read the menu aloud. "Medium is hot. Medium hot is very hot. Hot is very, very hot."

"Welcome to Duff's," Callie said proudly.

"It's not much to look at." Max glanced around the dark interior and low ceilings of the small dining room. "But it's got a good, authentic feel to it."

"They've franchised out and have several bigger, more polished locations, but this is the original, so I think it best to start here."

"I agree. You always want to start at the source of a story and work out from there," Max said, then frowned. "Then again, what do I know about sources?"

Callie did her best to ignore the comment. "Well, do you know what kind of wings you want to try?"

"What do you recommend? Despite what you saw in my car earlier, I have a relatively high pain tolerance."

Again Callie dodged the heavier topic and suggested, "Let's do one order of medium and one medium hot so you get a sense of the flavor and then the heat."

"Deal." Max put down her menu and let Callie place the order, but as soon as the waitress left, she started to get a little twitchy again, her gaze sweeping everywhere that didn't involve making actual eye contact.

Callie wanted to help. She wanted to know what was going on, but she felt as though she was dancing around a trapped animal too scared to let anyone get close enough to help. Her instinct to soothe was tempered by her own desire not to get bit in the process. She tried to tread carefully as far as Max would allow.

"I'm sorry we got interrupted back at the club."

Max's shoulders tensed, but Callie pushed forward gently. "I wanted to say that I think I messed up when I brought up your job. I think I made you feel pressured without meaning to."

"It's fine," Max said curtly, a warning in her tone.

Maybe Callie should have left it there, maybe she should've changed the subject again, but she couldn't shake the sense that something helpless lurked behind the low growl in Max's voice.

"I'm not always good at talking about things other than curling, but I was trying to show interest in your job because I know it's important to you. You've been so supportive of me in my job lately that I wanted to do the same for you, but I didn't convey that well."

"No, I misunderstood. I do that a lot more than I like to admit."

"I don't think so," Callie said. "I think you've worked really hard over the last month to try to understand curling. I know you don't share my interest."

"You mean obsession," Max teased.

Her heart stretched against its confines to hear a little sass back in her voice. "Sure. Obsession. I'll wear it, and you have done your best to humor me."

"To be fair, your obsession relates a little to my job."

She sighed. "Am I really that bad at showing a complimentary interest in something not related to curling?"

The corners of Max's mouth curled up. "No. I'm just bad at accepting it."

"Well, stow that long enough for me to say I'm interested in you. That's all I was trying to express back at the club. I wanted to know how your week went because I'm interested. Did I say that part all right?"

"Kind of," Max admitted, "but it's not terrible to hear twice."

The waitress returned with their wing orders and, after making sure they knew which ones would burn and which would scorch, left them alone again. The conversation faded as Max took her first bite of the medium wings and nodded appreciatively.

"This is in the top five of wings I've ever eaten." She chewed a little more. "Make that top three."

"Not too hot?"

She shook her head. "Good burn, but also good flavor. Smooth burn with a buttery texture."

"See," Callie said, in between her own bites, "here's the type of thing I should've led with earlier, but did you get into journalism because you always had a way with words, or did you learn to describe things like that because you're a journalist?"

Max frowned, and Callie's stomach tightened again, but the withdrawal she feared never came.

"Maybe both?" Max shrugged and grabbed another wing. "I think I learned to use my words early on, much to the chagrin of my family, who were more likely to use their fists or their intimidation."

Callie grimaced.

"Yeah, I didn't come from a high-class set of people." Max pushed on. "And I couldn't compete with them in their arenas. I was never going to be big or intimidating, but I could talk circles around them. I could tie them in knots, which didn't always end well for me at home, but it started to get me noticed at school. I had some teachers take an interest, and suddenly I wasn't just reacting. I was starting to make sense of things around me."

"I admire that," Callie admitted. "I wish I were better at making sense of things."

"You make sense of your world. You get people, know what motivates them. People trust you. They like you."

"I'm sure they like you, too."

"No." Max shook her head. "Sometimes they admire me. Sometimes they need me, and sometimes they find me interesting or amusing, but I think very few people actually like me. I get under their skin. I make them feel uncomfortable. I needle until they reveal things they don't always like to, and once I latch onto something, I don't let go."

"You're tenacious."

"I'm a polymath pain in the ass. I know enough to draw people in and then pick them apart."

"Sounds like a dangerous skill."

"It can be," Max said gravely, then reached for the medium-hot wings. "Should we take our taste buds up another notch?"

Callie noticed the change in subjects but didn't want to push. "Sure, same time?"

Max nodded, and they each raised a wing to their mouth and locked eyes. For a second she remembered the flash of connection, of staring down at Max in bed, of feeling their bodies pressed together in a way that went deeper than skin.

The heat spread through her before the sauce even touched her tongue, but the food certainly didn't help.

"Definitely hotter," Max said, as her eyes began to water.

"Too much for you?" Callie teased as she fared only slightly better. The wing still had good flavor, but it was harder to isolate over the burn across her lips and tongue.

"Not at all," Max said, even while reaching for her water. "I can take it."

"You don't have to," Callie offered. "It's not a competition."

"Everything's a little bit of a competition, isn't it?" Max asked. "I mean, maybe not with you, but with me. I always want to know where my boundaries are."

"So you can push them?"

"Maybe." Max grinned again. "Something we have in common."

"Is that why you chose to write about sports instead of going into a more general form of reporting?"

"It's part of it." Max relaxed again. "I think I also liked bucking stereotypes. Not a lot of girls in my school wanted to cover the sports teams. It was a boy's job, and even the school newspaper advisor didn't think I had what it took."

"I bet that went over well."

Max snorted. "Yeah, I don't like being told I can't do something."

"Shocking," Callie mused.

"Oh, you're one to talk. Besides, she wasn't totally wrong. I never did take to doing simple play-by-play summaries or reporting box scores. Before long, I transitioned into doing more in-depth pieces on the athletes or the sports themselves. Then I did an exposé on the funding of women's sports in relationship to men's sports in our school district."

"Impressive."

"The superintendent didn't think so when it got a Title IX complaint filed against him."

"Good for you!"

"Yeah, so while I found individual sporting matchups interesting enough, the people behind them were much more compelling for me. By the time I got to college, I'd found my niche, and I got bigger and bigger opportunities to delve deeper into the culture of sports and the psyches of the people who compete."

"And that's how you landed here," Callie concluded, grabbing one more wing and pushing the last one toward Max, who accepted but was no longer meeting her eyes.

"Something like that."

Callie internally kicked herself, but for what she wasn't quite sure. She'd obviously triggered the sadness in Max again, but she didn't know how to stop, and honestly she wasn't sure she wanted to. If something could shake a woman of Max's fortitude and presence this badly, maybe it didn't need to be exposed.

"So, how do you decide who gets to be a story? I mean, there are millions of athletes in the world. How do you decide which are interesting enough to warrant more research? The biggest? The fastest? The most famous?"

"Those factors help," Max admitted slowly. "They certainly guarantee a built-in readership, which is important, but they don't always ensure an interesting read."

"But how do you know, before you start, what will make for an interesting read?"

"I don't. No one knows where a line of questions will lead before it starts, or why ask the question in the first place?" She grew more animated as she gestured with her half-eaten wing. "I only know when something piques my own interest enough to start digging. That's part of the excitement. You never know what you don't know, and sometimes you find out even the things you think you know just ain't so."

Callie grinned. "I like that. Reminds me of my own life lately. I feel like I'm living at the intersection of what I don't know and what I thought I knew might not be true."

Max hung her head again. "I'm a big factor in that, aren't I?"

"Do you want me to lie or be honest?"

"Honest. Always honest."

"Then yes," Callie said. She quickly added, "Not that I'm pushing. I'm not. Your life, your feelings, your past, they're all yours, but the more I know about you, the more I want to know, and the more I know—how did you put it?—the more I suspect what I think I know, just ain't so."

Max still wasn't looking directly at her, but the side view allowed Callie to see the little twitch in her jaw, and the strain at the spot where neck met shoulder. Something was twisting her in knots from the inside out, and in that moment Callie wanted desperately to be the one to start untying them. Only she didn't know how.

Max finally broke the silence. "Are we ready to move on to the Anchor Bar?"

She nodded slowly. "I'm ready whenever you are."

Chapter Fifteen

The Anchor Bar was bigger than Duff's, and slightly more polished in that, instead of bare-wood paneling, the walls were covered in newspaper clippings about wings and framed photos of celebrities eating their wings. Max appreciated having something else to look at as an excuse for avoiding the questions in Callie's eyes.

Why did she have to be so perfect? So understanding? So gentle? Max had built all her defenses around being angry, and it had worked well until Callie had come along. Now, sitting so close to her, she'd started to forget why she needed defenses in the first place. She almost had the urge to try the "suicidal" wings just to feel the burn again, but Callie warned against it, and gave one order each of medium and hot. Mercifully, both arrived quickly.

"And?" Callie asked, leaning forward expectantly as Max tried one of the medium wings.

Max chewed slowly, taking in the crisp outer layer coated in a mix of tangy and buttery flavors. "I'm developing a preference, but I'm going to need a bigger sample size."

"Of course. Wouldn't want to rush to judgment." Callie feigned a serious nod, but the quirk of her lips gave her away.

This time Max selected one of the hot ones and took a big bite. Immediately the increased heat hit her sinuses. She wouldn't have thought she had anything left to clear out after the medium-hot ones at Duff's, but she stifled the urge to blow her nose. And yet, the fire never rose to a painful level. There was a distinct edge of hot pepper to this one, but it didn't completely sublimate the tang or the smooth finish. Duff's wings were great, top-contender great, but these were on a different plane.

"This one," she said, as soon as she swallowed. "These are better."

Callie raised a fist triumphantly. "We can be friends!"

"Wait." She laughed. "I didn't know this was a test."

"I told you we were doing a taste test."

"Yeah, taste test, not a friendship test."

"Who wants to be friends with people who have bad taste?"

Max laughed harder, the sound foreign to her own ears, the shake in her shoulders beginning to loosen some of the tension there. "Fair point, but I thought we were already friends."

Callie's smile turned sweet. "It makes me really happy you thought that. I mean, after everything that happened, and then everything else that happened today, I worried you hated me."

"No," she said quickly. "Callie, how could I hate you? Or more importantly, how can you not hate me? I mean, I know what you must think—"

"You don't." She cut her off. "You can't possibly know what I think, because I don't even know what I think. There are so many things I don't know about you and, again, I am not pushing. I am okay with not knowing every detail of your life, but please don't assume you know what's going on in my head. Or maybe, if you're so sure you do, then you should tell me, because I don't."

Max stared at her. "Um, that was kind of a lot."

Callie sat back. "Was it? Sorry."

"No, don't be sorry. You're right."

"I do love it when you say that."

She snorted. "Don't get used to it."

"I *am* getting used to it," Callie said, her tone a little lighter. "It's happening a lot lately, and I'm good with it happening more."

"What if I'm not around long enough for it to happen much more?"

"Unacceptable. You promised me a season, a full season. That's the deal. I'm not friends with people who break deals."

"Callie," she said sadly, "what Ella said today—"

"Was rude and hurtful and—"

"True. At least from a certain standpoint."

"Your standpoint?"

Max clenched her teeth. "Doesn't matter."

"I decide what matters to me, and you just won the wing test, and also I like you in other ways, too." Callie punctuated that phrase with a coy smile. "So if you don't want to talk to me, I get it. I can tell it's hard for you, and I hate that, but please just don't tell me it doesn't matter."

Max sighed. "Okay."

"Okay," Callie echoed. "Pass me the hot wings."

"That's it?" Max asked, sliding the basket across the table.

"Look, I told you, I'm ready whenever you are. That stands for multiple topics. Otherwise, yeah. It's wing time." And then she went back to eating as if nothing had happened.

Max stared at her, noticing the way her hair fell over her shoulders and how she had a little dab of hot sauce in the corner of her mouth, and how her perfectly smooth skin seemed more flawless than any of the glossy celebrity photos on the walls. Her own heart stopped hammering, her palms stopped sweating, and her jaw unclenched. No one was pushing her. No one was judging her. No one was making assumptions. Callie had called her a friend, and more than that, she'd treated her like one. She couldn't remember the last time someone had given her the benefit of the doubt. No one in her Rolodex of high-powered sports stars, no one in the wide field of famous sports reporters. No one, period.

"I fell in love with someone else's wife." The words just slipped out of her.

Callie glanced up, but didn't speak.

"I didn't mean to. I was working on a story about the hardships of being an athlete's wife. I mean, they are rich and privileged, and so many people would kill to be in their position, but the more I talked to them, the more I learned they didn't always have an easy road. Loving someone so driven means you have to share them with their passion. You might not even be the thing they love most in the world."

Callie nodded.

"And some athletes with long seasons are on the road more than they are home. Some of them don't see their spouses for two weeks at a time. Like in baseball or . . . hockey." Max blew out a slow breath. "That's how I met Sylvia Garrick."

Instead of immediately pushing for more information, Callie pushed the hot wings a little closer to Max, and somehow that was the perfect response.

"Her husband is kind of a big deal in hockey, and I knew of his reputation as a beast on the ice, but I never met him. In all the time I worked, and then socialized with, and then slept with Sylvia, I never once saw the man. He trained incessantly, and he was always off at preseason camps or traveling for games. On his off days, he always seemed to be traveling to meetings with trainers or doctors not affiliated with the team. I'd seen a lot of driven spouses, but his case seemed extreme, even to me."

"And, in your natural desire to find answers, you couldn't help but go looking for them," Callie supplied.

"That's the thing. I should've looked harder, but you know the old maxims about the simplest solution usually being the best one?"

Callie nodded.

"Well, Sylvia provided me with an easy answer. We had really bonded during my research phase, and we began to hang out. It was all very innocent at first. She called them 'girls' nights' and we'd do drinks or movies with a diverse group of women, from sports wives to stockbrokers to designers. Maybe it was hubris, but I never thought twice about being included in their ranks, and that was my first mistake."

"I would've never thought twice about your socializing with other powerful women."

"Thanks," Max said halfheartedly, "but eventually even I realized I didn't really fit in with anyone but Sylvia. Soon she and I started doing our own outings, and I still can't point to the moment those outings turned into dates. Maybe it would've been easier if it had happened all at once. Maybe some drastic shift would've thrown up a red flag, but it happened over months. We hadn't even slept together the first time she showed me a bruise on her arm and said Victor had flown into one of his rages again."

"Again?" Callie asked.

"She said it so casually, like it happened all the time. I was incensed at the thought of a hulking man tossing around this rail-thin woman who barely looked me in the eye. I told her it was unacceptable and if she wanted to leave, I would help her. She said he would come after her. I protested that I had the money and the connections to keep her safe. I also had access to the press. It was my fatal mistake."

"Any good person would have done the same, Max."

"But it wasn't completely altruistic. We slept together for the first time that night. She went on and on about how safe she felt with me. How I was so much better and gentler and giving than anyone she'd ever been with." Her face burned in shame. "I believed her, and more than that, I let it consume me. I got drunk from being needed. She became my drug of choice, but another month passed and she hadn't left him."

"Why not?"

"She kept saying she was too scared. I offered for her to move in. I offered to pay for the divorce attorney. I offered to pay for security, but she said he simply had too much power. His name carried more clout than mine. Every time we made love, she would cry afterward because she was stuck with him when she wanted to be with me more than anything." Her stomach still roiled at the memories, for so many reasons. "Then, one night, she brought me syringes."

Callie's eyebrows shot up. "Syringes?"

"A handful of them, all used. She said Victor used them all the time and wouldn't tell her why. Then she showed me another bruise and said he'd given it to her when she asked too many questions."

"Steroids?" Callie asked.

Max felt more than a little relieved that Callie had made the assumption, even though she knew how this story ended. "It makes sense, right? It more than made sense. It was the missing piece. All the meetings with doctors not affiliated with the team, his hulking stature, his violent fits, Sylvia's fear of him—steroids answered all the questions, and now I was standing there with a handful of used needles. It felt like she'd just handed me a silver bullet. I didn't even stop to think. I loaded the gun and cocked it."

Callie grimaced at the analogy.

"I'm not proud," she said quickly. "I wasn't a good reporter. I didn't verify. I didn't run tests."

"You had a lot of evidence."

"I had only one source."

"A source who should've been reliable. No one could've been closer to him."

"That's what I told myself. She'd been intimate with the subject of my report, but I left out the part where she'd also been intimate with me." She shook her head. "It was shoddy journalism, but at that point I wasn't thinking about craft or ethics. I saw someone struggling to get out of a bad situation. It tripped something deep-seated in me."

"Because of your own upbringing?"

She nodded. "I'd fought so hard to get myself out and up, and here was my chance to save someone else, someone I was head over heels for, someone who believed in me. It felt good, better than good. I felt like a hero, and I got off on that. I wanted to win her forever. I settled for the simplest explanation, and I ran with the story."

Callie hung her head.

"Yeah, you know how this ends, right? Within hours of the story breaking, Victor held a press conference and announced to the world that he had type 1 diabetes. He'd been aggressively managing his condition with the help of dieticians, specialists, and whole-health experts, but as his pancreas had deteriorated, he'd recently begun to inject insulin, a fact he'd hidden from the team for fear they would deem him too big a health risk and end his career. He apologized for keeping the secret, but said he'd rather admit defeat than let the world think him a cheater."

Callie's face had gone white, and Max suspected her own had turned hot-wing red. They must've looked like quite a pair, because the waitress hadn't come near them in a long time.

"I immediately printed a retraction, claiming I had been given bad information, but I still refused to reveal my source. After all, Sylvia had never told me he used steroids. I'd made the jump on my own. I hadn't done the legwork."

"But surely she apologized," Callie said. "Surely she wanted to help you."

"She stopped returning my calls," Max said flatly. "At first I thought she must be trying to protect me. Then I was wracked with worry that Victor had found out she'd been my source and he'd hurt her. I drove myself almost insane with fear for her, but I didn't want to put her at greater risk by pushing too hard to see her. I still believed everything else she'd told me about him, because . . . because I was an idiot."

"You were in love," Callie corrected.

"Same difference in this case. It took almost two weeks for the next story to break."

"Next story?"

"Oh yeah, it gets worse, because once my fellow sports reporters smelled blood in the water, they were all willing to eat each other trying to find the source. And they already knew I was the one who'd sounded the false alarm. It took mere days to trace me back to Sylvia. People had seen us together. The other sports wives we'd hung out with were happy to sing. My neighbors reported seeing her at my apartment regularly. Suddenly the whole city knew we'd been sleeping together, and the stories began to spin."

"What did you say to your fellow reporters?"

"Nothing!" she said quickly. "For all I knew, I'd just endangered the woman I loved. Now this man that I still believed to be a domestic abuser not only knew she shared his secret, but knew she'd also been having a lesbian affair. I sat quietly while my reputation swirled down the drain."

"You were willing to sacrifice everything you worked for to protect her?"

"Yes. I already told you, I was stupid."

"Some might say admirable."

"I slept with another man's wife and then published a false story in the hopes of rendering him powerless so that I could steal her away from him. Trust me, people called me a lot of things, but the word 'admirable' didn't come up."

"Is she still with him?"

Max snorted. "He divorced her quickly on the grounds of infidelities, plural."

"Oh no."

"Oh yeah. The court practically swooned as he described how his loving wife had sat stone-cold quiet through his diagnosis and early treatments, only to disappear when it became increasingly clear his time as a professional hockey player was coming to an end."

"She knew about the diabetes?"

"The whole time," Max said, some of her now-familiar anger beginning to swirl with the shame. "And while Victor jetted off to every specialist across the country, trying to find a way to stay on the ice, Sylvia began contacting every journalist she knew, trying to hedge her bets."

"But why?"

"I've wondered that a million times, but I think she was trying to broker a more favorable divorce. She must've thought that if she could tarnish his image, he'd be easier to break in court. She also knew he was lying to the team because he loved the game so much. She banked on him loving hockey enough to give her what she wanted. She had to be blackmailing him, but she overplayed her hand, and he came clean. She took an undisclosed settlement when it became clear she'd slept with multiple reporters."

"You weren't the only one," Callie said flatly.

"Not by a long shot. I was just the only one dumb enough to take the bait . . . all of it. I mean, as a writer I try to avoid clichés, but 'hook, line, and sinker' is a fitting image. I gave her the only thing she ever wanted from me, free press."

"She made love with you. You should've been able to trust her."

"Correction: She let me make love to her. It was always transactional for her. I was falling in love. She was working an angle to get what she needed. I was the only one willing to make the trade. Every one of my colleagues she approached either walked away or managed to get laid without getting emotionally involved. None of them developed feelings or hero complexes."

"Which is why they're covering football while you're sitting at the Buffalo Curling Club," she summed up neatly.

"Demoted, disgraced, and single while Victor has rebounded to an epic hockey season, and Sylvia has rebounded with the filthy rich son of a filthy rich Greek shipping magnate. They both ended up getting what they wanted. I got what I deserved."

Callie shook her head slowly. "I'm not sure you did. I mean, I can't say I agree with the affair part as those things rarely end well, but even if Sylvia hadn't slept with you, if she'd simply come to you as a friend and shown you bruises and syringes, wouldn't you have still wanted to help?"

She sat back, all the fight running out of her slumped shoulders. No one had ever asked her that question. "I don't know."

"Really?" Callie pressed.

She thought harder. It wasn't easy to separate out would've-beens and hypotheticals.

"What about this?" Callie tried a different angle. "What if I rolled up my sleeve and showed you bruises right now and said some man in my life was threatening me, or extorting me for money or favors, and I'm so broke that I can't see a way out?"

Her stomach roiled immediately. "Are you in trouble?"

Callie smiled. "No, but I think you just answered my question."

"I didn't."

"You did, with your eyes, with your body, with the fire in your voice. Max, you made a bad mistake, but you are not a bad person."

Tears sprang to her eyes completely unbidden. She hadn't cried for months. Not since she'd realized the woman she'd risked everything for had used her for her press credentials, then left without looking back. Not since she'd realized Sylvia had never cared about her. Not since reporters she'd considered close friends had published detailed reports of her personal failings. Not since it had become clear her name and her reputation and her life's work meant nothing to anyone anymore. No one, at any point in this whole thing, had ever cared about her own story, or her own heartbreak, her own remorse, at all.

No one except Callie.

Callie pulled her car into the curling club parking lot. The ride home had been quiet. Max hadn't seemed nearly as high-strung as when they'd left, or as despondent as when she'd poured her heart out, but neither had she returned to her normal self. She stared out the window, only occasionally turning so Callie could make out her strong profile under the yellow cones of street lamps. She still had her strong jawline, but the muscles were tight. She still had the same gray eyes, but the focus had left them. She still had broad shoulders, but they carried a more pronounced slope. Callie suspected the self-assured Max she'd been drawn to last week still existed somewhere, only buried under several layers of mental and emotional exhaustion.

"Thanks for the wings," Max said as they pulled up next to her car.

"It's never a burden for me to eat wings," she said with forced lightness.

"Then, thank you for everything else."

She unbuckled her seat belt. "It's what friends do."

"I don't have a lot of friends anymore."

"You've got at least one." Callie tried to keep her emotions in check. She wasn't sure Max could handle any more heavy conversations tonight.

They both climbed out of the car, and she walked around to meet Max between their two vehicles. "I mean it. I'm here if you ever want to talk, but you don't owe me or anyone else any other explanations."

Max shook her head. "What about Ella and the others?"

Callie glanced at their cars, all still in the lot. "I'll deal with them."

"You don't have to defend me."

"I know," she said, "and I'm not going to break your confidence in me, either."

Max shrugged. "Everyone already knows."

"No one else knows your side, but it's not my place to tell it. I'm just saying, I'm the skip. It's my job to take care of my team, and I will. You just worry about getting back to work."

"I've been trying to," Max said. "I thought I had, but—"

Callie pressed a finger to her lips. "Then go with that. You made a mistake, you faced the consequences, and now you're moving forward."

"Callie, I don't know what to say."

"Then don't say anything."

Max opened her mouth, then closed it. The two of them stared at each other for a long, slow minute, both seemingly waiting for a protest that didn't come.

Finally, Callie smiled slowly as the first hints of hope, and something more, stirred in her chest. Max mirrored the expression as they stood, mere inches apart, smiling at one another.

They were going to be okay. She knew it with the same certainty she felt when a perfect shot left her hand. Then she leaned in and kissed Max, a soft, sweet, gentle kiss she refused to let become anything more before she stepped back.

"I enjoy doing that," she said matter-of-factly.

Max nodded as her dark lashes fluttered back open.

"But I think we both have other things we need to work on before we give in to those impulses again."

Max nodded once more. "I take it you're going back to practice?"

"Yes, and I think you should probably call it a night."

"Agreed."

"But you're not going to disappear for another week." She purposely didn't phrase the comment as a question, and Max clearly noticed.

"Got it, Skip."

The hint of lightness in her voice did wonders for Callie's heart. She stepped back before she had the chance to change her mind, but that didn't stop her from standing there and watching Max pull away.

She took a few deep breaths and congratulated herself on her epic restraint. Standing there under a lone streetlight with Max's body so close and her eyes searching for one more affirmation, she'd wanted nothing more than to pull her close and kiss the world away. She might have caved if she'd gotten the sense that what she wanted and what Max needed aligned, but she knew deep down that stability would be more merciful than sensuality. Thankfully, she had plenty of experience providing that. Which reminded her, she had one more job to do tonight.

Turning back toward the club, she didn't relish the task ahead, but she hadn't been overstating her role with her team. Max might be a friend with the potential to become something more, and the faith she'd shown in her tonight meant more than either of them probably understood yet, but it didn't undercut the fact that Callie's first responsibility was always to Team Mulligan.

She squared her shoulders as she pushed through the door and immediately saw her team sitting around a small table to the side of the ice. None of them had removed their curling shoes, but the empty pizza box between them suggested they hadn't exactly been practicing the whole time Callie was off eating wings.

Layla was the first person to see her and started to rise, but Callie shook her head and strode up to the table. "We need to talk."

They all stared up at her expectantly.

194

"Max is here to stay."

Ella groaned but didn't interrupt.

"I'm not going to get into what she's done in the past. You can make your own assessments, or you can ask her yourself. You know I would never push into any of your personal relationships, and I know you all give me the same courtesy." She paused momentarily to let the full meaning of that comment sink in before she continued. "What does matter to me is this team. We are on a tremendous winning streak, and no one has the ability to mess that up but us. I have no intention of losing focus and have the utmost faith in you all to stay the course."

"Yes, Skip," Layla said.

"We are professional athletes. We have shown that on the ice. Now it's time to do the same off of it." She turned and pointed at Max's initial article on the board behind her. "Max has lived up to her end of the bargain. She's stayed attentive. She has opened her mind. She's shown up for work and written and recorded and studied and given us all ample opportunity to prove ourselves up to the challenge she threw down. I will not shirk from that challenge, not in any area of my job, and let me be clear, press is a part of our job now."

She made eye contact with each member of her team in turn. None of them so much as blinked.

"You all are the best team in professional curling. I know it, the other teams are starting to see it, and now it's time to show the world. Max is a huge part of that process. I don't expect you to like her. I don't even expect you to respect her, but please, for all of us, respect our goals enough to engage in the process like the professionals we all deserve to be seen as."

"Yes, Skip," Ella said, then with a sigh added, "I'm sorry."

Callie waved her off. "Don't apologize. You did what you thought was right given the information you had, but now I'm giving you new information and asking you to respect my call here."

"Of course, we will," Brooke said, more softly. "We're just worried about you."

"No need to worry. I'm curling better than ever."

Brooke grinned. "I would never suggest we were worried about your curling. The fact that your mind even went there right now only proves what a beast you are on the ice. I meant we're worried about you as a person."

"Oh." Her face warmed. "Well, don't worry about that either."

Layla laughed. "I make no promises on that front. It's what friends do, but you're right on every other point, and I think I speak for all of us when I say we're ready to get back to work."

The others all nodded and pushed away from the table.

"Thank you," Callie said, hoping the relief in her voice wasn't too evident. They really should be done by now. She'd kept them waiting for hours. They had every right to complain or want to head home to their families, but their easy acceptance of a return to curling went a long way toward bolstering her confidence.

Ella and Brooke headed for the ice, but Layla hung back. "You need something to eat before you head back out there?"

"No. I had wings."

"Where?"

"Duff's."

Layla raised her eyebrows.

"And the Anchor Bar."

A mischievous grin spread across her face. "I'm going to hear this story eventually."

"Probably," Callie admitted, shoving her toward the ice. "But not tonight."

Chapter Sixteen

"This is Max Laurens coming to you live from chilly Conception Bay, Newfoundland, where Team Mulligan has once again upset the competition to take their place as the only American team left in the quarterfinals of the Boost National."

"It's quite the surprise," Tim said as he smiled into the camera. "This team of young up-and-comers have certainly put the world on notice in the last few weeks with an exciting brand of curling, and today's match hasn't disappointed, even though they are facing much stiffer competition than they're used to."

"True." Max felt a little thrill at understanding his allusion. "Last year, Team Mulligan wasn't even in tier one of the world series of curling. They played a level lower on this section of the tour. For those of you new to the world of curling, that's like going from triple A baseball to the major leagues without a dip in your batting average."

"Very similar indeed. I think a lot of the credit goes to their able and affable young skip, Callie Mulligan, who is currently shooting over 90 percent in this tournament." Tim nodded to Callie, who was just stepping into the hack. "You've been following her for much of the season. Can you give the viewers an insight into her thought process?"

"She's a true professional," Max said without hesitation as something soared inside her. It had been so long since she'd been able to enthusiastically answer a question on air, and now, not only did she know what she was talking about, but she also felt good about the subject. "Very few curlers make enough money to live comfortably on, and most of them work close to full-time jobs to make ends meet. Callie's no exception on that front, but she still trains as long and hard as many athletes with million-dollar contracts."

"And you would know," Tim said, a hint of admiration in his voice. "How do you think a big-league basketball player or football star would feel to hear you say that about a curler?"

Max laughed. "They'd probably react the way I did to the comparison at first, but Callie is in the gym or on the ice seven days a week for hours on end. It's not the same as taking a beating on the gridiron, but I've watched her make the same shot the hundredth time at eleven o'clock on a Wednesday night all alone in a freezing warehouse. That takes mental fortitude, drive, and focus any top-tier athlete could respect."

"Well said, Max." They both watched Callie's stone skirt a guard and come to rest inches from the center of the house. "And another well-placed shot from Mulligan, taking one point with her hammer to keep the score knotted up at four points each. We're going to take a break for a few words from our sponsors, and you'll rejoin us in the second half of this quarterfinal match between the USA and world number one, Sweden."

With that the cameraman signaled they'd gone off the air, or off the internet, rather. Both of them sat back from the desk, and he slapped one of his giant hands on her shoulder. "You're a different person from the last time I saw you."

"Yeah." She shrugged. "I am."

He stared at her for a minute as if waiting for more of an explanation, but when she didn't offer, he just gave her shoulder a little squeeze and said, "Good."

Then he pushed back and began talking to the cameraman while Max tried to sort out all the thoughts and feelings the short interaction sparked in her. Very little about the facts of her life had changed in six weeks. She was still covering curling instead of the high-profile assignments she thrived on. She'd learned not to be totally inept in calling the games, but she still didn't carry any deep passion for or knowledge of the sport. She still didn't know what her future held beyond February. She still had plenty of detractors and very few fans. The only significant change she could point to was that Callie seemed to have moved from the former group to the latter.

Ever since the two of them had talked last week, she'd felt infinitely lighter in every sense of the word. Her limbs seemed to weigh less, and the unbearable press of stress, anger, and embarrassment had started to lift. The sun seemed to shine just a little brighter off the snow outside, and indoors, the lights of the camera seemed to bring everything slightly more into focus. She couldn't begin to count the number of times she'd replayed Callie's voice saying, "You made a bad mistake, but you are not a bad person."

Such a simple statement without any flowery language or dramatic delivery, but it had begun to loosen the chains she'd been wrapped in for months. She flashed back to Layla's earlier description of Callie's ability to lift people up. "When someone like her looks at you like you're special, like you're a winner, like you can do whatever it is she expects you to do, the funny thing is, you start to believe it. She's believed us right into the top tier." Was that what Callie had done that night over Buffalo wings? Had she believed Max right back to the top of her game?

She wasn't sure she'd go that far, but Callie had made her feel seen and heard and safe. She couldn't remember the last time she'd felt safe. Maybe never. Not in childhood. Not with Sylvia. Certainly not *since* Sylvia. Callie's easy, confident faith had allowed her to admit things she never had and be vulnerable in ways she'd never realized she wanted. In letting go, she'd taken a huge risk, and yet nothing horrible had happened. Callie hadn't shied away. If anything, she'd drawn closer, and as hard as it had been to relive the awfulness of the worst times in her life, she suspected she'd gladly do so again if only Callie would kiss her one more time.

"Ready?"

She blinked away her memories and saw both the cameraman and Tim eyeing her expectantly. She felt a minor rush of panic at having forgotten herself and her job so quickly at the thought of Callie, but as she glanced out at the woman standing tall and proud across the ice, all the anxiety faded. She smiled in a way that was far more fun than forced.

"Yeah. I'm ready."

"Good curling." The Swedish skip clasped Callie's hand.

"Good curling," she replied automatically. It's just what people said. Sort of like answering "fine" when a stranger asked how you were, even if you weren't. She knew she'd spend the next three weeks rehashing all the ways in which her performance today had fallen short of good curling. She'd missed two crucial shots, and she'd called a couple she wished she could go back and do over. She'd never know for sure what could've been, but they'd lost by two, and in some ways that was worse than getting clobbered, because it left plenty of room for second-guessing key moments.

"Let it go, Skip." Layla stood startlingly close behind her.

Callie spun around like a kid who'd been caught sneaking candy before supper.

"I don't know what you're talking about."

Layla laughed heartily, and the sound set off a war within Callie. She wanted to stay mad, and she both envied and hated how easily her best friend could bounce back after a loss.

"We left it all out there," Layla said. "We made it further than anyone expected us to this weekend and we hung in there with the number one team in the world for six ends."

She shook her head.

"No?" Layla asked and poked her gently in the ribs with the butt of her broom. "Where's the lie?"

She thought about the statement more carefully. She couldn't deny that they had far outplayed their ranking in the tournament overall. They'd beaten three teams ahead of them in the standings and outlasted the other Americans, so perhaps she had to concede that point. But today they'd been neck and neck right up until the end, which, now that she thought about it, was exactly what Layla had said. She sighed. "Okay, fine. No lie found."

"But?"

"But nothing. You're right. Everyone will be very impressed with us."

"Which isn't enough to make you happy," Layla said flatly.

"Nope." She knew it probably should, but it didn't. She'd lost a game she could've won. No amount of world rankings or outside expectations ever mattered as much as her own assessment.

"Okay, Skip, but what about that?" She nodded to the other end of the ice.

Callie followed her line of sight to see Max standing there, holding a microphone out to Ella, who seemed to be talking animatedly for the cameras. Warmth spread through her chest, and she exhaled a rush of negativity to make room for it.

"Does that make you happy?" Layla nudged her.

"Yeah," she admitted without hesitation, just as Ella said something that made Max laugh.

"You did that, you know?"

She shook her head.

"You did. You're a leader, and a damn good one. Don't second-guess your instincts just because they take time to work themselves out."

She sighed, but she didn't argue. "You're right. Thanks."

"Don't thank me," Layla said. "Listen to me. Cut yourself some slack. Take a break. Refill your cup."

"There's no time. We're more than halfway through the season, and now—"

"And now it's Christmas break." Layla cut in. "We've got three weeks to—"

"Cram. To practice. To get in top shape for the final push up to Nationals."

"They call it Christmas *break* for a reason. You're supposed to take time off. I'm not making that up. It's a thing. All the other curlers are in on it."

She continued to watch Ella's interview. They looked natural there, and anyone watching from home would have a hard time believing they had been at each other's throats less than a week earlier. Max looked back to the camera to say a few words before lowering the mic. Then she turned, and as if she knew she was being watched, immediately found Callie's eyes in the sea of people milling around. The heat began to spread through her immediately.

"Earth to Callie," Layla said.

"Hmm?" She hadn't given Max much thought during the match as she'd been too far away to hear and seated behind a desk, but now she looked so much closer and so much more compelling in her jeans and suitcoat, with a deep-blue dress shirt left open a button lower than any of the men in similar attire. Callie traced her eyes along the hint of exposed collarbone.

"Can I get a verbal commitment on at least trying to relax a little over the next few weeks?" Layla pushed. "I'm not saying no practice, but maybe try to do something you enjoy with someone you enjoy. Are you even hearing this?"

"Yeah," she said, the possibility of a smile tugging at the corner of her mouth. "Do something I enjoy with someone I enjoy. Got it."

"So you agree?"

"Yes."

"Good. Glad we had this talk," Layla said emphatically, then more quietly added, "In your mind you just agreed to fooling around more with Max, right?"

"Very much so."

"Okay then, that's what I thought. Make you a trade?"

Callie finally tore her eyes off Max to face her. "What's that?"

"You don't make us watch video of this match until next week, and I'll make an excuse for you not to come to the Patch with us tonight?"

Her grin widened into a full smile. "Deal."

⊙ ⊙ ⊙

Max had interviewed myriad players, officials, and coaches over the past few days, which was a bit of a surprise as, until this tournament, she hadn't even known curling teams had coaches. Turns out they didn't run practices or even always travel to small tournaments, but the national team kept them on retainer for major events. She was already planning a story on how different that was from other professional sports as she packed her personal camera and a set of notes she'd scribbled during the match into her backpack.

When she stood up and stretched her stiff back, she found most of the crowd had cleared out, and the only curler left at the other end of the ice was Callie. Max's heart beat a little faster at the sight of her sitting on a bench with her long legs outstretched, eyes closed, chin lifted to the ceiling. She'd covered her short-sleeved shirt with a full-zip jacket covered in Team USA logos and corporate sponsor patches. She looked like some kickass cross between a yoga instructor, a centerfold, and a race car driver.

Without thinking, Max slung her bag over her shoulder and strode toward her. She was tempted to just stop to appreciate the woman in front of her, but she didn't want to take advantage of an unguarded moment, so she cleared her throat and said, "Good curling, Skip."

Those hazel eyes fluttered open, immediately focused. "Could have been better, but you can't win them all, right?"

"True, but be honest. That maxim kills you a little bit inside, doesn't it?"

"Absolutely."

"For what it's worth, I think every serious athlete feels the same way."

"Really? Everyone acts like I'm so unreasonable to expect to win every time, but why not?"

Max shrugged. "I think the law of percentages or averages comes into play."

Callie stood. "That's all well and good if you're playing cards or flipping coins, but I don't trust luck or fate. Someone has to win every time out, and it's not like we're on a rotation or taking turns. The best team on any given day should win, and I train relentlessly to be the best. Why shouldn't I believe that if I'm the best on any day, I should have a chance to win every day?"

"You absolutely should."

"I do, and that means every time I fall short of the perfect season, I'm disappointed. Anytime I could've done better, I feel like I should have. I know me. I know what I'm capable of, and it's better than some law of averages."

"It's Olympic gold," she supplied.

"Yes," Callie said emphatically. "It's not about the hardware, though. It's about the game. It's about this game I love so much it hurts. It's about being consumed, but not owned. It's about chain reactions and building one brick on top of the other and climbing them like a set of self-made stairs all the way to the top of a mountain no one else has ever climbed. It's putting all the pieces together in the right order at the right time, and then doing it again and again and again until I master passion and productivity in equal measure and prove to myself, more than anyone else, that I can do what only I believe I can do."

The fire in her voice made the hair on Max's arms stand on end, much as it had in the moment Callie said, "I didn't choose any of it. This is who I am." She'd begun to suspect truer words had never been spoken, and damned if she wasn't getting sucked into that cool confidence once more. She wanted to get closer to it, and closer to the woman who stirred those emotions in her. "Are you going to the Patch tonight?"

Callie shook her head slowly. "I made a deal with Layla. I wouldn't make her think about curling anymore tonight as long as she didn't make me go pretend to be social or celebrate in a large, loud crowd."

"Good trade," she said, even as her heart sank and the cold seeped back into her skin. "I guess you earned a night to yourself."

"How about you?" Callie asked. "I didn't hear any of your commentary, but you looked more comfortable up there with Tim today."

"Yeah. All in all, today went pretty well for me. I mean, I'm not up to your standards of perfection yet, but after the last few months, any performance that isn't likely to get me mocked by my colleagues or fired feels like cause for celebration."

"Don't sell yourself short. I saw you got an interview with Ella. That's a victory of sorts, right?"

Max's chest puffed up with pride that Callie had not only noticed but cared about that massive step. "I won't lie. I was pretty shocked she agreed, and even more so that it actually went really well."

"Ella's always good on camera."

"I'll remember that, but I suspect she might not ever have given me the chance if not for you, so thank you. Seems like I'm saying that phrase to you a lot lately."

"You really are." She grinned. "And while part of me enjoys the idea of your being indebted to me, it's really not necessary. You're a professional, and so am I. It's in my team's best interest to maintain good working relationships with the only reporter who's given us any press in, well . . . ever."

Some little barb twisted in Max's chest at the purely utilitarian summation of her role here, but she couldn't argue the facts. Friends or not, they both had a job to do, and they needed each other to do it. "Either way, Ella wouldn't have spoken to me unless you'd pulled rank, and after everything you did for me and found out about me last week . . . well, yeah . . . I guess 'thank you' still fits."

Callie's smile grew as her eyes softened.

"What?"

"You're usually so good with words. I kind of like it when you stumble over them."

"Gee, thanks. I'm glad you find my bouts of ineptitude endearing."

"And now you're back on the big vocabulary bus." Callie gave her a little nudge with her elbow. "You never slip for long, Max. You always bounce right back into this totally put-together package, but sometimes it's good to see something human and fallible under your perfect head of hair."

"I thought I made my fallibility abundantly clear last week. Can we spend more time talking about my perfect head of hair?"

Callie threw back her head and laughed. "See, that's what I'm talking about. Right back into quick comeback mode."

Max flashed her a wolfish grin. "You didn't seem to mind that skill after the last tournament."

Callie's breath hitched and her cheeks flushed a faint shade of pink. "Oh, have we reached the teasing stage of this thing we're doing?"

Max raised her eyebrows. "This thing we're doing?"

"Sorry." Callie shrugged. "I don't share your superior grasp of the English language."

"No, actually, *thing* works as well as anything I've got in my thesaurus. We've got a thing, and yes, it does seem that we've reached the stage where I get to playfully remind you I haven't always been bumbling."

"You have not," Callie agreed, "but if we're in the 'we're adults who can casually joke about these things' phase, then I'm also in the 'mussing up your perfect hair' phase."

Before Max could even process the statement, Callie's hand shot out and tousled the front of her short and meticulously feathered layers.

"Whoa." She laughed as she ducked away. "I do not consent. That is not a privilege earned in one night. What do you think I am, some kind of hair hussy?"

"I was sort of hoping," Callie admitted. Her eyes which had burned only moments earlier now sparkled with amusement.

"Okay, well, maybe I could be loosened up, but not here in the arena for all the world to see. Hair mussing should be built up to—dinner, drinks, some low lighting and soft caresses."

"That's not how you felt last bonspiel, but never let it be said Callie Mulligan is a wham-bam-thank-you-ma'am sort of hair musser."

"I think we established that last time, and to be fair you did buy me two dinners last week. I think it might be my turn."

"Well, I wasn't going to mention it, Princess."

"Princess?" She laughed. "Now it's on. I saw a wing place down the street. Shall we?"

Callie grimaced. "That's adorable, but people from Buffalo don't eat wings in other places any more than people from Italy go to the Olive Garden."

"I have so much to learn. What do people from Buffalo eat in Canada?"

"Poutine," Callie said emphatically.

"You want me to eat your poutine for dinner? Wow. I mean, I thought we were slowing down, but after your princess comment, I think I'm about to rise to this challenge."

Callie laughed so hard she could barely talk, but she managed to squeak out, "Not *my* poutine."

"Someone else's? You are either way kinkier than I thought, or I have misunderstood this euphemism."

"The latter, or maybe both, but certainly in this context the latter. Poutine is a Canadian dish of awesomeness, protein and carbs."

"Sounds like the perfect thing to eat before a night of athletic prowess. Where do we go to consume such a thing?"

"Well, you can purchase it at just about any mid-level restaurant in this country, so we shouldn't have any trouble finding some, but when we do, let's get it to go. With the way this conversation is going, I'm not sure either of us will make it through a whole meal in a restaurant."

Max's heart rate increased at all the wonderful possibilities ahead. "I know I seem to be saying this a lot lately, but please, by all means, lead the way, Skip."

Chapter Seventeen

"Sweet mother of all things holy," Max called as Callie stepped out of the shower. Sadly, the door to the bathroom was still closed so the reaction must have been to the poutine.

"Did you start eating without me?" she asked as she toweled off.

"I had to test it. I mean, you're in my room. How could I serve you something I had never even tried? What if it was terrible or dangerous?"

"So you're just protecting me by eating my poutine?"

She could make out Max's snicker even through the door.

"That's what the dish is called. It's not dirty."

"I know, I know, I saw the menu, but I'm just not mature enough to adjust to the phrase 'eating my poutine' on the spot."

"So much for your chivalry argument. You're just eating my . . . food because you wanted to see what all the fuss is about."

"No. I'm just checking it. Curlers are celebrities in this country. What if some rabid fan tried to roofie you? I can't have you keeling over in here. I've had all the scandals I can handle for one lifetime."

She pulled on her yoga pants and a tight-fitting Curling USA T-shirt. "I see. You're not protecting me so much as your reputation."

"I don't see why we have to put such a fine point on things. The good news is that the poutine is both not poisonous and delicious."

"Good to know." Callie opened the door. "Thanks for letting me use your shower."

Max's eyes went a little wide, then flicked down to her shirt before snapping back up. "I get that we aren't overthinking this here, but I feel safe in saying you can use my shower anytime in the future."

Callie glanced down at her own chest and then rolled her eyes. "It's past bra o'clock. I didn't think you'd mind."

"I do not," Max said, without quite managing to sound serious. "This night keeps getting better and better."

Callie laughed. "You know, when you first showed up at the club, I thought you were a total hard-ass. If I'd known how easy you'd be to melt, I might have tried sooner."

"I'm going to pretend you didn't say that so I don't have to face the sadness of missed opportunities, and I encourage you to steal your own bite of poutine while I go change."

"Fair," Callie said, then as Max grabbed some clothes off the dresser and closed the door to the bathroom, she shouted, "Remember, past bra o'clock."

"How could I forget my new favorite time of day?"

Callie wandered over to the hotel room desk where Max had opened the takeout container of poutine and set out two hotel coffee mugs full of water and a couple of the paper plates they'd snagged from the communal continental breakfast area on their way in. It wasn't quite a candlelit dinner in a four-star restaurant, but right now she wouldn't have traded it for any meal anywhere. She snagged a gravy-coated French fry and sat back on the edge of the bed, testing the firmness of the mattress since that seemed to be where they were headed.

She smiled at the thought. She didn't know what had come over her, or rather what Max seemed to inspire in her. She didn't generally fall into bed with people. She'd had a few short-term girlfriends over the years, but everything hovered in that limbo between serious and not. She'd never had a real one-night stand, though if tonight went the way she now suspected, it would render their last encounter . . . what? A two-night stand? Or something more? The last time they'd ended up in Max's hotel room, she hadn't had time to think. The urge had been so sudden and overwhelming, she could only ride the wave, and she didn't regret it, but tonight felt different. Not only were they going slower, giving her little pockets of time and flashes of awareness, she'd also come in here knowing exactly where they were headed. She could hardly call this a lapse in judgment or the work of a moment. So, what would she call it?

Certainly they'd spent more time together since the last time, and she'd gotten to know Max better, too, but they weren't exactly dating. They might be colleagues with benefits, only they didn't exactly work together so much as adjacent to one another, distant enough to avoid any blatant ethical conflicts that might arise from sleeping with a teammate or competitor, but close enough that it probably wasn't a great idea for them to sleep together at all, much less with any regularity. Plus, they'd both been clear they prioritized their jobs over everything else in their lives. Why risk complicating them for someone they weren't even seeing seriously?

The door opened, and Max stepped back into the room wearing black sweats with a snug black T-shirt that showcased the subtle swell of her chest and the gentle curve of her hips. Her bare feet stuck out at the bottom, and a single strand of her coal-colored hair hung down across her forehead. She looked relaxed and open and so damn sexy. In that moment, Callie knew for certain why she was about to complicate everything.

"OMG, that was amazing." Max flopped back onto the bed, feeling warm and sated.

"Not going to lie," Callie said, "that's exactly the reaction I hope for when I go back to a woman's hotel room, but generally I expect it to reference me rather than the cheese curds, fries, and gravy."

Max rolled onto her side to stare at the woman in front of her. Callie was gorgeous as she propped herself up against the headboard, her long legs crisscrossed and her damp hair spiraling down over her shoulders.

"Well, to be fair, the night is young, but also you are the one who introduced me to poutine, so you get points for calling that shot as well."

"Calling shots is sort of my thing," Callie said with a grin.

"And you do it abundantly well. Something else that surprises me about the great game of curling—you all are way more commanding than anyone would expect from women who are largely doing housework on ice."

"Housework on ice?" Callie laughed. "Are we really going there again?"

"No, I just meant, like, my mom used to sweep our kitchen occasionally, but no one ever yelled 'harder, hard, yep, yes, hard' at her while she did."

"Yeah, well, I don't suppose she had nearly as much fun as we do."

Max shook her head. "Now that you mention it, I don't think she did. No one cheered for her, either."

"That's a shame. The cheering and yelling go a long way toward building a sense of urgency and importance. That's why I've gotten so good at it."

"Among other things." Max wrapped an arm around Callie's waist and pulled her down beside her on the bed.

"Why do I get the sense you're talking about a different skill set now?"

"I think they might be related," Max teased, giving Callie's side a little squeeze. "You were awfully commanding last time we were in this position, too."

Callie's eyes focused on hers, their lips only a few inches apart now. "You seemed to like me taking charge."

"I think 'like' is an understatement," Max whispered.

"Are you going to break out your thesaurus?"

"Who needs a thesaurus? I'm as good at words as you are at calling shots."

"Hmm." Callie gave a little hum of anticipation. "Prove it."

"You are stunning." Max kissed her forehead. "And alluring." She kissed her temple. "And captivating." She kissed her cheekbone and continued her way down, one kiss per descriptor until their lips met. Callie opened to her immediately as if she'd only been waiting for this moment all night. Max, on the other hand, had been anticipating this kiss since their last one. Even as they'd parted that night in the parking lot with an unspoken promise to focus on work, she'd known they'd be back here. The questions remaining between them now wouldn't interfere with what would happen next. That decision lay with Callie.

Max refused to push. They'd already established that the woman against her had a much better knack for calling shots, and she'd yet to let them down. It was rare for her to rely on someone else's instincts for once, but not unpleasant, as Callie's mouth moved hot against her own. Their breathing increased, and she had to steal her inhales from Callie's exhales.

Callie urged her flat onto her back, kissing her deeply before pulling away to stare down at her.

Max shivered at the intensity in those golden eyes. She'd seen it so many times during matches, but nothing compared to being the object of her attention. "You going to call a shot, Skip?"

The corners of Callie's mouth twitched up, but her gaze never wavered. "A takeout shot, on the pants."

"Yours or mine?"

"Yes." She kissed her again, and Max understood what her teammates must feel like in a high-pressure game. Callie's confidence inspired a desire to follow her even as the edge of her own vision blurred and her heart hammered in her own ears. It would have been easy to succumb to the endorphins, but Callie had called a shot, and Max was determined to execute, for both of their sakes.

Thankfully, her own sweatpants were loose enough not to offer a challenge. She merely had to lift her hips off the bed, an act which brought them into exhilarating contact with Callie's, albeit for much too short a time, before she lowered back to the bed and kicked her legs free. She allowed herself only the briefest of seconds to enjoy the slide of Callie's skilled tongue along her own before turning at least part of her attention to the waistband of the yoga pants she'd been instructed to remove from the beautiful body above her.

The Lycra clung tightly to Callie's flat stomach. Max decided that peeling would be more efficient and more fulfilling than pushing, and slipped her hands under the waistband. She slid her palms around and in, stopping to knead the perfect ass muscles contracting under her fingers.

"Magnificent," she mumbled against the corner of Callie's mouth, as she worked her hands lower, rolling back the pants as she did. Soon though, she reached the full extended length of her arms. Not wanting to stop, she broke away from the kiss and scooted lower on the bed. The shift allowed her to run her hand lower along the contracted thigh muscles helping to hold Callie perfectly in a plank position. It also put her mouth right in line with Callie's breasts. The thin T-shirt did little to restrain the evidence of Callie's arousal, and Max had never been one to waste such a blatant opportunity. Sucking through the thin cotton, she used her teeth to take hold of a nipple and thrilled at the gasp she pulled from Callie's lips.

Dipping her body lower, Callie egged her on, and Max wished she had a hand free to cup the other breast. As it was, though, both her hands were busy, and not with a lesser task. She ran her fingers along Callie's inner thighs, stripping away the yoga pants all the way down to her knees before realizing she'd have to go lower to finish the job. Thankfully, lower was exactly the direction she wanted to go.

Releasing Callie from her mouth, she scooted downward once more, pausing to place a hot kiss on the quaking abs above her before angling her head toward the heady scent of Callie's need. Just before she got there, though, a set of firm fingers in her hair stopped her progress.

"Oh no you don't. I didn't call the button shot yet." Callie brought up one knee and slipped off that leg of her pants before doing the same with the other. "And you came up just shy on the takeout shot."

Max glanced down at the lower half of Callie's body, now in all its fully exposed glory. "And yet there are no pants in the vicinity, so I couldn't have mucked up the call too badly."

Callie grinned down at her. "I swept you in. You're welcome."

"You're the best skip I've ever had."

"Best?" Callie teased. "Come on, Thesaurus. You can do better."

"Uh." Max's mind swam with so many words and emotions, but she wouldn't shrink from even the most playful of challenges. "*Elite, supreme,* the *crème de la crème*, the *paramount.*"

Callie adjusted her position so their eyes were level once more and their bare legs intertwined. "*Paramount* will do."

Max laughed. She'd never been with anyone like this woman. She was all confidence and legs. The combination made her heart throb in places other than her chest. Then Callie was on her again, only this time she used her entire body. They tumbled around, making a mess of the sheets. Callie's hair smelled like ice, and her hands felt like fire. Everywhere she touched, nerve endings incinerated, and Max's brain filled with a haze of smoke.

"Touch me," she panted.

"So soon?" Callie teased, as she licked a line from Max's jaw to her ear. "I thought I was in charge here."

Max growled. The game had been a fun little bit of foreplay, but she wasn't actually good at taking orders. Pushing up off the bed once more, she used both speed and surprise to roll Callie onto her back and pin her arms to the bed. She smiled down at her. "*Agility, dexterity, ingenuity,* in case you were looking for some words to describe that move."

Callie bit her lip as if trying to hide a smile. "You're adorable."

"Adorable?" She arched an eyebrow. "Don't you mean, *cunning, suave,* or maybe even *mesmerizing*?"

"I'm going to stick with *adorable* on this one," Callie said. "Also, you failed to clear the guard on your last shot."

Before she could even process the last part of the statement, Callie jerked both her wrists right out of Max's grip, not just freeing her own hands, but causing Max to pitch forward. Callie made quick use of her lapse in balance to sweep Max's knees wider. Then with one hand flat against her chest, Callie rolled her over and straddled her thighs.

"Holy hell," Max muttered from her newly prone position.

"Are you challenging my leadership style?"

She shook her head. "You are really strong."

"And you're quick." A new hint of admiration laced Callie's tone. "Not many people catch me by surprise."

"Then, I'd say we're even, 'cause not many people keep me on my back for long, but then again, I'm still on my back, so we don't actually feel very even."

Callie leaned forward and kissed her hard. Clutching Max's T-shirt in her fist, she pulled back up and brought Max with her until they both sat almost upright. Callie straddled Max's legs, her knees spread, and her chest right at eye level. "That position feel a little more equal to you?"

Max ran her hands over the subtle curve of Callie's waist and up her ribs, pushing her shirt as she went until the breasts she'd teased earlier broke free and firm. "This works for me."

"Good, because it's time to take round one."

Max's eyebrows shot up. "Button shot?"

"Button shot," Callie confirmed, then with a sly smile said, "I'm assuming you don't need me to point a broom in the general direction of where this particular button is located."

Max tried to sigh dramatically but couldn't quite pull it off with Callie naked and open and so very close. "No, I may not know curling the way you do, but I think I can find the button."

"You think?" Callie teased. "That's reassuring."

The sense of challenge surged in her again, and placing one hand flat against Callie's back, she pushed her into a magnificent arc. She set to work kissing along her chest and breasts, but she punctuated each kiss with words and phrases like, "familiarity," "considerable experience," and "some might even say *expertise*." But the playfulness had faded long before she reached the last one. Callie stayed, knees spread, back arched, but she began to grind

215

her hips. She moved, first in slow, small circles, then as Max sucked harder on a nipple, increased the pressure between them.

Max took the hint, with pleasure, and worked a hand between the point where their legs connected. She managed only a fleeting thought of Callie's earlier comment about pointing the way, because the wetness she found there more than did the job. Both of them moaned in confirmation as she slipped inside.

"Yes," Callie whispered through clenched teeth, as she moved her own body up and down.

Max clutched at her back, both attempting to help steady her and trying to touch as much exposed skin as possible. Everything about this woman was sheer magnificence. She managed to be both strong and supple simultaneously, and holy hell could she move. Her hips and ass made the most erotic circles, guiding Max in and out, up and down. Before long, Max's own body surged into the rhythm, thrusting forward and back in time to Callie's need. She didn't even know how long they'd been going at it—seconds, minutes, hours—and still Callie urged her on, tightening around her in every way.

"Yes," she hissed again, dragging her fingers through Max's hair and along her scalp. "Don't stop."

She had no intention of stopping until Callie collapsed, and maybe not even then. Working her thumb free from the press between them, she ran it along Callie's clit, causing her to jerk forward dramatically. Max's heart hammered against her ribs at the sense of power pulsing through her. She repeated the motion to the same result from each of them.

"Right there," Callie panted, holding her tighter. "Perfect."

Every part of her soared, both from the words and the crush of Callie's body flush against her own. Heat spread into a fire between them, muscles tightened to hold them both upright, and sweat prickled along smooth skin as Max zoned in on her target. She might have even thought she was in control of the situation if not for Callie calling out, "Harder, hard, yes, yes, hard all the way."

She couldn't have resisted the insistent blend of commanding and need, even if she'd wanted to, but no part of her did. She held firm even as Callie's steady movements devolved into spasms, and her voice, so strong and compelling, faded in groans. They rode out each wave in unison, fused and frantic until only after-shocks remained; then they rode those to completion as well before collapsing back to the bed.

Chapter Eighteen

Callie rolled over and snuggled closer to the warmth Max's body provided, but her new position also put her face toward the sun streaming through the windows. She tried desperately to ignore the pink tint on her eyelids, but a nagging thought urged her up. She threw her arms over her eyes, offering herself some prolonged darkness, but the vague unease wasn't as easy to banish. Her mind continued trying to fire through the haze. Sunlight . . . Max . . . warmth . . . sleep . . . morning . . . "Shit."

"Hmm?"

"We did it again," Callie grumbled.

"We did it several times," Max said, pride evident even in her sleepy tone.

"No. I mean, yeah. We did, but we also fell asleep."

"You earned it, Skip."

She smiled in spite of the situation. "Thanks. You, too. I meant it's morning, and I haven't gone back to my room. Layla's going to know, and if I don't make it down for breakfast, so will everyone else."

"Oh," Max said. "Wouldn't want that."

Something about the comment or its flat delivery made Callie open her eyes.

Max lay on her back, the sheet pulled only to her waist. Her revealed form was classically appealing, from the soft rise at her

218

stomach to her muscled torso and firm breasts. Her jawline seemed even stronger in profile, and her neutral expression made for smooth planes around her lips to her cheeks and even her forehead. Still, the picture didn't quite speak to serenity so much as a blank slate, and after the openness of their recent encounters, Callie craved something more.

"I don't want to just run off without getting to talk like last time," Callie said.

"It's okay." Max still didn't open her eyes. "We'll see each other at the club."

"But we don't really get to talk there, either."

"Right." Max sighed softly. "People might notice."

It was the second comment alluding to people not knowing about them, and while neither one had been sharp or pointed, she didn't like the feeling they left her with. As if sensing her discomfort, Max rolled over to face her, those gray eyes finally fluttering open. "Good morning."

The happiness that spread through her at those two simple words suggested this was how she should've started the conversation. Maybe this was how she should start every conversation, or at least every morning. "I'm sorry."

"About last night?"

"No!" The fact that Max could even think such a thing made her chest ache. "That I woke up in a panic . . . again. That I didn't take the time to kiss you awake. That I was already worried about other things before I got to thank you for last night."

"There's no need to thank me or apologize. I loved every minute of last night."

"But this morning—"

"Is what it is," Max cut in. "We're both adults, and unlike last time we didn't just get carried away in the heat of a moment. We both came here knowing what to expect."

"I don't know." Callie smiled. "I think I found a few things surprising last night."

"Well, maybe that time you took me up against the . . ." Max's face flushed, and she had to clear her throat. "We probably shouldn't rehash the highlight reel at the moment, or you'll never make your flight back to Buffalo. I only meant you and I are in very similar boats."

"We are?"

"Yes. We've got this kinetic energy that neither of us really seems able, or even inclined, to resist."

"So little resistance."

"I like you, Callie. I am attracted to you—like, off the charts attracted, and not just physically. You inspire me. You make me want to believe in things again. You make me feel like myself again."

She cupped Max's smooth face in her hands. "That makes me even happier than last night made me, and that's saying an awful lot."

"Good. Then my work for today is done." Max kissed her, too quickly for either of them to linger. "No more need to rehash or process."

"None?"

"None."

"No one is freaking out this time?"

"I'm not," Max said.

"No one is going to disappear for a whole week and not show up to the club until the next tournament?"

"The next tournament isn't until January. I can't promise I won't take some days off between now and then, but we both have work to do, and that's another thing we have in common. We both put work first."

She frowned at the comment. Not because it was untrue, but because it wasn't. She'd always put her team first, and she would do so again, but in this moment that didn't feel as good as it always had, maybe because she'd never had anything better in her life to choose work over.

"It's okay," Max whispered. "We're on the same page. I wasn't expecting breakfast in bed or out anywhere someone might see us. I know the drill."

More warning bells went off in her mind. Max talked about

this all so matter-of-factly because she thought she understood what Callie was thinking and feeling. She thought she'd been through this situation before. She'd take what they could get. She'd play second fiddle. She'd hide for the sake of her career and to protect Callie. She thought this was just like . . . Sylvia. "No."

"No?" Max stared at her.

"You don't know this drill, Max."

"Um . . . okay."

"It's not okay. I am not okay with leaving you like this."

Max shrugged. "I'm fine."

"Maybe you are," Callie said, "but I'm not, and honestly I'm not the kind of person who strives for just fine. I'm kind of an overachiever. I want great. I want awesome. I want everything."

"I thought I was supposed to be the thesaurus," Max teased, but her eyes were finally showing some focus, and that focus was squarely on Callie.

"You are not some dirty little secret to me," she continued. "You and I have this thing—I don't know what to call it yet because it's new, and it's complicated—but I'm not ashamed of you or of anything we've done."

Max tried to turn away, but Callie held her face close. "Don't pull away right now."

"I'm not good, Callie," Max said, in a voice that made her seem smaller. "If people found out we were—whatever it is we're doing here—it would only bring negative attention to you at a time when you should be the toast of your whole community."

She pursed her lips as a little prick of defiance stung in her chest.

"Don't look at me like that." Max sighed. "You remember how Ella reacted when I only made you frown? Imagine that times a million if anyone found out about this. Trust me. Go back to work. It's what we both know. It's what we're both good at. Nobody gets to have it all, especially someone who's made the mistakes I've made."

She was right. They both knew it. Neither of them could afford to lose focus, even for one minute.

She sat up and drew her knees to her chest, then smiled down at Max. "You're probably right."

"I am definitely right," Max said, in a way that was equal parts emphatic and sad.

"Yeah." Callie cast off the covers and pulled on her pants. She couldn't argue with any of Max's points, and if she was going to keep this thing quiet, she needed to go now. She needed to meet her team, catch a flight, review video, up her workouts, practice, practice, and practice some more. That was her life. Those were her priorities. And yet, when she listed all the things she wanted, shame wasn't on the list.

She grabbed her shirt and pulled it over her head, then turned back to face Max. "How do you feel about weddings?"

"Uh, I'm not looking to have one in the immediate future, and—holy shit, did I get you pregnant?"

"What?" Callie stared at her for a second and burst out laughing. "No, I wasn't proposing. I only mean . . . do you hate going to weddings?"

She shrugged. "I don't think I have strong opinions about them either way."

"Good, then you won't mind being my date to Ella's."

Max stared at her as if she'd spoken another language.

"I wasn't going to take anyone because I'm in the wedding party, but it's going to be kind of a big event, and if I know Ella, there will be lots of tulle, and probably some country music, and maybe a synchronized dance of some sort, and now I'm starting to think it might be nice to not have to experience those horrors alone."

The corners of Max's mouth curled up, but she still didn't speak.

Callie sat back down on the edge of the bed and reached for her hand. "I like you. And I'm not ready to put any label on us beyond that—Lord knows, I can't commit much time or energy to plans for the future, but I'm not ashamed of wanting more of this."

Max scooted closer. "I'm not ashamed, either, but if people find out about us they'll—"

"I don't care." Callie cut her off. "Honestly, the more someone tells me I can't make something work, the more I want to prove them wrong."

"I know that feeling pretty well."

She grinned. "I noticed that the first time you stepped onto the ice."

"You mean when I fell?"

"No, when you got back up."

"I always get back up," Max said.

"Good, then I won't have to worry about Ella's big curling wedding being the thing that finally breaks you."

Max snorted softly. "Only you would take a conversation about how we need to be careful and turn it into an invitation to the biggest social event on your calendar."

"Did I mention Ella picked out my bridesmaid dress?"

"I'm in," Max said quickly. "If you're going in an Ella-inspired dress, I would love to be your date."

"Date," Callie repeated, then kissed her quickly. "I like the sound of that."

Max breathed in a lungful of icy air and blew it out slowly, causing a translucent cloud to form in front of her. Who the hell had an outdoor wedding in Western New York on New Year's Eve? Jamming her hands in the pockets of her long, gray coat, she watched a couple of kids in khakis and dress shirts pelt each other with snowballs.

To be fair, everyone kept talking about how unseasonably warm the weather had been, but she'd never considered thirty degrees warm in any season. The Buffalonians must've been spawned from heartier stock, because everyone milling around outside the giant white tent that Ella and her fiancé had erected for the event seemed perfectly fine. Then again, it seemed like less than half of the people she'd met today were actually from Buffalo. The rest were all curlers, which probably explained a lot about their tolerance for the cold.

As if to illustrate her internal point, a group of curlers she vaguely recognized walked by wearing only light jackets, and she shook her head.

"Hello, Max," Pancakes called, as she and the rest of the Japanese team passed by on their way to the wedding tent.

She waved back, wondering what percentage of the world's top twenty curlers had convened for what appeared to be the social event of the season. She also marveled at how well they intermingled. Throughout the course of the day, she'd seen teams from all over the world joining in a variety of winter activities together, and everyone seemed to genuinely like one another. There were no butting heads or dominant personalities or one-upmanship on display, as far as she'd seen—another rarity for a gathering of this many top athletes in the same field.

"Psst."

She turned toward the sound.

"Max," Callie whispered, "turn toward the Winnebago."

She laughed at the phrase she'd never expected to have directed toward her, but followed the direction to see Callie's head poking out the door of the behemoth monstrosity on wheels.

She didn't even have time to crack a joke before Callie said, "We've got a hair emergency."

"What, is there a shortage of White Rain aerosol cans?"

Callie rolled her eyes. "Actually you're not far off. The bride's updo is starting to resemble the Leaning Tower of Pisa."

"I heard that," Ella called, a frantic tinge to her voice.

"Sounds serious." Max stepped closer.

"We're like, T-minus four minutes from a bridezilla-style massacre in here," Callie whispered.

"Need me to help you escape?"

"No, I'm not one to shrink from a fight."

"Which is how I ended up here," Max pointed out, despite the fact that no one had seemed too scandalized by her presence. "But, carry on. What's your plan?"

"I need you to run back to our cabin and get whatever magic

potion you possess that makes this"—Callie made a sweeping gesture toward Max's hair—"stay perfectly coiffed at all times."

"What?"

"Don't hold out on me, Laurens. I know you sports reporters all have some secret brotherhood of the hair."

"You know no such thing. I'm the only sports reporter who has this hair."

"Not true," Callie shot back. "I've seen Bob Costas interviews, and you'll never convince me you don't have a black-market connection for hair shellac. Don't be stingy."

Max laughed. "I'm not being stingy. I just think you're overestimating my hair-sticking abilities here. I mean, you've found a way to muss mine up several times in the last few weeks."

Callie's smile turned satisfied. "Well, yeah. First of all, I'm amazing."

She had no urge to disagree as a myriad of memories flashed through her mind.

"Second of all, Ella won't be taking part in that particular activity until *after* the ceremony," Callie continued, "and now we're T-minus three minutes from a meltdown, so make it snappy."

"On it." She turned and walked back toward a circle of cabins on the outer rim of an open field with the makings of a bonfire being assembled in the middle.

"I said snappy," Callie called after her.

She picked up her pace to something closer to a jog, but she wasn't going to run flat out across several inches of snow. She'd already pushed her fashion limits by wearing boots with slacks. The last thing she needed was to end up wet and shivering or having to change into jeans for a social event. Again, she wondered who the hell had an outdoor wedding in Buffalo this time of year, but as she swung open the door to their one-room abode, she couldn't actually summon any frustration.

The past forty-eight hours had been glorious in ways she couldn't have imagined before. Despite having a couple of weeks off from curling, Callie had still worked and practiced virtually every day, and while they'd shared dinner a few times, and a bed more than a few times, they hadn't had much more than that until they'd left the city two days ago. They'd driven only a short way, but the pressures that had burdened them had begun to slip as soon as the Buffalo skyline faded behind them.

She rummaged through her toiletries bag as she flipped through a mental scrapbook of the memories they'd made since they'd arrived. She had to give credit to Ella and Finn. They may have dragged half the curling world out to the middle of nowhere on a weekend most people usually headed for cities or their families, but they made sure no one was bored. Sledding, tubing, ice fishing, snowshoeing, a sauna, and plenty of booze assured there was something for everyone, and Callie had insisted they make use of it all.

Max grinned and snatched a small spray bottle out of her bag, then headed back toward the Winnebago dressing room. Callie apparently had no "low" setting and didn't seem to know the meaning of the word "vacation." She charged into every activity, from snow sports to bridesmaiding to building bonfires to having sex, with the same gusto she applied to curling—another thing Max was learning to love about her.

Her footsteps faltered, and she nearly tumbled down the stairs to their cabin. She hadn't actually said the L-word, but she'd thought it, and that was enough to make her blood run as cold as the air around her. She took a deep, steadying breath and blew out another cloud before starting off again. Yes, she loved Callie's gusto, her intensity, the way she threw herself headlong into whatever the day set before her, but that didn't mean she was falling in love with her. Because that would be bad, so very bad. Well, maybe not bad, but risky and complicated and so many other things she couldn't deal with right now. No, she could be attracted to Callie physically, and admire her, and have great sex with her, share some major world views, and even love some of her nonphysical attributes, too, but that didn't mean she had to lose her head for this woman. They had both been very clear about what their long-term goals were, and how a relationship would be incompatible with them.

And then they'd gone on a date to a very public event with all of Callie's friends and many of her colleagues—totally normal behavior for people who didn't intend to get serious.

She shook her head as she knocked on the door to the Winnebago.

"Thank God you're here." Callie's arm shot out of the door, caught hold of her shirt, and hauled her inside. "Did you bring the stuff?"

She nodded and extended the bottle in her hand. It was all she could manage as her brain had stopped working at the first sight of Callie in her full wedding attire. Stunning was an understatement. She wore a burgundy dress with thin straps that flared into a V-neck. A subtle ribbon of the same color cinched an hourglass waist before chiffon flowed freely down to her ankles. Elegant and classic would've been a profound understatement for the beauty it showcased.

Layla laughed from somewhere behind Callie. "I think Pencil Pusher is finally at a loss for words."

Her face flushed so hot she was certain everyone could see it, but she couldn't manage to dispute the charge, and the sweet smile caressing Callie's glossed lips did little to unscramble her brain.

"Remind me to come back to this moment later," Callie whispered, "but for now we have a job to do."

Max nodded again and followed her through a living area to a large bedroom.

"I brought reinforcements, and she brought a bottle of reinforcers."

Brooke and a woman who, judging by the resemblance, had to be the sister of the bride both stepped aside as Ella looked up from the mirror in front of her. When she turned her head, all the curls piled on top jiggled like Jell-O.

"Whoa, easy there," Max said, springing back into action. "I take it you've already tried pins?"

"So many of them I'm not sure I'll ever get through an airport metal detector again." Ella's voice shook with barely controlled panic. "The core is solid, but everything wrapped around the outside keeps shifting."

She nodded. "You've got fine hair. It's a challenge I'm familiar with. The trick is to give it enough texture to grip onto itself without plastering it down."

"Can you fix it?" Callie asked.

"I will admit I've never done anything this structurally advanced, but I'm kind of a pro at feathering and layering, which seems like a similar skill set."

"I don't care what techniques you use as long as they work."

Max extended her hand back and Callie placed the bottle in her palm. She set to work. A light touch, a fine mist, a couple of adjustments, a few more pumps around the other side, and she stepped back to survey her handiwork.

"It smells good," Brooke said hopefully.

"Yeah, but does it hold?" Layla called from up front.

Ella slowly tilted her head from side to side, then tentatively began to nod. When nothing terrible happened, she started to bounce. "Holy crud, I think it worked."

A collective sigh of relief whooshed through the vehicle.

Ella turned and grasped Max's hand. "Are you a flipping wizard?"

"I couldn't tell you if I were," Max shot back, but she smiled.

"What's that stuff called?" the sister asked, grabbing for the bottle.

"It's a homemade blend," Max explained. "Lemons, sugar, essential oils, and a touch of vodka."

"You make your own alcoholic hair spray?" Layla asked, sheer glee filling her voice. "You are never going to live this down."

"Ignore her," the sister said. "As soon as the groom kisses the bride you're going to have to tell me about this witchcraft."

A small girl popped up from the other side of the bed wearing a long-sleeved white dress with little lace daises all over it. "So, she really is a flipping wizard?"

"Whoa." Max jumped back in surprise.

"That's Emmie," Callie explained, taking her arm. "And that's the reason Ella says 'flipping' instead of a different word that starts with an *f*."

"Ella's going to be my new mom," Emmie said, and began to hop about. "I'm going to throw flowers, and she's going to kiss my dad, and then she'll always read me a story every night no matter where she is because we are going to be a family forever."

The sentiment of the bubbly statement hit Max in the chest, and suddenly she liked Ella more than she ever had. All those late nights of practice and driving to Buffalo and traveling to competitions and working in between matches, and she still found the energy to watch her language and pick out flower girl dresses and read bedtime stories to future daughters.

Max looked around the room for the first time, taking in the entire scene. Ella and Emmie wore white, Brooke and the sister of the bride wore navy, Layla and Callie's dresses were burgundy. It all came together to form a tastefully done Team USA color scheme. "I know this isn't an official curling event, but you all look so lovely. Would you mind if I took a few pictures to share on our network social media pages? I wouldn't post them until after the wedding, of course."

Ella's eyes lit up. "My wedding photos would make national sports news? Heck yeah!"

She hopped up and grabbed her bouquet, motioning for the others to gather around her. "Get one of just the girls, please."

Max pulled out her phone as the bridesmaids parted to let Emmie come stand up front. "Count of three, say 'wedding.' One. Two. Three."

"Wedding," they all said in unison. Well, almost unison, as Emmie sang out a little longer and louder than the rest.

Max snapped several shots in rapid succession before giving them the nod.

"Let me see." Ella sprang forward.

Everyone gathered closely around Max as she flipped through the various shots.

"Aww, they're perfect," Ella finally said. "And my hair is on point. Thank you!"

"Glad to help," she said, with a shrug, but she found that she was actually pretty happy to have been a small part of this event, in this moment, with these women. "I'll let you get back to the very important wedding prep."

With a wave, she backed toward the door, but halfway down the center hallway, she bumped into someone. Before she could turn around, firm hands clasped her hips, and a flutter of warm breath caressed her cheek as a familiar body pressed close.

"You just saved me from an epic meltdown," Callie whispered close to her ear. "I'll show my thanks properly when we get back to the cabin tonight, but for now this will have to do."

Then she turned Max around just enough to kiss her, full and quick on the mouth.

Somewhere behind them she heard a collective gasp, then a short whistle undoubtedly from Layla, but she didn't have time to process, much less react, before Callie nudged her out of the Winnebago and shut the door.

She stood there in the snow, fingers to her freshly kissed lips for several minutes. Callie had kissed her in front of her friends, in front of her team, in front of the people who mattered most to her. If anyone had harbored any remaining doubts about the nature of their relationship, Callie had just erased them.

Chapter Nineteen

"Yeah, so the Giants were down at this point," Max said to the group of guys standing around her by the keg. "Third and five on their own forty-yard line with virtually no time left for another drive if they didn't convert, so I'm thinking the odds are good this Super Bowl is about over."

"Oh man, this was one of the best nights of my life," one of the men muttered.

"Mine, too," Max agreed, with a little grin. "Probably for different reasons, though."

Callie shook her head. She'd never seen Max quite like this. Sure, she'd witnessed her way with words, her passion for sports, her attention to detail, but she'd never gotten to watch her in front of a crowd, and she was greatly enjoying the experience.

"So, I'm supposed to be on the Giants' sideline, but I figure the party is going to start on the Patriots' side in about one minute, and I'm young and dumb and just a college intern at this point. I'm not sure I'll ever get to another Super Bowl, so I say 'screw it,' and start sneaking behind this huge line of people just behind the end zone."

"I might actually kill someone to get to the end zone of a Super Bowl," someone else muttered.

"Yeah, and it gets better, because no sooner do I get to the other side when David Tyree makes this epic catch and the crowd goes wild, and I'm almost apoplectic because now they have four more downs to score this touchdown. Maybe I need to get back to the New York side, but then again, the Pats have been leading all night, so maybe I should just stay put."

"What did you do?"

"I just froze right there in the Patriots' corner of the end zone, and who just happens to come running up but Plax Burress with the game-winning touchdown. He ran right at me, caught the ball, and kept coming. Everyone else jumped out of the way, but I was still frozen."

"Did he hit you when he stepped out of bounds?"

"Damn near knocked me flat, but then he dropped to one knee, and his back foot was on top of mine with his spikes in my shin."

"What did you do?"

She laughed. "I yelped, but he stood up, looked right at me, smiled this huge grin and said, 'Sorry.'"

"I mean, it is kind of an honor to get spiked by a Super Bowl winner," one man said, and several others nodded.

"Totally. I think they should've given me a ring, but I did get an interview with him after the game, and I was the only lowly peon he spoke to, so it made a huge difference in my career."

"It would make a huge difference in my whole life," the first guy said, sounding thoroughly starstruck. "I would never stop telling that story."

Max slapped him on the back. "And obviously I never have."

Just then a tiny ball of miniature tuxedo came hurtling by. Before Callie could even process what it was, Max shot out a hand and scooped the ring bearer up, mere centimeters before he flattened himself against the bar.

"Whoa," Max said. "Easy there, sport."

"Emmie tried to kiss me." The little boy practically spat.

Max made a big show of looking around, her gray eyes dancing with a conspiratorial glint. "I think you're safe now. No need to endanger yourself again."

The little boy sagged in her arms. "Whew."

She set him down and started to turn back toward her crowd of admirers, but Callie caught her hand. "Nope."

"Nope?" Max raised her eyebrows.

"You've helped fix the bride's hair, took more pictures than the actual photographer, helped shore up the bonfire, regaled the guests with fascinating sports stories, and rescued a small child from imminent danger. Everyone is duly impressed except for your date."

"What? You're not impressed? I'm killing it tonight."

She couldn't actually disagree. Max had been more than anyone could ever hope for in a wedding guest, and the easy way she smiled now made Callie's heart do a little tap dance against her ribcage, which was all the more reason she wanted to get her out of this tent and all to herself. "I'd be more impressed if you came ice skating with me, unless skating is the one thing you aren't awesome at."

"Oooh." One of the guys elbowed her lightly in the ribs. "I think you just got challenged."

"I think I did," Max agreed, without taking her eyes off Callie. "And I accept."

"If you're going to fall on your ass, we'll come watch."

"She doesn't need an audience," Callie said at the same moment Max said, "I'm not going to fall on my ass."

The men looked mildly disappointed but stayed put as she interlaced Max's fingers with her own and tugged her out of the tent.

"Sorry if I wasn't giving you enough attention in there," Max said, as they strolled through the snow toward a small, frozen pond.

"No, you were fine." Callie sighed. "Actually, you were so much more than fine. You've been amazing this whole weekend."

Max's chest puffed up a little with pride.

"Don't get a big head. I didn't really know what to expect when I invited you to this wedding. I sort of leapt before I looked, and I don't regret that."

"Boy, you sure do know how to compliment a woman."

She rolled her eyes but gave Max's hand a little squeeze. "Fine, tease, but I don't get out as often as you do. I can't remember the last time I took off for a weekend without curling. I'm out of practice."

"If it makes you feel any better, every one of your top competitors is here, too, so you aren't exactly falling behind anyone," Max said. They reached the pond and sat down on one of the large logs ringing the outer edge.

"Yeah, we're all one big extended curling family. The other American team ahead of us in the standings even showed up and joined in the chicken dance, despite knowing we're trying to take their ranking from them in a few weeks."

"And their vice even asked you to dance. Don't think I didn't notice that."

"She's super straight with a husband and baby at home. She's just a nice person."

"She clearly feels the same about you." Max started picking up skates to find a pair close to her size. "You all seem to like each other."

"We do," Callie admitted, not sharing any of the surprise she heard in Max's voice. "Isn't that true in other sports?"

"I think athletes have a sort of camaraderie, yes, but I don't know. It's hard to put my finger on it. I don't think many star football players or basketball players would give up one of their only off weekends, and a holiday to boot, to attend the wedding of someone who wasn't a teammate or someone they really admired, even if they had the money to throw around."

"None of us have the money to throw around," Callie admitted as she found a pair of figure skates only one size too big. At least she'd been able to put on some thicker socks and leggings after the ceremony. "Maybe that makes us genuinely admire each other more. We understand what everyone else is dealing with."

"Genuinely." Max paused from lacing up her skates and cocked her head to the side. "I think that's it. These people are all genuine. You're here because of something you love, and you respect each other for that. I see it in the way people look at you."

"Me?" She laughed and stood, her legs a little wobbly until she pushed out on the ice. "I think it's everybody."

"To a certain extent," Max conceded as she took her own first shaky steps. "But I also think you cultivate that around you. People are drawn to you because of the way you carry yourself and the type of energy you exude."

"Hey, why aren't you falling?" Callie tried to ignore the compliment and the warmth it sent spreading through her core. "You always fall on the ice back at the club."

"Not true." Max laughed and slid a few more feet. "First of all, I haven't fallen at the club since you taught me about grippers, and second I am not in loafers right now. I'm on skates."

"And you know how to skate?"

"Why do you sound disappointed?" Max laughed. "Were you hoping I'd start the New Year bruised and broken?"

She smiled and shook her head. "Of course not. That would seriously inhibit the plans I have for us later, but I'll admit I did sort of hope you'd have to stick close enough to me that I'd have more excuses to have my hands on you."

Max extended her hand. "You don't need any excuses for that."

Callie accepted, and pulled so that both of them slid toward each other until the toes of their skates nearly touched. "Good. Shall we?"

They set off at a leisurely pace, making gliding loops around the small pond. All of the kids had either gone to bed or to thaw out, and they had the surface to themselves, save for one other couple who kept their distance. Callie took the few minutes of gliding quietly to admire the moon shining brightly overhead, the soft strains of music wafting out from the tent, and the even softer skin of Max's warm hand in her own. She couldn't have even imagined this kind of peace months ago, and if anyone had told her she'd find it with Max after their first meeting, she might have punched them.

She laughed a little at that mental image.

"What's funny?" Max asked. "Is it me?"

Callie turned to steal a glance at her profile in the moonlight.

"You are a lot of things, and sometimes funny is among them, but I was just thinking about how different you seem now from the first time I met you."

"Well, I am upright. That's different."

She smiled again. "And self-deprecating, which I prefer to stubborn and confrontational."

"Gee, I sure made a great first impression."

"It wasn't all bad. Like you said before, you got back up every time you fell. A lot of people wouldn't have finished that first game, much less stuck around. Why did you?"

"You want the honest answer?" Max asked.

"Always."

"I didn't want to. After our first meeting, I thought about bolting. I was hurt and scared and lost in more ways than one. Then, after I wrote that awful piece and you confronted me in the parking lot, I was actually pretty terrified of you."

"Of me?"

"Yeah. You're kind of intimidating."

"I am not."

"You totally are." Max laughed. "You're commanding. When you walk into a room, heads turn, and not just because you're beautiful."

"Now you're laying it on thick."

Max pulled her to a stop with a little tug on her arm that spun her around enough that they were facing each other once more. "Don't do that, Callie."

"Do what?"

"Shy away from the truth." Max lifted one hand to cup her face softly.

She leaned into the gentle caress.

"You're stunning and the camera loves you, but it's more than that. You embody everything good about the game of curling. You're compelling without being overpowering. You're competent and strong while still being approachable. You're fierce, competitive, hungry, and yet also genuinely friendly, self-effacing and fun. You're unexpected, inspiring, and strangely hypnotizing."

Max leaned close. "You are fire and ice, all wrapped up in one. You shouldn't make sense, but you do."

Callie kissed her. What else could she do with all the emotions exploding through her? It felt as though Max had melted her heart, melted her core. She didn't know how she hadn't melted the very ice beneath them, but she did know she'd never have Max's way with words. Maybe words didn't even exist to convey all the things she wanted her to know, but she would do everything she could to make Max feel what she felt.

Somewhere behind them music played and the bonfire burned, but it was Callie's kiss that warmed Max to her toes, and the sound of her own beating heart that offered the sweetest music to her ears.

Callie enveloped her senses. Her lips were like everything else about her, so full of the most wonderful contradictions. Firm and yielding, insistent and patient, sweet and salty.

"You are so very good at that," she mumbled when Callie pulled back.

Callie's smile was luminous as they began to skate slowly again. "You're no slouch yourself. If it weren't one of my best friend's weddings and New Year's Eve, I would've snatched you away from your fan club in there much earlier and dragged you straight to bed instead of onto the ice."

"Both valid options any night of the year if you ask me." Max tried to brush off the compliments in Callie's comment, but she couldn't hide from herself how good this weekend had been for her continued self-esteem bump. Despite significant fears fueled by her recent encounter with Ella, she'd felt completely welcomed at all the wedding festivities. At first, she'd written off Ella's turn-around as stemming from everyone's vast adoration of Callie, and perhaps their resounding affection for her had been the reason most people had been willing to accept her presence. But, once inside this circle, Max had made the most of the opportunity. She'd played and laughed and told stories and danced and felt more like herself than she had in nearly a year.

"Thank you," she said aloud.

"For what?"

"For inviting me. For having faith in me. For taking the time to listen to my story." She paused. Swallowed. "For kissing me in front of your team."

Callie sighed. "That was spontaneous, but I don't regret it."

"You sound surprised by that."

"I am." Callie laughed. "For reasons that have nothing to do with who you are or what you've done."

"Thanks?"

"You know what I mean. The kissing was totally about who you are, and how fond I am of you, but the fact that I'm surprised I kissed you in front of my team is another story."

"When was the last time you did that?"

"Oh, way back in never." Callie shook her head. "Layla has met people I've gone out with, of course, but Brooke and Ella and I have been playing together for five years, and I've never even introduced them to my dates, much less shown affection in front of them."

"Why?" Max asked, genuinely curious as to what about her would make a woman of Callie's caliber break her clearly well-established patterns.

"A lot of reasons. I don't like to complicate my work life. Dating always comes a distant second to curling. I never wanted to take time away from practice long enough to be social. I've also never gotten serious enough with anyone else to welcome them into my friend and peer groups." Silence fell between them except for the scrape of their blades against the ice for several heavy seconds. "I just made it sound like we're getting serious, didn't I?"

"You did," Max confirmed.

"I didn't mean to."

"You didn't mean to make us sound serious, or you didn't mean for us to actually get serious?"

Callie tilted her head to the side and seemed to give the question its due consideration while Max held her breath.

"Both," she finally said. "Is 'both' an option?"

Max nodded. "It should be, but I'm not certain what it means for us now."

"Well, you be sure to let me know when you figure it out."

She snorted. "You might have to wait awhile."

"I'm in no hurry." Callie gave her hand a comforting little squeeze. "I'm enjoying myself this weekend."

"As am I," Max said slowly, as if waiting for some disagreement to rise up inside her.

It didn't.

"And now you sound surprised."

"I've been to destination weddings and celebrity weddings and big family weddings, but this is my first curling wedding."

"Yeah? What's the verdict?"

"It's a lot to take in, but I think I'm a fan. There's been a great deal of fun and very little pretense."

"Is that your style?"

She shrugged. "A year ago, I would've said no. I liked the fast-paced and flashy. I would've said I wanted a big society wedding with high-end everything, the social event of the season, pull out every stop and impress all the people. You know, really make a statement in style."

Callie grimaced. "And now?"

"I don't know," she admitted. "Maybe my style is changing, or maybe I am, but I'm starting to think being surrounded by a handful of people I really like and trust, in a place where I could feel safe and loved might be the best way to start a new life with someone I could count on."

"Agreed," Callie said softly, and Max's heart began to beat faster.

Had she just planned a wedding with this woman? However vague and hypothetical, that didn't seem like a great idea. That's what had gotten her in over her head last time. As soon as she'd started dreaming, she'd stopped thinking. That's what had made her weak and vulnerable. She'd promised herself she'd never get stupid or sappy like that again, and now here she was, talking about weddings with a woman she'd known only three months.

Turning to look at Callie, her breath caught at the sight of her, eyes sparkling like the stars, hair stirring softly on the breeze, lips curled slightly upward. All the questions and fears blurred in the face of Callie. Surely, no one could blame her for getting swept up in her presence. How could any human hold her close and not fall for her?

She shook her head. No, no, no, she wasn't falling for her. She couldn't do this again. She was only supposed to be having some fun while covering curling. She had work to do. They both did.

They both did.

The internal phrase allowed some cold air back into her lungs. Callie was in the same boat. Callie had just admitted she always put her team first. Callie had her own life and priorities, just like Max. That's why they were drawn to each other. That's why they worked. Callie didn't want anything from her. She wasn't desperate or needy or asking to be saved.

She smiled almost ruefully at the thought of Callie being cloying or manipulative. Everything in her experience said the opposite was true. She was one of the most independent and driven women Max had ever met.

"Hey," Callie said suddenly, "it's almost midnight."

Max glanced at her watch to see more time had slipped away than she'd realized. "You're right. Want to go back to the party and ring it in with your friends?"

Callie looked back up toward the tent, then back at her. "Actually, I'm just mildly superstitious about how I start the New Year."

"And?"

"And normally I'd very much want to do so with the entire curling community around me, but this year maybe it's time to try something a little different."

"I'll defer to you," Max offered. "If the start of last year was any indication, I'm not so great at picking auspicious beginnings."

Callie squeezed her hand, this time pulling her all the way in until their bodies brushed against each other. "What if we didn't try to race up to the future, but we didn't hide from it, either? What if we just let it meet us, right where we are?"

"And we let it take us where we need to go?"

Callie shrugged. "It's not usually my style, but I've been breaking my own rules all weekend, and so far it's been working out pretty well."

Max's chest expanded at the warmth spreading there. She couldn't disagree with Callie's assessment, and even more so, she no longer wanted to. "Well, you know me. I'm not one to shrink from a challenge. If you can loosen your grip on the reins a bit, then I guess the least I can do is come along for the ride."

Callie leaned so close their noses brushed against each other before she pushed back off again and looked up at the vast winter sky. "Okay, future. Here we are. Come and find us."

Back in the tent a cheer went up, and even farther away fireworks sizzled and burst, but Max was only peripherally aware that anyone or anything else existed. For her, in this moment, there was only Callie.

Chapter Twenty

The sun's rays were already slanting down through the top of the blinds when Callie rolled over and opened her eyes. Normally that would've been cause to spring out of bed in a panic, but today she felt only gratitude for the way they illuminated the smooth skin of Max's bare back and shoulders. She would've thought she'd kissed and caressed every inch of her last night, or rather early this morning, but here in the full light of their tiny cabin she noticed the little indent where the curve of her spine met the white sheet between them.

Scooting lower in the bed, she pressed her lips to the hollow, relishing the warm, smooth slope and the faint hint of salt, a reminder of recent exertion. Pushing the sheet lower, she slowly followed its path with her lips, tracing each vertebra.

"Good morning to you, too," Max mumbled groggily.

"Happy New Year."

"Indeed," Max sighed, and rolled more fully onto her stomach.

Callie climbed onto her back and began to kiss her way up, dragging her body slowly across the length of Max's as she went. Her own muscles ached in places they usually didn't, but instead of slowing down, the reminder of their joint workouts only made her want more.

"You are insatiable," Max said, likely feeling the evidence of Callie's arousal against her back.

"Are you complaining?" She nipped at Max's earlobe.

"Not at all. Zero complaints," Max muttered into the pillow.

She rolled her hips forward so they ground against Max's firm ass.

"Actually, less than zero. Like, I don't know, negative complaints or subzero complaints."

She liked the low, husky quality of Max's voice in the morning. Sleep and sex added a rough edge to her normally smooth tones. She liked so many things about Max in the morning, actually— the way her hair feathered lightly across her ears, the way her body radiated heat, the pliant quality of her muscles before they fully engaged for the day. Why hadn't she noticed these things before?

Because of curling.

The answer came immediately, because she'd carried it with her for years, never letting it slip from her mind for more than a few minutes at a time. What did it say, then, that she'd forgotten it now for days? Not only had she not practiced since they'd left Buffalo earlier in the week, she hadn't worked out in that time either, not even yoga or push-ups. She hadn't watched video or studied strategy. She hadn't done anything even remotely related to practice or preparation, and what was more shocking, she hadn't wanted to. They were less than two weeks out from a major world event and a month out from the US nationals. She was a month from the confrontation that would likely seal her ranking and her funding for the next year, the year before the Olympics. This was exactly the time she needed to push herself hardest, and it wasn't like she didn't have that in her. For years she'd done nothing but work and push and practice.

Max shifted beneath her and pulled Callie into the present and the physical.

"Did anyone ever tell you you're the best blanket ever? Super warm and also super sexy."

Callie grinned and kissed the back of her shoulder. "No, can't say that anyone's ever mentioned those qualities to me before."

"Their loss is my gain. I think I'm going to wrap you around me and stay like that all day."

Callie waited for something inside of her to resist that idea, but it never came. Was this how normal people felt in the morning? When people talked about wanting to spend all day curled up in bed, she'd always been so confused. Turned out that disconnect stemmed from the fact that she hadn't yet met the right person to share her bed with. Then again, she wasn't sure the impulse applied only to bed. Lately, Max had made her want a lot of things she'd never wanted before.

The thought should've scared her more than it did, and certainly it raised plenty of questions, but for the first time they all seemed to start with "how" instead of "why." And the "how" seemed easier to answer this morning than ever before. Maybe she didn't have all the details, but at least they weren't hypothetical. She had seen other people make relationships work. They were here this weekend because Ella had managed to meet, date, fall in love with, and marry someone, all while curling professionally and working full-time. Plenty of curlers did the same things every day. Sure, there were challenges unique to her and Max's situation, but they'd already come so far from where they'd started.

She kissed along Max's shoulder to the soft line where her hair met her neck, as arousal and sentimentality met and melded inside of her. Max had already given her more in the way of trust and openness and vulnerability than any other relationship ever had. Shouldn't Callie at least try to do the same? She didn't want to let her foot off the gas when it came to her career, but surely if Max could make some concessions to follow her around, she could try to be more available.

Reaching the other side of Max's neck, she pressed her lips close to her ear and whispered, "I'm going to skip practice tonight."

Max's muscles tensed beneath her.

She laughed softly. "Oh sure, that gets your attention."

"I must have misheard you. I thought you said you were skipping practice after already taking three days off."

"You heard correctly." Callie bit her shoulder. "That is, if you want to stay here for one more day. I don't want to presume anything, but I thought we could go tobogganing, or cross-country skiing . . . or do other stuff."

"Other stuff, please."

"Yeah?" She rolled her hips again, enjoying the friction between them. "Want to be more specific there?"

"You're the one wrecking the plans. I think you should have to—"

Whatever she'd been about to say died on her lips as the shrill ring of a cell phone shattered the silence around them.

They both groaned.

It rang again.

"Leave it,." Max grumbled.

"That's not my ringtone." Callie rolled off her. "It's yours."

"Mine?" Max sounded confused. "No one calls me."

The phone rang again, and Callie reached across her to snag it off the bedside table. Glancing at the screen, she said, "It's someone called 'Flip.'"

Max sat up quickly and grabbed the phone, offering only the clipped explanation of "my boss."

"So much for leaving it." Callie rolled onto her back, and Max slipped out of arm's length to perch on the edge of the bed.

"Hey, Flip, what's up?" Pausing, listening. "Yeah, sorry . . . happy New Year to you, too." She ran a hand through her hair. "Of course. I'm always working."

Callie snorted softly. Max had most certainly not been working, but she didn't blame her for fudging on that fact. She stared at the exposed wooden beams of the cabin, listening to the only side of the conversation she could hear and waiting for the moment they could get back to the so-called work Flip had interrupted.

"Oh, I'm sorry to hear that . . . Uh-huh. Bad timing for his wife, too . . . No, it's not funny. Come on, Flip, you know I'd never make light of . . . well, any of it. I understand better than most how bad these things can be to live through."

Callie rolled onto her side as Max's voice turned serious.

"I am a professional."

There was another long pause while Flip presumably did all

the talking, but he must have been saying something big, because the muscles in Max's back tightened noticeably while her shoulders rose and fell more quickly with each breath.

"I understand. It won't be a problem. I promise. I'm so far past all that now. I can be in New Jersey tomorrow morning. I made my name there once. I can remake it there now."

Callie sat up. Had she heard correctly? Did Max just offer to go to New Jersey?

"I really appreciate this. I won't let you down again," Max said, her voice thick with emotions Callie couldn't read. Then she dropped the phone and flopped back onto the bed with a massive sigh.

Callie waited for some explanation, and when one didn't come, she finally said, "Um, that sounded . . . important."

"Yeah," Max croaked. "Sorry, I'm in a bit of shock. That was my boss at the network."

"I got that much."

"One of my former colleagues who covered the Giants, the football ones, not the baseball ones, got into a car accident this morning."

"Oh no."

"He's alive," Max said quickly, "but he may wish he wasn't before it's all over, because he blew twice the legal limit in a Breathalyzer, and the woman in the car with him at 2 a.m. on New Year's Day wasn't his wife."

"Uh-oh."

"Yeah. She's a stripper—the woman in the car, not his wife. His wife is a stay at home, society mother of three."

"This story keeps getting better and better."

"Actually, it does, not for him but for me, because there's now a pending investigation, or likely several of them, and he's been put on leave, which means the network needs someone to cover the Giants."

The pieces started to fall together. "And they asked you?"

Max nodded, her grin spreading. "They want me to cover the game this weekend."

Callie's heart beat a little faster, but she continued to speak slowly. "Wow, that's a big deal. You got your big break covering the Giants."

Max rolled over on her stomach. "You remembered."

"Of course." Callie reached out and tousled her hair. "In case you haven't noticed, I kind of like you."

Max captured her hand in her own and kissed the palm. "I kind of like you, too."

"But you have to go to New Jersey." Callie tried to keep her tone light.

"I do." Max sat up again. "This is a really big chance for me, and it would be kind of fitting if I got back to the top covering the team that got me there the first time around."

Callie nodded, not quite sharing the enthusiasm growing in Max's voice, but wanting to be supportive nonetheless. It was just one game, and if Max was getting back to work, she should probably do the same. They both began to pull on some of the various clothing items they'd tossed around the tiny cabin at different points throughout the last few days.

She smiled as she found one of her sports bras hanging from the corner of the radiator. She wished they could go back to doing whatever they'd been doing when it had landed there, but maybe they could pick up where they left off when they were both back in Buffalo. "So, you'll fly back here on Monday or Tuesday?"

Max stopped moving and turned to face her, her smile not quite reaching her eyes. "I'm not sure. We'll have to play that by ear, depending on if the Giants win or not."

Callie pressed her lips together to hold in the barrage of questions banging through her brain as she waited for Max to elaborate.

"They need someone to cover the rest of their season, however long that may be, so if they win this weekend, they'll play again next weekend."

"We play next weekend," Callie said flatly after doing the math in her head. "How many more weeks are in the playoffs?"

Max shifted from one bare foot to the other. "The Super Bowl is the first weekend in February. It's in Miami this year."

"That's the same time as the national championships . . . in Spokane." Callie sat back on the edge of the bed as the room began to spin. "You're not coming back, are you? Even if the Giants lose, you will have won. You're done here."

Max sighed. "I'm going to miss this, Callie."

She swallowed the lump forming in her throat.

"You understand, right?"

Callie nodded, even though she wasn't sure she understood everything, or maybe she understood more than she wanted to. Max had never been anything but honest about how much her career meant to her. It was one of the things that had brought them together, and yet Callie had been thinking about letting herself want more. No, she hadn't been thinking about it. She'd been acting on those desires. She'd shared parts of her life with Max that she hadn't shared with anyone. Sure, it had been only a short time, but the steps that might've seemed small to other people had felt momentous to her. It burned a little bit to realize they hadn't felt the same way to Max. Still, she fought to keep an even keel. "Yeah, I get it. I guess."

"Do you?" Max's smile twisted. "I know it's not ideal timing, but I kind of thought you of all people would be happy for me. I thought you'd recognize what a big deal it is for me to move up another level, or like six levels, because that's what the Super Bowl would mean for me."

"Six levels above what?" Callie found her voice. "Six levels above covering me and my team? Above covering the sport I kill myself working to perfect?"

"I didn't mean it that way." Max rubbed her face. "Look, I wish I could do both. I really do. If I could be in Miami and Spokane at the same time, I would, but we both knew this would happen someday."

She wasn't wrong, and as much as the little dig about levels stung, that wasn't even why Callie was upset. She couldn't even put her finger on all the reasons, but from the tightness spreading through her chest, she suspected it was much more complex than a scheduling conflict. She hadn't really expected them to live happily ever after, had she? No, she hadn't thought that far in advance, but she thought they had more than Max was conveying right now. Maybe that's what hurt most. The choice didn't seem to hurt Max at all. And it was a choice. Max had made a choice to end everything they'd had and everything they could have had without a moment's hesitation. How could she possibly convey her own muddled mess of emotions to someone who so clearly knew what mattered most to her?

"Yeah, I guess this was bound to happen eventually," she finally said, letting Max off the hook and hoping she could hold it together long enough to see her off without revealing how much she hated that fact. "Why don't you go ahead and take the car back to Buffalo? I'll get a ride later with Layla after we make sure Ella doesn't need any more help here."

Max stared at her again, her eyes once again the color of ice on an overcast day.

Callie didn't know what else to say, so she began to toss her own things into an open suitcase in the hopes it would speed Max's own departure. She might not know what came after this part, but she did know she didn't want to drag it out.

"Maybe I'll get some time off after the football season," Max offered as she collected her toiletries. "I could always come back to Buffalo for a vacation."

She recognized the comment as a peace offering, but the last word stuck in her like a splinter. "I don't think I'll have time for any vacations between the national championships and the world championship."

"Right, work. I understand." Max zipped up her bag and turned to face her again, a new emotion Callie had never seen in her eyes. Regret? Guilt? Pity?

She didn't need any of them. Despite whatever Max thought, her life wasn't some unfortunate subpar existence or pale shadow of brighter lights. She had a job she loved, people she trusted, a drive that gave meaning to her days, and sure, maybe lately she had let herself wish for something more, but that didn't mean she needed it from someone who met her passion with pity.

Max picked up her bag and moved toward her, then stopped as if second-guessing herself. Callie couldn't decide what would be worse, kissing her one more time, or not.

"Maybe I could come to the world championships and cheer you on." Max punctuated the offer with a fake smile.

She shook her head and forced the hurt from her voice. She couldn't take another awkward exchange, not after all the times everything had been so easy and natural between them. "Thank you, really, but I don't see the point of dragging this out. I'll be working at Worlds. You won't be."

Max grimaced. "Really? That's the only way this had any value? It only worked when we were both working?"

She considered the question. Was that true? They were only as good as their jobs? It didn't seem right. Maybe their jobs had brought them together and kept them there long enough to bond, but the last few weeks hadn't been about work. When had they become more? More importantly, could they still be? She didn't get the chance to fully form the questions, much less answer them, before Max shook her head.

"I can't believe this is happening again. I thought you were different."

"Different from what?"

"From Sylvia."

Callie took a step back. "Excuse me?"

"Here I was, worried about your feelings, and you're talking about work. Why not just come out and ask who's going to fill in for me on your press coverage? I'm sure Flip will send someone qualified, but I'd be happy to send you a text when I hear."

Her face burned, and the implications of Max's last few comments seeped through her confusion. "My coverage?"

"Sure. How could I have been so stupid? At least you were honest. You always said your team came first. I should've known that as soon as I wasn't a curling reporter anymore, I wouldn't be part of your master plan, either. Don't worry. I know how this goes. I won't play the fool this time." She put her hand on the doorknob, her shoulders up and her back rigid. She took a deep breath as if bracing herself to cross the threshold.

"How dare you?" Callie snapped. "Are you really going to say something like that and then walk away? You horrible coward."

If she thought she'd been hurt before, she didn't know what this new feeling ripping through her must be. Pain was certainly a major part of it, but sadness had succumbed to rage.

"I don't think—"

"Yeah, don't think." Callie cut her off. "Don't think you know what I'm thinking about. You're wrong, stupidly wrong, embarrassingly wrong, and if you think I'm like Sylvia in any way, you're not just wrong, you're offensive."

"You are so fixated on—"

"Stop," she snapped again. "You don't get to tell me anything else about me. You don't get to say things like you just said and then make pronouncements about me. You're the one who's walking out, not me. You're the one who used me as a stepping-stone to something you wanted. And I was going to let you go."

She laughed bitterly. "No matter how much it hurt my heart or my pride, I was going to shut my mouth and let you walk out the door, but you do not get to rewrite the narrative with your back to me. You don't get to become a fiction writer when it suits you. You're the one who took what you wanted as long as it was useful, and then dropped it the second you had a better offer."

"No." Max shook her head. "I'm not writing fiction. I was always honest about what I was doing here."

"Were you?"

A muscle in her jaw twisted. "I made no promises."

"Actually, you did." Callie folded her arms across her chest. "You promised me a full season. You promised me a fair chance. You promised me you didn't shy away from a challenge. You lied, Max. You're the one who let me down, not the other way around. You're just one more person in my life who sees curling as some

251

sideshow or hobby. You've never seen me as a serious athlete or considered my dreams as worthy as yours."

"I'm doing my job," Max said feebly. "I've always been honest—"

"No. You had a job to do here. You took this job. You said you took your work seriously. Walking out a month before you finish isn't serious unless you didn't think this assignment was a real job to begin with"—she snorted—"in which case, maybe I should take a page from your book and say, 'Don't worry. I've been here before. I know how this goes.'"

"That's not fair."

"But it's true." She pushed back, no longer fighting to hold her anger at bay. "Isn't it? You want to talk about how I'm just like everyone else in your life? Well, you're just a tired old cliché in mine, and I'm tired of people who don't see my dreams as on a par with their own. I have plenty of people in my life who don't think what I do matters as much as a 'real job,' or is too frivolous for the energy I give it, or don't think I have what it takes to be an elite anything. I don't need you to join that chorus with your 'real sport' refrain."

"I didn't mean that."

"Yes, you did. You can't say you're serious about your job and then switch jobs unless you didn't think the job you had was less valuable than the one you're leaving it for."

That little muscle in Max's jaw twitched again, and Callie knew she'd landed another blow. She might as well end this while she had her on the ropes, because if she had learned anything about Max, it was that when she got knocked down, she always got back up.

"I've always been honest with you, Max, and all I ever wanted from you was some way to make us work, in all our entirety. Maybe I was asking for a fairy tale, or maybe it was just stupid to ask for it from someone who was only killing time until something better came along."

She took a deep breath, hating the way her body shook as she exhaled. "Either way, I release you. I don't need your company, your pity, your guilt, your broken promises. You can take them all with you, but do me a favor and keep whatever fiction you're spinning to yourself on your way out."

Max scoffed and shook her head, but she kept her lips pressed in a tight line as she swung open the door and shouldered her duffel bag. Then with one last searing look from icy eyes, she heeded Callie's final request and walked silently away.

Chapter Twenty-One

Another bone-crushing hit sent three players crashing into the sideline with a spray of combined sweat. A tackle like that might've killed average humans, but the gladiators on the gridiron before her hardly fit the bill. All three men immediately hopped up and sprinted away.

Fast. Everything happened so fast here. Max shook her head, wondering if life had always felt this way, or if three months of watching curling had dulled her senses. A flash of guilt tightened her gut. What would Callie think if she knew she'd just thought that their time together might have made her duller and dumber?

The next emotion was one she'd grown reacquainted with in the last few days. Anger hadn't been around as much in the last few months, but apparently it was like one of those relationships that always sparked right back to familiarity even after months apart. She hated that. She hated feeling like she was back to square one emotionally, even if professionally she had vaulted several rungs up the career ladder.

A series of whistles and buzzers sounded, signaling the two-minute warning. Players hustled around her, calling out commands over the roar of the crowd. Behind her, cameras worth more than she made in weeks flashed and whirred, while overhead a jumbotron burst with high-resolution video of people she stood mere feet from. Why was she thinking about Callie right now? She was back in the big leagues, the very seat of power, pomp, and luxury. This was her real life.

"Excuse me, Ms. Laurens." One of the interns brushed up against her. Jimmy? Johnny? Jeremy? Too many lackeys around to learn all their names in three days, but they were all driven and connected and hungry, so she had to respect that. On the other hand, they all wanted something from her, which brought her right back to Callie.

She shook her head, and the young man's eyes widened. "Sorry, I didn't mean to interrupt. I can come back."

"No, it's fine. What?"

"The Giants are up two touchdowns with two minutes left to play."

"I can read a scoreboard."

"Right, sorry. I didn't mean to imply . . . anything. I only meant, do you want me to take you to the pressroom?"

She shook her head again, this time at him rather than her own memories. "I'm going to get a sideline interview with someone from the offensive line."

"But they usually go to the locker room, then the pressroom, and it's very hard for someone of your stature to get noticed in—"

She stopped him with a stare.

"A sideline interview sounds good." He changed course. "I'll get you a second camera and a live mic."

She didn't have to respond as he ran off through the crowd. She probably should've felt bad about intimidating the kid, but she sort of enjoyed being able to do so. Besides she'd felt bad enough lately, and about too many things. This job was supposed to be the one thing she was sure about. Lord knows she didn't have the same certainty about any other area of her life. She couldn't count the number of times she'd replayed her last conversation with Callie, and she still couldn't make sense of it all. Everything had happened so fast that morning.

Another player careened toward her sideline as if to prove "fast" was just a way of life for her now, and she barely managed to get out of the way. Another apt metaphor for her personal life.

She shook her head, disgusted once more that she couldn't seem to break free from that cycle of thoughts. Why should Callie have that kind of control over her when Max clearly didn't have the same effect on her? Callie had said herself she was willing to let her walk away. She would've been content to never see her again. She might miss her, sure, but not bad enough to want to see her again—if it conflicted with curling season, anyway. She hadn't even gotten mad until Max had made the connection between her and Sylvia.

Her stomach roiled again as she remembered the look on Callie's face when she'd made the comment. It had hurt her, and Max hadn't wanted them to end on that note. She hadn't really wanted them to end at all, but she hadn't had the chance to think. She hadn't had the chance to consider all her options. She'd had to make a choice in a moment, and she did, but she hadn't ever meant—

The final buzzer sounded, shocking her back into the moment.

She had missed the last two minutes of the game. She'd missed so many things. She had to stop running in circles around a memory. She had a job to do, one she'd fought and clawed her whole life for.

Grabbing the microphone from the intern without a word, she dove headfirst into the tide of players leaving the field. Most of them towered over her and could easily flatten her without actually seeing her, but she threaded nimbly between them. She hadn't gotten where she had without taking a few risks. Craning her neck upward, trying to recognize faces under helmets, she finally spotted an offensive lineman talking to another player. She practically hurled herself at him and prayed someone was behind her with a camera.

"Great game today." She shouted to be heard over the million other sounds around them. "Quick interview for Network Sports."

He blinked down at her as if trying to process her presence more than her request, which hadn't actually been a question. She didn't wait for his answer before arranging her shot. "Great. Just stand right over here with your back to the field."

She cast her first glance at the cameraman, who nodded his readiness.

"Your team held the opposing offense to only six points today, largely by controlling the receivers. Was that your game plan going in?"

He shifted uncomfortably and pulled off his helmet, revealing a sweat-soaked face, pink either from exertion or embarrassment. "Um, yes."

She raised an eyebrow, waiting for more explanation, but when one didn't come, she did her best to battle the dead airtime filling her report.

"Was your emphasis on containing the quarterback or on cutting off the receivers?"

"Yeah," he said, then seemed to realize he needed more, so he added, "Totally."

She pulled on every ounce of professionalism she'd cultivated not to roll her eyes. "And seeing how well that strategy worked, how do you think you'll have to tweak it for next week's matchup with the Rams?"

"Yes!" he said emphatically. "We will tweak it."

She stared at him for several more seconds, unable to believe someone had just given a "yes" answer to a question that started with "how," but she wasn't going to stand here any longer trying to squeeze thoughtful commentary out of a brain that had obviously taken too many blows.

"Well, thank you for your time, and good luck next week."

The guy grinned slightly. "Thank you."

As he jogged off, she turned back to the cameraman and intern. "That's totally unusable."

They both nodded.

"Get me someone else."

Jeremy, or Joshie, or whoever spun around, frantically scanning jerseys until he spotted one that meant something to him. He lunged to catch the player around the arm, or rather halfway around the arm, because his hand was tiny compared to the bulky biceps. Still, she had to give the kid credit for gusto.

"Interview with Network Sports?" he called.

The offensive lineman swatted him like a gnat. "Piss off, kid. I need a shower."

While Max couldn't disagree on the basis of hygiene—she could smell his stench from several feet away—her face did burn at the quick dismissal of a network reporter. Before she had a chance to reach her boiling point, her aggressive intern tried again with someone else.

This time he didn't even get a verbal response so much as a grunt and dismissive wave.

"Come on." Max caught the kid by the back of the shirt. "Let 'em go. We'll get to the pressroom."

He didn't argue, and they fell in silently with the sea of players leaving the field.

"Did you see that little prick from CBS trying to talk to me after that shit report he wrote?" one player grumbled. "I had to sit two weeks because of that asshole."

She checked the number on his back to confirm her suspicions that he had served a two-game suspension not for being rude to a reporter, but for beating his young fiancée senseless.

"Fuck 'em, we won," someone else said. "I'm getting laid tonight."

"I can get laid any night, but I don't get my bonus unless we make it to the league championships."

"Like you need more money," Max mumbled. The thought made her remember Callie having to work multiple odd jobs just to be able to afford the low-end hotel rooms that she split with Layla. What would she have given to have reporters pressing in on her after a big win? She certainly wouldn't have told them to piss off. And she wouldn't have given one-word answers. Would anyone care enough to ask her probing questions next week? Or would another win go largely unnoticed, like all the others?

The thought made her sad. She hadn't let herself feel sad very much, partly because all the other emotions were so much closer to the surface and partly because she worried that if she did, the sadness might end up consuming all the others. She couldn't let that happen. She couldn't pine over someone who probably wasn't even giving her a second thought.

"I'm going to be working." That's what Callie had said, and Max didn't doubt her. All this time, she'd thought they were both on the same track. The fast track, right to the top—that's what they'd both said from the very first moment. Clearly nothing had changed, no matter how different she'd felt around Callie. She supposed that should be a good thing. She hadn't really wanted to change. Despite Callie's accusation about broken promises, they had both been up-front about their goals. Neither of them had anything to feel bad about.

And yet, she did.

She missed her. She hated that she'd hurt her. She hated herself for caring more about their relationship than Callie did, again. Again. *Again.* The same thing over and over, and it didn't matter how many times she replayed Callie's little tirade about Max writing fiction. She still couldn't forget the fact that Callie hadn't had any problem letting her leave until she'd brought up the curling coverage and that stupid bet. She hadn't been able to summon any genuine excitement for Max's accomplishment or opportunities. Max had cheered for her, and studied and learned and celebrated with Callie for months, and yet when it came her time for a big break, all Callie could say was, "we have a tournament next week."

She couldn't ignore those facts. Not again. Not after last time. When was she going to learn that no one was ever going to care about her life and her dreams but her?

She spun and kicked the wall. "Fuck."

She turned to see not only her intern and cameraman, but also several other people staring at her. Her cheeks flamed all the way up to her ears as the horror of what she'd done slammed through her. She'd completely forgotten where she was, who she was with, and what she was supposed to be doing, all because of Callie.

It had to stop.

"Sorry," she said sincerely.

259

"It's okay," Jessie said.

The kid's name was Jessie, and she was damn well going to remember it from now on.

"We'll get a good interview inside."

She nodded. She would. It was her job, and she was good at her job.

"Welcome back to North Battleford, Saskatchewan," a sportscaster she didn't know said from behind Callie as she approached the hack. "Team Mulligan is two points down here in the final end of pool play, and their skip, Callie Mulligan, is looking for a little redemption after an uncharacteristically erratic tournament so far."

"Erratic is a good way to put it," Tim said, sounding almost embarrassed. "We've seen flashes of her usual brilliance even as recently as last end, but then she'll follow up fantastic shots with absolute clunkers."

She tried not to shake her head, but she might have rolled her eyes. Not at Tim, but at herself, because he wasn't wrong. She'd played terribly this whole tournament, and no matter what she did here, her team wouldn't make it into the playoff portion of the event. They'd already lost three matches in pool play so they were mathematically eliminated, but she still had her pride, and she didn't know why it hadn't rebounded by now. She should be totally focused on the end of Ella's broom, pointing her way toward at least one victory instead of listening to broadcasters state facts she already knew.

Focus. That's what she needed, and what she'd lacked all weekend. She tried to drum up some now as her eyes locked on the target and she pushed into her slide. Her back leg straightened, and the breeze brushed her hair back from her face. Externally everything went to plan, but internally nothing changed. She could still see clearly everything at her periphery, still hear even the voices of random people at the sidelines, and still feel the cold seeping through her skin. The world did not disappear. It didn't even fade. Trying frantically for some sense of control, she did a last-second calculation, noting her speed and trajectory. Then she released the rock, not at all certain where it would end up.

Her stomach dropped at the unknown, and instead of staying in the crouch she hopped up to chase after her rock helplessly.

"Sweep!" she and Brooke called at the same time.

Ella and Layla had already sprang into action, both clearly sensing disaster, but the more they swept, the more another problem revealed itself. The stone wasn't curling enough, and with each rapid scrub of the broom, its path stayed straighter. If they kept sweeping, it wouldn't curl enough to hit the button, and if they didn't sweep, it wouldn't have the distance. Classic curling damned-if-you-do-and-damned-if-you-don't, and she had only herself to blame.

Well, herself and Max Laurens.

"Off," she said.

The sweepers didn't hear or listen.

"Off," she called more loudly. "It's no good."

Both Ella and Layla glanced at Brooke, and Callie's face burned with shame. They didn't even trust her to forfeit correctly today. She should've been angry. This was still her team, but she hadn't exactly earned the right to make that argument over the last few days, so she too turned toward her vice.

Brooke lowered her head and shrugged in sad confirmation. "It's not going to get there."

Clenching her jaw, she strode over and shook the hand of the opposing American skipper. "Good curling."

"You too," Danielle replied automatically. "That shot in the seventh, mind blowing."

She appreciated the courtesy, but she knew she didn't deserve it, and she no longer had the energy to play the part of good sport or gracious looser. She merely gave a curt nod before moving on to shake three more hands as quickly as possible.

"Hey, Skip," Layla whispered as they began to pack their bags. "Tell me what you need right now."

261

"Get me out of here," she mumbled.

"You got it," Brooke said, kicking her shoes off and practically jumping into her sneakers. "Ella, you take the interviews. I'll go talk to the officials. Layla, get her to the car."

Everyone accepted their assignment without question, but before Ella walked away, she dropped a hand on Callie's shoulder and squeezed. "Everyone has bad tournaments. Don't be harder on yourself than you would be on one of us."

A lump formed in Callie's throat, but thankfully she didn't have to respond as Ella jogged off to intercept Tim and his new reporting partner.

Mercifully, Brooke only gave her a quick pat on the back before turning to go handle their official duties.

Layla merely picked up her bag and Callie's as well. Puffing herself up to her full but still unimpressive height, she acted as a human barrier between Callie and every single person they passed on their way out.

Callie climbed into the passenger seat of their rental, slammed the door, and immediately folded in on herself. She struggled to breathe evenly as a million thoughts screamed through her brain. They'd just been knocked out in the first round of a tournament by teams they expected to crush, and every one of their losses had landed squarely on her shoulders. She didn't know the exact stats, but she'd certainly been the weakest player on her team.

"This is going to hurt our rankings," she finally said.

"Yep," Layla agreed.

"And our wallets."

"Uh-huh."

"We didn't even make enough money to cover our hotels."

"We did not."

"I played like shit for four games in a row."

Layla didn't argue. "I do believe that's the worst event you've had since high school."

She drew her knees to her chest and rested her head against them. "I'm so sorry."

"I know," Layla said calmly. "So does everyone else, and I don't say this often, but Ella was absolutely right. You can't be harder on yourself than you are on any one of us when we have bad games."

"It was more than a bad game," she whispered.

"Okay, a bad tournament."

"It's more than these two days. It's been a bad ten days."

Layla didn't respond, and Callie tilted her head to look at her. Layla's big brown eyes were wide and sympathetic.

"Oh, are we ready to talk about this now, because you've damn near bitten my head off every time I've brought up 'She Who Must Not Be Named'," Layla said.

"I didn't want her to affect the team."

"And we can see how well that went." Layla laughed.

"It's not funny."

"It's a little bit funny," Layla said. "I mean, not that you got your heart broken. That sucks. But after years of ignoring anything and everyone who didn't relate to curling, you finally found the one person who can take your mind off the ice, and now you're trying to ignore that, too. That's some top-tier denial, my friend."

"Not true."

"Which part?"

"The part about ignoring things or the part about Max being the only thing to take my mind off curling."

"What about the part about you getting your heart broken?"

Her chest constricted so tightly all the air left her lungs in a rush. Why did it hurt so bad to breathe?

Layla's gaze softened. "That right there, that feeling? You can't ignore it."

"I don't have a choice. Max is gone. She got her chance to move on, and she didn't even hesitate."

"Not even a little?" Layla asked.

She shook her head. "I was there. It was a three-minute conversation, and by the end of it, she had plans to be covering football the next day."

Layla grimaced. "Did you say anything to her?"

"I said some things."

"Uh-oh."

"I tried. I promise I did. I faked a happy face."

"You faked it?"

The question sent another shot of pain through her. "Yeah, and she knew I was faking, but damn it, I'm not good at playing these games. What was I supposed to do? Jump up and down and say, 'I'm so glad all your dreams are coming true.'"

Layla shrugged. "I don't know. What would she have done if all your dreams had come true?"

This time the pain was too much, and she covered her face to hold in a sob. She couldn't answer, not because she didn't know the answer, but because she couldn't bring herself to say that Max would've been elated for her. Every time Callie had won, Max had cheered. In fact, the last time they'd beaten the other American team, Max had seemed more excited than Callie. Max had cared what happened to Callie even though she never really cared for curling.

"Yeah, that's what I thought," Layla said.

Callie groaned. "Don't make it harder. I admit I have regrets. I should have reacted better. I should've realized how big an opportunity like the Super Bowl would be after everything she'd been through, but in that moment I only felt a creeping fear that I would never see her again."

"That's good. It's human. Did you tell her that?"

"No."

"Oh, Callie." Layla sighed. "You made it about curling, didn't you?"

"What? No!" She chewed her lip for a moment, and then quieter, "How did you know?"

"Because you make everything about curling. Your jobs, your family, your friends, anyone who challenges you. It's like other people have emotions, and you have curling. What did you say to Max instead of, 'I don't want to lose you'?"

"Maybe I implied I was worried about my tournament schedule . . . and our press coverage if she left."

Layla groaned.

"I didn't mean to!" She balled her fists as the helplessness washed over her again. "Honest to God, it all came out wrong. You said yourself, I'm not good at big emotions. I only meant to set her free because the dynamic was changing, and I didn't know what to do, so I said we both had different jobs now, and she took it the wrong way. Everything spun out of control. She thought I was only interested in her for what she could do for the team, and I never for a second felt that way."

"There." Layla pointed at her excitedly. "What you just said, it's perfect. Call Max right now and tell her what you just told me."

"I can't. Maybe I could have if the conversation had ended right there, but it didn't. Things were said that can't be unsaid, and not that I'm keeping score or anything, but Max leveled some way worse accusations at me. My screwups came from fear and slow processing skills. She compared me to a lying, conniving, adulterous bitch who destroyed multiple lives and careers."

Layla winced. "Okay, yeah, I see how those sorts of comments might complicate a conversation."

They'd complicated a lot more than one conversation. Those comments haunted her. They kept her awake at night and jarred her out of focus even during matches. They hurt every time she relived them, and the hurt hadn't lessened with time. Callie might not have been perfect, and she would certainly have done things differently if she'd had the chance, but she didn't know if she could ever get past the fact that Max held such an offensively low opinion of her. Besides, even if she could get past those assessments of her character, and even if they could find a way to make their totally different lives and priorities mesh, she had no reason to believe Max wanted to.

And that hurt too.

"People say things they don't mean when they are confused or scared or sad," Layla said.

She nodded. "That thought has occurred to me. How couldn't it after I admitted I didn't handle things the best that I could, either?"

"So, see? You're a mature adult, and Max, despite some early indications otherwise, seems to be a pretty solid human too."

"She knows what she wants, and she goes for it without apology, which is why no matter how I spin it, I can't get around the fact that she didn't hesitate to leave. She didn't show any remorse for the unfair things she said. She hasn't tried to contact me since then either," Callie continued, even as the depression pressed down on her back and the emotions tightened her throat. "If Max is someone who goes after what she wants, I have to conclude she doesn't really want me."

Chapter Twenty-Two

"So the thing no one wants to tell you is, this whole thing is kind of bullshit."

Max blinked at the top tight end in the NFC and his complete *non sequitur*.

"You know what I mean?" he asked, staring down at her, his green eyes dull and a little bloodshot.

"Sorry," Max said, without really knowing why. "I'm not sure I do. I just asked if you thought you deserved to be elected to the Pro Bowl team this year."

"Yeah, people keep asking me that, but no one wants to talk about the fact that I'm not getting paid enough to play in this charity game."

"By charity game you mean the Pro Bowl?"

"That's what I said." He shook his head and rolled his eyes like she might be dumb.

"Right, but being chosen by your coaches, other players, and fans as an all-star to represent your league?"

"It's not *my* league. I'm a one-man league. I'm here doing this dog-and-pony show, and I'm here to tell you I might only make $28,000."

"Oh, is that all?" Max could no longer keep the disdain from her voice. This man might be pure magic on turf, but he was a real asshole off of it, and his piss-poor attitude during this press conference didn't even rank on the long list of reasons why.

"Twenty-eight K is chump change. How many professionals do you know who want to fly halfway across the country and give up their first week of vacation in six months, to sit in a chair answering questions about deserving this and past offenses just to play a meaningless game?"

Callie's image sprang to mind just as clear and beautiful as ever, even after three weeks apart. What would she have given for the type of opportunity this man was spitting on? "I can think of a few."

He scoffed. "Not for twenty-eight grand, when that's even less than they make doing their real job."

"Or, perhaps, even less than they owe in domestic abuse settlements and fines?" Max offered.

A collective gasp went up from the pool of spectators and reporters around her, but he only threw back his head and laughed. "That's what I'm talking about."

A league official stepped onto the stage and announced the press session had ended. Several reporters glanced at their watches or phones to confirm what she already knew. They'd had at least a couple of more minutes left, but the league didn't want another scandal to mar their two-week Super Bowl party. She thought about calling them out on the hypocrisy of protecting the images of wife beaters when they did little to actually protect their wives, but that was a losing battle, along with so many others, in the NFL.

She stood and stretched, shading her eyes against the glaring sun overhead. At least she was warm for the first time in who knew how long. If she had to be surrounded by assholes, Miami was as good a place as any.

Another little twinge pricked at her chest as that thought was followed by the realization that she didn't really have to be surrounded by assholes. There were good people in sports. Hell, there were even good people in football, but the culture here seemed to breed, or at least cover for, more sins than many others she'd reported on. Basketball was better. Baseball was better. Tennis was infinitely better. And curling—her heart clenched—curling was better. Dare she say it? Maybe the best.

She didn't see any reason to deny the obvious, even though no one had actually asked her to. Or had even asked her a question. She was merely having another useless conversation in her own head, the way she'd had for weeks anytime the damn interns left her alone long enough to hear herself think. And those internal monologues always led her back to the same place. When someone talked about conditioning, she thought of kissing Callie's spectacular shoulders. When someone mentioned passion, she saw the glint in Callie's eyes. When someone bitched about not making enough millions of dollars, she thought of Callie working odd jobs just to keep playing the game she loved.

Whenever she was confronted with the culture that allowed grown men to behave like spoiled toddlers with impunity, she remembered Callie buying drinks for the team that beat her, or curlers lining up to wish a competitor well on their wedding day, or the unabashed respect with which both teammates and opponents regarded each other on the ice. Every one of them was dealing with so much more than the players parading across the stage in front of her today—families and school, day jobs and training routines, practice schedules and travel schedules, and competition at the highest levels, but they did it all without making enough money at curling to support themselves.

They did it all for love.

The thought caused an ache to spread through her chest. She closed her eyes and tilted her face to the sun. When was the last time she'd done something for love?

The phone in her pocket rang, and for one stupid second her heart thudded with the hope it might be Callie. She fumbled with the lock screen as she hopped out of her chair, but she'd only made it two steps away from the press area when she noticed the caller ID bore the number of the network headquarters in New York.

"Hello."

"Hey," Flip said. "Got a minute?"

Her stomach flopped with disappointment, and she kicked herself internally. "Sure, uh, let me get someplace quieter."

She lowered the phone and strode toward a small cluster of palm trees, but even when she'd stepped into their shade, she gave herself the luxury of a few extra breaths to even out her erratic heartbeat.

When would she stop hoping every time the phone rang? Callie wasn't going to call, and even if she did, what could either of them say? They'd both used up all the words in their last encounter. Three weeks of perspective was plenty of time to foster a great many regrets, but it didn't change the facts of their situation. They both still had jobs to do, and they'd both chosen them over each other.

Raising the phone back to her ear, she said, "I'm here. What's up?"

"I just read the story you sent in last night."

"Yeah?" She tried to keep her tone even until she knew where he intended to go.

"It's damn fine writing, Max." He laughed. "Like, Pulitzer-grade prose."

Her lips twitched up at the first positive emotion she'd felt in a while. Pride. With everything else going on inside her and around her, she'd almost forgotten what it felt like to do something well. She might not have Callie's passion for the sport or the people she happened to be covering, but she was still a damn good sportswriter, and people all over the country would hear what she had to say. "Thanks. Glad we'll get the word out."

"Yeah, about that," Flip said, then paused.

"What?"

"It's a great piece."

"But?"

"It's 12,000 words long."

"It's nuanced."

"I don't disagree, but I've got nowhere to put it. I even showed it to a friend at *Sports Illustrated*, and they've got nowhere to put it."

"So I need to cut it down."

"For starters, and then maybe, I don't know, lighten it up a bit."

"It's about human trafficking and sex workers in Super Bowl cities. How do I lighten that up?"

He sighed. "Yeah, I know, but I'm not publishing the *Atlantic*, or even *Rolling Stone*. I know you love the in-depth stuff, but really I need a blogger right now. No one wants long-form journalism, at least not in this format."

"Then what format should I use to tell more complex stories?"

"I don't know. Documentaries had a big year, but that's not the work of this network, and you still want to work for the network, right?"

"Of course," she said, without even thinking.

"Good. Because you're still one of the best, but right now I need short snippets and teasers to add to the human interest angle for the big game next weekend."

"But what if these people are not actually interesting humans?"

Flip laughed, but Max didn't see the humor. "I'm serious. I've already filed a story on the guy who works for Habitat for Humanity, and the one who's still in the National Guard, but for every one of them, there are two players beating their kids or getting stoned with hookers or doing nothing but complaining all the time."

"I'm sure you'll find something. Hell, you managed to make curlers sound interesting for three months." He laughed again, but her shoulders drooped as the full weight of that realization settled over her. She'd had both an easier and a more fulfilling time covering the people she'd worked to get away from than covering the people she'd fought to get back to, and she'd given up a shot at something real in order to do it.

"Who did you get to cover the curling, anyway?"

"Hmm. Actually, I can't remember his name. Nobody I'd ever heard of before."

"Is he any good?"

"Seems adequate."

271

Her jaw twitched. "That's a ringing endorsement."

"Yeah, well, he's no you, but it's just curling. Besides, what do you care what happens over there? I'd have thought you'd be eager to leave that assignment behind."

She would have thought so, too. In fact, she *had* thought so. She'd been so damn quick to get out of curling, she'd hurt Callie. No matter how hard Max tried to focus on Callie's comment about work, she hadn't quite been able to forget the pain she'd seen on her face. She wanted to leave all of that behind as well, but even here, weeks later, in the shade of palm trees and power, she had failed to do so.

"The thing is," she said slowly, "curling may not be much to watch at first, but the people there ended up being much more compelling than I anticipated. They live their sport in ways and at levels some of these millionaires can't even imagine. And Callie, the skipper, she's this true force of nature. She's electric in every setting. She's got this drive that's singular and as pure as the driven snow. She makes everyone around her better than they ever even dreamed of being. And that spills over off the ice."

"Yeah, I'm going to have to stop you right there," Flip said. "I get that you're fond of waxing poetic, but, and I say this with all professionalism, whatever's going on with you and this woman, you need to save it for your therapist."

Her face flamed instantly. "What?"

"Look." Flip took on a patronizing tone. "I can't touch any part of your personal life. I'm not a counselor. I'm not your drinking buddy."

"Right," she said flatly, trying to hide the embarrassment from her voice. They weren't friends. She didn't have any friends. She had a boss, she had colleagues, she had interns, and she had a bunch of selfish, overpaid, overprivileged assholes to cover. This was her life. This was what she'd told herself she wanted, over and over and over again, until she couldn't see herself anywhere else. "Sorry, you're right."

"Good," he said, "then you'll get back to writing those short, happy pieces?"

"Yeah," Max said, then sighed and added, "through Sunday."

"All right," he said, then seemed to really hear what she'd said. "You're there for two more Sundays."

She shook her head, not because he could see her but to try to clear the remnants of old dreams from her mind. "I'll finish covering the Pro Bowl, but then I'm done."

"What do you mean?" he asked, incredulously. "Done with what?"

She smiled in spite of the trepidation she felt growing inside her. "Writing fiction."

Chapter Twenty-Three

"This one's for all the marbles, kids," Ella said as they stepped onto the ice.

Callie didn't know whether to choke her or hug her. The choking impulse came from the fact that she didn't really want any more attention brought to the fact that they'd somehow made it to the finals of the United States Women's Curling Nationals. Six months ago, that wouldn't have blown her mind. She'd expected to be here, right up until three weeks ago. Now she was surprised, and more than a little ashamed, that she had done less than any other member of her team to put them in this position, which, of course, was where the urge to hug Ella came from.

She wanted to hug Brooke and Layla, too. They had played phenomenally all week. They had become the team she'd always known they could be—passionate, persistent, and with a precision that continued to wow everyone watching. As she looked across the ice at the first-place American team, she knew they must be feeling the same mix of emotions. Nervousness, a desire to protect what they undoubtedly thought of as theirs, a shaken confidence, and a confusion that this team might be a threat even without Callie at the top of her game. The conflict of pride in her friends and disappointment in herself was just one more to add to the long list of things tearing her apart.

"Hey, Skip," Layla said softly, as the clock began ticking on their official nine minutes of warm-ups. "A word?"

She paused, looking from her best friend toward the hack. "Sure it can't wait?"

"Yeah," Layla said, with unusual seriousness.

She stepped back, motioning for Brooke and Ella to continue their slides. "What's wrong?"

"You got enough regrets."

The comment hit her square in the chest.

"I know you're trying to compartmentalize, but it's not working."

Suddenly it hurt to breathe. "You waited until now to do this?"

Layla grinned, but it came off looking more sad than anything else. "Timing matters. Once the minute is gone, it's gone. And you've been working your whole life to be in this minute right here."

"Do you honestly think I don't know that?"

"Yeah. Or maybe you knew it, but you forgot, because I can tell from the glassy glaze over those tiger eyes that you are not here right now."

"I'm here," she said emphatically.

"You're not. You're reliving every other game, every other mistake, and I suspect you're reliving a conversation that took place three weeks ago."

"I'm not." Or at least she hadn't been, but now that Layla mentioned it, all the pain and confusion of those moments rushed back to join the pain and confusion of the present. She hung her head.

"You don't get a do-over on any of it," Layla said softly. "You can't go back and say things differently any more than you can pull a rock back into your hand once you've released it."

She nodded. She knew this. She knew all of it with body-crushing certainty. She didn't need anyone else to tell her those mistakes would haunt her for the rest of her life.

"But you can change shots you haven't made yet," Layla continued. "You can use those regrets to help you ward off others."

She lifted her eyes as a hint of something stirred inside her.

275

"Don't try to hide from the pain. You already tried that. It hasn't worked. You're going to have to embrace it."

"It hurts too much."

"Use that. Grit your teeth, accept it, and then let it fuel you."

"I don't know how."

"Yes you do." Layla pushed.

She shook her head.

"Callie, you have turned every doubt, every naysayer, every slight and sting you've ever suffered into more logs on the fire." She locked eyes with Callie. "Do it again. You need to stare your regrets in the face and say, 'You've taken enough. You don't get to steal this dream, too.'"

A whoosh of air left her lungs.

"Come on." Layla nudged her with her broom. "Say it."

"You don't get to steal this dream, too," Callie whispered.

"Give it more," Layla urged. "The past doesn't define my future."

"The past doesn't define my future." Her heart rate responded to the mantra by kicking up a few notches.

"There you go." She nodded. "You don't get a do-over, but you get to decide where you go from here."

"I get to decide," she said more convincingly, as she felt the blood pumping through her limbs.

Layla punched her in the shoulder. "No more regrets."

"No more regrets," she agreed, and this time she really meant it. "I'm ready to leave it all out on the ice."

"Then, let's do it." Layla made a sweeping gesture toward the hack, and Callie took her position.

Clutching a stone in her hand and eyeing the button, she straightened up, then swung back. This time instead of trying to block out the pain, she breathed it, the ache spearing up under her ribs once more. She welcomed it, channeling everything that had scared her and pressed in on her and kept her awake at night. With an exhale, she pushed off, and the world whisked away. It was as if she'd blown all that negativity out into a cloud before her and then propelled herself right through it. Everything blurred for a brief second, then a space at the end of the tunnel came into sharp focus as the rest disappeared.

She was back.

Somehow time managed to both slow and speed up at her will as the match began. She seemed to have all the hours in the world stretching before her, but she no longer needed them. She could anticipate a shot before it left someone's hand, and she could counter a play before it came to fruition, which was a damn good thing, because everything her opponents set out to try seemed to hit. One golden shot after another landed exactly where they wished, and her team matched them blow for blow.

Somewhere behind her, the scoreboard showed the balance teetering on one point here, another there, with no lopsided numbers to be found. She didn't need a scoreboard to tell her what she'd known all along. Her team was every bit as good as the number one team, even on their best day.

By the ninth end, little had given way, not the score, which now had them up five to four, or her team's determination or the sharp shard of grief pushing in her ribs. As she strode down the ice, she met first Brooke's eyes, then Layla's, then Ella's. This was the moment she'd led them to. The moment she'd inspired them to, the moment she'd promised them. More than that, though, it was the moment she'd promised herself. The moment she'd studied and fought and worked and sacrificed everything for. Would it all be worth it?

She settled into the hack, ready to find out.

She raised her eyes to home in on the spot Brooke indicated with her broom. She couldn't relive her misses. She didn't have time for doubt or room for speculation. She couldn't even begin to consider what the other team would do with the hammer. She had one shot to make.

She pulled back, pushed off, and whispered, "No regrets."

Then she let go.

She didn't hold her breath or squint or stay low. She didn't have to.

"It's perfect," Brooke called, but even that confirmation was unnecessary. The rock would land exactly where she'd willed it to. Vindication, at least for now, said she should have been elated. She'd done no less than the best anyone could do, and it was out of her hands, both literally and figuratively.

She smiled a subdued sort of smile and stepped to the side as the number one skipper in the world clutched a hammer in her hand.

"You didn't make her job easy," Layla said, coming to stand behind her.

"No."

"I'd rather be us than them right now."

She couldn't disagree, but neither could she summon much glee. She couldn't summon much trepidation, either. She didn't feel much of anything, actually. It was a hollow sort of sensation after a lifetime of emotion around this sport—and several weeks of internal chaos.

The final stone was released by someone else, in a moment she couldn't control, a moment completely separate from who she was and all she'd ever done. Someone else got to make the final call, and she watched with detached interest as the rock smacked a guard that then careened into the outer rings before bouncing off of another stone. It continued spinning wildly into the rock she'd just placed on the button until it pushed Callie's stone out and sat squarely in her place.

A series of groans and cheers went up around her as the realization of what they'd all seen rippled like shock waves through the arena. Down on the ice, the same emotions erupted in amplified jubilation and agony, but Callie felt little of either as Danielle rose and walked toward her, hand outstretched.

"Good curling, Callie," she said, with abundant emotion, the primary one seeming to be relief.

Callie clutched her hand tightly, and sincerely meant it when she said, "You, too. You earned it."

Danielle laughed weakly. "Not by much."

Mercifully, her teammates caught up to her in a rush, mobbing her with praise and allowing Callie to slip back from the fray, right into Layla's arms.

"I'm okay," she said, as her best friend squeezed her tightly.

"You played flawlessly," Brooke said from the side.

She nodded. "Yeah."

"You couldn't have done any more than you did today," Ella piled on. "It was a frickin' honor to be out here with you."

She smiled weakly and stepped back far enough to meet Layla's sympathetic gaze. "I have no regrets about this game."

Layla nodded and then swallowed, as if too overcome with emotion to acknowledge the entirety of that statement.

Callie released a shaky breath. "I put everything I had up against the best in the world, and I just came up short." The thought didn't make her sad. She merely felt numb at the realization that her best wasn't enough. It hadn't been enough today. Maybe it never had been. She wasn't the best curler. She wasn't the best skipper. She wasn't the best person.

The last item on the list was the only one that hurt.

She had paid a heavy price to learn that lesson, and while she now knew for certain how it felt to leave everything she had to the game, she couldn't say for sure if that knowledge had been worth what she'd surrendered, and she likely never would.

Turning slowly around to look first at her friends, her teammates, and her colleagues, she widened her gaze to sweep over the crowd of other players and spectators watching them. This community had given her so much. It was impossible to fault them. Any lack undoubtedly existed in herself. The numbness spread until it nipped the tips of her fingers and toes like the cold she'd lived in for so long. Still, she continued her deliberate turn until, when she nearly reached the place where she'd begun, her eyes swept across a familiar image, and her heart beat so hard it cracked the ice encasing her.

There in the front row, edging her way along the banister toward the stairs, eyes locked on her own . . . she might not have believed it, if not for those eyes.

"Max," she called. Then she ran.

⊙ ⊙ ⊙

279

If she'd thought her heart had stopped beating the moment Callie saw her, the impact of their bodies colliding jolted it back to life with a shot of pure electric energy. They clutched each other tightly as Max teetered on the bottom step of the bleachers. She wasn't sure she would ever regain her balance around this woman, and she wasn't sure she cared, if only Callie would hold her this tightly forever. Still, she had things she needed to say, and she'd had enough spectacle to last her a lifetime. She didn't need to subject either of them to a grand public declaration, so she slowly steered them away from the riser and around the corner, far enough that no cameras could follow.

"You came back," Callie whispered into her neck.

"I couldn't stay away." Max kissed her temple.

Callie turned her head and returned the kiss fully on her lips.

Her knees nearly buckled at how amazing that felt, but Callie pulled back quickly.

"I'm so sorry," she said, her cheeks flushed. "I didn't mean to do that. I mean, I did, but I didn't mean to presume. I know I made so many mistakes, Max."

"Not as many as I did. I broke my promise."

"You worked so hard for that opportunity, and I knew how much it meant to you. I should've been happier for you. I should've celebrated with you. I should've been happy for what you were gaining instead of focusing on what I was losing."

"You had every right to be mad at me."

"That's the thing." Callie cupped her face in cold hands. "I wasn't mad at you. I was sad and scared of losing you. I didn't want to admit that, not to myself and not to you, so I fell back on the only thing I've ever fallen back on, and I made everything about curling. I didn't lie exactly, but I didn't tell you the whole truth either, and I have regretted that every minute since you walked out the door."

"What's the whole truth?" Max asked, then held her breath.

Callie bit her lip as her eyes began to water, and Max's heart hung suspended on whatever those tears meant.

"So help me, God," Callie finally whispered, "the whole truth is, I'm crazy about you, even crazier than I am about curling."

"That's pretty crazy," Max said, pulling her in tightly once more.

"So much crazy," Callie mumbled against her shoulder, "and I don't even know what that means for us. I know it doesn't solve a damn thing, and you still have your job, and it's still a priority for you. I don't want to lose the things I love either, even if things are shifting for me, and I'm willing, but . . ." Her voice drifted off as their bodies shook. "Are you laughing?"

"I am," Max admitted, the trembling between them only growing. "I'm sorry. It's not funny, but I can't help it. I was so scared, and now I don't know what to do. This is *not* the reception I was expecting."

Callie leaned back and wiped a tear from her eye. "But it's a good reception, right? Please say it's the reception you hoped for."

"Way better." Max tried to bite back a smile. "Even if you did steal my thunder a little bit."

"What thunder?"

"I thought I was the speechwriter in the couple," she teased. "Then you have to go and outshine me there, too."

"I didn't make a speech." Callie sniffed. "I don't write speeches."

"Well, if you just ad-libbed that, I feel even less secure in my abilities, because the speech I've been writing in my head all week pales in comparison."

The corner of Callie's mouth twitched up. "I want to hear yours."

"Oh no, it's not nearly as good. I was going to apologize for walking off a job that, as it turns out, was way better than the one I left it for." Shame crept up and warmed her cheeks. She wished they could just skip this part and go back to kissing, but Callie deserved to hear it as much as Max needed to get it off her chest. "Then I planned to tell you how you were right all along about everything, about curlers and your team and the sport as a whole being a hidden gem of really awesome people—er, athletes."

Callie rolled her eyes.

"No, I'm serious. I meant both people *and* athletes. I know I've said that before, but this time I'm going to prove it because I'm selling my apartment in New York. I bought a really good camera, and I'm going to make a documentary about curling and about you specifically if you'll agree to let me follow you all the way to the Olympics."

Callie shook her head, her expression filled with a sadness Max had never seen there before. "I just came in second at nationals. My best wasn't good enough. It might never be. And even if it is, I'm going to start next year in the same position I started this one in. I'm a very long way from the Olympics."

Max shrugged, then hooked a finger under Callie's chin and gently tilted it back up. "It can be a very long movie. You have time, and so do I. We both do, together, if you want it."

Callie sniffed back another crying jag. "That's a pretty good speech."

"Yours was better."

"Why?"

"Oh, you had all these emotions, and you kissed me, and—"

"No." Callie laughed. "I wasn't asking for a speech analysis. I mean, why would you give up all your high-powered contacts and contracts to follow me around?"

"Well, two reasons. One, turns out that making a documentary about someone interesting actually appeals to me a lot more than shouting questions at people I don't particularly like."

"And the other reason?"

"I love you."

This time there was no restraint in Callie's smile. It was almost a shame to smother such a radiant expression, but Max kissed her anyway.

Epilogue

Callie took one more deep breath of the steam-laden air in the tiny hotel bathroom. The tension had begun to lift from her shoulders the moment her last rock had left her fingers three hours earlier, but the wet heat of her extra-long shower had gone a long way to accelerate the process. Now she planned to finish decompressing with the incredibly sexy woman waiting on the other side of the door. She opened it, buzzing with anticipation, only to roll her eyes at what she saw.

Max stood a mere two feet in front of her, still fully dressed in her on-air slacks and deep red button-down shirt with her now ever-present video camera lifted to her eye.

Callie wanted to be annoyed that she'd finally left behind four days of tournament work only to find Max hadn't gotten the "out of office" memo, but she couldn't contain a little smile. She found that happening more and more these days.

"How does it feel to be the Players' Champion?" Max asked in her most professional voice.

"They don't call it that," Callie said. Stating the obvious, she added, "And you cannot use any documentary footage in which I am wearing only a towel."

Max's grin grew wider than the edges of her video camera. "I'll only shoot from the neck up. Now answer my question."

"Well first of all," Callie said, wrapping her towel a little tighter around her chest, "my *team* won the Players' Championship."

"And what did you shoot throughout the tournament?"

"About 97 percent."

"Is that a record?"

"I don't know. You'll have to look it up."

Max turned the camera around so the lens faced her. "Note to self: Look up official records to prove Callie is the greatest Players' Champion who ever lived."

"Again, not a thing," Callie corrected. "My whole team won the tournament called the 'Players' Championship,' and it's not the same thing as the national championship, which we lost, or the world championship, which we didn't qualify for, you know, because we lost nationals."

"And who won the world championships?" Max prodded.

"The Swedish national team."

"Oh interesting." Max played a little dumb, and Callie felt a setup coming on. "Remind me: Who did you beat today in the final game of the tournament?"

"The Swedish national team."

"Players'... wait for it ... Champion!"

Callie finally laughed. How could she not? Never in her whole life had she shared these moments with someone who seemed to relish them even more than she did. Over the last six and a half months, Max had gone from adversary to reluctant curling convert to Callie's biggest fan. And in the two months since their reunion, both of them had gone on a tear, both professionally and personally. Team Mulligan had won four of the five bonspiels they'd entered while Max's stellar and charismatic coverage of those events had helped secure preliminary funding for a documentary that would follow them through the entirety of next season and hopefully into their Olympic year.

More than that, though, they'd worked together, eaten together, traveled together, and virtually moved in together. While many of Max's belongings were still in storage back in

New York City, she'd turned in the keys to her hotel room and was spending all of her nights in Buffalo curled up at Callie's side.

"What?" Max asked, as she pushed the camera button Callie had come to recognize as the zoom.

"Nothing."

"Come on, your eyes got all dreamy. Were you remembering the moment in the sixth end when you played a triple takeout to sit two?"

She shook her head.

"The push back onto the button in the fourth?"

She bit her lip. If Max's increasing fluency in curling speak wasn't so damn endearing, she might have cut her off sooner.

"The shot you called that Brooke didn't think would work, but totally did?"

"Nope."

"You know," Max finally said, "this is going to be a long, boring documentary if you refuse to reflect on your matches with me."

"Lucky for your viewers the documentary doesn't officially begin for another six months, and lucky for you the dreamy look you caught on camera had nothing to do with curling."

"Oh." Max managed to appear a little sheepish. "Care to elaborate?"

"Care to turn off the recording?"

Max must have heard something in Callie's tone that caught her attention, because she pressed another button and snapped the lens cap back in place. "Tell me, please."

"I got a little dreamy thinking about how much I love having you with me every night. It doesn't matter if we're working, or traveling, or trying to catch up on sleep, or—"

"Which we are very bad at," Max cut in.

"Only because you keep looking at me the way you are right now, even when we're both exhausted."

The corner of Max's mouth quirked up. "Hey, I tried. I put the camera between us and everything, but you're in nothing but a very thin hotel towel. It's not as if you're projecting the air of someone who wants to spend the evening reviewing video from her triumphant performance or plotting the opening scenes of the film."

She pressed her lips together and shook her head.

"Okay then." Max shrugged. "I never really expected to be the half of this relationship who was more interested in talking about curling, you know."

Callie laughed lightly. "No, and don't get me wrong, that makes me almost stupidly happy. I don't want to rain on your parade, but you do know today's win does very little to help our national ranking."

"But it helps a bit."

"We're certainly on a winning streak, but the season is practically over, and we are still going to start the next one in basically the same position we did last year."

Max leaned a little closer, those gray eyes filled with focus and a hint of defiance. "Except for one small difference."

Callie arched an eyebrow.

"This time you've got me with you."

"My, someone is awfully fond of herself."

"I am," Max admitted without a hint of chagrin, "and I'm more than fond of you, but more importantly, I'm fond of *us*, you and me together, and how far we've come. Think of who I was the first day at the club."

Callie smiled immediately.

"Okay, okay." Max laughed. "You don't have to enjoy the memory of me busting my ass quite that much."

"You're the one who brought it up."

"Only to prove a point," Max explained with an earnestness that never failed to pull Callie closer. "We grew so much over the course of the last season. We're not the same people we were the day we met. We're not even close, and if we could come that far in the last six months, imagine what we can do in the next six months, and the six months after that. Even if we grow only half as much, even if we're only half again as strong or committed every six months, there's no limit to what we can do, both on our own and collectively."

Callie couldn't resist the passion in Max's voice. It stirred her in more ways than she could fathom, and instead of growing immune to it over time she found herself more captivated with each ardent speech. She didn't care how hot Max burned. She wanted only to draw closer to the flame.

Releasing one arm from its tight grip on the towel, Callie gently cupped Max's cheek in her palm and pulled her closer. Running her thumb along smooth skin, she stared deeply into those intense eyes. "You really believe all that, don't you?"

Max leaned into her touch, but never broke her gaze as she said, "How can I not, after everything? Callie, you and I are fire and ice. If we can fall in love and make it work, nothing is impossible."

What could she say to that kind of perfection?

Nothing.

Or at least nothing she couldn't say better with a kiss.

As she wrapped her arms around Max fully, the towel pooled on the floor at their feet.

Acknowledgments

This book is another sports romance. Like *Heart of the Game*, *Edge of Glory*, and *Love All*, I combined my love of love and my love of sports to hopefully give you something compelling on both fronts. Unlike those other books, though, *Fire and Ice* showcases a sport that is both more and less familiar, in that curling is more familiar to me than snowboarding or tennis, because I actually play it regularly, and likely less familiar to many of you, who judging by statistics probably don't. Curling generally gets a blip of notoriety every four years during the winter Olympics, then disappears off the sports radar for most Americans. I am not most Americans. Through the initiatives of a small but enthusiastic curling community in Buffalo, New York and Niagara Falls, Canada, I got hooked on the sport about five years ago. I am a proud member of a constantly evolving roster of the Lusty Shams, who play once a week all winter at the Buffalo Curling Club. The Shams are not what anyone would call good, but we have a lot of fun, and more importantly my experiences with them have taught me so much about the amazing community and culture that surround the sport of curling. I am honored to be able to share that world with all of you, dear readers.

I want to thank the curling community for all the love and welcome, support, and positive energy you all have surrounded me with. From Danielle Buchbinder, the very first curler I ever spoke to, who continues to build me up in the sport even when I play terribly, to all the curlers at the Buffalo Curling Club who offer tips, encouragement, and food after matches, I feel blessed to be part of such an affirming circle. Seriously, you all are the best. To my Shams, Dustin, Anne, Susan, Melissa, Bitty, and now Jackie, thank you for letting me be your skip. We might not win many matchups, but to me you are the best. To the professional curlers, who so willingly give their time and energy to answer questions and hold workshops, and even accept phone calls from writers they've never heard of, I don't know any other sport where top-tier athletes are so willing and open with fans, despite juggling so much in their own lives. I especially want to thank John Shuster for taking some time amid a busy weekend to talk to Jackson about a few of the finer points of his slide, all of which I took copious notes on, and some of which appear in this book. And I owe an even greater debt of gratitude to Aileen Geving, who took a considerable amount of time during a curling season and impending motherhood to talk with me at length, not only about the nuts and bolts of curling, but the day-to-day life and struggles of a professional curler. Your insights helped take Callie from a concept to a compelling character and gave life to a broader world I couldn't have accessed on my own. I simply cannot thank you enough.

Then, as much as I love my team on the ice, I also love my team off of it. From my ever-awesome beta readers Barb and Toni to my kick-ass substantive editor Lynda Sandoval, every single one jumped headfirst into the world of curling and the details of these characters. My Bywater team—Salem, Marianne, Elizabeth, Nancy, and Kelly—all added their eagle eyes and their enthusiastic support to this project. I kept waiting for someone to say, "Is a romance centered around ice and brooms really the best idea?" but none of them did. Ann McMan, fabulous designer and Lammy-winning author, not only made one book cover, but two (a curling cover within a romance cover) because she is the best. Thank you to Will Banks, aka Big Papi, for my author photo and for all-around excellence. Thank you to my fellow authors, who keep me on my toes and help me continue to refine my craft and my opinions on writing, especially Jenn and Anna. Thank you also to my final line of defense, my proofreaders, who never fail to see things everyone else has missed.

And thank you, as always, to the most wonderful friends and family in the world. There are too many of you all to possibly name, and isn't that a lovely problem to have? I am blessed to be surrounded by love, the bulk of which comes from Jackson and Susie. Jackie, I have loved watching you take to the game of curling with the same gusto and intensity you apply to everything. Sharing this game with you has been pure joy. And Susie, my vice, my partner, my first reader, and the only opinion that ever really matters, none of this would be worth doing without you. Thank you for standing by me, come what may.

Finally, thank you to the One who has given me so many things to be thankful for, *Soli Deo Gloria*.

About the Author

Rachel Spangler never set out to be an award-winning author. She was just so poor during her college years that she had to come up with creative ways to entertain herself, and her first novel, *Learning Curve*, was born out of one such attempt. She was sincerely surprised when it was accepted for publication and even more shocked when it won the Golden Crown Literary Award for Debut Author. She also won a Goldie for subsequent novels *Trails Merge* and *Perfect Pairing*. Since writing is more fun than a real job and so much cheaper than therapy, Rachel continued to type away, leading to the publication of *The Long Way Home*, *LoveLife*, *Spanish Heart*, *Does She Love You*, *Timeless*, *Heart of the Game*, *Perfect Pairing*, *Close to Home*, *Edge of Glory*, *In Development*, *Love All*, *Full English*, and *Spanish Surrender*. She is a four-time Lambda Literary Award Finalist, an Independent Publisher (IPPY) medalist, and the 2018 recipient of the Alice B. medal. She plans to continue writing as long as anyone, anywhere, will keep reading.

Rachel and her partner, Susan, are raising their son in Western New York, where during the winter they make the most of the lake-effect snow on local ski slopes. In the summer, they love to travel and watch their beloved St. Louis Cardinals. Regardless of the season, Rachel always makes time for a good romance, whether she's reading it, writing it, or living it.

For more information, visit Rachel online at www.rachelspangler.com or on Facebook, Twitter, or Instagram.

Other Titles by Rachel Spangler

Learning Curve
Trails Merge
The Long Way Home
LoveLife
Spanish Heart
Does She Love You
Timeless
Heart of the Game
Perfect Pairing
Close to Home
Edge of Glory
In Development
Love All
Full English
Spanish Surrender

Bywater
BOOKS

At Bywater Books we love good books about lesbians just like you do, and we're committed to bringing the best of contemporary lesbian writing to our avid readers. Our editorial team is dedicated to finding and developing outstanding writers who create books you won't want to put down.

We sponsor the Bywater Prize for Fiction to help with this quest. Each prize winner receives $1,000 and publication of their novel. We have already discovered amazing writers like Jill Malone, Sally Bellerose, and Hilary Sloin through the Bywater Prize. Which exciting new writer will we find next?

For more information about Bywater Books and the annual Bywater Prize for Fiction, please visit our website.

www.bywaterbooks.com